$\mathcal{V}$OICES OF THE $\mathcal{S}$OUTH

The
Golden Weather

LOUIS RUBIN

The Golden Weather

LOUISIANA STATE UNIVERSITY PRESS
Baton Rouge and London

*To my mother and father
and to Dora Rubin*

Now, if this earthly love has power to make
Men's being mortal, immortal; to shake
Ambition from their memories, and brim
Their measure of content; what merest whim,
Seems all this poor endeavour after fame,
To one, who keeps within his steadfast aim
A love immortal, an immortal too.
Look not so wilder'd; for these things are true
And never can be born of atomies
That buzz among our slumbers. . . .

JOHN KEATS *Endymion*

CONTENTS

PART ONE

The Near Meadows

1. I WAS NEVER SURE WHY I ALWAYS LISTENED FOR THE launch. I did not enjoy hearing it pass by. I knew that if ever I saw it by daylight (which I never did, for it must have made its return trip in the very early hours of the morning) it would almost certainly be a forlorn, clumsily painted wooden craft with several frayed automobile tires slung along its sides, and very likely called the *Lucy H.* or the *Martha S.* or some such humdrum name as that. I was glad that the night hid it, so that all I could see through the laden branches of the water oaks beyond my bedroom window was, at intervals, a tiny pinpoint of light on the river. Each evening I would lie in bed and wait till I heard, far away, the faint pulsing of its gasoline engine. It took a very long while to round the wide bend upstream and creep down toward our house, so slowly it moved, the persistence of its feeble engine sounding unimaginably dreary to me. Then, finally, a dim little lamp was faintly visible out in the channel. Still I would wait, until it toiled on downstream, and at last gave a wan toot of its klaxon for the railroad bridge to open. I would hear the clanking of the machinery as the center span turned on its axis to a position parallel to the channel. By the time the bridge machinery went into action again to close the span, the launch was out of earshot. I was always glad of it.

So unimposing was the launch that I seldom thought of it during the day. Once, however, I did think to ask Major Frampton, who knew all about such matters and who must certainly also have heard it at night sometimes, what cargo it was that the launch carried on its nightly journey. And

3

even the Major did not know, which was final proof of the utter inconsequence of the launch. But even so, when I went to bed I would always listen for it. I wanted to have it pass by, I suppose, and its sound safely dispatched for night, so that I could listen for better things.

After the launch had disappeared, the train would arrive. It too came regularly each night, rolling into the city across the trestle from the south. No matter how far behind schedule it might be operating, eventually I would be able to pick out the wail of its whistle miles away across the river. After a time it would draw near, moving ponderously and steadily, until the sound of the wheels would become a low rumble and I would know the locomotive was lumbering along the approach to the trestle, pulling a string of freight cars behind. As more and more cars rolled onto the trestle, the deep roar would increase, and I would listen carefully for the sudden rise in pitch which told me that at that instant the locomotive was moving directly across the closed draw-span. Then the train would come clattering into the city itself and hoot for the crossing at Rutledge Avenue. The whistle made a tremendous din, audible, I was sure, all over the city, even far downtown by Colonial Lake where my Aunt Ellen lived, and I wondered whether she too was listening. Above the clatter of the train I would now be able to make out the clanking of the alarm on the flashing signal at the crossing, joined with the deeper, less strident bell of the locomotive itself as, slowed now to a crawl, the night Seaboard freight glided into Charleston. Finally the sound would die out as the train disappeared in the railroad yards far to the east along the Cooper River. By now our cook, Viola, can hear it in her house, I would think. But I would be unable to hear it any longer myself.

I knew that my parents listened to the train, because sometimes my father complained about it at breakfast.

4

"I don't understand why they have to blow that whistle like that," he would say. "That's what they've got the crossing signal for." My father would then declare that he was going to write a letter to the Seaboard Air Line Railroad that very day. But if he ever did, it was to no avail, because each night the train would rattle into the city as usual, sounding its whistle. I never understood why my father objected so to it; I liked to hear the train whistle at night. So, for that matter, did my mother.

"I don't mind it," she would tell my father. "I think it's nice. Besides, half the time you don't even hear it anyway, you're so sound asleep."

"Damn locomotive," he would mutter, unheeding. "Sounds like it's coming right in through the window."

Sometimes I used to wonder what it would be like if a train actually did come through the window. Suppose, I imagined, a hurricane were to blow our house a mile through the air and right onto the railroad tracks at the moment when the evening freight was coming. I thought about it and decided that what I would do would be to open my bedroom window and try to jump down onto the top of a boxcar as it went by underneath—though since the hurricane winds might still be blowing, it would be a fairly difficult leap. I would attempt to time my jump in order to land just behind one of the brake wheels atop the cars, so that I would have something to hold onto. Then I would simply turn the wheel and stop the train. However, since there had not been a hurricane to strike Charleston within my memory, the chances of this happening were not too great, I decided.

Though my father would rage over the noise of the night freight train, he never expressed any concern over the sound of the trolley cars. For some reason, perhaps because it was more persistent and somewhat less dramatic, the clatter of the cars on the Rutledge Avenue Line, just five blocks away, appeared not to bother him at all, though it seemed to me that the trolleys made at least as loud a din.

Rutledge Avenue, along which the streetcars operated, was five blocks to the east of our house. The Rutledge Avenue Line was one of three in the city, in addition to the bus routes along Meeting Street. There was the Belt Line, which ran far downtown, and aboard which my Aunt Ellen rode to work each morning from her apartment by Colonial Lake to the legal district on Broad Street. There was the King Street Line, which stretched from downtown to Hampton Park, a mile south of our house just beyond the Seaboard tracks. For the King Street Line, though I seldom rode on it, I held a certain affection. It operated along King Street just under the auditorium windows of the James Simons School, and the trolley cars would sometimes come clattering by just when our singing teacher, Miss Mason, was teaching us a new song, and she would be forced to wait in exasperation until the car passed on down the street.

And finally, there was our line, the Rutledge Avenue. It was the longest in the city, running from Broad Street where my Aunt Ellen worked, only a few blocks from the harbor, all the way uptown past our street and the city limits a block farther out, up to the end of the line at Magnolia Crossing. After the trolleys passed Hampton Park on the uptown run, there was apt to be very little automobile traffic along Rutledge Avenue, especially at night, so that if a motorman chose to do so, he could operate his car at quite a rapid clip.

The Marvelous Ringgold often chose to do so. As I listened to the trolleys at night, I could always tell when the motorman was the Marvelous Ringgold, for then the sound the trolley pole made as it rolled along the catenary would be one of furious and intense hissing, until it seemed that at any moment the cable must surely be ripped from its moorings. Whenever the car stopped it would be with a wild screeching of brakes, and the air valves would explode loudly as the folding doors shot open.

The Marvelous Ringgold—where did he get that name? I asked my father once.

"I don't know," my father replied; "it just fits him, I suppose."

The Marvelous Ringgold knew every one of his passengers by name, occupation and ruling passions. Knowing that rose gardening was my father's chief activity, he would be sure to discuss that with him whenever my father rode on his trolley. When, on alternate Sundays, my Aunt Ellen rode his car up to our house from downtown, to have dinner with us, she and the Marvelous Ringgold would discuss the doings of our family, including all the out-of-town relatives—such as my Uncle Ben, who was a movie writer in Hollywood. With my mother, the conversation would concern itself with grocery prices and shopping experiences. With Major Frampton, he would join in reminiscing about the good old days. With me—for unlike many adults I knew, the Marvelous Ringgold did not disdain to converse with persons my age—he would discuss baseball and school work. No matter who the rider was, the Marvelous Ringgold could soon search out a topic of conversation. And sometimes, on evenings when I happened to be walking along Rutledge Avenue and would look up to watch him pilot his trolley along, he would seem, if the car was empty, to be talking to himself.

In all respects he was the exact opposite of the other regular motorman on the Rutledge Avenue Line, Mr. Zinzer, who seldom spoke to anyone. In contrast to the Marvelous Ringgold, Mr. Zinzer went about operating a trolley car in as routine and unexciting a fashion as possible. The sound of his streetcar in the night was a low deathlike monotone. He crept up and down the line on his appointed course, either on schedule or a little behind, with never a variation in his routine.

In school that winter we read the poem entitled "Dover Beach," and one evening as I lay in bed listening to Mr. Zinzer's trolley the notion came to me that the nearest thing I knew to the ocean surf that would "begin, and cease, and then again begin, with tremulous cadence slow, and bring the eternal note of sadness in," was a trolley car on the Rutledge Avenue Line at night piloted by Mr. Zinzer.

2. THE IMPUDENCE OF MISS WILHELMINA MASON, I thought, was an outrageous thing. Billy Cartwright and I discussed it often in early April, as we cycled to school together. It was I who usually brought up the topic, because I would inevitably think of it as I sat astride my bicycle outside the Cartwrights' house each morning, waiting for Billy to come out and join me. The sun would be shining on the marsh and the thickets across Peachtree Street toward Devereux woods, in the yellow flare of early morning, and at once I would find myself repeating the words: "Awake, awake, ye dreamers, The cuckoo loudly calls!" The song would go through my head involuntarily, unfailingly. And it was Miss Wilhelmina Mason's fault, for it was her song.

What so mystified Billy Cartwright and myself was the abruptness of the change in Miss Mason. Only the previous year she had first come to the James Simons School to teach us singing, as replacement for the aged Miss Clara Von Lehmann. Miss Mason was slight, with a round face and very large, round eyes, and her red hair came down in brisk bangs over her high forehead. Ordinarily her complexion was a pasty white, but with the exertion of singing and beating time, her face soon grew flushed and moist. She spoke in the clipped, nasal tones of an outlander, for she was from Bridgeport, Connecticut, and when she sang, her voice was a high, wavering soprano.

At first Miss Mason had been welcomed enthusiastically. Her predecessor, Miss Von Lehmann, had been an ancient lady with a German accent, who my father said was *his* singing teacher when he attended Bennett School thirty years before. He would sometimes mimic the way that Miss Von Lehmann used to sing "My-eee hartz en der high-lenz, a-ghaz-ing der dee-err, my-eee hartz en der high-lenz, my-eee hart iss nod hee-err!" By our time, however, Miss Von Lehmann could no longer sing a note. She carried a long wooden pointer, with which she would gesture at musical notes crayoned on a chart of faded cheesecloth, and beat time furiously as she directed us. "Ah VUN, ah DOO, ah DREE, ah FOUR! Ah-DON ah DROB der FIN-al NODE!" We did not care for the songs she taught us, which were all about bluebirds, and robins in the treetops gaily singing, and the fir tree grew in the forest cold.

Then one day a considerably younger woman appeared on the auditorium stage at song time. She carried a much shorter baton, and no cheesecloth charts at all. Instead she handed out mimeographed sheets with the words to new songs on them. This was Miss Wilhelmina Mason and, to our delight, the songs that she began teaching us were not about robins in the treetop gaily singing and fir trees in the forest, but "Home on the Range," "Goodbye, Old Paint," and "Old Black Joe." Such songs were a distinct improvement, acceptable even to the most carping among us. We were soon full of praise for our new singing teacher.

To be sure, Major Frampton was skeptical from the start. The Major was Billy Cartwright's grandfather and lived with the Cartwrights. He was eighty-nine years old, and a Con-federate veteran, and as soon as we told him that our new singing teacher had a Yankee accent, he was suspicious.

"Don't trust her," he advised us. "They're a tricky lot."

We assured him that Miss Mason was far too nice for that; her choice of songs proved it. But the Major was right. For after the first year, a change came over Miss Mason's singing methods. She did not revert to the cheesecloth charts that Miss Von Lehmann had used, but each new selection of songs on the mimeographed sheets was increasingly less palatable. There was no more "Home on the Range" and "Goodbye, Old Paint." Instead we were now taught to sing about country gardens with whirlpools of color flowing in eddies while the light wind plays a rippling tune, and about the sweet and low, sweet and low wind of the western sea. Between such songs and robins in the treetop gaily singing, there was very little to choose.

Particularly we disliked still another song—from Italy, land of music and laughter, it came, Miss Mason said—entitled "Santa Lucia." The last word was pronounced Lu-chee-uh, Miss Mason told us. There was something about the closing lines that enraged my friend Billy Cartwright:

> *Hark how the sailors cry,*
> *Joyful, the echoes nigh*
> *Sa-an-tu-uh Lu-chee-uh,*
> *SAN-TAAA Lu-chee-uh!*

"Echoes nigh!" Billy Cartwright kept saying. "Who ever heard anybody talk that way?"

For myself it was the *Lu-chee-uh* that irritated me most. The only L-u-c-i-a I knew was our English teacher, Miss Lucia Jahnz, who was a friend of my Aunt Ellen's, and *she* pronounced her name LU-sha. Furthermore, though Miss Lucia Jahnz had a dark, Latin-looking face, she was at least fifty years old, with gray hair and a large, pointed nose, so that I could not remotely envision the sailors wanting to cry *Hark!* to her.

In any event, there was general displeasure with *Santa Lu-chee-uh*, and an increasing loss of respect for Miss Wilhelmina Mason.

The Major, of course, who by this time had learned from us of Miss Mason's fall from grace, was not surprised. "Didn't I tell you so?" he demanded. "The instant you told me she was from Connecticut, I knew she was up to no good. They're

11

sly ones, they are. You can't trust them one bit." He shook his finger warningly. "The next thing you know, she'll have you singing 'Marching Through Georgia,'" he said. "You just wait until the next meeting of the P. G. T. Beauregard Camp," he told us. "I'm going to keep a sharp eye on her."

Actually the Major was the only living Confederate veteran in Charleston, and the P. G. T. Beauregard Camp, United Confederate Veterans, had long since gone out of existence, but in the heat of argument the Major sometimes tended to forget it.

It was a week or so later that the ultimate provocation came. On a clear April morning Miss Wilhelmina Mason distributed mimeographed copies of a new song which she told us we were to learn so that we might sing it on graduation day. It was entitled "The Cuckoo Song," and the first verse was as follows:

> *Awake, awake, ye dreamers,*
> *The cuckoo loudly calls!*
> *The sun peeps o'er the treetops*
> *And shines on garden walls.*
> REFRAIN:
> *Cuckoo, cuckoo, cuckoo, cuckoo!*
> *Cuckoo, cuckoo, cuckoo, cuckoo!*

It was the refrain that enraged us. Miss Mason had gone too far this time.

There were murmurs of protest, but Miss Mason ignored them. We would now, she declared, learn "The Cuckoo Song," and she proceeded to run through it on the piano, singing over her shoulder at us in a fluttering soprano voice. The tune seemed even more obnoxious than the words.

"Now," she said, "all together—let's go! One, two, three—"

But only Miss Mason and the girls in the class sang. The male students were silent.

Halfway through the refrain Miss Mason held up her hand.

"What is the difficulty?" she demanded. "Let's have no holding back, boys and girls. All join together. Readyyyyy? One, two, three—"

Again sound came only from Miss Mason and the girls, though one or two boys halfheartedly murmured the words.

Miss Mason's face was now fiery red, and her round eyes glowed. "Now, you boys listen to me. This is a lovely song, and you are going to learn to sing it. Do you understand? You'll sing it, or you'll come back after your classes until you do. I want no more nonsense from you!" She stamped her foot. "Now, ready! One, two, three—'Awake, awake, ye dreamers—'"

Several of the boys droned the words out faintly, but most of us simply could not bring ourselves to sing. Midway through the refrain the music again quavered to a stop. Miss Mason glared furiously at us.

Billy Cartwright turned to me. "Look at her face," he whispered. "She looks like a traffic light."

So she did, but unfortunately, she was at that moment looking directly at us, so that she saw Billy Cartwright speak, and me turning my head to listen.

"You two!" she said, pointing to us. "Why weren't you singing?"

Neither of us replied.

"Come up here to the front," she ordered. "Now you two will stand in front of the boys and lead the singing, while we try again." She looked at me. "What is your name?" she asked.

"Omar Kohn," I stammered.

"And you?"

"William Cartwright."

"Very well. Now you two will lead the class in singing the song."

Red-faced, we stood before the class and prepared to sing. A streetcar passing in the street below brought us a momentary reprieve, but as soon as it had moved beyond earshot Miss Mason signaled us to begin, and with faint voices we quavered the words. But our classmates in front of us sang almost inaudibly, and before the end of the song the effort collapsed. Miss Mason was scarlet with anger. The boys in the class would return to the auditorium after school, she announced, and would continue with "The Cuckoo Song" until we had learned to sing it properly—all afternoon if necessary. Never before in her career had she encountered such arrant rudeness, and she was not going to stand for it. She had put up with us long enough, and from now on she meant business. So saying, she dismissed us.

We went out through the side door and down the iron fire excape that led into the school yard, grumbling to ourselves. "That old bag," Billy Cartwright said. "Who does she think she is?"

Another classmate, Wallace Riley, who was the son of an army sergeant and the most hardened member of our class, was equally indignant. "Pooey on her and her coo-coo-ke-doo!" he declared.

"Coo-coo, coo-coo," said another. "How stupid can you get?"

We came back that afternoon as required, and after one or two attempts managed to sing "The Cuckoo Song" with sufficient volume to satisfy Miss Mason. She too wished to go home for the day, and so she accepted our token surrender. "Well," she told us, "that's better. Now you have decided at last to behave like good children and not like little ruffians. The class is dismissed."

The worst of it was that, once learned, "The Cuckoo Song" stayed with me. I could not banish it from my thoughts. At odd times I heard the melody running through my head. When I saw the trees brightened by the sun in the morning while I waited on my bicycle for Billy Cartwright, automatically I would begin humming "Cuckoo, cuckoo, cuckoo,

cuckoo" before I was aware of what I was doing. The thought that this enforced saturation with "The Cuckoo Song" must go on at least until graduation in June, two months away, that three times a week until then we should be made to sing it, with goodness only knew how many involuntary recitations of my own between times, seemed almost too much to bear.

3. WINTER WAS FOR MY FATHER A TIME OF WATCHING and planning, of readying the forthcoming spring campaign and securing gains previously made. My father was a fervent gardener. He wore old clothes and a broad-brimmed straw hat, scanned seed catalogues avidly, invested in gardening equipment, rose early and went to bed early in the evening. He struck up an acquaintance with the county agricultural agent and spent hours discussing problems of soil and growth with him. His trips downtown became infrequent now—generally just once a week, on Friday mornings, to take care of business matters, and occasionally in the evening to attend meetings of the American Legion post, of which he was adjutant, or to make social calls with my mother. His interest in the weather, always strong, was now directed toward its agricultural significance. He would study the skies and the direction of the wind. "Cumulo-nimbus clouds. We ought to get some rain in the next twenty-four hours," he would say to my mother. "The tea roses could certainly use it."

My father concentrated his interest on landscaping and flower gardening. He set out bushes, shrubs, evergreens. He built trellises, planted trees. He sought for variety and for exotic specimens, searching the catalogue for unusual plants not ordinarily grown in our part of the country. He had a Temple orange tree that already was beginning to bear a little fruit, a grape arbor, a ginkgo tree. When he read of a new variety of elm, a fast-growing tree called the North China, he immediately ordered one, taking care to inform the newspaper gardening editor that it would be the first to be planted in the area.

16

My father went in especially for roses. He converted the sizable area within the horseshoe driveway exclusively into a rose garden. He planted dozens of varieties of roses, nurtured them with special composts, treated them with insect sprays. He set out trellises, arbors, copings, flagstone walks, stone benches. He joined the American Rose Society, and watched its monthly bulletin for announcements of new types of roses, which he immediately ordered and set out to grow. He read books on rose culture, visited commercial hothouses to discuss the techniques and varieties with professional horticulturists. In two years' time he had a thriving rose garden, and the display during the previous autumn had been such that strangers began driving up into our driveway on Sunday afternoons just to see the roses. He always kept the newspapers fully posted on the state of blooming, so that visitors would be encouraged to come up and inspect them.

After the fall rose season was over, he began making plans for the next year. It would be the first really spectacular blooming season, for now most of the various kinds of roses he had planted were well rooted and thriving. Mounted on the wall in the basement was a large-scale map of the garden area, on which my father diagramed his campaign. Not only was the location of every bench, trellis, arbor and flagstone in the garden indicated here, but he had noted the position of each rose bush and, with water colors, had painted in the over-all color scheme he wished to achieve. It was not a map of what he had grown, but of what he wanted to grow.

He was impulsive, given to instant decisions. Sometimes this caused consternation in the family or among his associates, as when, the previous fall, he had decided in his capacity as adjutant of the American Legion post that a great deal of the assorted materiel in the basement of the Legion armory should be cleaned out. In particular there was a bulky wardrobe of uniforms, somewhat tarnished but still quite elegant, which had once belonged to the Charleston Light

Dragoons, a crack military company now defunct but once the pride of the Charleston gentry. The American Legion post had inherited the uniforms but could make no use of them. My father fretted over the matter, then telephoned the director of the Jenkins Orphanage, a local Negro institution, and offered the uniforms for the orphanage band. The gift was accepted with alacrity, and the uniforms cut down to fit the youthful musicians of the band, who thereafter appeared regularly on King Street resplendently dressed in what was once the martial finery of an exclusive Charleston troop.

He approached gardening in the same way. He was always suddenly transplanting rose bushes, moving shrubs about, relocating trellises. He would gaze at his garden map, note what seemed to him an imbalance, and straightaway begin digging and relocating. My mother would come home from downtown to find that the garden had been switched about drastically. "Why did you move the tea roses and the trellis to the other end of the garden?" she would ask my father.

"Looks better," my father would say. "Too much yellow down at that end of the garden."

The only part of the garden my father was strictly forbidden to manipulate was the flower beds immediately adjacent to the house. These were my mother's preserve; she spent hours weeding and pruning, planting and watering. Garbed in overalls, a straw beach hat, and cloth gloves with wide gauntlets, she sat low to the ground on a little wooden bench. Unlike my father she worked deliberately, carefully, without haste or impatience. She grew nasturtiums, phlox, gardenias, azaleas, hollyhocks, tulips, violets, zinnias, peonies, lilies, marigolds, primroses, daffodils, hydrangeas. She was unconcerned with total color schemes; each cluster of flowers was an end in itself.

My father's occasional suggestions that she might transplant this or that shrub, or set out new beds here and there, were not heeded. "I've got some crocus bulbs over there," she would say. If my father continued his argument, contending that the crocus bulbs could be transplanted over by the coping where they would provide a better border arrangement, my mother shook her head. "Now, they've been trying so hard, and they've just begun to grow, and I don't want to discourage them," she would explain. "They've had a hard enough time as it is, this past winter. I think I'll just let them grow in peace this spring, and enjoy themselves."

Such reasoning baffled my father. The plants were for him simply means to an end, which was the total appearance of the garden; he had no compassion for the plants themselves. They were there for his benefit and by his tolerance, to grow where he wished them to grow, and he was not interested in their possible discomfort.

As the spring season approached, my father grew uneasy. He did not trust the soil in which the rose garden was located. It was too humid, with too much sand in it. Furthermore, it was low-lying, and after a heavy rainstorm tended to collect pools of water that required days to drain off properly. My father had soil tests made by the county agricultural agent's office, and consulted with the agent about ways of effecting better drainage. Still he was unhappy. He had been building toward a spring crescendo of roses of unparalleled glory, and he feared that the disadvantageous soil conditions might dull it.

I came home from school a little later than usual one April day to find my father and mother already seated at the dinner table. "I don't care," my father was saying. "It's got to be done. It's now or never."

"But all those beautiful roses," my mother objected. "They'll be ready to bloom in a month's time now. Why don't you wait till summer?"

"Too late," my father declared. "Spring's the time to transplant roses around here. I'm going to pull them all out, set them along the back fence for a few weeks, and dig the whole

19

plot up. I'll get some decent soil in there. By fall you'll never know the difference, and I'll have a blooming season in September that'll beat anything in town."

"All right," my mother said, "you do what you think best. Only you're going to miss your pretty roses this spring."

"Can't be helped," my father said. "You have to take the long-range view sometimes. I've got too much money and time invested in that garden to piddle around."

That afternoon my father made arrangements to dig up his entire rose garden. He asked our cook, Viola, whether she knew of someone who wanted a month's employment working in the yard. Viola said she knew someone, and my father arranged to have him start work the coming week. He called a building supply company and ordered truckloads of black soil and some crushed rock, to be delivered in a week's time. He marked off a plot of ground near the side fence for setting in the rose bushes until the new soil was in place in the garden. He ordered grass seed, a new shovel and hoe, and a supply of crocus sacks for transplanting. It was a bold step he was taking, but he was resolute.

4. On Saturday mornings, when I went downtown to Sabbath School, I always waited, if there was time, for the Marvelous Ringgold's streetcar. For while with Mr. Zinzer at the controls a trolley-car trip into the city was always a slow, deliberate occasion, with the Marvelous Ringgold each trip was new and adventurous, a wild and perilous ride during which the bell clanged incessantly, the trolley pole sang along the wire, the brakes hissed and moaned, the iron window-guards rattled in chorus, and the car rocked like a ship as it sailed down the tracks. Even in the matter of recording fares on the register overhead, the Marvelous Ringgold was a virtuoso. He could make a three-cent children-under-twelve fare sound like a silver dollar as he reached over, twirled the pointer to its proper position on the indicator dial, jerked down the wooden handle of the waxen bell rope with an emphatic ring, and then let it fly upward with a satisfying *whack!*

"Hop aboard the chariot!" he would call as he ground his car to an abrupt stop at a corner where a waiting passenger stood, and flung the doors open dramatically. He would always have a greeting and a remark or two for me. "Going to temple?" he would ask. "I took your mother down to her sewing club yesterday afternoon. How's your father's rose garden?" And so on all the way downtown.

Sabbath School was an hour of tedium. We sat in the small, chilly tabernacle auditorium, listening to the announcements and singing the opening hymn, the first line of which was "We meet again in gladness"—a sentiment I did not think especially applicable to the situation. After that we retired to our individual classes for a half hour with Jewish history. There were three of us in the confirmation class—though it would be several years before we were confirmed. The teacher was a middle-aged housewife, originally from New York City, who had been reared in an Orthodox rather than a Reform Jewish congregation. The three of us delighted, whenever the chance arose, in asserting our subtle superiority to Orthodox ritual and Jewish lore in general. For to be Orthodox, it was well known, was to be "Uptown," and to look Jewish and alien, and to talk in a thick foreign accent, and to operate little stores on King Street above Calhoun, or to run pawnshops, and to wear peculiar little black skullcaps in synagogue, and to listen to bearded cantors who wailed bizarre Near Eastern litanies, and to observe all manner of mysterious and illogical dietary restrictions, and, in short, to be Jewish.

To be Reform, on the other hand, was to be fair-complexioned, and not look Jewish and alien. To be Reform was to come from families of professional people, journalists, realtors, businessmen; to eat whatever we wished; to attend temple rather than synagogue, to have an organ and choir and to sing hymns; to speak in the same accents as our friends, and not to comprehend the guttural familiarity of Yiddish—to be, that is, not Jewish, but as it was customarily put, of the Fine Old Jewish Families of Charleston.

There were very few of Us still left, as compared with a great, swarming multitude of Them. Our Sabbath School contained no more than three dozen children at most, ranging in age from tiny toddlers to the three of us in the confirmation class, who were twelve and thirteen years old, and would be confirmed when we reached the ages of fifteen and sixteen. We learned our lessons grudgingly for the most part, though sometimes the historical aspects interested me. I was, therefore, for want of a better one, the scholar, so to speak, of the class.

After Sabbath School there were services in the temple. The services lasted fifty minutes—our rabbi, Dr. Raskin, ordinarily dispensed with a sermon on Saturday mornings—and were attended by the three of us and from ten to fifteen adults, mostly women but with a few retired businessmen sometimes showing up.

My classmate Jack Marcussohn and I were detailed to take turns on alternate Saturdays at assisting Dr. Raskin in the ceremony of reading from the Torah—a large, cumbersome parchment scroll encased in a velvet jacket and adorned with silver ornaments and plates. At the proper moment, Dr. Raskin would nod, and I would walk up to the altar, spring up the carpeted steps, and help him carry the heavy scroll from the ark at the rear. I would place the ornaments and jacket on one chair, and then sit down on another and wait while he unrolled the scroll and read from it, translating the words into English as he went along. When he was done, we would replace the velvet cover and the ornaments on the Torah, and I would bear it to my seat and hold it while Dr. Raskin read from the Haftarah.

The year before, when I had first been entrusted with this duty after the confirmation of the older Sabbath School class, it had seemed an honor, a sign of increasing manhood, and I used to wait my turn with eagerness. But now, after many alternate Saturdays of assisting Dr. Raskin, both Jack Marcussohn and I had long since lost any sense of being privileged. It was a chore, or if not quite that, then at best a perfunctory ritual which we performed habitually and with no great spiritual dedication. I would sit on the altar, holding the scrolls of the Law, and listen to the commotion of the busy downtown city out beyond the banked temple windows. I hoped then for one of two things: for the appearance on King Street of the Jenkins Band, or for the Marvelous Ringgold's trolley to be caught in a traffic squeeze on King Street. In the spring, either was quite possible.

The Jenkins Band customarily performed downtown on Saturday mornings, with a squad of the smallest Negro orphans circulating among the shopping crowds to pass the hat while their larger brothers tootled away on much scarred but brightly polished instruments. I could hear the band music far up King Street, and as the temple services progressed, so did the band progress southward. It was my earnest hope that the band's movement would be swift enough so that at some point during the service it would reach the corner of Hasell and King Streets, a half block from the temple, preferably while I was still seated on the platform. Though of course I could not actually see them, I could imagine how the band looked out on the corner, the Negro youths attired in the braided glitter and plumes of the dragoons' uniforms my father had given them, working away intently at their music. Though the orphanage musicians lacked finesse, they could sometimes achieve considerable volume, and Dr. Raskin would have to compete mightily to make his words heard by the congregation. Sometimes, indeed, it would become necessary for one of the adult members of the congregation to go outside and ask the band to move farther down the street—which it always did willingly. There would be several minutes of quiet, and then we would hear the band strike up a tune once more, a block down King Street, and successive numbers would gradually grow fainter as the musicians continued southward toward Broad Street and the Battery, where they would attempt to tap the resources of the tourist trade.

If the chances of the Jenkins Band's putting in an appearance outside the windows during the temple services were fair, the odds in favor of the Marvelous Ringgold's doing so were even better. For temple services lasted fifty minutes, and by the logic of the Rutledge Avenue Line's schedule, each motorman on duty must, at least once during that period, round the corner at Wentworth Street in his trolley car and proceed along King toward Broad. King Street was narrow and curving, with automobile parking permitted on only one side. Even so, there was a matter of only several inches of clearance for the streetcar, and if a motorist parked his car only a little out of line and away from the curb, that was enough to block the trolley tracks thoroughly.

When that happened, most streetcar motormen—Mr. Zinzer, for example—were forced to sit patiently in the car, occasionally tapping on the alarm bell, until the careless motorist came back to move the offending automobile. Or the motorman might enlist the help of a few passers-by to help ease the automobile a trifle closer to the curb, and thus clear the tracks.

The Marvelous Ringgold, however, scorned these procedures. He considered the blocking of trolley tracks an offense against all heaven and earth, and when it happened he would stand indignantly in the cab, his hands on his hips and his left foot planted firmly on the bell pedal, so that the clamor could be heard for blocks. Not until the unfortunate automobile owner had come hurrying back and moved his car would the Marvelous Ringgold consent to withdraw his foot from the bell pedal and guide his trolley car on down the street. At those moments the silence, after such clamor, would seem unbearable, and Dr. Raskin's voice, droning on through the services, almost unreal. Finally the prayers for those in mourning would come, and the prayer for peace, and at last the benediction, and I would then hurry outside, eager for the commotion and bustle of the shoppers on King Street, the excitement of their coming and going.

5. In Felder's Palace Barber Shop electric clippers droned, straight razors scraped stubble from chins, ivory-handled brushes clunked thickly against the lathered rims of shaving mugs. The light-skinned Negro barbers conversed in low tones with their somnolent clients. In the background a radio played. By the lead chair near the door a thin, curly-headed barber toiled with loose, long-bladed shears, snipping away at my hair. Above the broad, beveled mirror behind him was a framed sign: OLIVER—LUNCH HOUR 1–2:15. On the shelf by the mirror a stuffed owl with blank eyes looked knowingly out from an oval glass case.

Along the opposite wall, facing the tier of barber chairs, coatless men slouched in high-backed wooden chairs with black leather padding. Their shirt collars were open and neckties hung loose on their shirt fronts or were discarded entirely. One man, however, in all that crowd sat erect, already shaven and spruced—Major Frampton, who by prearrangement waited there for me to complete my haircut.

Each Saturday morning, while I was at Sabbath School and temple, the Major rode downtown on the trolley with Billy Cartwright. At King and Wentworth Billy descended, bound for the cowboy movie and the serial chapter at the Majestic Theater. He never accompanied us on our weekly walks. The Major, however, remained aboard the streetcar for two more blocks, alighting at Market Street for his weekly shave and tonic at Felder's. Picking his way carefully but firmly across King Street, he strode past the saloon on the corner, rounded the striped barber pole outside the shop,

26

and pushed open the double glass doors. With a nod of his head he stepped precisely down the wooden steps onto the tiled floor and looked about him to receive the greetings of the barbers and the clientele. Gravely he removed his coat and placed it on a brass hook along the wall, disdaining the help of the shine boy who stood by. Standing silently before the mirror, he loosened the wide knot of his red necktie, slipped it from about his throat, extricated the gold stud from his high collar, and placed the collar itself in his coat pocket. Then he selected a vacant seat, settled lightly and accurately into the high-backed oak chair, and prepared to await his turn in the barber chair of Dash, a thin-faced Negro with a gray mustache, who, save in emergencies, was the only one of the five barbers at Felder's in whose hands the Major's tonsure was ever placed.

After he was done the Major would replace his collar and tie, put his coat back on, and wait for me. I would hurry to Felder's from temple, and we would go out for our walk. On those fourth Saturdays when my own hair needed trimming, however, I would take a seat myself, and wait for Oliver, my special barber. While I sat waiting, and then when Oliver was ready for me and I ascended the chromed Koken barber chair and was tucked in for my haircut, the Major would engage in conversation with other clients.

Until I was done and ready to go, we affected never to notice each other. I would sit in the barber chair and listen while the Major talked. The discussion always had to do with old times in Charleston, and especially this year, with the War between the States, and the soon-to-be-held ceremony commemorating the seventy-fifth anniversary of the firing on Fort Sumter in 1861. Alone of those present, the Major remembered that day, for as all who knew him were well aware, he was the last living survivor of the Confederate forces who had opened artillery fire on the Fort and launched the war.

27

Properly the celebration should have been held on April 12, the day when the bombardment of Fort Sumter had begun, but because the President of the United States—a Democrat, running that year for his second term in the White House—had consented to speak on the occasion if the date could be postponed until late July, when he would be returning from a fishing trip in the Caribbean, it had been decided to delay the ceremony until then.

No matter. It was to be held, and that was all the Major cared about. He had waited eighty-nine years, he said, and he could wait three or four months longer. Indeed, for the past half year, as Billy Cartwright and I knew so well, the Major had thought and talked of little else. Not only had the Major played an important role in the firing on the Fort in 1861, but, as he had told us in vivid detail, he had participated in many of the war's most exciting engagements after that—under Joe Johnston from Dalton to Atlanta; with General John Bell Hood in an attempt to break the stranglehold on Atlanta; in the ill-fated Tennessee campaign against Thomas; and once again under Joe Johnston, in the retreat through the Carolinas. Finally he had stacked arms at Greensboro and saluted for the last time as a soldier the bonnie blue flag for which he had bravely survived so many hard-fought battles.

All the subsequent distinctions of the Major's life—he had ridden with Hampton's Red Shirts, he had been married twice and fathered two ample families, for many years he had piloted a ferryboat between Charleston and Mount Pleasant across the Cooper River, and he had served as alderman and civic leader—had been no more than aftermath to those four years of wartime glory. In his own eyes as well as in mine, he was, and always would be, Major William Izard Frampton, C.S.A.

More than my father, more even than the Marvelous Ringgold, the Major was my hero, my friend and my confidant. Now, as I sat in the padded barber's chair while Oliver worked away at my hair, I listened to the Major telling the other men in the shop about the plans for the Fort Sumter ceremonies, and I was proud of his renown among them and of the respect they seemed to have for him.

"I hear the Marine Band's coming down from Washington to play," someone remarked.

The Major nodded. "Yes, eighty strong. The finest military marching band in the world. And not only that, but a regiment of infantry from Fort Benning, too, and they'll bring along *their* band."

"Are the Citadel cadets going to march?" he was asked.

"Not all of them, but a detachment will. Unfortunately, it's their vacation time, you see. But the Citadel Band will be on hand. Mr. Metz has assured us of that. And also two Legion Post bands, and the Fort Moultrie Band, too. Oh, there'll be plenty of good, stirring martial music, all right, that day!"

"How about the Navy, Major? Will the whole fleet be in port?"

"Not all the fleet, but a number of vessels. The President will be aboard the cruiser *Indianapolis*. He will spend the two weeks before the celebration on a trip aboard her."

"Going to catch some fish, huh?"

"Yes, sir," the Major said, "and he deserves the vacation, too, after all the hard work he's put in these past four years." The Major was a Democrat, and often declared that never once had he failed to vote the straight ticket, though "It was mighty hard to bring myself to it sometimes when that jackass Bryan was running." But he had stuck by his party—"And now, thank God, we've got that scoundrel Hoover and all his crowd out of there, and a good Democrat in the White House. And we'll keep him there again this time, by God!"

The fact that the President was a Yankee from New York, which might ordinarily have troubled the Major, was excused by the fact that "He's a good *Democrat*. And besides, the Vice-President is a Texan and a good one, yes, sir."

By now Oliver had completed his trimming job on my hair and had applied the tonic that he termed "bug juice." Deftly he combed my locks into place, stepped back to admire his handiwork, dusted powder about my neck with a soft, long-bristled brush, then removed the gray-striped sheet. "Step down," he said, and flapped the sheet. "Next gentleman."

I handed Oliver my quarter and went over to where the Major sat.

"All ready?" he asked. This was the first overt sign that he recognized me.

"Yes, sir."

"Very well, young man," he said, and bracing his bony hands against the oaken arms of the chair for support, he rose to his feet. "Good day to you, gentlemen!" he called out. Barbers and clients chorused goodbye, and we left Felder's Palace Barber Shop.

On these Saturday excusions of ours, it was customary for us to journey to one of two places. Either we went down to the waterfront, where the Major would explain the defense of Charleston Harbor during the War to me, or we went eight blocks westward, past Colonial Lake and the Warwick Apartments where my Aunt Ellen lived, to the foot of Beaufain Street. There, on a mud flat along the Ashley River, was the rotting hull of the ferryboat *Sappho*, which many years ago the Major had skippered on the Mount Pleasant run. The Major liked to walk out along the narrow planked catwalk, enjoying the sunshine, while he told me about ferryboat days.

We had been there on our last outing together, however, and so I was not surprised this Saturday when the Major proposed that we "journey down to the waterfront and see what's doing in the shipping world today." We waited for the streetcar, and I hoped that the Marvelous Ringgold would be the motorman who would heave into sight around the bend at Beaufain Street. It was Mr. Zinzer who came along, however. We climbed aboard the trolley, the Major paying our fares and requesting transfers to the Belt Line car for us, and we took our seats as the car nosed along King Street's narrow thoroughfare.

We got out in front of the Post Office, at Broad and Meeting. Broad Street was the legal and financial district, and most of the lawyers, bankers, realtors, insurance men, brokers and cotton factors who peopled it spent much of the day standing outside the nondescript office fronts talking with each other. Everyone on Broad Street knew the Major, and his stroll down the sidewalk toward East Bay occasioned a chorus of greetings and salutations. He could hardly take a dozen of his deliberate but sturdy paces—he was a tall old man—without someone else coming over to shake his hand and inquire after his health. The Major was always careful to introduce me to everyone. "This is my young friend Omar," he would intone. "He and my grandson William are my color guard these days." I would wait while the Major and his friends exchanged pleasantries, and then we would continue down the street until the next interruption. It always pleased me to see how well known the Major was. Sometimes I wondered why I enjoyed the proof of his eminence so much; it was as if the knowledge bore out my faith in him.

Often on Broad Street we would meet my Aunt Ellen, who was secretary to a lawyer there. The Major and my Aunt Ellen were old friends. My aunt would always inquire about the forthcoming Fort Sumter Celebration, and the Major would proudly give her the latest news. There would also be others that I knew—Mr. Simons, who lived in the house across from our own; my "Uncle" Theobald—not my real uncle but a friend of the family—with whom I some-

31

times attended Municipal League baseball games during the summer. Sometimes, too, I caught sight of the famous Dr. Chisholm, a round-faced man well known as a poet and historian, who lived in the same apartment building as my Aunt Ellen. He was one of the few people who evidently did not know the Major, for they never spoke. I often wondered about this, for I knew that Dr. Chisholm was a member of the commission staging the Fort Sumter Celebration, just as the Major was, and it struck me that they certainly must have met each other. But when Dr. Chisholm passed by he seemed not to recognize the Major at all.

Finally we would reach East Bay Street, and cross over to the narrow cobblestoned alley that led to the waterfront. To our left, when we cleared the last building, were the Clyde Line docks, where on Saturdays a small passenger liner, the *Cherokee*, was moored, masthead pennants flying. To our right was Adger's Wharf, where a number of the shrimp trawlers were tied up, and where the snub-nosed, red tugboats of the White Stack Towboat Company were berthed.

We walked over to the seawall along the wharf and looked southward toward the harbor. Some distance to our left, beyond Castle Pinckney in mid-harbor, a small gasoline-powered ferryboat moved slowly across the bay toward Mount Pleasant. It was operated, I knew, by a man named Captain Baitery, and the sight of the little craft never failed to throw the Major into a rage. "A skiff—that's all it is," he said. "It's not even big enough to be a good-sized launch. Why, the *Sappho* or the *Pocosin* could have run it down in a fog and not even felt the impact!"

He shook his head indignantly. "You should have seen *them* in service, my boy," he would tell me. "Now, *they* were ferryboats! Steam-powered, they were. They had walking beams larger than Baitery's whole deck! And as for the *Palmetto* and the *Lawrence*—why, either one of them would have dwarfed Baitery's tub into utter insignificance!"

The latter two ferries I remembered faintly. Both had been
taken from service some seven years before, when the Cooper
River Bridge had first been opened to traffic. By that time
the Major had long since retired from active ferryboating,
but he never ceased to berate what he considered the abso-
lute folly of building the bridge.

"That monstrosity!" he would mutter, gesturing upstream
to where the massive steel spans of the Cooper River Bridge
arched high over the river. "What in God's name do they
need that for? It can't even pay for its own upkeep, not to
mention the bonds it cost to build it. A million-dollar white
elephant," he declared. "Pure window dressing, that's all.
There wasn't a thing wrong with the *Palmetto* and the
Lawrence. Finest ferryboats in the world. I remember the
day they first put the *Palmetto* into service. I had retired
several years previously, but they asked me to pilot her
across the harbor on her first run, just to see that she han-
dled correctly. Obeyed like a dream, she did.

"Of course, there'll never be another boat like the *Sappho*
for me," he continued. "That's only natural; she was part of
my life for thirty years, and for me she'll always be close to
my heart."

The Major stared out at the harbor. "All gone, all gone,"
he intoned. "And nearly all the men who skippered them
as well. Yes, sir."

He shook his head wistfully. As he did, he caught sight of
Captain Baitery's gasoline ferry again, now only a tiny
shape off to the east.

"Goddamned putt-putt boat," he growled.

Beyond the tiny silhouette of the ferryboat was the Cove
Bridge and the low shore line of Fort Moultrie, and the
Major's eyes fastened on it. I watched his gaze as it hung

there for several seconds, then moved southward to the squat bulk of Fort Sumter in the center of the harbor. The Major looked at Fort Sumter for a while. Occasionally he would turn his face a little so that his glance rested on Fort Johnson, on the western rim of the harbor, and then back to Sumter itself. I knew what he was thinking. I could repeat what was coming by heart, yet once again I found myself waiting eagerly for him to begin his recitation. The Major cleared his throat.

"But still," he began.

> *"But still, along yon dim Atlantic line,*
> *The only hostile smoke*
> *Creeps like a harmless mist above the brine,*
> *From some frail, floating oak.*

> *"Shall the Spring dawn, and she still clad in smiles,*
> *And with an unscathed brow,*
> *Rest in the strong arms of her palm-crowned isles,*
> *As fair and free as now?*

> *"We . . . know . . . not; . . . in . . . the . . . tem-*
> *ple . . . of . . . the . . . Fates*
> *God . . . has . . . inscribed . . . her . . .*
> *doom . . ."*

The Major's voice grew low and hushed as he neared the end. He spoke each word deliberately, solemnly, shaking his head from side to side to emphasize the gravity.

> *"And, . . . all . . . untroubled . . . in . . . her*
> *. . . faith, she waits*
> *The . . . triumph . . . or the . . .*
> *tomb!"*

Awed by the rhetoric and the occasion, I stood silently with him, looking out at Charleston Harbor. As for the Major, his face was stern and sharp, his carriage straight as a ramrod, his shoulders flung back, his fists clenched at his sides.

"It was over there," he said finally, pointing, "just beyond the point of Fort Johnson. Can you see?"

"Yes, sir," I said, straining my eyes to make out the tongue of land along the horizon just at the mouth of the bay.

"That was where we fired the shots that started the war. And over *there*—" he gestured seaward, beyond Sumter— "over *there* the *Star of the West* first hove into view. It was Cadet Haynsworth, from Sumter—the town, that is, not the Fort—who pulled the lanyard. 'Shall I fire, sir?' he asked me. 'Fire away, sir!' I told him. The shot burst just over the masts of the ship. Yes, I can see it just as if it happened yesterday."

"Did you hit it on the next shot?"

The Major shook his head. "No, no, we didn't. You see, we didn't really *want* to sink the ship. We just wanted to warn her off from reinforcing the garrison on the Fort. As a matter of fact, she continued on to *there*—" he gestured off to the left—"and the guns at Fort Moultrie opened up on her. It was then that she turned tail and steamed back out beyond the bar—about where the jetties are now—and returned back North whence she came."

The Major waved his hand seaward. "Thus began the War for Southern Independence," he said, "April 12, 1861, a bloodless battle. Two men were wounded after it was over, while firing a salute. Otherwise not a scratch." He shook his head. "We little knew the bloody, deadly ordeal we were embarking upon. I remember when Colonel Wigfall and I rowed out to the Fort on the second day to call for the surrender. 'Have you any casualties, Major?' Colonel Wigfall asked Major Anderson. 'None, sir,' he replied. 'Then thank God for that,' the Colonel said, and each of us breathed a silent prayer."

The Major continued to gaze seaward. "And those cowards," he declared, "those pusillanimous cowards aboard the fleet just beyond the bar. They stood at anchor, and they watched our guns pounding away at Fort Sumter, and they did not fire one shot in all that time. We felt *ashamed* for the old flag, we did. It grieved our hearts, loyal Southerners though we were, that American seamen could be so craven, so blind to all the demands of honor and chivalry."

I should have liked very much for the Major to continue with his description of the firing on Fort Sumter, but I knew that it was getting on toward one o'clock. "Hadn't we better be going back home, sir?" I asked.

The Major nodded, but it was some seconds more before he could turn his eyes away from the harbor and back toward the city.

"It will be a great day this July," he said as we walked slowly across the open field toward East Bay Street, a block away from where we would catch the trolley car for home. "A great day. Five bands will be on hand, including the Marine Band, and the President of the United States will be the speaker. Seventy-five years. A great day. You just wait and see."

6. THERE WERE, AFTER ALL, MORE IMPORTANT MAT-
ters than Miss Wilhelmina Mason and "The Cuckoo
Song." The Fort Sumter Celebration was much more interesting than school doings. And the song, as I kept reminding
myself, was only one small item, unpleasant though it might
be, in what was really something quite exciting—graduation
from the seventh grade of the James Simons School. More
than that, the three months of summer vacation—thirteen
weeks, an eternity of days—stretched out one after another as
if they were stone steps leading over a rolling green hill on
a bright day. Summer. Faced with the prospect, I was
satisfied, even pleasantly enthralled with what remained to
be done at school before vacation time. I did not even mind
Miss Wilhelmina Mason too much. Despite her action in
singling the two of us out for special rebuke, neither Billy
Cartwright nor I were especially resentful. It was not the
first time that such things had occurred at school. One had
to take one's chances. Billy and I might have done no more
than sulk a bit during singing practice for the remainder of
the term—until one May morning when all was changed.

So accustomed had I become to "The Cuckoo Song" that
as I waited outside Billy's house that morning I thought only
momentarily, and with no great distaste, of the sun as shining on garden walls. Together we went wheeling off to
school. We were earlier than usual in leaving, and we took
our time in the warm spring morning. We paused to examine
the excavations for the new sewer line along Peachtree
Street, listening to the squat little gasoline pumps noisily
sucking the water from the clayey ditches, watching the

Negro workmen sloshing about the wet trench in their mud-spattered hipboots. At Martschink's Cash-and-Carry we stopped for a supply of chewing gum. Billy Cartwright always insisted on this, because the newspapers had advertised that the Wrigley Man was in town, and anyone who was carrying a package of Wrigley's gum would receive a dollar bill if the Wrigley Man stopped him. We had both been carrying packages of Wrigley's gum for several weeks in the hope of meeting him. Unfortunately, we could never refrain from chewing the gum, and every day we had to purchase a new supply. We had already bought and consumed at least ten packages each, and if the Wrigley Man did not show up soon, little profit would come of the transaction. We bought a new supply of gum and continued on our way.

In the school yard, there was time to witness a masterful yo-yo exhibition by Wallace Riley and others, before Miss Lucia Jahnz stepped out from the side door of the brick school building and clanged the brass bell to summon us indoors for study. "Hark!" cried Billy Cartwright, "Santa Lucia!" and in we went.

To our surprise, however, we found no teacher to greet us as we came into the first classroom. Miss Delia Lathrop, our hygiene teacher, famed for her two protruding yellow front teeth that gave her the general appearance of a beaver, seemed to be late. Minutes went by, and we began to realize that if our teacher was not here by now, it was quite possible that she might be absent that day.

Finally the hall door opened, and Miss Lucia Jahnz thrust her dark head inside. "Miss Lathrop is sick today," she announced. "The substitute may not be here for a half hour or so. Study your lessons quietly in the meanwhile."

For perhaps two minutes after Miss Jahnz had made her announcement and withdrawn, the classroom was almost silent, while each member of the class permitted the import of this almost miraculous development to filter into his or her consciousness. Then gradually discussion arose, became louder, grew boisterous in tone. Soon there was even some informal scuffling among certain of the scholars grouped around Wallace Riley over near the windows. In five minutes widespread disorder had broken out, with the girls in the class looking on and giggling appreciatively while the boys followed their own individual inclinations.

It occurred to me, seated as I was with Billy Cartwright near the back of the room and close to the hall door, that it might be prudent to glance into the corridor in order to make sure that no authorities were approaching. I got up to make the reconnaissance, and as I turned my back to the classroom to peer out the door, I felt a sharp sting on my neck. From previous experience I recognized this at once as being caused by the impact of a small wad of paper, thoroughly moistened and chewed and expelled with considerable velocity through a small tube of paper held to the lips.

I whirled around. "Who did that?" I demanded.

My question was greeted with snickering from that corner of the room where Wallace Riley was seated, and renewed giggling from some of the girls. I sat down, abandoning plans for the reconnaissance, and as I did I heard another thud of flying spitball upon exposed flesh, and Billy Cartwright, seated next to me, grabbed at his ear and swore loudly, "I saw you, Wallace!" he accused, and ripping off a strip of paper from a writing tablet, began preparing a retaliatory missile.

Someone else in the far corner of the room stood up and, with no attempt at concealment this time, brazenly fired still another spitball at us. Missing its intended target, it thudded against the window of the door behind us. Thereupon a general bombardment ensued. Billy Cartwright and I and several neighbors were under fire from the Wallace Riley faction, all the while replying vigorously ourselves. The air was filled with flying spitballs, with neither side asking or receiving quarter.

The girls and a few of the fainter-hearted boys scattered along either wall of the classroom to remove themselves from the line of fire.

Abruptly, just as both Billy and I were standing, paper tubes held to lips, in the very act of discharging another salvo, we saw our antagonists hastily dive for their seats, and we heard the door behind us opening.

With constricting hearts we turned to confront the red, frowning face of our old friend Miss Wilhelmina Mason.

"So!" she declared. "This is how you behave when your teacher is ill!"

Stricken, we made as if to resume our seats.

"No, you don't," Miss Mason told us. She looked at us closely, and recognition came. "I might have known that you two troublemakers would be the ones to be misbehaving this time, too. Well, both of you can just march right out of here and straight up to Dr. Higginson's office!"

"But—" Billy Cartwright began.

"You heard me! I saw you both quite clearly. Go to the principal's office this minute!"

We slunk out of the room. Neither of us said a word as we walked along the dingy calcimined corridors and up the staircase to the office of the principal. There was no getting around it; we had been caught red-handed.

Timidly we opened the door that led into the reception room of Dr. Higginson's sanctum.

"What is it?" the secretary asked crossly, looking up from her typing over her black-rimmed eyeglasses.

We told her.

"Sit over there and wait quietly for Miss Mason, then," she ordered, and returned to her work.

We sank into the red plush chairs in the corner, next to the potted palm. Disaster, swift and terrible, had come. I scarcely dared think of what might happen to us. Always Dr. Alexander O. Higginson had seemed to me a dire and angry creature, whose mission in life, and passion as well, was the visiting of stern judgment upon sinful boys. I remembered—and trembled at the memory of it—his customary speech at the first assembly period each fall. He would call upon all of us to mend our wicked ways, and then, with a dramatic gesture, raise before us a short, mean-looking bamboo stick.

"I'm going to break up the old cane now," he would announce, and with his bare hands snap it squarely in two, "and I hope that I won't have to break out the new one."

For three years now I had watched him go through this fearful ritual, and each year he had been forced soon afterward to bring the new cane into action. How often in the past had I seen certain of my classmates shuffle painfully out of the classroom in obedience to the exasperated command of the teacher, only to return somewhat later, faces flushed and eyes puffed from recent shedding of tears, and with chastised hands clutched gingerly to their sides.

"Did it hurt very much?" they would be asked later.

"I'll say it did! That old Higginson, he really lays it on!"

And so now it was my turn.

The door to the hall opened. We looked up in terror. It was Wallace Riley, who straightaway joined us in the corner, omitting even to explain his presence to the secretary. "Forrest Beckman told on me," he whispered. I saw Billy Cartwright flinch at his words, and I remembered then that Billy and Forrest Beckman had the highest grades in our class and were generally considered to be the leading candidates for the Julian Mitchell Achievement Medal, awarded each year to the outstanding member of the graduating class. Now, no matter what else might happen, Forrest Beckman would surely win.

"Wait till I catch him after school," Wallace Riley whispered to me.

"Be quiet!" Dr. Higginson's secretary said.

Again the door opened, and this time it was Miss Wilhelmina Mason herself. The quarter hour that had elapsed—or so the clock on the wall indicated; it had seemed hours—appeared in no way to have calmed her wrath. She glared at us.

"Go right on in, Miss Mason," the secretary said.

"Come along," Miss Mason told us.

Tremblingly we followed Miss Mason through the door and into the very presence of the dreaded Dr. Higginson. He was seated at his desk, his huge bulk framed in the sun from the thin-curtained windows, fearful in his terrible dignity. "Cuckoo, cuckoo," I thought miserably, hating myself for the wan, involuntary attempt at levity at so agonizing a time.

As Miss Mason recited the horrendous story of our crime, not neglecting to mention that she had already found Billy Cartwright and me to be troublemakers once before, the furrows increased along the high arc of Dr. Higginson's domed brow, and his countenance grew steadily darker. Afterward there was an awful silence, while Dr. Higginson glared at us in tight-lipped indignation, and we felt like the veriest worms about to be crushed under the heel of a vengeful giant.

"Well," he asked finally, "what have you to say?"

We were too stricken to reply.

"Only think of it," he declared, pronouncing his words carefully, resoundingly. "Members of the seventh-grade class, about to graduate, behaving like little children. How shameful!"

"You, William Cartwright," he went on, addressing himself to Billy, "comporting yourself like this! With *your* record —and your father a member of the School Board. Blowing spitballs, just like a baby. What is your father going to think when he hears about this?"

"I don't know, sir."

Dr. Higginson looked at me. "And *you*—Omar Kohn, of all

the boys to be involved in something like this! What will *your* parents say?"

I hung my head. I knew all too well what my parents would probably say.

"*Why* did you do it?" Dr. Higginson demanded.

I sought desperately for a reason. "Sir," I managed to say, "I threw in self-defense."

Dr. Higginson shook his finger at me in exasperation. "*There is no self-defense with a spitball!*" he thundered.

Next Dr. Higginson turned to Wallace Riley. For him he affected no surprise at his presence there, for Wallace Riley was a hardened offender.

"You again?" was all Dr. Higginson said.

"Yessir," Wallace Riley replied.

Dr. Higginson shook his head slowly. He sighed. His gaze traveled slowly across our frightened faces, like a searchlight delineating an artillery target in no man's land.

"I declare, I don't know *what* is to be done with boys like you all," he told us. "There is no possible extenuation for your conduct."

For a half minute longer he trained his eyes upon us. Then he spoke. "Go on back to your class," he ordered. "I'll have to think about the proper action to take in your case. Report back here after school."

We trudged back to our classroom, downcast, wretched, flushed with our shame and sick with apprehension. The morning hours passed by in a haze. Trancelike I sat, insulated as it were from all humanity, and I knew that beside me Billy Cartwright was equally grieved. As if from far away I heard the various teachers as they talked; occasionally I heard my own voice reciting when called upon, automatically, unthinkingly, severed from my real self which existed all the while in another universe, one of empty, hopeless misery, where all was gray and fallen.

Only Wallace Riley seemed amazingly undisturbed by the

disaster. Seated several rows in front of us, he was whispering to his friends, grinning, carrying on much as usual.

The recess bell rang. We went out into the schoolyard. Neither Billy nor I could bear to voice the thought that was tormenting us—that we would not simply be caned, as we had innocently feared at first, but, far more serious, that we might actually be suspended from school, sent home to face our parents with the catastrophic news that we could not after all be graduated next month, that instead we should have to attend summer school and go slinking into high school that fall with the shameful mark of our iniquity forever entered on our record. The idea was almost beyond enduring, not least because we could readily imagine what severe and lasting penalties our parents would be sure to visit upon us for our misdeeds. And not only that; I could imagine how hurt and disappointed my Aunt Ellen would be, and how hard my friend the Major would take this news of the disgrace of his color guard. Instead of the imminent season of joy that the coming summer months had seemed to us short hours before, with thirteen golden weeks of vacation, baseball, the beach, above all the Fort Sumter Celebration, now the forthcoming vacation season might be transformed into a dark, purgatorial time.

Occasionally one of our friends would come up and attempt to engage us in conversation. We answered briefly, in monosyllables, not wishing to talk with anyone about anything. The recess softball game, in which Billy Cartwright and I should ordinarily have been the most active of players, went on as usual across the yard, but we did not care. Games now seemed far away and unimportant, and all amusement mockery. Not even the long-anticipated arrival of the Wrigley Man interested us now. We watched our classmates thronging about him, waving their chewing gum packages aloft, the softball game abandoned, and we did not even see fit to remark on it.

Recess was over, and we went back into the classroom to sit through the final hours before our dreary and inexorable rendezvous with Dr. Higginson. We watched the minute hands of the schoolroom clock moving steadily, incorruptibly, toward the appointed time. Two hours became one, one hour became thirty minutes, became fifteen minutes, ten, five—until the dismissal bell rang out shrilly, harshly, and our time had come.

Billy Cartwright and I looked at each other desperately. "Let's go," I said.

He shrugged, and we rose to leave.

But we reckoned without Miss Lucia Jahnz. Our final class of the day had been with her, and now, as we moved toward the door to meet our fateful appointment, she motioned to us and to Wallace Riley who had sauntered over to join us.

"You three wait right here," she ordered. "I'm going upstairs myself first."

She disappeared through the door. Billy and I stood silently. Wallace Riley went over to the window and looked outside, humming a tune. The minutes dragged by.

After what seemed hours, we heard Miss Lucia Jahnz coming back down the corridor, the leather heels of her shoes clacking emphatically as she walked. The door opened.

"I have talked with Dr. Higginson," she told us, "and I explained that you didn't realize the seriousness of what you were doing, and besides, you probably weren't the only ones. So he agreed with me that this one time you're to be let off. But don't you *ever* do anything like this again!"

Miss Lucia Jahnz smiled.

The weight of the world was abruptly lifted from our shoulders. Most ardently we thanked Miss Jahnz, tears in our eyes. Fervently we pledged that never again would we wander from the way of virtue. Thankfully and joyously we raced out into the warm, bright afternoon, drinking in the scented May, reveling in the glad sunlight. Happily we leaped upon our bicycles; in soaring arcs we pumped for home.

"Hark!" I shouted at Billy Cartwright.

"Santa Lucia!" he shouted back. Joyful the echoes nigh.

Late that night, when I had turned off the reading lamp and lay in bed listening to the night sounds, I was filled with gratitude. For Miss Lucia Jahnz, who had intervened so nobly in our behalf. For Dr. Alexander O. Higginson, who had consented at the last to temper justice with mercy. For Billy Cartwright, for Wallace Riley. For the Major, who would have been saddened by our disgrace, but who alone perhaps would have understood and stood by us. For the Marvelous Ringgold, whose trolley car clattered so gladsomely along out there in the dark and filled the May evening with joyous movement. For kind souls and generous natures everywhere.

7. Though it would be six o'clock and later before my Aunt Ellen would return from her office, I arrived at the Warwick Apartments where she lived by five. Whenever I was invited to have supper with my Aunt Ellen I came early, for I enjoyed waiting for her almost as much as the suppertime itself. Her apartment was on the third floor, overlooking Colonial Lake and the downtown city. I borrowed the passkey from my friend Mrs. Bready, who owned and operated the apartment house. She was a sturdy, firm-jawed lady with a pleasant New England twang to her voice, and I enjoyed talking with her about books and literature. She was always waiting in the downstairs hall of the building, seated on one of the thick-cushioned marble benches under the racks of brass-paneled mailboxes. She would hand me the passkey in a paper bag, and then we would sit and talk until duty summoned Mrs. Bready elsewhere, as it always did, whether it was a delivery boy who needed rerouting through the side door or a tenant who required some linens. Mrs. Bready would sigh. "All right—just a minute!" she would call out, and get to her feet. "They always want something," she would say, and go padding off down the hall. Then I would spring up the sharp, winding staircase to the third floor, open my aunt's apartment door, replace the passkey in the paper bag, and drop it down the stairwell, watching it plummet to the bottom, to the first-floor hall.

My Aunt Ellen kept her apartment stifling hot. Though it was May, the heat was on, and the silver radiators by the windows were ticking. I flung open the green French doors to the balcony, placed the roses my father had sent her in a

47

vase on the kitchen drainboard, and went into the parlor.

I knew by heart what I should find there, but I always enjoyed exploring the room even so. It was a medium-sized room, with a great deal of unstuffed furniture with light-green upholstery. On the walls were old, browning photographs of Greek statuary, a small snapshot of a five-masted lumber schooner, three tinted Neapolitan scenes, oval portraits of my grandfather and grandmother, both of whom had died long before I was born, a photograph of my Uncle Ben, my father's and Aunt Ellen's older brother, in his lieutenant's uniform from the World War, and, over the desk and dominating the room, a large gray engraving showing an American doughboy kneeling before the Goddess of Liberty, with the legend COLUMBIA GIVES TO HER SON THE ACCOLADE OF THE NEW CHIVALRY OF HUMANITY, and my uncle's name—awarded him, as my aunt often explained, for having been wounded in action during the attack on the Argonne Forest.

In the two small bookcases, one by the big Atwater-Kent radio and the other against the wall near the door, were an assortment of books in faded jackets or none. I had inspected them all, and I knew the titles by heart. I liked to repeat them to myself. There were novels by Anatole France; several orange-covered copies of the *Virginia Quarterly Review*; an illustrated edition of *In Memoriam*; volumes of plays including *Dulcy*, *Green Pastures*, *The Passing of the Third Floor Back*, *The Second Mrs. Cheney*, and some of the Burns Mantle theater yearbooks; Woollcott's *While Rome Burns*, in a new, bright-red cover without a jacket; several Joseph Hergesheimer novels; a copy of *Ships That Pass in the Night*, which my aunt had told me once belonged to my grandfather; assorted prayerbooks and Passover manuals; copies of the *Atlantic Monthly* and *Harper's*; McFee's *Casuals of the Sea*; *The Story of Philosophy*, by Will Durant;

The Age of Innocence by Edith Wharton; a little volume by
Barrett H. Clark with an oft-inspected page devoted to my
Uncle Ben's plays; gray-covered librettos of operas my aunt
had once attended at the Metropolitan in New York; a scrap-
book of press clippings about my Uncle Ben's plays; a number of worn novels such as *Lorna Doone, Miss Gibbie Gault,*
and *Little Dorrit;* books of poems by Tagore, Lanier,
Shelley and Browning; a thick, green-covered edition of Bul-
finch's *Mythology;* several editions of *Alice in Wonderland,*
my aunt's favorite book; and, finally and prominently, a
group of books and pamphlets about Charleston, including
Mrs. Ravenel's *Charleston, the Place and the People;* a
boxed edition of a large work entitled *The Carolina Low
Country,* to which my aunt's employer had contributed an
essay; a book entitled *Sea-Drinking Cities;* and an inscribed
copy of *The State That Forgot: South Carolina's Surrender
to Democracy,* by Dr. Ball of the *News and Courier.*

When I tired of looking at the books I went out onto
the balcony and sat down in one of the green wooden porch
chairs. Below me in the semicircular court that overlooked
Rutledge Avenue and Beaufain Street there were several
palmetto trees, and the paperlike fronds rustled in the
breeze from the harbor. A few automobiles moved along
Rutledge Avenue. Occasionally one of the Belt Line trolleys
came bumping along—sluggish, uninteresting cars, I thought,
by comparison with the Rutledge Avenue Line which turned
into Wentworth Street and headed downtown a block north
and out of sight from where I sat. Mr. Zinzer, I thought,
really ought to be assigned to the Belt Line run; it would be
far more appropriate for him. The destroyer fleet was in port,
and it was possible to see the mast tips in the Ashley River
above the rooftops beyond Colonial Lake, swaying slowly as
the invisible vessels below them rocked at their moorings in
the harbor tide.

To the east and south the rooftops of the city stretched away. Above them rose the four downtown church steeples —the Unitarian church, St. John's Lutheran, and St. Philip's clustered together, and the thin white spire of St. Michael's standing all alone off to the right. As I looked out I heard St. Michael's bells tolling six o'clock, the notes dissolving liquidly in the faint, warm downtown air.

Meanwhile I watched the various tenants of the Berkeley Apartments coming home. There was Dr. Chisholm, the poet and historian, stepping briskly and importantly along the avenue, tipping his hat to several elderly ladies who stood talking at the corner as he passed. There were the Misses Altman, who occupied the temple pew just behind ours on Saturday mornings. There was Dr. Cheek, a tall, fat-faced gentleman who was a professor at the medical college.

Finally one more automobile came up Rutledge Avenue, turned the corner into Beaufain at the Berkeley, and my Aunt Ellen got out, busily conversing all the while, a process that involved several minutes from the time the automobile door first opened to my aunt's final wave to the driver. Ostensibly my aunt took the streetcar to and from work, but almost always some acquaintance would call to her as she waited on the corner for the homeward-bound trolley and give her a ride.

My aunt started up the walk, her oversized, thickly stuffed pocketbook slung under her arm. Then she looked up, saw me watching her from the third-floor balcony, and waved enthusiastically. "Hello, my love!" she called up to me, and skipped up the steps into the front entranceway. I listened then, and could trace her progress through the building and up the stairway. There were brief intervals of shoes clacking along the marble hall and stairway, and much longer periods of talking—with Mrs. Bready down by the mailboxes, with various residents as she passed their apartment doors, with other residents who came out to exchange news when they heard her voice down the hall, until finally, after a last stop of several minutes at the apartment just opposite her own to deliver an extended message and receive another, she flung open the door, plunged breathlessly into the room, and rushed out onto the porch to embrace me.

8.
DR. CHISHOLM IS COMING TO HAVE SUPPER WITH us," Aunt Ellen told me.

"I've told him all about you, and he wants to meet you." Going into the kitchen, she saw the roses that my father had sent. "Oh, how nice! I'll put them in a vase on the supper table!" As I watched, she went about arranging the flowers, preparing supper, setting up a table for three in the living room, and tidying up. At intervals various neighbors came in to visit with her.

"I can only stay a second," each one warned, and then settled down for from five to ten minutes of monologue, with my aunt listening and occasionally adding a comment while she worked away. Eventually the visitor departed, always remarking first, "I've simply got to go, I can't stay another second!"

Finally, when dinner was ready on the stove, and all preparations made, my aunt and I went out onto the balcony to watch the darkening city.

Presently there was a knock on the door, and my aunt hurried inside to open it. Dr. Chisholm entered. He was small, nattily dressed, and round-faced, with thick pince-nez on the bridge of his arching nose. Though I had never formally met him, I knew him well by reputation, as did all Charlestonians. By profession Dr. Chisholm was a librarian, and was employed at the Charleston Library Society. His major renown, however, was as an author. He had written two volumes of poetry, both of which I had seen displayed in the windows of bookstores downtown, and a book entitled *Gracious Yesterdays*, about plantation life in the Carolina

Lowcountry before the Civil War. From time to time the newspapers reported that he was addressing this or that organization near Charleston on the events of the War between the States. I knew he was a member of the Fort Sumter Seventy-fifth Anniversary Commission, the same as Major Frampton.

"Well, well, young man," he said as soon as my aunt introduced me to him, "your aunt has told me about you. So you are interested in the War between the States, are you?"

"Yes, sir, sort of."

"Splendid," Dr. Chisholm said. "It's always encouraging to find our younger generation concerning itself with our history."

"How is the Celebration coming?" my aunt asked.

"Very nicely, I think. Our plans are all set, and we expect considerable public response. It should be quite a tribute to the memory of the Lost Cause. Of course," he continued, "I deplore the circus atmosphere of some of it—all the bands and the like, but I suppose some of it is necessary."

"Isn't it nice," my aunt remarked, "that the President is going to speak?"

Dr. Chisholm frowned. "Oh, yes, I suppose so," he said, "from the standpoint of tourist interest, at least. Though for my own part I should much have preferred to have a speaker somewhat more appropriate to the occasion. After all, the President is not a Southerner, and certainly his views on so many important issues are not those of the Southern people. It is quite true, however, that the President's presence will attract a great deal of national publicity for the occasion. Besides, the most important thing after all is not a political speech, no matter who the speaker is, but the over-all spirit of the observance, and the honor being paid to Confederate history. From my own point of view at any rate, I am far more concerned with the interest that the Celebration is sure to stimulate in Southern history. It should make our people, especially our young people, think a little more about the lessons of the past. As you may know, I've been engaged myself in preparing a modest little history of the defense of Charleston, as my own small contribution to the Seventy-fifth Anniversary observance."

"Yes, indeed," my aunt said. "I've heard so many people talking about it."

"People are very kind," Dr. Chisholm said, smiling in deprecation. "It's nothing important, just a small volume. But I like to think that I have caught just a little of the spirit of the Lost Cause, and what it meant to our forebears."

"Have you chosen a title for the book, Doctor?"

"Yes, as a matter of fact, I have. I'm calling it *The Triumph or the Tomb*."

I recognized this at once as being the last line of the poem that the Major always recited whenever we went down to Adger's Wharf and looked out at the harbor. "I know that," I ventured. "It's from a poem by Henry Timrod."

"So it is!" Dr. Chisholm declared, a pleased tone in his voice. "You are quite correct. I didn't know that our young people read Timrod any more. How nice that you know his work!"

My Aunt Ellen beamed proudly. "Oh, Omar reads poetry often," she said. "He writes it, too." I flushed in embarrassment.

"Does he now?" Dr. Chisholm replied. "What sort of poems do you write, young man?"

To my extreme discomfort my aunt got up and went over to her desk. "I've got one right here!" she said. She handed Dr. Chisholm a magazine.

He glanced briefly at the title of the magazine. It was called *Young Israel*, and at that moment my poem suddenly seemed very inane to me, and rather silly. Dr. Chisholm turned the pages. "Let's have a look, now," he said, and his face assumed an expression of gravity as he read.

The poem was one entitled "Mountain Kingdom," which I had written over a year before. "Ah," said Dr. Chisholm after a minute, "very interesting. Have you been to the mountains often?"

"No, sir."

"You must have your parents take you to Flat Rock sometime. Simply sublime, the Carolina Highlands. How often have I watched them at dawn. The most peaceful country in the world. Next, of course, to the Lowcountry." He laughed. "You know what they say about us Charlestonians—when we die and go to heaven, it won't be satisfactory for us unless it smells like pluff mud! Ha, ha, ha, ha, ha!"

My aunt and I joined in the laughter, as expected. "If you two gentlemen will excuse me, now," my aunt said, "I'll get supper on the table. Would you care for a little cocktail, Doctor, while you're waiting?"

Dr. Chisholm scrambled to his feet. "Why, yes indeed, Miss Ellen, I would love one. We two will just have a little poet-to-poet talk while you're getting ready. What do you say we go out onto the balcony, young man? We can talk there while we take the evening air."

I followed him out onto the porch. For some reason, though I was quite thrilled at being called a fellow poet by so august a person as Dr. Chisholm, I felt very uneasy, as if I were posing, pretending to be something that I actually was not.

Dr. Chisholm breathed deeply. "Look at this lovely city," he declared.

> "They tell me she is beautiful, my city,
> That she is colorful and quaint, alone
> Among the cities . . ."

Below us the traffic moved along Rutledge Avenue. Some children were playing hopscotch on the sidewalk across Beaufain Street, by Colonial Lake. It was dusk, and beyond the rooftops I could see the tiny red lanterns on the masts of the destroyer fleet in the harbor.

"Beautiful lines," Dr. Chisholm commented. "An exquisite poem, by a true poet. Do you know Mr. Heyward? A talented man, though I confess I think he leases his muse to Mammon too readily. You know, we Charleston poets are fortunate—to live in so lovely a city, endowed with so many beautiful memories. Why, we breathe the very atmosphere of poetry from birth onward. It's no wonder that we've produced so many poets among us."

"Yes, sir."

Aunt Ellen came out on the porch and handed Dr. Chisholm a highball glass. "Thank you, ma'am," said the doctor and took a generous sip.

"You know," he resumed, "hardly a day passes by for me without some tangible occasion for poetry presenting itself. I keep a notebook with me at all times, simply in order to jot down images and lines as they occur to me while I go about my day." He lifted a tiny brown leather book from his inside coat pocket momentarily, to show me, then replaced it. "Do you do that, young man?"

"No, sir."

"Oh, but you must," Dr. Chisholm declared, taking another swallow from the highball. "All serious poets have to keep a kind of storehouse, a treasure trove of golden moments, so to speak. Later we can turn them into our songs— emotion recollected in tranquillity, as Dr. Johnson said. The important thing is to seize and pin down the fleeting instants of insight as they flash upon our inward recognition. You must learn to do that. Then when you sit at home, in the solitude of the study, you can take pen in hand and gather the harvest."

"Yes, sir."

"Oh, there is so much poetic material out there, almost at

your finger tips!" Dr. Chisholm gestured toward the down-town city and the harbor. "All you have to do is reach out and take it, you know!" He had emptied the highball glass by now, and he set it down on the arm of a chair.

Aunt Ellen came to the door of the balcony. "Won't you come in and have supper?"

"Yes, indeed," Dr. Chisholm replied. "We've been admiring the beauty of the city at dusk together, haven't we?"

I followed Dr. Chisholm inside, and we took our places at the table. "I've just been remarking to our young friend how fortunate he is to be a Charleston boy," Dr. Chisholm said. "The sea, the harbor, the old city—these young people just don't know how privileged they are, do they, Miss Ellen?"

My aunt handed Dr. Chisholm a bowl of curried shrimp, and the doctor spread a liberal helping over his rice. "Do you do any sailing, young man?" he asked me.

"No, sir."

"What? Not sail? A Charleston boy? Why, when I was your age I lived on the water from April to October."

"Did you have a boat of your own, sir?" I asked.

"I certainly did! Every Charleston boy should own a boat. Don't tell me that you don't."

That started Dr. Chisholm reminiscing about his boyhood. He told Aunt Ellen and me about the various boats he had sailed, the trips he had taken about the harbor, the adventures he had enjoyed. After that, the conversation shifted to his historical researches about the harbor in the course of writing his new book, and he described the studies he had conducted, using maps, charts and old documents, and even taking depth soundings himself to determine the actual spots at which the various events of the defense of Charleston Harbor during the War had taken place.

"You know, it was a very strange feeling—thank you." He helped himself to more curried shrimp. "My own great-uncle, Colonel A. R. Chisolm—he spelled his name without the second *h*—was aide-de-camp to General Beauregard during the time of the bombardment of Fort Sumter. As I moved about the harbor on my own researches, I felt a strange sense of recapturing the past, a kind of racial or ancestral memory, so to speak. I am not ashamed to tell you that my work in preparing my little book seemed to take on for me a kind of symbolic meaning, as if in writing it I was expressing, in the only way that I could, my own allegiance to the cause my great-uncle fought for."

"How interesting," Aunt Ellen said.

"It's just a little monograph, of course, and I don't flatter myself that it will cause any great stir. Though it *will* be the definitive account of the defense of Charleston Harbor, and all the earlier work on the subject will be rendered obsolete when it comes out."

"Oh, I'm sure it will be very successful," my aunt said. "When will it go on sale?"

"Two weeks from now, if all goes well. I delivered the last of the page proofs to the printer on April 15. The bound copies are due back any day now."

We had finished dessert by then, and Dr. Chisholm rose. "Well, Miss Ellen, I hate to be one of those people who eat and run, but as I warned you when I accepted your gracious invitation last night, I do have a board meeting of the Seventy-fifth Anniversary Commission. I do hope you'll forgive me this time, and I promise you I shan't let it happen again."

"Oh, of course, Doctor," Aunt Ellen assured him. "I know that Omar is simply thrilled to death that you could even come at all. Isn't that right, Omar?"

"Yes, sir."

"It was a genuine pleasure," Dr. Chisholm declared. "Young man, we'll have to see more of each other, now that we've met. And remember—keep that notebook! Capture those flashes of insight when they come to you!"

Dr. Chisholm shook hands with Aunt Ellen and me and departed.

"Well," Aunt Ellen said after he had gone, "I'm so glad that you and the doctor hit it off so well together. He's a very interesting person, isn't he?"

"Yes'm."

"And do you know, his poems are very highly admired. I've heard that some of the best editors in New York have said that his work is quite distinctive."

Aunt Ellen began clearing away the dishes, and I helped her carry the silverware and plates into the kitchen. After we had finished we went back into the living room, but before we could sit down there was a knock at the door. "Come in!" my aunt called.

It was Dr. Chisholm again, with a book in his hand. "I just wanted the young man to have this," he said. "A slight thing, but mine own, as they say. Wait a moment now, and I'll inscribe it." He opened the book, drew a large green fountain pen from his inside coat pocket, and prepared to write. "How is it that you spell your name now?"

"O-m-a-r," my aunt told him. "Omar Kohn. This is very nice of you, Doctor, and I know Omar will be thrilled."

Dr. Chisholm wrote in the book for a minute, and then, after blowing on the page to dry the ink, snapped it shut and handed it to me. "There you are," he said. "Must be running; I'm late now. Bye-bye!"

"Thank you very much, sir!" I said.

"Think nothing of it. A pleasure. 'Bye!" and Dr. Chisholm disappeared down the hall. I could hear him hurrying down the circular staircase, his patent-leather shoes clacking rapidly along the marble steps.

"Now, wasn't that nice of Dr. Chisholm?" my aunt asked. "Think of it. Now you have an autographed edition, inscribed by the author!"

I opened the book to where Dr. Chisholm had written, in a small, precisely lettered hand, these words:

> *To my young friend Omar Kahn,*
> *These products of some few flashes of insight.*
> *Horatio Chisholm*
> *Charleston, May 13, 1936*

The volume was entitled *Sandpiper Soliloquies*; it was thin, with light-blue binding and a black-and-silver jacket. The poems were all quite short, and were neatly printed, one to a page.

"You must be sure and keep it carefully," Aunt Ellen said. "It may be quite valuable some day."

I rode home that evening on Mr. Zinzer's trolley car, but for once I did not mind. The long, deliberate ride up to Versailles Street passed soon enough. I sat by myself, alternately reading the poems in the book that Dr. Chisholm had given me, and thinking about the events of the evening. I had met a real poet and talked about poetry with him! He had actually presented me with a personal, inscribed, autographed copy of one of his books. A real author, and I knew him personally, even if he wasn't sure how to spell my last name.

After I came home and showed my autographed, inscribed book of poems to my parents, I went on upstairs to bed. It was quite late, and my mother told me that I was not to turn on the bed lamp and read that evening. I took the book with me to the bathroom, and read a little there, but I found I was still too excited to read for very long at a time. So I lay in bed, thinking some more about my talk with Dr. Chisholm, trying to remember everything he had said. I promised myself that I would do just what he had suggested: I would get a little notebook and think about poetic things and write them down. I would work hard at it, and perhaps one day soon I would have a chance to show him the results. . . .

The launch had long since passed by our house and gone down the river. I heard the train coming into the city toward the bridge. I began thinking about what Dr. Chisholm had said about sailing, and how every Charleston boy should have a boat. Where was I to get one, however? I had no money to purchase one, and I knew my father would not for a moment think of buying a boat for me. Yet I must have a boat, even if I had to build it myself.

That was it! I would tell Billy Cartwright about it tomorrow morning, and we would build a boat ourselves. There was no reason why not. It would be the easiest thing in the world to steal some lumber from the new house being built on Pendleton Street; we had taken some just last week to build a tree house. We would get some lumber and nails and construct a boat of our own and float it in the marsh, mooring it at the old wharf behind Mr. Simons' house.

A sailboat would not be very practical in the marsh though. Besides, we had no canvas for a sail. Then I remembered a photograph I had seen in a set of picture books that Billy Cartwright owned, showing a boy a little younger than ourselves afloat in a small boat equipped with paddle wheels. The very thing! The Major could tell us how to do it; he had often talked about the great paddle wheels that had powered the ferryboats he piloted many years ago. The boat would be long, and low, and white, and we would go churning about the marsh and out into the river, with the paddle wheels revolving, revolving. . . .

In the distance I heard the Seaboard freight train rumbling across the bridge into the city, but my mind was on other things that night. I thought of boats, and poetry, and the defense of Fort Sumter, and Dr. Chisholm, and the Major, and

61

gradually they all blended together in one pleasant and sunny panorama. I dropped off to sleep only dimly conscious of the locomotive bell tolling far away, and the trolley cars on the Rutledge Avenue Line coming and going, humming as they moved along.

9. WE COULD NOT START ON THE BOAT ON SUNDAY. BILLY Cartwright was away at Sunday School and church during the morning, and there were too many visitors driving past the new houses in the afternoon. But I found some sheets of smooth brown kraft paper, and with ruler and pencil I designed a long, low-slung craft with an arched bow tapering gracefully to a point. A sturdy planked deck extended three feet back from the bowsprit, and a handsome pennant was to be mounted upon it, with a palmetto flag. The paddle wheels were eight-bladed and set amidships. The boat was to be painted a bright white, with a blue streak along the side—I carefully filled in the colors with watercolor paints. There would be seats for three people: one at the stern, for manning the rudder, another in the center, at the paddle wheels, and a third one forward, just short of the deck, for looking over the bow. I imagined the Major occupying that seat, giving us the benefit of his long experience afloat as we churned along the marsh creeks and out into the Ashley River.

Aunt Ellen was having dinner with us that Sunday, and proudly I showed her my drawings. To my surprise, however, especially since she had been present the very night before and had heard Dr. Chisholm tell me that a Charleston boy *had* to have a boat, her response now was less than enthusiastic. "Aren't you afraid you'll fall in and drown?" she asked. I assured her that such a boat as I planned could never under any circumstances capsize, and besides, as good sailors, we intended to take every precaution. She would be able to see for herself when she went for a ride with us, after the boat was completed. But Aunt Ellen declared emphatically that she did not go out in small boats, no matter how well built. "The solid earth is good enough for this gal!" she said, and laughed. "The Belt Line trolley car will take me anywhere I want to go!"

Billy Cartwright came over in the early afternoon. I had already told him my plan earlier that morning, before he left for Sunday School. He had not seemed enthusiastic at the time, but this was because he had just found out that a girl cousin from Philadelphia would be coming down to spend the summer months at his house, and this had cast a shadow over his plans for a carefree vacation. Billy sometimes got into such moods, but I knew he got out of them fairly quickly; and sure enough, when he showed up after Sunday dinner he was willing and eager to begin work.

One hitch in our plans appeared at the start: the Major was away on a three-day visit to relatives in Orangeburg, and would not be back until Wednesday. So we would have to manage the paddle wheels by ourselves, unless we wanted to wait—and the idea of a three-day wait before completing our craft was unthinkable.

Not until after supper was it sufficiently dark outside for us to begin collecting the lumber we needed. We sat around impatiently during the long May afternoon, planning our project and imagining the many exploits that would be possible once the boat was finished. The first day we would take a trial run along the edge of the river. After that there would be voyages across the Ashley to the sandbanks along the western shore. Once school was out and our days were unencumbered, we would begin making trips all the way down the river and to the harbor. We saw ourselves proudly rounding the point at High Battery, waving to spectators gathered along the iron railing to watch us, and continuing on to Adger's Wharf, where we would put ashore. There was no

64

telling what we would be able to do, once the boat was built.

Billy was intrigued with the commercial possibilities of the boat. "We could run harbor tours from Adger's Wharf," he said. "We could take two people at a time, at fifty cents apiece. In less than a month we'd have enough money to buy a large boat, a launch. Then we could run sight-seeing tours out to Fort Sumter. The Major could go along and describe the battle. Boy, we'd soon be rich!"

Meanwhile we assembled tools and collected sawhorses. At first my idea had been to build our boat in the basement of our house, where my father's workbench was handy. My father, however, vetoed this plan emphatically. "I've got to mix rose spray all day tomorrow," he said, "and I don't want the basement all cluttered up anyway. You'll have to build your boat out under the side porch." So we set up operations there and waited for dusk to come.

"We'd better get some life preservers," Billy said. "It might get rough all of a sudden, or a storm might come up." We decided to get some old automobile tubes from a gas station and patch them up.

"What are we going to name the boat?"

"I don't know," I said. "How about the *Star of the West?*"

"Maybe."

On second thought I decided that this would not do, since the *Star of the West* had been a Yankee boat, and the Major would not approve of such a name. We thought of various other possibilities, but none of them seemed right.

When suppertime came it was still light. Afterward, however, the shadows finally grew long enough so that we thought we could begin. With a small red wagon borrowed for the occasion we set out for the new houses. We stacked some long boards of white pine on the wagon and managed to haul them back. Then we returned for nails. We could find no white paint, but there was one half-used can of red lead under the toolshed of the house, and we appropriated that, adding, for good measure, several more pine boards and an assortment of smaller slabs of wood. By the time we had finished it was dark, and there was no electric light under the porch, so we were forced to postpone the actual boat building until the next afternoon.

As things turned out, our boat when completed was somewhat different from the craft I had planned. We found first of all that it was impossible to keep the pine boards bent firmly into a curve for the pointed bow. Not only did they buckle awkwardly and unevenly, but they were forever springing back into their former uncurved shape and pulling loose all the nails we had driven into them. My father explained why: the lumber had not been treated so that it would remain in shape. It would be necessary, he told us, to build a blunt-nosed craft without a pointed bow, if we wanted it to hold together.

He also suggested that it would be very difficult to float such a boat as we planned in the marsh, except at extremely high tide. "What you boys want to build is a little two-man bateau—something you can handle," he explained. We had not bothered to tell him our plans for traveling downstream to the harbor, for obvious reasons, but it did seem logical that we should build a boat small enough to use in the marsh when we wished. We decided to build a bateau such as he had suggested, and then later on to build still another boat, a much larger one, which we would keep moored at the edge of the river, using the bateau to get to it from the shore.

The boat we built was a short, squat affair, with high sides and square bow and stern—to be exact, a wooden box without a top. The deck I had envisioned, with a place for a palmetto-flag pennant, was missing. Boards were nailed across the top fore and aft, as seats. Our boat was painted solid red, with no trim.

At the point when we had been about to start nailing the planks into place, my father, who had been out in the side yard pruning his North China elm tree, had come by and made a suggestion. "You've got to have calking," he said.

It was a term we did not know. My father explained that it was necessary to place calking between the planks, so that they would swell up when wet and seal off the water. We would have to buy some at a ship's store downtown, he said. Then he returned to his task of pruning the elm tree.

Billy Cartwright thought a minute. "Why couldn't we use tar?" he asked. We walked around the new houses, hoping to find some, but nothing of the sort was available. Finally I noticed a half-used roll of tar paper lying in the grass near the toolshed.

"Do you reckon we could use that?" I asked.

"Sure, I don't see why not," Billy said.

The workmen were about, but we managed to tear off a large piece of tar paper without being noticed, and took it back home. Cutting it into strips, we placed the tar paper between the planks and nailed them into position as snugly as we could. Then we began painting.

There remained the matter of the paddle wheels. We found a long, rusty iron rod designed for reinforcing concrete, and bent a tuck into it for a handle. Onto each end we fastened a board, and fixed four slabs of wood to each. We attached it to the boat by driving long, thin nails into the top of the planking and bending them over the rod. There remained only the rudder, and we decided to dispense with that for the time being and to steer by means of a paddle.

Our craft was ready. It was still light, and we wanted to take it down to the creek and launch it then and there, but the tide was low and the creek bottom was mostly mud. So we postponed the launching operation until the next day.

We did not yet have a name for our boat. We thought of calling it the *Sappho*, in honor of the Major, but we were not sure the Major would approve of that, either, since his *Sappho* had been a great, majestic affair and ours was so small and insignificant.

It was Miss Lucia Jahnz, of all people, who finally supplied a name for it. In English class the next morning she was telling us about the poet John Keats, and she read us some passages from a poem called "Endymion," including one that described a man in a boat:

> And, as the year
> Grows lush in juicy stalks, I'll smoothly steer
> My little boat, for many quiet hours,
> With streams that deepen freshly into bowers.
> Many and many a verse I hope to write,
> Before the daisies, vermeil rimm'd and white,
> Hide in deep herbage, . . .

"We can call it the *Endymion!*" I told Billy Cartwright as we were changing classrooms. This seemed especially appropriate to me, because while there were no daisies or herbage in the marsh, it was filled with stalks, just as in the poem. Billy agreed that it did seem a good name. The more I thought about it, the more I liked the idea. It was an imposing name, and poetic—Dr. Chisholm would doubtless approve heartily.

That afternoon I painted the words, *Endymion of Charleston, S.C.*, in block letters on the stern of our boat, and we prepared to launch it. We loaded it onto the wagon and tugged it down to the wharf. With a couple of long boards for runways, we pushed it off the edge of the dock into the creek. The tide was going out, but there was still ample water to float our craft. It rode high upon the surface of the creek, rocking slowly, and we observed it with considerable pride and satisfaction. It was not exactly a graceful-looking boat, it was not even especially boatlike in appearance, but it was ours—we had built it. We broke a jar of Koolaid across its bow after several tries, and felt quite pleased with our efforts. Now we could take to the water like true Charleston boys.

The *Endymion of Charleston, S.C.* soon proved to be something less than perfect. For one thing, the strips of tar paper we had placed between the plankings did not keep out the water; instead they worked out of place and floated around in the bottom of the boat, and we soon found ourselves ankle-deep in water, thus necessitating frequent bailing. The *Endymion of Charleston, S.C.* also tipped and rocked considerably, and whenever either of us stood up a precarious balancing operation was necessary.

From the outset the paddle wheels proved impractical. Not only did they propel the boat very slowly indeed and require much exertion, but on their upward revolutions the flat blades splashed great quantities of water into the boat and onto the person seated on the rear seat, so that we were soon drenched from head to toe. Regretfully we abandoned the paddle wheels in favor of long paddles made of strips of board with slabs nailed to either end.

We did not venture very far from shore that first afternoon because the tide would soon be too low to float us. The next day, however, we hurried home from school, took to the water right away, and poled and paddled our way up the sluggish creek, threading our way through the marsh grass toward the river. It was a much longer distance than we had anticipated, and the insect life buzzed irritatingly about us as we poled, pushed, and bailed in the sun. Each bend in the creek revealed still another ahead, and it was a long time before we finally rounded one more wide, sweeping curve and saw ahead of us the open waters of the Ashley River.

69

Up to the creek mouth we paddled, pausing at intervals to bail, with the *Endymion of Charleston, S.C.* rocking in the current. The river seemed awesomely wide and deep. For the first time we realized the boldness of our notion of taking to the river. Feeling very insecure, we sat there in the boat, clutching at some reed stalks to keep from drifting off, and contemplated the great flowing channel before us.

"Let's just paddle along the edge of the marsh for a while," Billy suggested finally.

Hesitantly we directed the *Endymion of Charleston, S.C.* around the point of the marsh and into the main current of the river itself. Our blood pounding, we edged along the border of the marsh grass, moving upon currents far stronger than we had ever traveled, on waters we knew would be far over our heads if we were to capsize. And we had forgotten to get the life preservers too.

A hundred feet we paddled, down to a channel marker along the marsh. Catching hold of its concrete base with our hands, we rode there, astonished at our own audacity, awed at what we had done. For this red boat was supporting us, was rocking and pitching as it lifted us over each wave, was wooden, was secure, was—though it leaked, though it was clumsy, ungainly, inelegant—a boat, and we ourselves had made it.

10. For the first time since Sabbath School had begun the previous fall, Saturday morning was free. There would be the final children's services next Friday night, when the awards and prizes for the year would be made, but the class work was over. The closing of Sabbath School was a sign of the imminence of summertime, a perceptible, undeniable token. Not for two more weeks, when the public schools shut down and we graduated from the seventh grade, would summer actually come. It was still May, not June. But now we knew the long school term was almost over, and summer vacation, once a nebulous, far-off abstraction, was a definite thing, an event certain to occur soon.

Now the low hum of insects filled the green jade marsh, the thin cattails waving their tan plumes, the tide light on the marsh, so still, so clear. Oak trees along the banks were heavy in leaf, the thick brown trunks cool, humid to the touch. The air was summer-sweet in breath of fern, wildflower, cherry laurel, marsh grass. The red boat swung at the landing. In the torpid pluff mud of the creeks the midmorning sun stirred hot life, popping little rainbow bubbles of slime on pocked fiddler coves, baking the ragged lacework of silt to dry crust. Below the velvet surface of the water crabs glided secretly by, scuttling sidewise along the receding bank. A school of mud-minnows fanned out in the pale recesses of the creek, slowly, their forward motion almost suspended; then drawn by an invisible cord they flashed away in unison through the current. Nearby in the snail-leeched reeds an unseen bird loudly picked its way among the stalks. In the oaks overhead the

71

branched boughs swished together, their thick waxed leaves murmuring in tens of thousands.

Beyond the marsh and the houses, toward town, the fields were hazy and sweet in the scented sharpness of fennel and pokeberry, the ground thick-woven with bramble, garlanded in white flowering blackberry vine. Paths through the thickets wound among rough weeds, carpeted with spongy crabgrass, the cool earth springy to the touch. Roads, sandy and tight packed to coarse hardness, stung the bottoms of bare feet, and the easy prickle of the regained crabgrass was soft balm to the sole. Along the roads the ditches were steeped foot-deep in rain water from last week's showers, their clouded depths swarming with black tadpoles already beginning to sprout minute limbs. Scooped out in the hands they lay wriggling and cool, their compact, curled intestines visible through the transparent skin of their filmy bellies. In stagnant ponds frogs warbled.

Up Pendleton Street there was the steady thumping of hammers from a house under construction, the wheeze of a sharp bandsaw rasping through raw lumber, the slap of flat boards banged together, the sound of workmen whistling, singing, calling to one another. A truckload of bricks rumbled heavily down Versailles Street, the truck jouncing over the ruts and the red clay bricks clinking brightly to each jolt and dip of the swayback frame. In the lee shade of a toolshed two bird dogs lay wearily, one with mouth open and curling tongue lolling in heated pant, the other with eyes closed and legs stretched sidewise in morning sleep. Overhead a high blue sky, with an occasional puffed cloud drifting serenely across. And above all the land, a shimmering haze of heat, moistened and hovering in its faint undulation.

I saw it all. I was there, listening, seeing, breathing in all that weather. Through the fields and woods I went. The bird dogs, roused from their nap, came with me, darting off into the bushes to flush startled birds from thickets, criss-crossing in the rutted path up ahead, racing along the trail for a moment, noses down, then bolting off into the high brush once again. Deep into the woods of Devereux I made my way, treading carefully down a narrow pathway, bending to avoid overhanging thorn bushes, pushing aside cherry laurel and bramble, stepping down to the marsh's edge to sit on cool grass banks while the dogs sprang lightly through the boggy reeds until only their tails could be seen cutting excited arcs above the rushes. In the still glade I sat for a while, hearing the noise of house-building far off, the humming of insects, a car lurching down the street in the distance, the sound of my own breathing. Three months of summer were ahead, each day like all the rest, hot, jeweled, somnolent.

Dominique came from the West Indies. He was of medium height, with huge shoulders and arms that bulged with purple clusters of muscles. His skin was deepest black in color, and his teeth were glistening white. On the finger of one hand he wore a ring of unusual brightness.

He came to our house to work on my father's rose garden. He was a friend of our cook, Viola, and ordinarily he worked at the fruit company dock at the waterfront, unloading bananas. His speech was strange to my ears, for he had grown up in Jamaica and spoke with an English accent. For all his great physical bulk and strength, however, his voice was low and soothing. When Viola conversed with him, as she began to do at lunchtime, it was she who seemed to do most of the talking.

The fruit boats arrived from Central America on Mondays, Wednesdays and Fridays, so Dominique came to us on Tuesdays, Thursdays, and Saturdays. When he worked for us he would spend all morning under the fierce sun, hacking at the hard earth, shoveling spadefuls of it into a barrow, until he amassed a load that seemed surely too heavy for any single man to move. He would then lay down his shovel, take hold of the wooden handles of the barrow, and without straining, cart the dirt away, depositing it in a neat mound in the street. Though the temperature was moving up into the nineties by late May, he stopped only occasionally to get a drink of water. He would labor away, his head protected only by a soiled handkerchief, the upper half of his torso bare save for a frayed undershirt.

At noontime Viola would call to him from the side porch, and he would put down his spade and go in where there was shade and be served lunch. Most days Viola would sit with him while he ate, talking away while Dominique listened, until his work time came again. Then he would get up, return to the garden, and work all afternoon, steadily, tirelessly, until the shadows reached out across the yard and it was past five o'clock. He would gather up his tools then, deposit them under the porch, collect his pay, and go home.

With my father supervising, he dug up all the rose bushes, taking care to keep the roots packed in balls of earth, and set them in along the fence. Then he excavated the entire garden area. He spread first pebbles, then the new earth, watered the area, planted grass seed, fertilized it. Then, with my father carefully measuring distances and consulting diagrams, the rose bushes were removed from their temporary beds and placed back in position. Next came more fertilizing, raking, watering.

Soon the new grass began showing through the black soil. The rose bushes took hold again. My father strode about the garden, noted each sign of renewed growth, signified his approval. If all went well, the rose garden would be back on its normal schedule by the time the really hot weather came, and well able to hold its own during the dry season of July.

When September arrived, it would be ready to put out bloom as never before.

My father turned his attention to other gardening matters. His North China elm tree needed attention. There was work to be done in the side yard as well, and several concrete arbors to be built. Dominique was kept on to help. It was too good a chance, my father explained to my mother, not to get the whole property into first-class shape. Dominique dug, shoveled, hauled, raked. On the days he was there, Viola sang to herself as she worked.

Sunday morning I saw a sailboat on the river, and thought of Dr. Chisholm. It had been more than a week since I had talked with him about poetry, and he had given me the volume of his own poems. I had read it through several times by now, and despaired of ever being able to emulate it. The trouble was that when I looked at things, I did not *see* what Dr. Chisholm saw and put down in his poems. I had even bought a little notebook to jot down those golden moments Dr. Chisholm had spoken about. But no golden moments ever came. I would look at a rooftop and think to myself that I *ought* to have a fleeting instant of insight, as Dr. Chisholm had said, about the way the sunlight fell upon it. But all I thought of to write in the notebook were things like "the red roof is bright" or "the yellow sun is on the red rooftop," which would never do. Reading Dr. Chisholm's book, I felt my utter lack of poetic vision; where I saw only a few trees or fields or creeks or houses, Dr. Chisholm saw all kinds of similarities and allusions to foreign lands, romantic places, famous events.

How many times had I been down to the waterfront with the Major and looked out toward Fort Sumter, and yet all I had ever thought of was the low shape of the fort in the center of the harbor. Yet Dr. Chisholm's book contained a

75

poem called "View from Adger's Wharf"—precisely the point from which the Major and I always observed the harbor—in which he described Fort Sumter as

> *That thick-walled bastion, bristling now with steel,*
> *Searching the feckless sea for hostile keel,*
> *In timeless vigil over the surly deep,*
> *That the sunned palmettos of the land may sleep.*

Try though I might, I could never think of things like that. I knew the Fort's history, of course, but it never would have occurred to me to imagine that the Fort might still be keeping watch like a sentinel over the harbor, as if it were alive and had a memory.

There was also a poem about marsh grass in Dr. Chisholm's book, and this was the most discouraging poem of them all. For marsh grass was something that I saw right out in front of my house every day of my life. To me it had always been —marsh grass, green in the spring and summer, brown in the fall and winter. I liked to sit down by the edge of the marsh and watch it sometimes, because it always seemed so calm and tractable, and when the tide was unusually high in the spring and fall the spears of the grass were almost submerged by the water, giving a kind of needlepoint effect to the clouds and sky reflected in the water. Sometimes it seemed as if the clouds were almost fastened to the surface of the marsh by the reeds, and I would imagine that they were trying to tear themselves loose, like clothes on a line on a windy day. But how could things like clotheslines and needlepoint be made into poems?

I went upstairs to my room and got Dr. Chisholm's book —the cover was already becoming soiled, I noticed, because I had been handling it so much—and walked down to the wharf. I looked at the marsh—the tide was quite high—and then I opened the book to Dr. Chisholm's poem and read it aloud:

MARSH GRASS

It is a carpet, gay in green and gold,
For clouds to sleep upon at high noonday,
As if some Persian merchant-god unrolled
A prayer rug there, then wandered far away.

Now herons weave the corners to the land,
And river currents curl about its side,
Till what was loomed and turned at Samarkand
Is raveled by the ebbing of the tide.

I would never be able to do that. How many times had I
too seen the herons at the edge of the marsh, ankling along
on their stilted legs; yet never had they seemed to me remotely to be weaving a rug. As for Persian merchant-gods and
faraway cities like Samarkand, I had never thought of anything like that. In fact, the marsh simply did not look at all
like a rug to me. Not at all. It was just . . . well . . . marsh.
That was the trouble with doing what Dr. Chisholm had
said, and capturing the golden instants of insight. I just
didn't have any golden insights to capture! The marshland
was the marshland, and Fort Sumter was Fort Sumter, and
things like merchant-gods and Samarkand and herons weaving and hostile keels and the like never crossed my mind.

Yet Dr. Chisholm had praised my poem about the mountains. But there were no golden moments of insight in that.
I had made it all up. I had never even seen a real mountain.

I felt that I had taken the book of poems from Dr.
Chisholm under false pretenses. He had thought my poem
was about real mountains, like the one about the Great
Smokies in his book, when the truth was that I had fabricated
the whole thing. I had fooled him into thinking that I had
looked at some actual mountains and had captured a golden
moment of insight, as he did when he looked at the Great
Smokies, or the marsh, or at Fort Sumter—fooled him so

77

completely that he had acted as if I were a fellow poet and had talked with me about golden moments. If only he knew. If only he knew!

I went back up the bluff to my house and up to my room. "In the solitude of your study," Dr. Chisholm had told me. It was one more token of my fraudulence, for it was no study, only a bedroom with a desk by the window and one red bookcase. "Take pen in hand," he had advised—and I, I wrote my poems on a typewriter, a big, unromantic old Underwood No. 5 that my father had bought from a used office supplies store for twelve dollars. "Gather the harvest" —but there was no harvest there for me to gather.

I put a sheet of yellow paper in the typewriter. P O E M I typed out.

> *What I see by the edge of the creek*
> *Is not a sailboat, lovely and sleek,*
> *But a little red boat with seams that leak.*

For a half-minute I stared at what I had written. Then I reached out and jerked the sheet of yellow paper from the typewriter, balled it up, and fired it at the wastebasket across the room. It ricocheted off the wall and plunked into the basket. Billy Cartwright was surely home from church by now, I thought. I got up and went to find him.

11. WE WERE THE CHILDREN OF ISRAEL. I ALWAYS thought of Sabbath School in those terms. There was a kind of nobility, a silent dignity to the words, a sense of proud yet unobtrusive kinship that we all shared. I felt a sad, mystical, beautiful loyalty, a vision of brotherhood with a band of lonely and quiet men with sad, luminous eyes through which a deep brilliance shone. There was a hymn we sometimes sang at Sabbath School that always obscurely thrilled me:

> *There is a mystic tie that joins*
> *The children of the martyred race*
> *In bonds of sympathy and love*
> *That time and change cannot efface.*

I liked the idea of the bonds of sympathy and love that lasted throughout all time and change, and I was proud of my possession of those bonds.

I was, for that matter, proud of our Sabbath School and temple, and my attendance there. I did not particularly like what we studied at Sabbath School—biblical history, Jewish history; but I did like the sense of a continuity extending far back into the past, a kinship with scholars, poets, philosophers living in Germany two centuries and more ago, in Holland and Spain before that, in northern Africa, Rome, in the Near East, far off along the Black and Caspian Seas. The thought that I, in bright and sunny South Carolina across the great ocean, bore in my blood so tenuous yet inescapable a heritage pleased me.

It was the custom for the children of the Sabbath School

to participate in one evening service every year, during which awards were made for achievement during the past term. I looked forward to this evening service with considerable anticipation, for I knew that I was to receive the prize for achievement in our class. It was not that I was a devoted scholar; rather, of the three of us in the class, I was the only one interested in history at all, and such lukewarm concern was more than enough to distinguish one in our class.

The ceremony of the presentation of prizes would therefore be something of a triumph—my only triumph of the season, for I had already found out that I was not going to win the American Legion medal for achievement in American history at public school, and I was in no way a contender for the Julian Mitchell Achievement Medal. This, despite our near-disaster of two weeks before, Billy Cartwright still hoped to win. Since there would be no chance of my being in any way singled out for commendation at the public-school graduation exercises, the Sabbath School prize would be my single opportunity for glory. I would be summoned up to the altar last of all, I knew, after the various awards for the lower classes had been made, and before my parents and the adult members of the congregation who never attended Saturday morning services but were always present on Friday evening, I would be presented with a book. I was sure of this, for I had seen the little presentation card with my name on it on Dr. Raskin's desk in his study the week before.

I did not fail to inform Billy Cartwright of my impending honor. Indeed, since I knew that if he won the Julian Mitchell Medal it would give him a distinction far beyond mine at graduation next week, I felt impelled to magnify the importance of my own small victory as much as possible. On Thursday afternoon I alluded to it again with studied casualness, this time in the presence of Billy's mother, who was driving us downtown to the movies.

To my consternation, however, Mrs. Cartwright not only

caught up my remark at once, but asked whether the Cartwrights might attend the services the next evening to watch
me receive the award.

Now this was considerably more than I had bargained for,
because I was in no way anxious to have the Cartwrights, who
were Presbyterians, involved in any function in which my
separate religious and racial identity would be emphasized.
I tried therefore to pass off Mrs. Cartwright's suggestion
without reply. But Mrs. Cartwright insisted, and taking my
silence for consent, promised that when she got home she
would telephone my mother about it. I hoped devoutly that
she would forget to do so, but to no avail.

My mother was of course delighted to have the Cartwrights accompany us. When I suggested that perhaps there
might not be room for visitors at Friday night services, she
pooh-poohed the suggestion. "There's always plenty of room
at temple," she said, "especially now that so many people
have already moved over to the island for the summer."

I tried to think of further objections but could not. My
mother saw that I was not enthusiastic, however, and scolded
me for it. "Anyone would think you were ashamed of your
religion," she said. "There's nothing wrong with the Cartwrights' going to services with us. It will be very beautiful
when you all march in with the candles, and they'll enjoy it.
Besides, you know how much the Major will enjoy seeing
you receive the prize."

The Major! That was even worse. I had not realized until
then that he too would be going along. "Oh, *he* wouldn't
like it," I said. "It'll be hot and stuffy in there, and he goes
to bed early anyway."

My father laughed. "Don't you worry about the Major,"
he said. "He's sat through a lot worse than that in his time.
And anyway, until that Fort Sumter Celebration takes place,
not even hell and high water would put the Major out of
commission."

81

"But he's so old," I insisted. My mother became irritated at my attitude. "Now you just hush up this minute!" she told me. "If the Cartwrights and Major Frampton want to come along, they're perfectly welcome. The very idea of being ashamed of your religion! You should be proud that your friends want to come to temple with you."

That was Thursday evening, and I was not proud. By the next day, however, I had begun to think differently about the matter. For I came to feel that the services that evening would serve to enhance my triumph, affording it a general recognition that would extend beyond the private boundaries of the "downtown" Jewish community. I thought now of how impressed the guests would be with the services, particularly by the ceremony of the reading from the Scrolls of the Law.

At dinner that evening I was anxious to be off. Even Viola noticed it. "He got the fidgets so bad he can't eat," she remarked. I kept urging my parents to hurry up with their dressing, so that we would not be late. After we had called for the Cartwrights and Major Frampton and were driving downtown, I felt as if I were a functionary, soon to take part in a solemn and momentous occasion, and I listened impatiently to the small talk that my parents engaged in with the Cartwrights as we drove along.

We students were to gather in the tabernacle building and then march into the temple two by two, bearing candles, with the younger children coming first and the older ones bringing up the rear, ourselves last of all. The Sabbath School teachers began handing out the long tapers, arranging us in ranks, making sure that we understood that we were to hand the candles to the teachers who would be standing at the altar rail. Dr. Raskin himself came in for a moment to see that all was set. Our teachers straightened the ties and garments of various children, and listened for the sound of the organ next door in the temple.

Several minutes passed. At last we heard the organ music, prelude to the ceremony. "Let's go!" the teachers in charge called, and we began moving in double file out of the tabernacle building and along the hedge-lined walk toward the temple steps, where we were to wait until the hymn began that would summon us inside. The organ played on, in the low, reflective manner customary during those moments when the congregation was taking its seats. Then abruptly the music modulated into the opening chords of the hymn. We heard the shuffling of feet as the congregation rose, the inner doors were flung open, our teachers gestured to us, and up the stairs we began moving in hesitant processional, past the vestibule, through the open doorway, into the temple itself. With quavering voices we sang:

> *Happy who in early youth,*
> *While yet pure and inno-cent,*
> *Stores his mind with heavenly truth,*
> *Life's unfailing orna-ment.*

Up the center aisle we walked, bearing our flickering candles, conscious of the adult faces turned toward us. From the corner of my eye I saw my parents and the Cartwrights standing in our family pew by the windows at the left, the Major and Billy Cartwright there with them, watching intently as we paced solemnly along.

> *Thine, O God, these souls are thine,*
> *Undefiled they come to Thee.*
> *Guard them with Thy love divine,*
> *Heirs of immortal-ity.*

Two by two we walked up to the altar rail, where several of our teachers waited to take the candles from us and set them in the brass candlesticks. Then we moved back and filed into the pews at the very front of the temple nave. We stood there, singing the hymn, until the organ ceased to play and Dr.

Raskin nodded for the congregation to resume its seats.

The service began, the invocations and responses differing somewhat from those used on Saturday mornings, with which I was so familiar. Self-consciously I followed the service in the prayerbook, reciting the appropriate responses, not daring to turn my head and look back at my parents and the Cartwrights seated in our pew. After a while it was time for the reading from the Torah. On Saturday mornings the passage that Dr. Raskin read at this juncture was from the 24th Psalm:

> *Who shall ascend into the mountain of the Lord?*
> *And who shall stand in His holy place?*

Whenever I heard those words, an automatic chill of apprehension would always rise for a moment in the pit of my stomach, whether or not I was scheduled to assist Dr. Raskin that day. *Who shall ascend? Me,* I would think to myself. This time, however, the words were quite different, and in any event did not involve me, and I continued reading from the prayerbook.

"He's nodding for you!" Jack Marcussohn suddenly whispered. "Go on!"

Startled, I looked up, and indeed it was so. Dr. Raskin was looking at me. I stared at him to be sure I had not misunderstood. But Dr. Raskin gazed steadily at me and, as if he had read my thoughts, he nodded again, unmistakably, clearly. My heart beating violently, I rose and edged past the others in the pew.

I walked out into the aisle and up along the altar rail, staring in acute self-consciousness at the carpet along the steps, noticing the gray-green fabric and the slight rip at the seam along the top step. I had helped with the scrolls half a hundred times, yet now I racked my brain to remember what I was supposed to do first, so unnerved was I at this unexpected summons to perform before the congregation, my parents, the Cartwrights, Major Frampton, everyone.

I stepped up alongside Dr. Raskin, turned toward the ark at the appropriate time, moved slowly toward it with him as he spoke the prayers. The scrolls were encased in rich purple velvet embroidered in gold. Instead of selecting the smallest of the five sets, as he always did on Saturday mornings, Dr. Raskin reached into the ark and picked up one of the largest. We moved slowly back to the pulpit, Dr. Raskin bearing the Torah. I stood by him, received the silver ornaments and breastplate as he handed them to me, placed them carefully on the high-backed, velvet-upholstered chair. Over the arm of the chair I laid the purple, gold-embroidered cover, and then I took my place in another chair.

I did not dare to look out for more than a second at a time at what seemed the unprecedentedly vast evening congregation. Instead I concentrated on watching Dr. Raskin as he read. He was a small, kindly little man, with a gentle voice, and with just enough of a foreign accent to give a pleasant, musical quality to the words as he spoke them. As he read he marked his progress along the lines of Hebrew characters with a long silver pointer, at the tip of which was a small, pointing hand, held securely in his grasp with the silver chain wrapped about his wrist and fingers. How impressive, how learned Dr. Raskin seemed, standing before the congregation reading the Hebrew script aloud and translating into English as he went, without a halt or a break.

Finally he was finished. The choir began to sing. I rose quickly and handed him the velvet cover, helping him slip the tightly fitted jacket down the long scroll and over the polished wooden disks at top and bottom, then presenting him with the silver ornaments one by one. Firmly he fitted each into place, and finally looped the chain of the pointer over the adorned handles of the scroll. He gave the Torah to me. I bore it carefully to my chair, sitting lightly down in the seat and placing the sacred scroll upright in my lap.

On the handles of the scroll a pair of large, globular silver ornaments were affixed, much like the topmost ornaments on a Christmas tree. They were hollow inside, with numerous flaps and lids that jingled. With the scroll upright in my lap, the silver globes were in front of my face and I found I could peek between them and look directly at the congregation. I saw the Sabbath School children in the front rows, the teachers, the intent faces of the congregation, among them my various aunts and uncles, and in our own pew my parents and the Cartwrights. Billy Cartwright was watching Dr. Raskin, listening curiously to his words as he read. Occasionally Billy would turn and look at me as I sat there on the altar, and though I knew he could not see my face, instinctively I lowered my eyes. As for the Major, he was settled back against the wall, surveying the entire performance with an air of assured dignity.

Dr. Raskin read on, his voice sober and hushed, pronouncing the sacred chronicles of the Children of Israel, as rabbis of my faith had been doing for thousands of years, in dark days and bright, in far countries, among alien peoples, openly or in stealth. Now I, myself a chosen youth of the Children of Israel, was in my own day and time seated before the company of elders, taking part in this most hallowed of rituals. The temple was quiet; little of the noise of King Street that on Saturdays was so audible was heard now. I was particularly glad that the Marvelous Ringgold was not on duty at that hour; his customary wrangle with the autos on King Street would mar so solemn an occasion.

Now Dr. Raskin was closing the large Bible, with its white leather binding and gold edges, and was leading the congregation in prayer. Then as the choir took up the refrain, he motioned to me. Grasping the heavy scroll upright, I rose to my feet and joined him. Together we walked back to the ark and stood there. As I walked at his side, our backs to the congregation, I felt especially proud.

86

The choir ceased its hymn. We turned again toward the congregation. "Thank you," Dr. Raskin whispered to me, and I walked down the carpeted altar steps and resumed my place among the other Sabbath School children.

Dr. Raskin had begun his sermon. He spoke of children, and of how vacation time was the happiest of times for them, and how the children of the Sabbath School looked forward to the carefree months of rest and play. Yet during that bright time, he said, our education for adulthood did not cease, for the family circle was the center of Jewish life. In the good Jewish home, the upbringing of the child was always foremost in the parents' minds, and the children were given the loving tutelage there that would enable them to grow up to be good Jews and good citizens. For to be the one, he said, was to be the other. It was in the home that the Jewish child received the guidance and instruction in the precepts of his religion, so that eventually he could take his place as a responsible member of the congregation and the community. He was proud that so few Jews were guilty of crimes in later life, and this, he said, was due most of all to the firmness of the religious life of the Jewish home. He hoped that in the months of joy that lay ahead of us, we would never lose sight of God, but keep him in our thoughts at all times, and that in the autumn, when we returned to Sabbath School, we would come back with renewed interest and desire to learn the truths of our religion. As rabbi of the congregation, he said, he was proud of us all, and confident that in the years to come we would never stray from the teachings of our religion, and would always be good Jews and good Americans.

It seemed to me that it was of myself, most of all, that he talked.

12. THERE WERE NEW DEVELOPMENTS CONCERNING THE Fort Sumter Celebration. The last American Legion meeting of the season had been advanced one week in order to discuss them. What they were, no one knew; if my father, who was adjutant of the Legion Post, had been informed, he gave no indication of it. There was an air of secrecy about the whole thing.

School was over. Graduation would be held in four days, and we were free. Furthermore, we could now go to bed much later in the evening. I took advantage of this new status at once, by persuading my father to let me go along to the Legion meeting. Billy Cartwright would be going, too; his father was a member. The Major was also coming along. Of course his war had been an earlier one, but the meeting had to do with the Fort Sumter Celebration, and the Major considered himself entitled to attend any discussion having to do with that topic. The Fort Sumter Commission itself had met the previous week, but he had been too tired to attend, and so he was all the more anxious to come to the Legion meeting now.

The Legion post was housed in an old gymnasium that had once been the city high school. The Post Commander started by announcing that he had advanced the date of the meeting one week at the request of the Celebration Commission, which faced an important decision and wished the advice of the various participating organizations before acting. The Commission had been informed that if the celebration was held in early July as planned, the President of the

88

United States would not be able to attend as scheduled. If, however, the ceremonies could be postponed until the first week in September, the President could and would speak. The Commission was undecided whether to postpone the event until September, in order to have the President speak, or to go ahead as planned in July.

While the Post Commander was speaking, I watched the Major. He was sitting forward in his seat, listening intently, his lips set in a tight line. I turned to Billy Cartwright. "Did the Major know about this before now?" I whispered.

Billy shook his head. "He was too tired to go to the meeting the other night. First one he's missed."

Someone from the audience began to speak. He was in favor of going ahead, he declared. The plans were all made, and President or no President, he did not want to delay any further. After all, the ceremonies should by all rights have been held in April, the actual date of the firing on Fort Sumter. They had waited three months so that the President could speak; if he was unable to come now, then it was just too bad.

He sat down. Another man rose to his feet, a small, red-faced individual whom I recognized as someone I had seen on Broad Street while walking with the Major. "I want to second the motion just made," he said. He had been against tailoring the Fort Sumter Celebration to suit the convenience of the President's political schedule in the first place, and he was darned, he said, if he was willing to sit back and let the President mess things up a second time. "He ought not have been asked in the first place," he declared, his face growing redder as he spoke. "I vote that we withdraw the invitation and instead invite a real, genuine, hundred-percent Southerner, the honorable Harry Flood Byrd of Virginia, to speak in his place—in July! There's too much New Dealing in the country as it is, without inviting the biggest New Dealer of them all down here to speak, and then bow-ing and scraping and changing dates all around to suit his tastes, like he was God Almighty himself!"

Various people were on their feet and waving for attention. The Post Commander was banging his gavel on the rostrum and calling loudly for order.

A man in the front row was recognized. He regretted to see the issue of the Fort Sumter Celebration being dragged into politics, he said. He himself was a good Democrat, but he thought he could safely say that even if a Republican President still occupied the White House, which God forbid, he would be in favor of having him as a speaker for the Fort Sumter Celebration. It was not the man or the party that was being honored, but the office.

The next man to speak was Billy Cartwright's father. "I think the last point is well taken," he said. "There is nothing political about this celebration. The question is entirely one of when is the best time to hold it, and whether it is better for the city and for everybody concerned to go ahead with our plans for July or to wait until September. What about such things as programs? And hotel reservations? And weather conditions? Shouldn't we find out about that?"

The Post Commander spoke up. "I am advised by the Fort Sumter Commission that the official programs are still in the proof stage, so that they can be changed if necessary. As far as available hotel space is concerned, the Commission checked on that too. The hotel people say there's very little difference between July and early September in that respect.

"As for the weather," the Post Commander continued, "you know what's involved there as well as I do. September is hurricane season, and July isn't. On the other hand, we haven't had a hurricane in a long time, and otherwise September is pleasant and mild, while you know how hot it's going to be out on that Fort in July. So there you are."

The Post Commander's words carried weight. The members began discussing what he had said among themselves.

Finally someone got up. "Mr. Commander," he said, "I think we ought to wait. Everything else seems equal, so why not wait and have the President as the speaker? We'll get more national publicity for the city from that than from anything else we do, short of opening fire on the Fort again!"

There was laughter. "I move we take the second alternative," someone shouted, "and this time I will personally pass the ammunition!" The laughter was redoubled. There was a delay before the Post Commander could restore order.

Then the little red-faced man who had sounded off about the New Deal and the President spoke up again. "Mr. Commander, I just cannot see it! If we postpone this thing again, it'll run into hurricane season, and the first thing you know we'll be holding it on Christmas Day! We don't need the President or any of the rest of that bunch in Washington. The Fort Sumter Celebration is the South's celebration; our Confederate heroes don't need a New York-born President to be properly honored. Let's honor our own, I say, and to hell with the whole crowd of them up there! *They* didn't kowtow to Washington in their day; why should we?"

There was an uneasy silence, as if the vehemence with which the choleric little man spoke had embarrassed everyone.

Then I saw people looking toward where we sat, and I realized that the Major had risen to his feet and was waving his hand. "Mr. Commander," he was saying, "I am not a member of your organization, but I wonder whether I might say a few words?" He was standing straight, swaying just a little, his hands clenched in front of him, his lip trembling a bit.

"It is always a pleasure to hear from you, Major Frampton," the Post Commander told him. "We should be very happy to have your thoughts on this matter."

"Last winter when we had to postpone the Fort Sumter

91

Celebration from April to July," the Major said, "I was very disappointed, but it seemed to me then that it was worth doing it.

"I still feel that way. I am a Democrat, Mr. Commander, and I have always been a Democrat, and I think there could be nothing finer than having a great Democratic President speak on this great occasion.

"I realize that there are people in here who don't feel that way about our President, but I'm not one of them. Back in 1861, if we'd had a Democrat like him in the White House, there wouldn't have been any war."

I watched him, standing there so straight and tall, his old hands clenching and unclenching, his eyes shining. There was no one else in the world like him, I thought proudly.

"The way I see it, we ought to have nothing but the best for this celebration," he continued. "A big parade, plenty of bands playing, and the President of the United States for the speaker. I've waited seventy-five years for this day, and I can wait a couple of months longer if I have to, if it means that the President will be able to come!"

The Major sat down, his back still straight, his jaw firm, breathing heavily, while the Legion Post burst into applause. When the cheering finally died down, someone in the center of the hall rose. "Mr. Commander," he said, "I move that the Fort Sumter Seventy-fifth Anniversary Commission be advised that this Post is in favor of postponing the date of the ceremonies until early September, so that the President can take part."

"Second the motion," several voices shouted.

"Question!" some others called.

"The question has been called for," said the Post Commander. "All those in favor of the motion to wait until September, signify by saying 'Aye.' "

There was a chorus of *ayes*.

"Those opposed, no. . . ." There were some *noes*, but

not nearly enough to matter. "The *ayes* have it," the Post Commander said.

I looked at the Major again. He was still breathing hard, but now he was smiling.

There were other items of business to be taken up that hot May evening. The Post Commander's voice droned on, the audience grew restless. From time to time there was the noise of shoes being shuffled and the creak of wooden chairs. The Major's eyes were closed all the way now, while his breath was coming quietly and at regular intervals.

"Is there any new business before we adjourn?" asked the Post Commander finally. My father, on the rostrum, was already gathering up papers and pencils.

Someone across the hall got up. "Mr. Commander," he said, "I have one more suggestion to make about the Fort Sumter Celebration. Unless I am mistaken, this Post has in its custody the dress uniforms of the old Charleston Light Dragoons, and I regret that their colors will not be represented at the Fort Sumter exercises. Mr. Commander, I would like to move that an honor guard, made up of members of this Post who were members of the Light Dragoons before 1917, march in the parade wearing the old uniforms and carrying the colors."

I watched my father as he sat on the platform; his face was a deep crimson. Billy Cartwright nudged me with his elbow, but I did not need his reminder; I knew that it was the Light Dragoons' uniforms that my father had given away to the Jenkins Orphanage last year.

I saw my father lean across the table and whisper some words to the Post Commander, who turned to speak with him before addressing the membership again. "I regret to say that we don't own those uniforms any more," he announced after a minute.

"What happened to them?" the man who had made the suggestion asked.

"They were given away when the armory basement was cleaned out last year," the Post Commander explained.

At this point, up jumped the same little red-faced man who had argued so heatedly against postponing the celebration so that the President could speak. "Given away?" he asked. "By what right?"

"Surplus property belonging to the Post."

"That's not my idea of surplus property," the little man said, his face flushed and moist. "By what right were they declared surplus? Who's got them now?"

The Post Commander turned to my father again. "They were given to the Jenkins Orphanage Band," he announced after a brief consultation.

"The *what?*"

"The Jenkins Orphanage Band."

"Mr. Commander, that is not only an outrage, but it is an insult to the memory of every man who ever wore the uniform of the Light Dragoons!"

By now there was an excited buzz in the audience as the members realized that another real dispute was in the offing. My father rose to his feet from behind the table, and asked for permission to speak.

"Those uniforms weren't doing anyone the slightest bit of good, collecting dust and moth-holes down in the basement," he said. "The Jenkins Orphanage is a deserving charity, and they needed uniforms for their band very badly, so I gave them the old uniforms. They were just going to pieces down in the basement, and this way somebody could still get some use out of them."

"*Use!*" the little red-faced man shouted, brandishing his finger. "Mr. Commander, this is a disgrace. Mind you, I don't have anything against the Jenkins Orphanage, but to give the uniforms of the Light Dragoons to a bunch of

94

nigger musicians to parade up and down King Street on Saturday begging for money is a goddam shame!"

The Post Commander flushed. "I see no need for that kind of language!" he declared. "The adjutant will strike those words from the record!" The adjutant, of course, was not keeping any record whatsoever at the time, but was standing at the Commander's side.

The little red-faced man was not to be silenced. "I want to know who the adjutant thinks he is, giving away those uniforms! I don't know what the adjutant's people were doing during the Civil War, but my grandfather fought for the South from 1863 to the end of the war, and I'm here to tell you that he would turn over in his grave if he knew that somebody had given Confederate gray uniforms to some nigger musicians!"

Now my father's face was white. He stepped up to the edge of the platform.

"Just hold it right there," he said. "I had full authority to dispose of any surplus property I wished, in any way I wished. And as for what my people were doing during the war, my Great-uncle Julius was wounded five times fighting for South Carolina, and left for dead on the battlefield of Gettysburg. And if *your* grandfather," he said, pointing at the little red-faced man, "is so narrow-minded as to turn over in his grave because a bunch of moth-eaten old uniforms were given to some poor, needy Negro orphans, then for all I care he can spin like a top from now till Kingdom Come!"

Now Billy Cartwright's father was on his feet, waving frantically to the Post Commander, who saw him at last and gratefully recognized him.

"Mr. Commander," Billy's father said, "isn't this all a little silly? I used to belong to the Light Dragoons myself before the war. I wore one of those uniforms. In the first place, they aren't Confederate uniforms. They were bought about twenty years ago, I think, right before the Mexican

Border trouble, and there is nothing historical or sacred about them in any way. So if we want to have the Light Dragoons represented in the Fort Sumter parade, we can have some new uniforms made for the occasion. They'd be every bit as appropriate as the ones that the adjutant gave away. As for myself, *I* certainly don't object to the orphans having those old uniforms, and I'm certain that most of the other members of the old Light Dragoons would say exactly the same thing."

Incredibly, throughout this exchange Major Frampton had been sleeping peacefully. Now, at last, he woke up. He blinked his eyes and looked around him in perplexity.

"What's all the excitement about?" he asked.

"They gave the old Light Dragoons' uniforms away to the Jenkins Band," Mr. Cartwright whispered, "and now somebody wants them worn in the parade."

"Let the Jenkins Band wear them in the parade then," the Major snorted. "The more bands, the better!"

Mr. Cartwright grinned. "Mr. Commander," he called out, "Major Frampton has made a good suggestion. Why not invite the Jenkins Band to march in the parade wearing the uniforms?"

Everyone laughed. "Second the motion!" someone shouted. "All in favor, signify by saying 'Aye,' " called the Post Commander. There was a loud chorus of *ayes*. "Opposed, 'No.' Motion carried!"

The meeting was adjourned with everyone still chuckling over the Major's master stroke.

Driving home after the meeting, my father was still angry. I had never seen him so angry before. "That stupid little so-and-so," he kept saying. "Who the devil is he?"

"I think his name's Skinner," Mr. Cartwright told him. "I believe he works for the post office."

"Was he in the Light Dragoons when you were?"

"Hell, no," Mr. Cartwright said. "He was never a member of the Light Dragoons at any time; I'm sure of that. He's not even from around here."

After we dropped the Cartwrights and Major Frampton at their house and were driving around the block to our own, I asked my father a question.

"Are they really going to ask the Jenkins Band to march in the Fort Sumter parade?"

My father chuckled. "Why not?" he asked. "It certainly wouldn't do any harm. Besides, as the Major says, the more music, the better."

13. THAT MISS MASON WOULD HAVE HER TRIUMPH! THAT we would sit obediently upon the stage of the James Simons School, and sing "The Cuckoo Song"!

It did not seem fair.

The episode was over, but we could not forget. Both Billy Cartwright and I agreed that she had caused us difficulties out of all proportion to our wrongdoing. Another teacher would have known that we were only two of a number of offenders. But not Miss Mason. She had accused *us*, and but for Miss Lucia Jahnz's providential intervention, we might have suffered grievous harm. Despite what Dr. Higginson had declared when I had put forth my feeble attempt at an alibi, we *had* been the attacked rather than the attackers; we *had* thrown the spitballs in self-defense.

Yet it had all ended without mishap. We should have forgiven her crimes and forgotten them. We were graduating; we would never again be forced to submit to her tyranny; she was only a silly old woman. Why then did we continue to brood over what she had done and been?

The afternoon before graduation we bicycled over to the grounds of The Citadel, to see the final dress parade of the cadets. It was, as always, a stirring occasion. The long ranks of Citadel cadets, resplendent in their gleaming white uniforms and white-plumed shakos, executed their maneuvers. They stood at attention while the bugles blew retreat and the sunset gun was fired. A white cloud of smoke curled over the drill field as the colors came swinging down from the flagstaff and the band played "The Star Spangled Banner."

Afterward the cadets marched off for the barracks, chorus-

ing loudly in cadence count, the shouted numbers rever-
berating throughout the campus as they trooped along.
HUP-HOOP-HEEP-HOH! they chorused, HUP-HOOP-
HEEP-HOH! their left arms swinging rhythmically as they
marched, the white gloves rising in blurred arcs. HUP-
HOOP-HEEP-HOH! HUP-HOOP-HEEP-HOH!

At that moment Billy Cartwright turned to me, and I
turned to him. Our glances met.

Graduation morning. I was eager to be off. My father and
mother had to go downtown before the exercises, so it was
agreed that I would go to school by myself on the streetcar
and meet them afterward. My mother inspected me before
she left. "For heaven's sake don't soil your white trousers,"
she said. "Watch where you sit. Get on the streetcar and go
straight to school, and stay out of mischief."

An hour before time to report at school I left the house.
"Remember what your mother said," Viola called to me from
the dining-room window as I set off up Versailles Street for
the car line. "Stay away from dust, dirt and trouble, till you
walk off that platform with the piece of paper in your hand!"

On so auspicious a morning I could not bear to ride in Mr.
Zinzer's trolley, which was moving down toward the corner
as I reached Rutledge Avenue. So I stepped back to wait for
the next car, which would certainly have the Marvelous Ringgold for pilot. Soon I saw it rocking along in the distance,
dipping and swaying as if the tracks were not steel but heaving
waves.

"Climb aboard, young fellow!" the Marvelous Ringgold
shouted after he ground to a halt at the corner and flung
open the French doors. "All set to graduate?"

Magnolia Crossing, near the end of the Rutledge Avenue Line, was not a prepossessing place. It consisted of a dirt
street with car tracks down the middle, an asphalt highway

perpendicular to it, the railroad tracks beyond the highway, a few produce stalls, an ice plant, a fertilizer factory set back beyond the fields to the north, a gasoline station, and barren acres in every direction. Across the railroad tracks was a monument works, and beyond that, Magnolia Cemetery, where my grandparents were buried.

It was the presence of the railroad tracks that made the end of the line infinitely interesting to me. For though the chances were not too good, there was always the possibility that during the minutes that the Marvelous Ringgold's trolley car lingered there before commencing the downtown run, a railroad train —not merely a switching locomotive—might come by.

Today, graduation day, there was no train in sight. I helped the Marvelous Ringgold reverse the wicker seats, taking care not to get my clothes dirty, and after he had reset the trolley pole and transferred his operating paraphernalia to the other end of the car, we were off for the city.

I got off the trolley at Moultrie Street. "Don't forget to walk up and get your diploma when they call out your name!" the Marvelous Ringgold called to me as I stepped down from the cab. "Otherwise you'll have to go back next fall and do it over again!"

When I arrived at the schoolyard, Billy Cartwright was already on hand. "I've been telling everybody," he told me. "It's bound to work."

"Are you sure," I asked, "that we ought to do it?"

"Sure I am! Aren't you?"

"I guess so . . ."

"What could they do to us? It'll be all over by then," he said. "Besides, it's all set. Wallace Riley's in favor of it. The others will be afraid not to now."

The graduating class of the James Simons School trooped onto the auditorium stage and took its appointed places along the rows of folding chairs, the boys attired in blue jackets and white trousers, the girls in gauzy white dresses with pink ribbons. Our parents were all there, crowded awkwardly into the cramped auditorium seats, busily pointing out their own children to relatives and friends. There were my mother and father, there was Billy Cartwright's mother. There was the Major, immaculate in a white suit with red tie. My Aunt Ellen was also on hand. The only person who should have been there but wasn't, I suddenly thought, was Viola.

Our teachers, dressed in their summer finery, occupied places of honor along the front row. Miss Wilhelmina Mason, pertly garbed in a starched white suit with a tiny corsage of violets pinned to the lapel, proudly and effusively led us in the singing of the national anthem. Dr. Alexander O. Higginson presided, his stentorian tones now grown mellow, welcoming friends and parents to this proudest of moments in the just-budding careers of their children.

First, the awards, and he was happy to announce that the Julian Mitchell Achievement Award for all-around excellence in scholarship and deportment went to—William Frederick Cartwright, Jr.! Billy walked up, blushing, to receive his prize. Next, the American Legion Medal for excellence in American history—won by Forrest Beckman. Though I had long known I was not to be the winner, still I had vaguely hoped that at the last minute there would be a change—the discovery of a mistake in grades perhaps—so that I would be the winner, and I knew a momentary disappointment.

Now the graduating class, under the direction of Miss Wilhelmina Mason, would sing an Italian folk song, "Santa Lucia." Sing it we did, sweetly, lowly. Hark how the sailors cry, joyful, the echoes nigh. Rapturously Miss Mason led us, her smile serene, her hands fluttering, her round eyes narrowed to slits, as if the light were too beatific to be let in all at once.

Next, the commencement speaker—a special privilege indeed for those present, for it was none other than Mr. William Frederick Cartwright, Sr., a member of the City School

Board, whose own son had just been awarded so deserved an honor.

Then Dr. Higginson again, with the presentation of diplomas. One by one we filed up to the rostrum, were handed a document neatly rolled into a scroll and fastened with black and gold ribbons, and returned to our seats.

Finally, Dr. Higginson said, the members of the graduating class, under the capable direction of Miss Wilhelmina Mason, would sing an old English air, "The Cuckoo Song." And our moment had come.

We did not sing "The Cuckoo Song"; we *shouted* it. Under the horrified gaze of Miss Wilhelmina Mason, the puzzled looks of Dr. Higginson and our teachers, and the vainly suppressed laughter of the assembled parents and guests, we roared out the words at the top of our voices. AWAKE, AWAKE, YE DREAMERS! we chorused at topmost pitch, THE CUCKOO LOUDLY CALLS! THE SUN PEEPS O'ER THE TREETOPS, AND SHINES ON GARDEN WALLS!

And in lusty cadenced shout: COO-COO! COO-COO! COO-COO! COO-COO! Again, even more deafening than before: COO-COO! COO-COO! COO-COO! COO-COO!

Her face flushed in anger, Miss Wilhelmina Mason began talking to us in a loud whisper as we sang, gesturing with her hands for *pianissimo.* To no avail; throughout the small auditorium the sound of our singing blasted, vigorous as the cadence count of the Citadel cadets, violent as the rumble of the thundersquall that had begun to mount beyond the windows outside. COO-COO! COO-COO! COO-COO! COO-COO! COO-COO! COO-COO! COO-COO! COO-COO!

There was a vague attempt at applause when we had done, but the audience was for the most part too busy laughing or attempting to refrain from laughing. Raging, Miss Wilhelmina Mason stood there on the stage, her jaws working with-

out sound, her eyes round in blazing light. Dr. Alexander O.
Higginson hastily stepped to her side and nudged her toward
the wing. Slowly, reluctantly, she retreated. Then Dr. Higginson quickly called upon a minister for the benediction. We
bowed our heads in prayer, and then to the recorded music of
"Pomp and Circumstance" we marched off the stage. As Billy
Cartwright and I swung by, we caught sight for a moment of
Miss Wilhelmina Mason standing in the wings, livid in
powerless anger. Her face was blood-red, and her eyes burned
like coals.

"Why did you sing the last song so loud?" my mother
asked as we drove home along Rutledge Avenue. The Cartwrights and the Major were with us, except for Mr. Cartwright, who had to go on downtown to work.

"That's the way it was supposed to be," I mumbled.

"It seemed awfully noisy to me, too," Billy's mother said.

"Well, she asked for it," Billy replied.

"It was almost as if you were shouting instead of singing,"
my mother declared. "I've never heard of people being taught
to sing *that* way before!" She looked around at me. "What
are you giggling about?"

"Nothing," I said. "Not a thing."

Billy Cartwright was staring out the window of the automobile, biting his lip and intently observing the sidewalk
across the street.

I glanced at the Major. He was sitting in front with my
mother and father. From where I sat in back, I could not tell
for sure, but I was almost positive that the Major was grinning
from ear to ear.

14. For graduation the Major presented me with a dollar bill, crisp and new. I knew at once what I would use it for. I had never flown in an airplane, and for one dollar it was possible to circle the airport in one. It was agreed that on Sunday morning we would drive out to the airport and I would take my first flight. Billy wanted to come, too, but his mother insisted he stay home to greet his girl cousin from Philadelphia and her mother.

I received another present that day that especially pleased me. It was a copy of Dr. Chisholm's new book, *The Triumph or the Tomb*, which he had been telling my Aunt Ellen and me about, that evening when he had had supper with us. Now the book was published, and Aunt Ellen had purchased a copy for me. On the jacket was a picture of Fort Sumter, with a shell bursting just over it. "Next time you see the Doctor you can ask him to inscribe it for you, just like the one he gave you," Aunt Ellen said.

On Sunday morning I found myself at the airport, walking out toward one of the yellow airplanes, following behind a tall, slender man who was to pilot me on my trip. I was quite nervous and even a bit frightened. Feeling extremely self-conscious as we walked along, I tried to appear as solemn and unconcerned as possible. The pilot opened a flap on the side of the plane, boosted me up inside the cockpit, and then took his seat ahead of me. A mechanic in stained khakis came over and spun the yellow wooden propeller. The motor coughed into action, and soon we were bumping and jostling along the runway toward the far end of the field. Slowing to a halt near a clump of pine trees, we wheeled about and faced into the runway down which we had just come.

There was a moment when the motor raced, then eased down, and I heard the wing cables creaking and the tail flap banging behind me. Then straightaway the motor roared into renewed frenzy, and we went streaking along the asphalt runway. There was a sensation as of the floor of the plane pressing up beneath my feet, and I looked down below to see the black strip of the runway drop away. Then I saw grass, then the tops of trees, and then we were aloft.

There was a curious instant in which our forward motion seemed abruptly suspended, and after that it was the ground far beneath us that appeared to be moving, while we remained still, fixed in the air. Instead of the sensation of great speed that I had expected, all was calm and tranquil; the noise of the throbbing motor seemed low and far away, and a deep, throttled hum pervaded everything.

The pilot turned around to me and pointed at his throat. "Swallow!" he shouted, his voice sounding faint and far off. I took a breath and swallowed, and the noise of the engine became much louder again.

Far below I saw dark green timberland, with a wide, slate-gray river twisting off ahead in the distance, while directly beneath was the thin band of a highway, along which toy vehicles slowly crawled. Then the plane banked sharply to the right, and I realized we were over the Cooper River north of town, while the other, silver river over to the southeast was the selfsame Ashley that flowed by our house.

As I watched I saw how the Ashley executed a wide, lazy bend on its seaward path. It was there, no doubt, that I first picked up the sound of the launch at night. Beyond, strung out on a narrow point of land between two widening rivers, was—the city! I could even make out, just below us, the green roof of our house, and near it the marsh and the meandering creek along which the *Endymion of Charleston, S.C.* had ventured.

I looked to my left again. Behind us were the installations of the Navy Yard, the giant cranes now looking so small, the gray destroyers moored there, the railroad yards with tiny chains of freight cars along the ribboned tracks, and here and there the smudge of smoke from locomotives. Oil tanks closer to town seemed flat saucers arrayed in orderly rows along the ground, bedded in a green felt tablecloth. In triple strands the tracks led into the city, past Magnolia Crossing, where I saw a streetcar, tiny now and snubnosed, and lost themselves among a spread checkerboard of rectangles and squares. Trees were everywhere, crisscrossed in honeycombs along the streets. Houses were precise designs of white, red, green, their flat roofs set out for inspection in laid planes. The double winged arch of the Cooper River Bridge hinged the eastern islands to the city. Along the waterfront the wharves seemed like jagged teeth, sawtoothed to irregular fringe, the apertures occasionally clogged with the toy frames of ships. And there, last of all, was Adger's Wharf, the trawlers and tugboats clustered about it like the glistening ornaments of a Christmas tree.

Everywhere, in all directions, sprawled the harbor, widening out beyond the point of the city like an enormous fan, the city itself a small tongue tasting the bay's immensity. Seaward the harbor unfolded, flooding into yellow-green banks, verging to dark, then finally to deepest blue toward the ocean horizon. The coastal islands were strung-out alabaster chains rimming the sea. Behind the islands the marsh was folded, a frayed rug of pale jade, with mud-black creeks embroidering the pastel fabric in sinuous coils.

In the center of the harbor was the Fort—Fort Sumter, her pentagonal walls resembling a heaped castle of mud, beleaguered, cut off, surrounded by flats of water. How small, how ordered it seemed! Was it along these waters that the Major had rowed about while the bombardment was under way? that Dr. Chisholm had boated like his ancestor while

preparing his new book? that in July—no, in September—
the President would visit to make his speech? Did those things
happen *here*, where everything was so contained, so precise
from where we soared high above the bay? Looking beyond
the harbor once more as the airplane banked for a turn, I
marveled again at the blueness of the deep ocean, really blue
as I had so often read but never seen, with the rocks of the
jetties set across the harbor like a frail, stationary wave. In
shaded folds the ship channel wound carelessly through the
bay toward the glistening city.

I thought at that moment that I could spend a lifetime and
not exhaust what I saw. I promised myself that I would know
city and country and bay, shade and shadow, every arranged
point of light, each secret part, until it would all become so
completely my own that we should be one another, my mind
forever suffused in summer and amber air. Sea and sun, sand
and city, all woven together in one fabric, a carpet of reds,
blues, greens of a thousand hues; the matchless color of light,
a universe of gradations, unrolled before me in every direction,
bathed every bit of it in translucent brightness, all of a golden
weather, held forever in my all-seeing eyes.

PART TWO

The Hot Season

1. I READ DOCTOR CHISHOLM'S BOOK AT ONCE. THE very night after the plane trip I took it to my room and went all the way through it. In my mind's eye I tried to keep a picture of the harbor as I had seen it from the airplane, but I found this difficult, for Dr. Chisholm's book had a kind of groundness to it, and at all times there was the feeling of looking out from land over water—toward the fort, toward the sea, toward the shore. Nor did the characters in the book seem like people I knew. All of them went about making speeches and pointing across the water at the enemy. The most important person was General Beauregard, who was always issuing proclamations about Southrons and Liberty and Your Homes and Sacred Honor. His picture was in the book —a little man with a pointed beard and thick gray eyebrows. I repeated his name over and over. Pierre Gustave Toutant Beauregard. Pierre Gustave Toutant Beauregard.

But there was something much odder than that about Dr. Chisholm's book. Not once did the book mention the Major! And this despite the fact that almost every one of the adventures that the Major had told me about were in the book, just as he had described them. There was the firing upon the *Star of the West*, and all about Cadet Haynsworth and the others. There was the first shot of the war, from Fort Johnson, and Captain James's gun crew that fired it. There was the story of Colonel Wigfall rowing ashore to ask for the surrender of the Union garrison on Fort Sumter, and even the business about his drinking the glass of poison and having to have his stomach pumped out then and there.

The Major had described all these things to me; he had

told me of running out to get a stomach pump and how it had saved Colonel Wigfall's life. It was clear that the Major knew what he was talking about—Dr. Chisholm's book was proof, because every detail of what the Major had told me was there in print. Yet he was not even mentioned.

It seemed to me that Dr. Chisholm *must* have known about the Major's part, could not have helped knowing about it. What, then, was the explanation?

Billy Cartwright's cousin from Philadelphia had arrived, along with her mother. I had forgotten that they were coming, and when I went over to Billy's house on Monday morning, I was surprised to find her there. She was slight of build, with long, light-brown hair. She had freckles, a rather sharp chin, a small, turned-up nose, and she wore glasses with tortoise-shell frames. At first sight she was not particularly pretty, but her features were delicate and pleasant, her eyes were a lively blue, she had a small, perfectly formed mouth, and when she laughed her whole face seemed to fill with brightness.

When I arrived she was telling Billy Cartwright about a game called lacrosse, which she and her friends played at school. She was the same age as we were, thirteen, but she attended a private school. I had never before known a girl who was interested in sports, and soon Billy and I were telling her about the baseball teams in the Municipal League that we went to see play every weekend. After that we talked of boats, and when Billy mentioned that we had built a boat of our own, Helen wanted to see it at once. So we walked over past my house and down the hill to the water, where our boat was tied to the wharf. Its rough, boxlike appearance, with the red paint spread over the raw boards and the clumsy lettering in uneven black across the side, seemed quite unattractive at that moment. Helen did not seem to think so, however.

"The *Endymion!*" she said. "What a clever name!"

"It's from a poem," I explained.

"Oh, yes, I know. We studied it last year, about the little boat sailing through the daisies vermeil rimmed and white," Helen told us. "It's a wonderful name for a boat. I've always wanted to have a boat named Lucasta."

"Lucasta? Why?" I asked.

"That's from a poem, too. Do you know it?"

I shook my head.

Helen recited part of it:

> *If to be absent were to be*
> *Away from thee;*
> *Or that when I am gone,*
> *You or I were alone;*
> *Then, my Lucasta, might I crave*
> *Pity from blustering wind or swallowing wave.*

"And so on," she said. "It's by a man named Richard Lovelace. We read about him in our English class last winter. He was very gallant."

"I don't know about him. Do you know about a poet named Henry Timrod?"

Helen shook her head. "No, I don't."

"He's the Major's favorite poet," I explained. "He wrote a poem about Charleston Harbor during the war. It goes—"

Billy Cartwright interrupted. "I thought we came down to look at the boat, not to recite poetry."

I flushed. "Let's go for a ride," I proposed.

"Oh, let's!" Helen agreed.

"The boat will only hold two people," Billy Cartwright declared.

"You go ahead," I suggested hastily. "I'll wait here for you."

"No, you take Helen out in the boat," Billy told me, with a smirk to his voice. "I can't anyway, because I've got my good pants on to go to the doctor's this morning."

113

After a perfunctory protest, I untied the *Endymion of Charleston, S.C.*'s rope, and climbed aboard. Billy Cartwright held the boat next to the dock and Helen stepped down into the front seat. I grasped the homemade, two-bladed paddle and swung the *Endymion* around, and we set out along the creek. Now as I sat in the boat alone with Helen, paddling, I felt self-conscious and began apologizing for the way the seams of the boat let the water in. But Helen talked about the marsh, and how she liked the soft colors so much. I told her that a friend of mine had written a poem about the marsh grass, in a book he had given me. Helen said that she had always wanted to know a real poet; her grandfather—not the Major, but her father's father—had known Walt Whitman when he was an old man living across the river from Philadelphia in Camden, New Jersey, she said. Did I know his poems? I told her that we had read a poem called "O Captain, My Captain" in class, and that the teacher said it was about Abraham Lincoln. "Oh, you should read the one called 'Out of the Cradle Endlessly Rocking,' " she told me. "It's about the sea, and a seabird calling for its dead mate, and a little boy listening, and you can just feel the surge of the waves and the breakers." I told her about my Uncle Ben, and how he was a writer for the movies out in Hollywood.

We were almost at the point where the creek began twisting and bending, halfway to the river, and I swung about to return. I could see Billy Cartwright standing by the bank, poking at the fiddler dens in the mud with a pole. We moved along the creek lightly, gliding shoreward with the incoming tide. When at last we reached the wharf, Billy had come back and was waiting to help tie up the *Endymion of Charleston, S.C.*

As we walked back up the hill I wished devoutly that I owned a real boat. But all we had was the *Endymion of Charleston, S.C.* I must show Helen Dr. Chisholm's book, with the poem about the marsh. I wondered whether Helen wrote poems too, but I had no intention of reintroducing the subject now, with Billy Cartwright there. "Do you like baseball?" I asked instead.

"Oh, yes. Sometimes we go over to North Philadelphia and watch the games. Daddy likes the Athletics the best, but I like the Phillies. They play so hard, and always get beat, but they never stop trying."

I told Helen that she would have to come with us to see the Municipal League games on the weekends. I explained to her about the teams, especially the Tru-Blu Brewers who were Billy's and my favorites. She could see for herself this weekend, we told her, when the Tru-Blu Brewers played their next game.

"Oh, look!" Helen said, pointing toward the front of Billy Cartwright's house. "There's Grandfather!" She was pointing to the Major, who was standing at the edge of the marsh, looking out toward the river. She ran ahead of us toward him and up to his side. The Major put his long arm around her shoulders and was smiling down at her as Billy and I came up.

"Have you boys been showing this little girl about the neighborhood?" the Major asked us.

"Showing her!" Billy Cartwright told him. "Omar rowed her halfway to the river in the boat. I thought they were going to spend the day out there."

"What do you say," the Major proposed, "that we go and sit up there on the porch, and Helen can tell us all about Philadelphia?"

We walked up the steps, with the Major bringing up the rear, ascending slowly but firmly behind us. "Now then," he said, "here we all are. You sit right by me, Helen, here on the glider." He drew her alongside him. "So you went out for a boat ride, eh?"

"Yes, sir, we did. Right out there in the marsh."

"Did I ever tell you," the Major began, "about a boat ride

115

I once took in Charleston Harbor, right under the guns of Fort Sumter, while the first battle of the War between the States was in progress? I'll bet she's never heard about that, eh, boys?" He looked at me and winked.

"No, sir," I agreed.

"Oh, please tell me," Helen urged. "It sounds awfully exciting!"

"Well," the Major said, "it *wasn't* exactly the kind of boat ride that you'd want to take every day. It was on the night of April 13, 1861. You see, at midnight the previous evening, we had been stationed on Fort Johnson, at the southern tip of the harbor, waiting for the word from General Beauregard, and shortly before midnight . . ." And the Major was off once again on his favorite subject. I listened as he told the story of the trip to the besieged Fort Sumter with Colonel Wigfall, which Billy Cartwright and I knew so well. But this time I kept thinking about Dr. Chisholm's book, with its account of the same adventure. All the details that the Major included in his version had been in the book, and more besides. He must have been there! And yet . . . Dr. Chisholm had left him out.

Presently Billy Cartwright's mother called up to him from the basement. "Billy, you'd better come along now, or you'll be late for your doctor's appointment!"

"All right!" Billy called back, and stood up to go.

"Helen, how about you?" Mrs. Cartwright called. "Do you want to come too? Your mother and I are going shopping while Billy's at the doctor's."

Helen got up. "I'd better go tell them I want to stay here with Grandfather," she declared. "Don't tell any more of the story for a minute," she said to the Major. "I'll be right back."

She followed Billy Cartwright inside, and there was a moment of silence, while I heard her go down the front hall toward the basement and down the steps.

"Sir," I began, "I was reading Dr. Chisholm's new book about Fort Sumter last night . . ."

"Oh, you did, did you? Has he got it all written down right?"

"Yes, sir." My heart was in my throat. "Only not all of it." I hesitated. "You see, he—uh—didn't know about your part in the battle."

The Major frowned. "Is that so, now?"

"Yes, sir. Probably you never told him."

Major Frampton nodded his head for a moment. "No, I never did, as a matter of fact," he said. "But it doesn't matter. Now, I'll tell you, Omar, the Doctor's all right, and all those authors are all right, but they've got one trouble when they get to writing about things that happened a while back. You see, all they know about is what the generals and the colonels and the commanders-in-chief did. They don't know anything about the ordinary soldiers, like me. Now, I was just a rear rank private at that time, and nobody wrote books about the buck privates. Why, unless you were actually there and remembered how it was, you'd think the whole war was just a matter of generals and colonels, and never hear a word about the lads who did the marching and pulled the lanyards. But if it hadn't been for them, what could the generals have done? Think about that for a minute."

"I don't know," I said.

The Major removed a long cigar from his inside breast pocket, and lit it carefully with a long kitchen match, whipping the head of the match deftly across the sole of his neatly shined shoes. "So Chisholm has written a book? (*puff, puff*) Well, well!"

"I'm sure he didn't mean to leave you out intentionally," I said again.

The Major laughed. "I don't imagine he did either, Omar. You see, all he knows about the defense of Charleston Harbor

117

is what he's read in other books. And if I didn't tell him, how could he have known about me? Now those books are all right. I used to have a whole bookshelf full of them at one time. Yes, they're all right, but all they ever tell about is what the generals and colonels did. But as for me, now, I'll match what I know about the Battle of Fort Sumter against all the books in the world. Yes, sir." He puffed on his cigar several times to keep it lit. "And that's not all I know about, either. Did I ever tell you about the time that General John Bell Hood tried to outflank General Schofield? It was in November of 'sixty-four—the war was three years old then, and we were mighty tired of it—and our boys were up in Tennessee, along the line of . . ."

Helen came back onto the porch at that moment. "Now go on with the story, Grandfather," she said. "You had just landed on the sandbar outside the fort."

"Hmm?" The Major frowned as he tried to recollect where he had left off with the previous story. "Oh, yes. Well, we pulled up on the shore, and I jumped out to haul our boat up on the sand. Colonel Wigfall was the next one to disembark. The Union sentinels were standing there, their rifles at port arms. 'Where's the officer in charge?' the Colonel demanded. One of the Union soldiers stepped forward and saluted . . ."

And the Major talked on, drawing on his cigar all the while, as Billy Cartwright's cousin and I listened. I felt much better about the whole thing now.

During the next several days, I spent a great deal of time in the company of Billy Cartwright's cousin. I showed her the book of poems that Dr. Chisholm had inscribed for me, and in particular the one about the marsh grass. She thought it was beautiful, and even made a copy of it for herself. And my hunch had been right; she *did* write poems, too. They

were much better than mine—she wrote several out for me—
and she used words that would never have occurred to me.
They were about snow on the ground, and old ladies at the
library, and the forest animals in winter. So learned and polished did they seem that I was embarrassed to show her my
own; but when I finally did, she seemed to like them. When
she went back home at the end of the next month, we decided, we would send each other the poems that we wrote.
But July and August, I thought happily, lasted a long time.

As for Billy Cartwright, he scorned our talk of poems. He
would snort in disgust when we insisted on speaking about
such things, and often he would go off and leave us. Otherwise, though, he seemed to be enjoying his cousin's visit as
much as I was. On the weekends we took her to the ball
games. We pointed out all the players to her, especially those
on the Tru-Blu team, and soon she could recognize them all.
Her principal charm in Billy's eyes, however, rested in her
willingness to play endless games of Monopoly with him.
Monopoly was Billy's favorite game. He played it with a con-
suming passion, totaling up his profits with great satisfaction,
and even keeping a record of them from day to day in a
notebook.

My parents soon began to tease me about Helen. "Omar's
poet love," my father called her one day as we sat down to
the dinner table. "Yes, sir. Cupid has shot his arrow into the
air, and it fell to earth, and Omar knows where!" I blushed,
and my father, thus encouraged, continued. "Have you ever
recited to her the poem that goes

> *"Lips that touch wine jelly*
> *Shall never touch mine, Nellie?"*

He roared with laughter, and my mother giggled, and even I
had to grin. "Or maybe," my father said, "she would prefer

> *"Lips that touch watermelon*
> *Shall never touch mine, Helen!"*

119

"Now don't tease him so," my mother told my father.

"Oh, I wouldn't do that," my father assured her. "How about the one that goes

> *"An epicure, dining at Crewe,*
> *Found quite a large mouse in his stew.*
> *Said the waiter, 'Don't shout*
> *And wave it about,*
> *Or the rest will be wanting one, too!'"*

Again he laughed uproariously, and kept asking me whether my "poet love knows that one?" I attempted to ignore him, but it was difficult to do, because just when I would think he had dropped the subject, he would introduce it again.

"You'd better not go out in your boat when the tide's too high, Omar," he said. "It's very dangerous now." I knew better than to ask why, but I could not resist finding out what he would say.

"All right, *why?*"

"Because if your boat was to tip over, instead of romance it might be a case of Helen high water. Ha, ha, ha!"

I got up from the table in disgust and stalked out of the room. But my father fired a parting salvo as I went. "Sweet Helen, make me immortal with a kiss!" he recited, and the roar of his laughter followed me up the stairs.

2. Meanwhile, despite poets and poetesses, airplane trips, books about Fort Sumter and visions of cities, there were the streetcars and the motormen who piloted them, my chauffeurs, my companions on trips into the city and back uptown to Versailles Street. For twenty hours of each day, the Rutledge Avenue trolleys came and went, passing five blocks from my house at their nearest point, in the daytime all but unheard in the confusion and activity, but at night resuming their identity from among the general hubbub of the city, asserting themselves, their singsong iron vigil the last sound in my ears as I drifted off to sleep.

In the morning, on days when I went downtown to the movies or to the library, they were there to carry me, boxlike, colored orange, with large black numerals on side, front and rear; serrated brackets of iron along the windows, trolley arms bent rearward like thin plumes atop their curve-rimmed, flattop roofs. At night, when I came back home from my aunt's or from a softball game downtown, I spied the single yellow eye of light moving steadily down the dim-lit street, stolidly, inexorably. One time the journey to or from the city might be slow, with Mr. Zinzer at the controls, never varying his pace, puttering along at the same monotonous clip, night or day, rain or shine. Or it might be a madcap, helter-skelter dash along the quiet city streets, with the Marvelous Ringgold coaxing, cajoling, urging the trolley car to greater and more pandemonic effort. I always hoped for that, but too often my hopes were disappointed, and as I waited, it would be Mr. Zinzer's car that would heave into view down the street, easily recognizable by the forlorn lack-luster of its unambitious gait.

Mr. Zinzer's appearance was as unexciting as his driving style. He was a short, plump man—so short, indeed, that he used a thick green satin cushion on the operating seat in order to let him see over the cab front. His complexion was an un-sunned cheese-white, and his face almost a perfect egg shape, its symmetry disturbed only slightly by his receding chin, thin, pursed lips, and little round eyes that stared through reddish, granulated lids. He had small, stubby hands, and wore dully glossed black shoes that dangled above the floor, for the seat cushion elevated him too high for his feet to reach the wooden floor of the cab. Whenever he wished to operate the bell pedal, he had first to climb down off the seat. But he seldom rang the bell.

He almost never spoke with anyone. People who had ridden in his car for ten years and more were known to say that the most Mr. Zinzer had ever condescended to reply to their greetings was a grunted "H'lo." His round face was absolutely expressionless; nothing ever seemed to evoke a response from him.

Once, in early July, this complete stolidity was demon-strated to me very forcibly. I was riding his car late one eve-ning, returning from supper at Aunt Ellen's, when a small, red-faced woman got aboard at Calhoun Street. She took the seat opposite Mr. Zinzer and at once began jabbering away at him. I was seated in the unoccupied motorman's seat at the rear of the car—there was no one else aboard—and could not hear all of what was being said because of the noise of the wheels, but it was evident that the woman was angry at something, for she was gesturing wildly and talking away in an almost hysterical tone. At first I thought she must have some grievance against Mr. Zinzer, but after a while her harangue grew so monotonous that I decided she was simply crazy. Whichever it was, however, it did not seem to disturb

Mr. Zinzer; throughout her tirade he continued to stare blandly ahead, just as if she were not even there, giving at most a perfunctory nod of his head now and then. What might have unnerved another man was as nothing to him. Eventually the woman got off the car, and we continued on our way, with Mr. Zinzer's face as expressionless as ever.

He was almost the exact opposite of his colleague on the Rutledge Avenue Line. The Marvelous Ringgold was, like Mr. Zinzer, a short man, too—but at that point the resemblance ended. The Marvelous Ringgold was thin, wiry, with a great deal of nervous energy about him. Far from being expressionless, his bony face was a reflection of swiftly changing emotions, his forehead alternately furrowing and smoothing itself, his eyes deep and glittering, his wide, thick-lipped mouth breaking into a broad grin that displayed a twisted and dazzling array of gold teeth. On his balding head he wore a high-peaked motorman's cap, and he was always dressed in a somewhat foxed and shiny black uniform with dull gold buttons. His uniform bulged at the pockets with paper-wrapped rolls of nickels, dimes and quarters, and was always in disarray. His hands were large and horny, with long, yellowed fingernails. For comfort's sake his shoes were often untied, and they were always scuffed. No wonder, for he moved about constantly, habitually standing in a slight crouch as he operated his car, shifting his feet like a boxer to tramp boisterously upon the alarm bell or, at the slightest hint of a shower, to kick the sanding pedal.

And he talked. He talked to anyone, everyone. He talked with me, finding out about all my doings, telling me about his family, giving me his opinion of the pennant races, the state of the world, the good life. He asked about the Major. How was he taking this hot weather? Wasn't it remarkable the way the Major kept as alert as if he were thirty years younger, never confusing the past with the present as some old men did? Mr. Zinzer, he said, had a wife who was half insane and who plagued his existence. I remembered the woman I had seen on the trolley a few evenings before, and thought that must have been her. The notion that Mr. Zinzer was human enough to have a wife, even a crazy one, seemed almost unbelievable to me.

My idea of the proper conclusion to a summer evening spent downtown was to board the Marvelous Ringgold's trolley and to take a seat up front and watch him as he operated the car and talked with other passengers. I would talk with him myself when the other passengers got off, all the while feeling the humid night air of July flowing through the barred, open windows, and seeing the framed rectangles of light from the parlors and halls of homes set back in the dark on either side of Rutledge Avenue. Finally I would get off myself at Versailles Street and step out alone in the warm darkness. I would walk homeward then along the deserted dirt street, watching my shadow grow shorter and thinner as I neared and extend itself again as I passed under the solitary street lights at each corner, and hearing the insects whirring in the thickets, a dog barking off in the distance. All the way home I would listen to the sound of the Marvelous Ringgold's trolley, growing fainter, but still distinct in the night, as it rolled along to the end of the line.

3. "I THINK," SAID MAJOR FRAMPTON TO ME ONE MON-
day morning, "that we ought to show Helen the
Sappho, don't you?" The *Sappho* was the old ferryboat that
the Major had captained many years ago, the wooden hulk
of which now lay half sunk in the marsh beyond Gadsden
Street, near where my Aunt Ellen lived. Mrs. Cartwright
wanted to drive us downtown in her car, but the Major refused.

We set out for the car line, walking slowly to keep pace with
the Major. It was a bright day and not oppressively hot, and
we were all in high spirits. Soon the trolley rounded the bend
a block north of Versailles Street and came toward us. In
keeping with the spirit of the occasion the Marvelous
Ringgold was at the controls. When we climbed aboard, the
Major introduced Helen to him. "Oh, I met this young lady
last week," the Marvelous Ringgold responded. "How's everything up in Philadelphia?" he asked her.

At Rutledge and Wentworth we got off and walked down
toward Gadsden Street and the *Sappho*. The old ferryboat
was imbedded in the marsh a hundred yards offshore, behind a large yellow frame residence belonging to a man
named DeVries, who was the city coroner. Mr. DeVries had
purchased the ferryboat hulk some years ago, long after it
had been taken out of service, and had arranged to have it
towed at high tide up into the marsh behind his home and
moored there. A plank catwalk had been built between the
Sappho and the bank, and the ferryboat served as a dock for
several sailboats and rowboats. It had long since settled per-
manently in the thick mud, and at low tide there was water

only at the end that faced toward the river. All the *Sappho's* superstructure had been stripped from her save for a little shed with a galvanized metal roof at the far end. For safety's sake the stairways leading below the deck had been removed and the entryways boarded over. The edge of the deck extended far over the hull, and on each side there was a large gap where the paddle wheels had once been housed. Before we left for downtown the Major had shown Helen an old photograph of the *Sappho*, one that I had looked at many times, and which showed it with tall smokestacks, windowed cabins with pinnacled wheelhouses at either end, an elongate, diamond-shaped walking beam, and graceful, covered paddle wheels. "You'll hardly be able to recognize her now," he had warned Helen, "but she was a grand old ship in her day."

The walkway to the *Sappho* was a swaying affair of sagging double planks, crossing over the shining black marsh mud with its filigrees of fiddler trails and pockmarked dens. The little crabs stretched out by the thousands in the sun, some with yellowed single claws as big as their entire bodies, others with two tiny pincers pressed against the fronts of their square little torsos. At our approach they scurried off in waves, retreating into their dens. Beyond range many more thousands of them rested unperturbed on the surface of the mud.

We made our way along the catwalk in single file, the Major in the lead. The unsteadiness of the footing seemed to bother him not at all; he walked slowly, carefully, stepping with precision. We followed behind him, our eyes trained on the planking beneath us. The walkway led under the overhanging deck of the *Sappho*, with a stairway built up to the deck through one of the empty paddle-wheel gaps. Up the steps we clambered and onto the open deck, with its wide, weather-beaten timbers, some dry and mealy, others exuding little tarred droplets of moisture that glittered in the light.

Before us the Ashley River fanned out in a wide bend, with Wappoo Cut visible far across the stream. To the left, a quarter mile away, there was the lighthouse station, with the three ships, the *Cypress*, the *Mangrove*, and the red-painted *Relief*, tied alongside the dock, and with large black-and-red channel buoys lying on their sides atop the wharf and along the adjacent shore. Off the point, scores of white sea gulls dipped and soared in mid-air. Halfway across the river, in midstream, a launch moved slowly upstream toward Elliott's Cut, its gasoline motor thumping steadily. Its roof must have been newly tinned, for it flashed so dazzlingly in the sunlight that I had to turn away.

"Do you suppose that could be the launch that comes past our house every night?" I asked the Major.

He shook his head. "No, too big. That's a Palmer engine. That launch that goes downstream every night's got a Lathrop engine. You can tell by the sound. Hear how regular that one is? A Lathrop's more rough sounding—thump, thump, thump, thump. You've heard it. Beside, that's the sugarboat out there."

"What's the sugarboat?" Helen asked.

"It's a launch that operates between Charleston and Savannah. The Dixie Crystals Company runs it."

"Was that what your boat did, Grandfather?" Helen asked.

The Major laughed. "No indeed, child. The *Sappho* was much bigger than that little craft. Let's go sit over there in the shade, under that shed, and I'll tell you about this old lady you're standing on. Of course, Omar and Billy know all about it, and I expect they'll want to find something else to do, instead of listening to the same old story again." The Major knew quite well, of course, that I would not for the world miss hearing him talk about ferryboating in the old days, no matter how many times I had been told the stories. Billy, however, wandered off on some interest of his own.

"No, child, the *Sappho* was too big for that. She was a harbor ferry. For close to fifty years she plied back and forth between Hungry Neck—that's Mount Pleasant now—and

127

Charleston, across the Cooper River. And for more than forty of those years, I was her skipper." He puffed on the cigar. "Yes, she was quite a gal, quite a gal. . . ."

I knew the story, and all that followed, by heart, but that did not keep me from listening willingly while the Major talked on. He told us about the *Sappho's* first running-mate, the *Pocosin*, which everybody called the Pokey Slow. He told of the *Pocosin's* replacement, the *Commodore Perry*, and of how the coming of automobile traffic necessitated flattening out the *Sappho* at the ends. He told of the later ferries, the *Lawrence*, with its great tall stacks, and the *Palmetto*, which was built right there in Charleston and made the run along with the *Lawrence* until the Cooper River Bridge was opened to traffic—"on the morning of August 8, 1929"—after which the ferries were soon driven out of service. He told of the trolley cars that used to meet the ferryboats at Mount Pleasant and take passengers on to Fort Moultrie, Sullivan's Island, and the Isle of Palms. And the Major talked on, while Helen and I sat next to him, asking questions now and then, listening to the extended replies that followed. Sometimes I watched him as he spoke; at other times I looked out at the river, the broad, flowing river, that swept by us and out of sight past the lighthouse docks, toward the harbor and Fort Sumter. After a while, in the mounting heat of the day, the Major grew tired. He yawned. "Well," he said, "that's enough about ferryboating for now, I suppose. Why don't you two go exploring a little, while I sit here and rest a bit before we go home?"

So we left the Major there in the shade, and walked together back along the deck of the *Sappho* toward the catwalk. Just as we reached the stairway I looked back, and saw that the Major was already asleep, his white head bent forward and his back propped against one of the wooden roof posts.

*   *   *

We set out down the steps and along the narrow plankway to the shore. The Major was not there to slow us up this time, so we walked swiftly, and the wooden planking swayed under our feet.

It was hot now. The heavy plant growth along the edge of the marsh seemed to exude a sticky radiance of moist heat. Perspiration clung to us in a heavy film, and insects swirled and darted about the foliage along the path back to the De-Vries yard, where the coroner kept a small menagerie.

Several cages, protected from the sun by chinaberry trees with wide overhanging boughs, were set among some oleander bushes. In one cage there was a raccoon, grayish-brown in color, which lurked in the dark far corner of the cage, eyes almost closed, with its black cheek patches set in a knowing scowl, and its striped tail curled fringelike around its body. In another cage some red squirrels, tails thinned for the summer's heat, cavorted about. We watched them for a while as they scampered over the forked trunk of a sawed-off tree mounted within the enclosure, then flung themselves against the fine wire mesh of the cage. Their sharp claws took instant grip of the wire and the squirrels held firmly there while the cage rattled under their impact. I gathered up some dry pecan shells that had fallen under the cage, and amused myself by tossing them over the side and through the wider mesh at the top, while the squirrels scampered after them. Helen wandered over to a third cage, near a low garage, where several tropical birds, somewhat bedraggled in appearance, hissed and whistled at her as she drew near. I watched her talking back to them, delighted at their excitement.

I heard the raccoon begin chewing at its cage for some reason, and I went back to look. It was crouched in the front corner now, and was thrusting its tiny, wrinkled black fingers about in the mesh as if to find someway out of the cage.

At that moment I heard a sharp scream. I looked around,

129

startled. Helen was standing beyond the bird cage, at the corner of the garage, her hand over her mouth, her face white.

"What's the matter?" I asked, and started toward her.

She backed away from the cage, then turned and ran toward me, her hands raised before her, her eyes wide and round.

"There's a—skeleton—in there!" she whispered. "A—human skeleton!"

Then she began to cry, her face blanched with fright. I put my arms around her, and we stood there a moment, her face pressed against my arm and shoulder.

I looked around me. The animals were still and quiet in their cages, the oleander bushes stirred lightly in the breeze. The garage, its exterior pale brown in color, was bathed in sun. I tried to peer into the shaded interior, but from where we stood I was too far away to see anything. I could feel Helen's hot tears spreading in the fabric of my shirt. I did not know what to say.

I heard sounds behind me, and turned my head to see Billy Cartwright come walking up along the path. He was grinning at first, and then he saw as he came closer that Helen was crying.

"What's wrong?" he asked.

Helen looked up at him and started to reply, then broke into sobs again. I felt quite helpless.

"She says there's a skeleton in there."

"A *what?*" Billy asked, looking over toward the garage.

"A human skeleton. In the garage."

"Let's go see," Billy Cartwright said. I disengaged myself from Helen, and Billy and I went over to the garage and peered gingerly inside.

We saw it, there in the corner. It *was* a human skeleton, propped up against the inside of the garage, the head sunk over the chest as if asleep. A numbing sensation, as of ice, spread along my backbone.

"I'll be darned," Billy whispered. "It sure is."

We edged a little closer, staring at the dry, shiny whiteness of the bones, the caged ribs, the curved hollowness of the hip bones, the heavy dome of the cranium with its vacant eye sockets and the bared, yellow, grinning rows of teeth.

"What do you suppose it's doing here?" I asked.

Billy Cartwright did not reply, but continued to stare at the skeleton. Then all at once he stepped over to it and bent down.

"It's been wired together," he said.

I went over and looked. Sure enough, the white bones of the skeleton were fastened in place with rusted metal strands.

I reached out and touched the long arm bone. It was dry, hard.

"It's probably been dead a long time," I said.

"Maybe they got it from the medical college," Billy suggested. "I wonder if it's worth anything?" He lifted a wrist and raised up the arm, its long, jointed fingers extending loosely before it. Several joints were missing from one hand.

I remembered then that we had left Helen standing outside, and I went back to the yard. She was over by the oleander bushes, looking toward us, no longer crying but her face streaked from the tears.

"It's just an old skeleton," I told her. "It's all wired together."

"Why is it in there?"

"I don't know. Probably came from the medical college. It's nothing to be frightened of."

"Let's go away from here," Helen said.

"It won't hurt you, Helen," Billy Cartwright called, coming part way out of the garage. "Come look at it. It's all wired up."

Helen shook her head. "I don't want to see it," she told me. "I don't like it."

"All right, then," I agreed. "Hey, Billy," I called, "come

on and let's go wake up the Major."

Major Frampton was already roused from his nap, however, and was stepping carefully along the planked catwalk toward the shore when we reached the bank. While we waited there for him, Helen removed a small handkerchief from the pocket of her blouse and dabbed at her face to remove the traces of the tears.

The Major laughed when we told him what we had found. "Probably some old cadaver DeVries found once," he said. "That's what coroners have to do, you know. Most likely he had it wired up as a joke, or something like that. Don't worry about it."

"Do you think it's valuable?" Billy Cartwright asked.

"I doubt it," the Major told him. "Anyway, it belongs to DeVries."

And we walked off toward the streetcar line.

On the way home we rode quietly, the Major and Helen seated together, chatting a little, while Billy Cartwright and I sat farther back in the car, immersed in our private thoughts. The motorman was Mr. Zinzer, and he piloted the streetcar slowly and steadily up Rutledge Avenue.

I thought about what we had seen and done that morning. I remembered the way the skeleton had looked when we first saw it, propped against the side of the hot, dusty garage. Oddly, there was superimposed upon that image, in my mind's eye, the sight of Major Frampton, as I had seen him when I had looked back for a moment as Helen and I were about to descend the *Sappho's* stairway. Both had seemed asleep.

But then I thought of Helen, and of how I had held her in my arms in her fright, and of how, against my shirt and skin, her tears had felt moist and burning.

4. IN THE HOT DAYS OF LATE JULY DOMINIQUE WORKED in our yard three times a week, laboring from early morning until the shadows grew deep in the late afternoon. I never saw him grow tired, never saw him lay down his pick or shovel and seek the shade. His body in a half-crouch, he grasped the handle of his pickax with his great, flexible hands, swung it in a fast chop over his shoulder, sent the point plunging into the hard, caked turf near the fence. He placed the blade of the long-handled shovel, set his heavy foot atop it, drove it deep into the ground, shoved the handle back, grasped it firmly, looped the loose earth into the wheelbarrow. He was powerful, sinewy; all day long he dug, hoed, raked, shoveled, carted earth away.

Often we would stand out in the yard and talk with Dominique while he worked. His voice was low and gentle. The West Indian accent, English in inflection, gave his words a musical quality strange to our ears. He was always quite willing to talk, though never for an instant did he break the stride of his work as he did so. Only very occasionally would he stop his labor, and then it would usually be to reach down in the grass nearby and pick up a frog that had wandered along. For some reason he seemed to be fascinated by frogs, with which our garden was always plentifully supplied. He would thrust his hand out swiftly, deftly, seize one with his long fingers and place it on the palm of one hand, lightly stroking its mottled brown back with the fingertips of the other hand. Oddly enough, the frog would seldom make any effort to free itself so long as Dominique held it. It would lie docilely in Dominique's hand, its little bright eyes glinting in the light, as bright as the silver ring Dominique wore,

133

which always seemed to glimmer with an unusual luster. When at length Dominique stopped stroking its back and deposited it carefully on the grass, the frog would hop away calmly.

The first song I ever heard Dominique sing—Helen was along, and she asked him whether he knew any songs—was about a frog. "Yes, mum," he had answered. "I know a song called 'La Pluie Tombe.'" Helen asked him to sing it for her, and he did so:

> *La pluie tombe,*
> *Crapeau chante,*
> *Oin, oin! oin, oin! oin, oin!*
> *M'a pale baigner moin.*
> *La pluie tombe,*
> *Marin-gouin crie,*
> *M'a pale noyer moin.*
> *La pluie tombe,*
> *Marin-gouin crie,*
> *M'a pale noyer moin.*
> *Oin, oin! oin, oin! oin, oin!*

"How lovely!" Helen cried. "Where did you learn it?"
"In Haiti," Dominique said. He pronounced it High-TEE.
"What kind of language is it?" Billy Cartwright asked him.
"That is French."
"What does it mean?"
"It tells about the rain falling, and a frog croaking, and a mosquito making answer," Dominique said.
"How did you learn to speak French?" I asked him.
"For a long time I lived in Haiti," he said.
"Do you know any more songs?" Helen asked. But at that moment Viola called from the porch to tell Dominique that his lunch was ready, and he laid down his shovel and went off to eat under the porch.

Billy Cartwright and I would urge Dominique to tell us

stories of his life in the West Indies. He was born and grew up in Jamaica, but he had lived in Haiti for a long time, and he had served as a guide for the U.S. Marines when they went into the jungles to fight bandits there. He told us of guiding platoons of Marines along the narrow trails through the thick rain forests, of how they would engage in fights with rebel sharpshooters in the jungles, and how they would surprise rebel bands and kill or capture them.

On one of Dominique's arms there were some serrated marks that formed a pattern on his dark, purplish skin. They looked like scars, and I asked him how they got there.

"One time I was accused of committing a crime," he said, "and they whipped me."

"The Marines?"

"No, this was in Jamaica," Dominique said, shaking his head. "I was working on a sugar plantation with my brothers."

"Did they beat you with a stick?"

"With a leather whip."

I shuddered, imagining to myself the curling thong of the whip snaking around the dark biceps, drawing blood as it cut into the skin. "Did it hurt very much?"

Dominique shook his head again. "No, not so very much."

We did not often talk with Dominique during his lunch hour, however, because most of the time Viola sat with him. Viola was always in especially good spirits on the days when Dominique was working for us. She would sing at her chores, and her voice, high-pitched but melodious, could be heard all over the house and yard. It seemed to me that she was always hovering near the windows while she cleaned and dusted. My mother loved to hear her sing. "It's the way they sing out on the sea islands," she would say. "The old-time songs." Most of the songs were mournful in nature, having to do with watery graves sinking down, and going along lonesome roads, but Viola sang them happily.

135

One afternoon when my parents had gone downtown and were late in returning, the telephone rang and Viola answered it. I paid little attention until I thought I heard Viola ask, "You coming out here to work tomorrow?" Why, she is talking to Dominique! I thought. Later I heard her say, "Well, I'll be seeing you directly after I come home," and soon after that the conversation ended.

"Do you suppose," I asked Billy Cartwright one day, "that Viola and Dominique are in love?"

"They might be," he said.

"They always talk together at lunchtime, and he calls her on the phone sometime on the days when he's not working out here."

"That doesn't cut any ice," Billy said. "Why does it matter anyway?"

"I don't know. I was just wondering."

One morning during the week that followed, Viola came to work several hours late—something she rarely did, for usually she was either absent all day or there on time. When she finally arrived, there was a long gauze bandage on her forearm. My mother asked her what had happened, and Viola said she had fallen at home while preparing dinner and had cut herself with a carving knife. My mother pressed her for details, but all Viola would say was that the knife had slipped from her grasp and gashed her arm.

"Well, be careful with it," my mother said. "You don't want it to get infected."

But the wound did not seem to get better. Viola's arm became sore, and my mother told my father to take her down to Roper Hospital and have it examined. The doctors there gave Viola some medicine to put on it, and the soreness in her arm got no worse, but the wound did not improve.

During this period, Viola's disposition was not of the sunniest. She seldom sang at work any more. She did her tasks and said little. I noticed, too, that when she would bring

Dominique his lunch on the days when he was working for us, she did not chatter away at him as before. Usually she would still sit with him, to be sure, but neither of them spoke very much, and sometimes Viola would not even stay down under the porch with him for his whole lunchtime, but as soon as he finished eating would take his tray back upstairs. If romance there was, I decided, it was less ardent now.

As for Dominique, I noticed no change in him at all. He was as hard a worker as ever, and as ready to tell Billy, Helen and myself stories of his life in the West Indies whenever we asked him. Helen once asked whether he knew any more songs, and he sang one about a monkey:

> *If you want to see*
> *De monkey dance,*
> *Bus' a pepper in he tail;*
> *Monkey play de fiddle,*
> *Baboon play de banjo,*
> *Yard-o, yard-o,*
> *Bella in de yard-o,*
> *Massa dead, he lef' no money,*
> *Missis have to work all about.*

He sang this song and others in a strange half tune, not quite a melody, with some words pronounced very rapidly, others drawn out in a wavering, almost eerie chant. Helen was enthralled with them, and said it was too bad that we could not make a phonograph record of Dominique singing.

"Do you notice," Billy Cartwright said once, "the way he looks at a frog? His eyes get all bright, and he stares at it like it was magic or something."

Helen and I had both noticed it, too. Whatever the reason was, Dominique was interested in frogs. He never failed to pick one up and stroke its back when he saw it. It was the only thing that could ever make him pause in his yard work.

*   *   *

All the while Viola's disposition grew worse, and her housework began to suffer. Ordinarily the most thorough of cleaners, she now began to neglect her chores. My mother, puzzled at the change, had several times to remind her of duties she had neglected.

Viola did not reply. My mother said, "You're not doing your work any more. You walk about as if you were in a trance. What's the matter with you?"

"I don't know, ma'am." Viola looked down at the floor.

"Is your arm hurting you? Does that wound still worry you?"

"No, ma'am."

"It certainly is hanging on for a long time. Is it any better?"

"No, ma'am. But it doesn't bother me none."

"Well, then, what *is* the matter? Are you worried about something?"

"No, ma'am."

My mother sighed. "Well, try to do better, then."

"Yes, ma'am." Viola answered in a listless, unconvincing way, her eyes still on the ground. My mother watched her for a moment, shook her head helplessly, then went into the next room. Viola resumed her work.

After Viola had gone home that evening, my parents talked about her. "I just don't know what can be the matter with her," my mother kept repeating. "She's not herself half the time any more. Some days she'll be all right, and other days she goes around like a walking corpse or something. I asked her whether that wound was still bothering her, and she says no. But *something* is."

"That wound never has healed up, has it?" my father asked.

"No, it hasn't. It's the strangest thing. It doesn't seem to get any worse, but yet it doesn't seem to improve."

"Does she take care of it?"

"She seems to. She has a fresh bandage on it almost every day."

"Well, I don't know. I'll take her back down to Roper Hospital if you want."

"That doesn't seem to do any good, either."

I was considering what my mother had said about Viola's being better on some days than on others. I thought back over the past week. "You know," I said, "she wasn't so bad yesterday, was she?"

"No, she wasn't," my mother agreed. "Some days she's almost like her old self. Then the next day she'll be back in a daze again."

"And the day before yesterday, she was acting peculiar," I said. "But the day before *that*, she was all right."

My mother thought a moment. "Yes, I believe you're right. Wednesday was when the Sewing Circle was here, and she was so dazed that she even forgot to set the table in the dining room. But Tuesday was when I went shopping downtown, and she did her work all right that day."

I began to see it now. "It's when Dominique is here."

My father and mother stared at me. "What?"

"The days when she's worst are those when Dominique is working in the yard. He was here Wednesday, and today, and Monday. He wasn't here Tuesday and Thursday. Don't you see?"

My parents looked at each other. "What has Dominique got to do with it?" my father asked me.

"She's in love with him." They did not seem to comprehend. "Viola's in love with Dominique," I repeated.

My father frowned. "That doesn't make any sense," he said. "If she's in love with him, why does she act so queer on the days when he's out here?"

"Maybe *he* doesn't love *her*," my mother suggested. "Perhaps Omar is right."

"I'll be damned!" my father said. "Maybe that's it."

"Well, if it is," said my mother, "you'll just have to get rid of him. I can't have her going on like this. The house will

139

be in ruins in another month's time."

"But it's not his fault," my father said. "Why should he be made to suffer?"

"How do you know whose fault it is?" my mother asked. "Besides, it doesn't matter who's to blame; I simply can't afford to have Viola going on like this. If Dominique is worrying her, then he'll have to go."

"Well, I don't know," my father said. "He's a mighty queer one, all right. From the West Indies, you know. They're mighty strange down there."

"How do you mean?" I asked. For some reason the way my father said this made me uneasy.

"Oh, they go in for voodoo, and all sorts of things. They get it from the jungles."

"What's voodoo?"

My father laughed. "It's a kind of worship. They believe in witch doctors, and spells, and magic amulets, and they put the Evil Eye on people."

"How do they do it?" I felt the hair rising on the back of my neck.

"Oh, there are lots of ways. They use herbs in a jar, or certain kinds of powder in little sacks called goofer bags, or they make effigies and stick pins in them—I don't know. I used to hear about it when I was a kid. Most of the Negroes around here don't believe in that sort of thing any more."

"Wasn't there something about frogs?" my mother asked.

My heart was in my throat.

"I believe there was," my father replied, laughing. "They were supposed to have some kind of magic power over frogs, and they could use them to make charms."

I remembered how Dominique would reach out and pick up frogs and hold them in his hand. I remembered his long fingers stroking the back of a frog, and his eyes as he looked at the frog, and the glint of the silver ring he wore.

I realized suddenly that my parents were staring at me.

"My lord!" my father exclaimed. "What's the matter? You're as white as a sheet!"

"You've scared him with all that talk!" my mother said. She came over and put her arms around me. "Don't take it seriously, sweetheart. It's just superstition, anyway."

My father got up and chucked me playfully under the chin. "Come on, boy," he said, "don't worry about it. There's nothing to it all. I was just kidding."

He explained to me that primitive, uneducated people sometimes believed in magic, and that it was a way for them to explain the movements of the sun and the moon and the seasons and the crops, whereas we knew the scientific explanations of such things. "It's only ignorance," he said. "It was brought over from Africa, and on some of the West Indian islands where the natives aren't around educated people very much, and haven't been thoroughly civilized, they cling to the old voodoo superstitions, and believe in witch doctors and charms and magic. But it's dying out. Nobody much takes it seriously. Even twenty years ago you'd see lots of the Negro houses in the country with the shutters painted blue, but not any more."

"Why were they painted blue?" I asked.

"It was a superstition that the Evil Eye couldn't come into houses if the windows and doors were painted blue. So they'd touch up the shutters and sills with blue, and paint a blue cross above the doorsill. The cross was Christian, you see, and no witch doctor would dare walk underneath it."

"What kind of things could the witch doctors do?" I asked.

"They couldn't *really* do *anything*, of course. It's all superstition. But they used to scare ignorant Negroes into believing that they could bring bad luck, or cause sickness, or prevent wounds from healing, or—good God, what's wrong now?"

I felt the chill run up and down my spine; the objects in the room reeled before me.

141

My mother hugged me. "Omar, stop it! What's frightened you? It's just ignorant superstition; you know better than to believe all that!"

I tried to say the words, but my throat was thick, and my teeth chattered. "The—the—wound!" I quavered.

"The *what?*" my father asked. "What are you trying to say?"

"Viola's wound!" I blurted out. "The one that won't heal. You said that—"

My father and mother looked at each other. "My God!" my father began. "Could it be that—"

Then my father began to laugh. I had never heard him laugh so hard before. He slapped his knee, he threw his body back, he leaned over his chair, he gripped the arms of the chair to keep from toppling over; his laughter rang through the house, the tears rolled down his cheeks as he tried help-lessly to stop laughing. "Wound—!" he kept repeating. "Witch doctor—Viola—!" He held his sides. "My lord, what an imagination!" It was some minutes before he could regain his composure.

As for myself, I began to feel sheepish about the whole thing. I laughed a little, too, though I did not know what was so preposterous about it.

My mother, who had joined in my father's mirth, hugged me again. "Darling, you have too much imagination for your own good," she told me. "Now why don't you run upstairs and change into your good clothes, and we'll all go down-town to the movies? We've had enough of witch doctors and voodoo for the evening. Viola will be all right."

"Witch doctor!" my father said, still laughing. "Good God!"

I got up and went on into the hall and up the stairs to my room. Downstairs I could hear my father still chuckling as he and my mother went into their room and began getting dressed. It *was* pretty foolish, now that I thought of it. I even joked about it a little as we drove downtown.

But in bed that night, I remembered again the evening's conversation. I thought of Dominique, and the frogs, and of Viola's strange conduct, and the wound on her arm that would not heal up, and I remembered the look my parents exchanged just before my father suddenly saw humor in the episode. I thought of the Evil Eye, and the blue crosses painted on the doorsills to ward off its presence. Outside, beyond my window, the trees and the fields were dark, and the moon was masked behind the clouds. I heard a mourning dove calling in the distance. And a disturbing picture kept intruding—the skeleton in the garage, lying there propped against the wall, its empty-socketed head bent forward as if asleep. The darkness about me seemed close, oppressive. I turned my reading light back on, and opened Dr. Chisholm's Fort Sumter book and read for a while. When finally I went to sleep it was very late; the evening train had long since come and gone, and even the trolley cars were silent.

5. THERE WAS A COOLER SPELL TOWARD THE END OF July. The days were still hot, with the temperature in the eighties, but in the evenings it was pleasant, and several nights we even slept under light blankets. For my father it was something of a triumph, for some weeks ago he had predicted that we would have a brief period of cooler weather during the last week in July, and now he could remind everyone of his forecast. For all of us the change in the weather was invigorating, enjoyable. My mother welcomed the respite from the hot season and worked all day in her flower garden. Once again my father tried to persuade her to move the crocus bulbs away from the walk, but she refused to do it. "They're doing well where they are," she said. "They don't deserve to be pulled up and moved."

Only the Major looked at the skies and frowned. "I've seen it like this before," he said, "just before a hurricane: high sky, and fleecy clouds, and the like." But of course that was irrelevant, because no sign of a hurricane had been reported in the Caribbean, and the hurricane season was a month distant at the very least. The Major was looking forward to September, however, when the twice delayed Fort Sumter Celebration would finally take place, and he did not like anything that reminded him even remotely of the possibility that there might be bad weather then.

"I wish you and your mother could stay for it," he told Helen. "It'll be a wonderful occasion." But Helen's school began the first week in September, and she and her mother were scheduled to leave for Philadelphia during the third week in August, when her father would have returned from

144

a business trip to Europe. The thought of Helen's leaving, nearly a month away though it was, seemed disturbing. I wished that the summer might go on forever.

We sat on Billy Cartwright's front porch, overlooking the marsh and the river, the tide quite high before us—Helen, Billy, the Major, and I. The Major was telling Helen what would take place during the Fort Sumter Celebration. "It's going to be a great day," he said, as he had said so many times. "Six bands, a solid mile of troops, the Atlantic fleet in port, and the President himself for speaker of the day."

"Will they fire on Fort Sumter again?" Helen asked.

"Ha, ha!" the Major laughed. "Not very likely. Once was enough."

"Why did they do it the first time?" Helen asked.

"Because South Carolina had seceded from the Union, and Northern troops held the fort."

"But wasn't it a Union fort?"

"Not any longer," the Major said. "It was on our territory, and once South Carolina was no longer in the Union, it was natural that the fort couldn't be, either. At least that's what *we* thought. *They* didn't think so."

"Why didn't the North let the South have the fort?" Billy Cartwright asked.

Helen answered at once, even before the Major could reply. "Because the Union had to be preserved."

"But it was the South's territory, not the North's," Billy objected.

"No, it wasn't," Helen said. "Our history teacher said that the South tried to break up the United States of America, and the Union had to be saved. Besides, there were slaves in the South, and they had to be freed."

"The slaves were happy, and most masters were good and kind. *Our* history teacher said *that!*" Billy Cartwright declared. "She said that most Southerners didn't even own slaves."

145

"Then why did they care if they were freed?" Helen asked.

"Because the Yankees had no right to tell the South what to do," Billy replied.

"Well, I think it was wrong for the South to own slaves, and I'm glad the North freed them, no matter whether they had a right to or not."

"That's because you're a Yankee," Billy Cartwright told Helen.

"Wait a minute there," the Major said. "Now don't you go calling your cousin Helen a Yankee, Billy boy. She's my grandchild, just as you are, and no grandchild of mine can be a Yankee."

"But she lives in Philadelphia, and that's in the North, so she's got to be one," Billy insisted.

"Not if she's my grandchild. It's not where you live, but who you are that counts. Isn't that right, Omar?"

I had been staying out of the argument, because my emotions were mixed. On the one hand I agreed with Billy about the North's starting the war, but on the other hand I wanted to be on Helen's side in any argument that occurred. "Yes, sir," I said.

"The North started the war," Billy Cartwright insisted.

"No, it didn't," Helen answered. "The South fired on Fort Sumter, and that started the war."

"Tell us about the *Star of the West*," I suggested quickly to the Major. "Helen's never heard about that, has she?"

"No, I haven't," said Helen, who seemed equally anxious to change the subject. "What a lovely name, the *Star of the West*. What is it?"

"Well, now, I'll tell you," began the Major. "The *Star of the West*," he said, as he commenced the process of lighting one of his cigars, "was the name of a ship. On January the ninth, 1861, in the early dawn, it steamed across the bar into Charleston Harbor." He held a kitchen match to the cigar and began drawing on it. "We were stationed on Morris

Island—a battalion of Citadel cadets and some of us older men. I was in command of the battery. When we saw the *Star of the West* out in the ship channel, my executive officer turned to me and—"

But I listened no more. For suddenly the import of the Major's story, which I had heard many times, struck me. "I was in command of the battery," he had said, and "My executive officer" . . . but that time when I had told him about Dr. Chisholm's book, and that he was not in it, what had he replied? That he was just a rear-rank private! But if he had been only a private soldier, then how had he been in command of the gun crew that fired on the *Star of the West?*

Was Dr. Chisholm right, and had the Major not been in all those adventures, after all?

I looked out at the river, flowing on and on as always. I heard the Major talking, his familiar voice saying the same words that I knew by heart. The names, the stories, just as Dr. Chisholm had described them in his book. Surely the Major must have been there, must actually be remembering them, to know them so well, in all the details. But what had he said about his executive officer turning to him? What did it all mean?

I became aware that a pause had come in the Major's narrative. I knew that it must be the moment when he was describing how the first shot had exploded over the masts of the *Star of the West*, and that I was expected at this point in the story to ask, "Did you hit it on the next shot?" so that he could explain that they didn't really want to hit the ship, but only to make it turn around and withdraw from the harbor. But I could not say the words.

I leaped to my feet. "Maybe we could show her!" I said. "Maybe Billy and I could get in the rowboat and be the Union crew and paddle along the marsh, and you and Helen could be the Confederate garrison on Morris Island!"

The Major looked at me, startled. "Well, now," he said

147

after a moment, "maybe we could at that."

"Look!" I pointed toward the marsh, talking rapidly. "See, the creek there could be the channel, and this could be Morris Island!"

"By gosh," said the Major, "that would be a fine idea. Now, Helen, do you see where the land curves around there, by the hill?"

"Yes, sir," Helen said. The Major was pointing to a clump of woods called Devereux, several hundred yards or so down the shoreline and extending well out into the marsh. Devereux was famous as a lovers' lane, and from my window at night I could sometimes see the headlights of automobiles driving up to park there.

"Now, we can imagine that little island right off the point there is Fort Sumter. Billy and Omar can come paddling along in their boat, representing the Union crew. You and I will be the Confederate defenders of Charleston Harbor."

"But I don't want to be a Union crewman," Billy Cartwright declared. "I want to be a Confederate defender!"

"I'll go in the boat," Helen said. "I want to be in the crew of the *Star of the West*."

"Very well," the Major said. "Billy and I'll be the defenders, and Helen and Omar will be the crew of the *Star of the West*. Is that all right with you, Omar?"

"Yes, sir," I said. I forced myself to pretend impatience to begin the game while the Major explained in great detail what we were to do. But what I really wanted to do was to get away, out in the boat if need be, but away from the Major and his stories. "Come on," I said to Helen as soon as the Major had done. "Let's go!"

I hurried off, sprinting toward the grove of trees in front of our house that led toward the wharf where the *Endymion of Charleston, S.C.* was tied. Helen came running after me.

We stepped down the grassy bank to the dock, where the *Endymion of Charleston, S.C.*, its red rectangular hulk rocking in the current, waited. I got in and hastily bailed out the water that covered the bottom, then untied the rope. Helen, who was still breathing hard from the precipitous descent down the hillside, climbed in. I pushed off from the dock and we set off over the reed grass; the tide was so high that it was hardly necessary even to follow the creek channel. We glided right over the marsh with no difficulty at all.

"Look! There they are!" Helen cried, pointing toward the shore. The Major and Billy Cartwright were standing at the edge of the water, just in front of Billy's house.

"Hello there, Confederate defenders!" Helen called across to them.

"Hello yourself," the Major called back. He held up a walking stick and pointed it at us, as if it were a weapon. "Fire!" he said.

Billy Cartwright was not content with gesturing. He picked up a rock and heaved it in our direction.

"Hey, watch out!" I yelled at him.

"Number two battery!" Billy shouted, and fired another stone. This time it landed no more than six feet away, and water splashed on us.

"Billy!" the Major said. "Watch what you're doing!"

"Full speed ahead!" Helen shouted. "On to the Fort!"

Billy Cartwright threw another stone; this time his aim was considerably short.

"I wish we had an American flag to wave!" Helen said. "Oh, isn't this great fun?"

Devereux was heavily wooded, with a trail through it that led up onto the hill overlooking the marsh and then down again to a clump of oak trees at the water's edge. There was one tree in particular that arched far over the marsh in which Billy and I had built a platform the previous summer. Just offshore was the small island in the marsh, thickly covered with underbrush.

"Is that Fort Sumter?" Helen asked, pointing toward it.

149

"Yeah."

"And the hill over there, that's Fort Moultrie?"

"Uh huh."

"Oh, how exciting! This is just like we were actually fighting in the battle!"

"Uh huh."

"And just think, Grandfather remembers it all! He was actually there. Isn't he a wonderful old man?"

"Uh huh," I said.

Helen frowned. "What's the matter with you?" she asked. "You're so quiet all of a sudden. Don't you feel well?"

"Oh, I'm all right."

"Well, you certainly don't act like it. Don't you think this is fun?"

"Sure," I said. "Of course I do."

For some minutes the Major and Billy Cartwright had been out of sight behind Devereux woods. Now they reappeared, Billy first, on the crest of the oak-laden hill.

"There they are!" Billy shouted. "There's the *Star of the West!*"

"Fire away!" the Major said, and raised his cane again.

"Aye aye, sir!" Billy called. He picked up a large rock and with two hands he heaved it at us. It fell far short, crashing down into the trees below the summit of the hill.

"Now you've got to come about and steam out of the harbor!" Billy called to us. "Else we'll sink you!"

"Never!" cried Helen.

"Battery two!" Billy Cartwright yelled, and sent another large rock crashing into the marsh just beyond the trees.

"Turn around," he shouted, "or we'll blast you out of the water!"

But at that moment a strange thing happened. Two adults, a man and a woman, suddenly emerged from the trees below the hill. "What the hell's going on here?" the man shouted, glaring at us. He was tugging at his belt.

We stared at them.

"Goddam kids!" the man swore. So far he had not noticed Billy and the Major on the crest above him. Now he looked up at the bank and saw them standing there.

He stared at the Major for a moment. "Come on, let's get out of here!" he said to the woman. The two of them went hurrying off through the thickets, with the woman attempting to straighten out her clothing as she walked.

There was a long pause. The Major and Billy Cartwright stood there on the hill, while Helen and I sat in the boat as it rocked gently in the water.

The Major coughed. "Well, children, uh, I guess we'd better be getting back," he said after a minute.

"All right," I said. I plunged the paddle into the current. The *Endymion of Charleston, S.C.* swung about.

"We have met the enemy," yelled Billy Cartwright, "and they are ours! Three cheers for the South!"

It was hot now; the pleasant air of the earlier morning had changed into full late July heat. From the reed grass a salty fragrance rose as the green stalks, wet from the receding tide, began drying out in the sun.

The encounter with the man and the woman drove all thought of the Major's conflicting stories out of my mind. Instead, I felt curiously exhilarated now, with an odd tightness in my stomach. I was embarrassed by what we had seen, but there was also a kind of excitement, a feeling of suspense. It was not simply what had happened, but that Helen too had seen it, that she and I were there together when it took place. Now as I sat in the stern of the *Endymion*, pushing away with the paddle, I watched Helen seated in the bow, looking out at the river. Until now, though I liked her very much indeed, I had not quite noticed her as an individual, thought of her as a girl. Now I saw her slight, square shoulders, her fine, light-brown hair which stirred a little as the *Endymion* swayed in the current, her thin, tanned arms, the sharpness of her firm body, her small feet in the faded blue tennis shoes she wore. I remembered my father's jest: "Sweet Helen, make me immortal with a kiss!" The thought was at once intensely embarrassing. I had to say something.

I could not stop. I told her about the Major then.

Helen only laughed. "Oh, he's a dear old man, and perhaps he gets his stories mixed up a little, but I still love him so. And you," she said, "you're the apple of his eye. You mustn't let it bother you because his memories don't always seem to make perfect sense. After all, he's eighty-nine years old."

I felt then that if Helen wished it—because she did—then surely I could believe it, could feel that affection.

We tied the *Endymion of Charleston, S.C.* to the dock, and walked back up the hill. As we crossed the lawn, the sun beat down on us, and our feet made small, flat footprints in the dry grass. I turned off at my house, and as I went up the steps, I wondered what Helen was thinking.

6. YET I COULD NOT FOR LONG FORGET THE MAJOR'S slip, could not dismiss his contradictory statements as being only the forgetfulness of an old man. That afternoon, looking over Dr. Chisholm's book again, I kept trying to tell myself that it didn't matter, that it was all of no consequence, that he was an old man, as Helen had said, and that old men are forgetful and hazy about events that happened a long time ago. It was not good enough. Either the Major was not telling the truth, or Dr. Chisholm's failure to mention him was deliberate.

What made the matter more difficult was that I was to have dinner at my Aunt Ellen's that night, downtown at the Warwick Apartments. That was where Dr. Chisholm lived too, and I was afraid I might run into him. How quickly things changed! I had so enjoyed talking with him the last time, had been so thrilled by the talk of poems and poets and Charleston Harbor and boats, had so looked forward to the next meeting—and now here I was, only two months or so later, hoping anxiously that I would not encounter him.

When I arrived at the house I paused for my customary visit with Mrs. Bready in the lobby, but for only a very short time—the Doctor might come home early and I would have to confront him. Once upstairs I stayed off the balcony, too, because if I sat outside I would be sure to see him and he might notice me as well. But as luck would have it, Mrs. Bready called up to me that my father was on the phone— the one in the entrance lobby. While I was talking to him, Aunt Ellen came in with Dr. Chisholm.

"How are you, young man?" the doctor asked.

"All right, sir."

"How's the poetry coming along?"

"Fine, sir," I lied.

"I was just telling your aunt," he said, "that I wanted you and her to take dinner with me in my apartment next week."

"Won't that be nice?" Aunt Ellen asked.

"Yes, sir."

"What do you say to Tuesday evening?" Dr. Chisholm suggested.

"Why, that's a good night for me," Aunt Ellen said. "How about you, Omar?"

"That would be fine," I said.

"That will be lovely, Doctor," Aunt Ellen told him. "I'm sure that Omar's been looking forward to talking with you again, haven't you, Omar?"

"Yes, sir."

"Good enough!" Dr. Chisholm declared. "And, young man, why don't you bring some of your poems along this time, so that we can go over them together? Two heads are always better than one, you know."

"Yes, sir."

Aunt Ellen and I went back upstairs to her apartment. "It certainly is nice of Dr. Chisholm to show so much interest in you," she said to me as we went in the door. "He was very much impressed with you last time. He has told me so several times."

Later, as I left my aunt's apartment, she came out onto the balcony to wave goodbye to me. "Watch out for the steamboats!" she called. I laughed; it was a long-standing joke we had, stemming from an occasion when I had told her I was going on an excursion boat trip to Fort Sumter and she had immediately urged me to watch out for steamboats. I strolled down the long walk through the courtyard, her voice following after me, out into the street, past the hedges and the palmetto trees, whose fronds now rustled murmurously above my head.

Quietly and pleasantly I traversed the block to the corner where I would board the streetcar—through the soft, luminous night, under the oak trees and past the large white homes with their white columns and iron rail fences, the sugared oleander bushes just inside the railings, the stained-glass hall windows beyond that. At the corner I sat down on the iron stoop of the A&P store, its interior dark except for a single light left burning in the recesses of the building, the outside woodwork red, flaked and warm under the street lamp. Automobiles passed by, their windows open to the summer evening. I heard voices, the laughter of a girl, the momentary blare of a car radio. A delivery boy wheeled by on his bicycle. Negro cooks and maids strolled past on their way home from their jobs, late work finished, laughing and chattering as they went. Then all sound died out and I sat there in the silence, enveloped in the hush of the city at evening, part of its great tranquil being that lived and breathed softly in the night.

Fifteen minutes and more passed before I caught sight of the single amber headlamp of the streetcar making its way along Wentworth Street toward me. I climbed aboard to find the Marvelous Ringgold at the controls and only a couple of other passengers on board. I took a seat across from him. By the time we reached Race Street the other riders had alighted and only the motorman and I were left. Whereupon the Marvelous Ringgold said, "Come here, and I'll show you how to operate one of these."

I went up to his side. He pointed to a lever. "Let it out easily," he said.

I moved the throttle forward. "Not too fast," he cautioned, "or you'll jog the car too much." I did as he instructed. "Now keep a steady, even speed . . . that's right . . . keep it steady now."

And the trolley car wound along.

The Marvelous Ringgold spied someone waiting to board the car. "Ease it down, now," he told me. I edged the throttle uncertainly back along the rim of the base. "Easy, now— easy, easy. Now take the brake handle here"—he indicated an iron lever—"and nudge it in, slowly, slowly . . . that's right . . . not too fast! Not too fast! Easy . . . don't bump it now. Push the throttle all the way shut, all the way. . . ." And the car shuddered to a stop at the corner.

The Marvelous Ringgold flipped the throttle to open the folding doors, told me to move back a little, and accepted a fare from the new passenger, a sallow-faced man who took a seat midway back in the car. "Just showing the lad here how it's done!" the Marvelous Ringgold remarked to him.

He closed the doors. "Okay, now catch hold of the brake handle there and release it," he said. "That's right." The air brakes hissed open. "Now move the throttle two notches out . . . right there . . . that's the way! Open it more now. Give it some power. Let her have the current now!"

We were rocking along the tracks now at a good clip, with the Marvelous Ringgold carefully and volubly supervising my every move, and with my heart thumping in excitement. He peered ahead up the tracks, alert for possible developments. "Oh-oh," he said, catching sight of the headlights of an automobile several blocks ahead of us, past Grove Street. "Give him the gong. Step on that pedal there."

I reached over with my foot and trod timidly upon the bell pedal.

"No, no, no! Mash it down *hard!* Got to give them plenty of warning, or they won't hear you! Step on it with all you've got. That's the way!" The alarm bell clanged fitfully. "No, don't slacken your speed yet. He's still a ways off. Just let him know you're here." We sped along, the bell clanging.

The automobile continued toward us, and when the distance between us was no more than a city block, the Marvelous Ringgold took over the controls. "Here, let me get it for a minute," he said, and he grasped the throttle and began pumping on the bell pedal with renewed violence, meanwhile fingering the brake lever nervously.

At the proper moment the automobile moved past the rocking streetcar, whereupon the Marvelous Ringgold let go of the brake lever and settled back with a sigh. "You've got to watch motorists like a hawk," he told me. "Never know what some crazy driver will do next."

Just beyond Grove Street there was a stretch of double track, and there another trolley car sat waiting for us to pass so that it could proceed downtown. The Marvelous Ringgold slackened the speed of the trolley to switch to the spur, drew up alongside the waiting car, and stopped for a moment. Inside the other trolley car Mr. Zinzer was seated at the controls.

"Everything all right?" the Marvelous Ringgold called across from his window. Mr. Zinzer nodded.

The Marvelous Ringgold opened up the throttle, our car sailed along the double track, and clattered back onto the main line. "Here, you take it again," he said. I moved in front of him and gripped the throttle.

There was one more stop, at Poplar Street, to let the other passenger off, and after that we moved unimpeded up the line toward my own destination, with the Marvelous Ringgold instructing me as I guided the trolley car. At Versailles Street I pulled the car up to a stop, not without a perceptible lurch, and opened the folding doors for myself.

"Well, there you are," said the Marvelous Ringgold. "How did you like it?"

"That was fun," I said. "Thanks a lot."

"Nighty-night," he told me. "Next time you can try it again. Yes, sir, all you need is a little experience, that's all."

I stepped to the ground and waited for the Marvelous Ringgold to depart. He slammed the doors and the streetcar leaped into motion. I watched its orange bulk slide past under the street lamp, saw the black numerals "403" stenciled on the side. The lights of the car receded up the street; briefly the car flared orange again as it passed beneath another street lamp half a block away, and then it rounded the bend and disappeared from view.

I walked home with the sound of the Marvelous Ringgold's trolley car still swirling through the dark as it headed for the end of the line. Now he is slowing for the switch beyond Mount Pleasant Street, I thought. Now he is picking up speed again. He is nearing Herriott Street and is applying the brakes to edge the car around the corner. He is moving along Herriott Street to the end of the line. Now he is releasing the throttle and pushing down the brake lever to bring the car to a full stop at Magnolia Crossing. Now the trolley has halted, and the Marvelous Ringgold is opening the folding doors. He has stepped outside and has proceeded to the rear of the cab and is lowering the trolley from the wire. The lights in the cab are out. Now he has walked to the other end and is raising the forward trolley up to the catenary for the return trip. The lights have come back on and the motor is idling again. Now he has gone back into the cab and is transferring his paraphernalia to the controls at the other end of the cab.

Now he is drinking creamy coffee and munching on a sandwich, waiting for the time to begin the downtown run.

I listened. There was not a sound. Then faintly in the still evening I thought I could hear the *clump-clump-clump* of the wicker seats as the Marvelous Ringgold reversed them two by two for the return trip.

7. OVER THE FIELDS, THE MARSHLAND, THE LIGHT WAS intense, searing. Sunrise came early, a great hollow yellowness with dark smears of red against the gray. I rose early and watched it from the windows at the rear of the house—the sky already a glazed blue, a few clouds trailing over the trees and distant rooftops and the cantilevers of the Cooper River Bridge along the eastern horizon. Birds streaked their monotonous way, flying low and fast across the sky. Industrial smoke curled up in black smudges from factories along the Cooper River. The sun climbed steadily higher, quickly dispelling what little dew and moisture remained from the night. It was going to be a clear, dry, intensely hot day.

We were to go downtown—Helen, myself, Billy Cartwright. We had planned to ride our bicycles since the Major was not coming along. My mother attempted to dissuade us from going. "You'll get sunstroke," she declared. "Why don't you stay home and play in the basement where it's cool? This is no day to be going downtown."

I did not answer.

"I guess Viola's not going to show up," my father said after a while. "The heat's probably got her, too."

"I just wish she'd get someone to phone when she's not coming," my mother said.

"They just won't do it," my father told her. "You can't get them to let you know. You just have to put up with it."

It was a dialogue I had heard repeated on other occasions. When Viola decided not to come to work, she simply did not show up. The following day my mother would ask her to send word by telephone the next time she was ill, and Viola would always promise to do so. But she never did.

"It's probably that Dominique," my mother said. "He's got her all worked up. Now that you have the yard in shape, let him go. He can always get another job."

My father maintained that he would never be able to find as good a man for the yard. My mother insisted that Viola's services were more important than Dominique's. "You can get another yard man," she said, "but where can I find another Viola?"

My father shook his head sadly. "Only laborer I ever saw that I had to keep from working too hard," he said.

We went downtown on the streetcar. Helen's mother had insisted upon that, if we were determined that we must go at all. We got off the trolley at the corner of Broad and Meeting, by the post office, where the Major and I always debarked during the winter. In the shaded archway of St. Michael's Church, across Broad Street, Negro women were standing with baskets of flowers. "Oh, how lovely! Let's buy some!" Helen exclaimed, and ran toward them. The flower women crowded about her, waving bunches of zinnias, petunias, foxglove and nasturtiums. Surrounded by the coaxing Negro women with their tiers of flowers, Helen could hardly make up her mind what to buy. "Why don't you wait till we come back?" Billy Cartwright kept asking her. "You can't carry a bunch of flowers around with you all morning." But Helen paid him no heed. "I'll take some of those," she said, pointing to some petunias, "and a bunch of those," indicating some nasturtiums. She paid for two large bunches of flowers, and after she had combined them into a single parcel, we set off toward the waterfront.

We had proceeded along Broad Street for no more than half a block, however, when I heard a call from across the street. "Omar!" someone shouted, and I saw my Aunt Ellen waving at us. She hurried across the street, stepping almost directly in front of an automobile, which obligingly slammed on its brakes to let her cross. Aunt Ellen nodded her thanks to the motorist for his courtesy, then greeted us enthusiastically. "And how are you, Helen?" she asked. "What lovely flowers!"

"I just couldn't resist buying them," Helen explained. "They were so beautiful, and so inexpensive."

"Pure waste of good money," Billy Cartwright insisted. "They'll all be wilted before we get home."

"Why don't you let me put them in a vase for you at my office?" Aunt Ellen suggested. "Then you can pick them up on your way home."

"That would be wonderful," Helen said.

"Where are you children going?" Aunt Ellen asked as we walked along. "Down to the waterfront?"

"Yes, ma'am," I told her.

"You must stop and see the Clyde liner," Aunt Ellen said. "It's in port today, you know."

"I want to go over to Adger's Wharf," Helen remarked. "I've heard so much about it."

Just then we saw Dr. Chisholm step out of the brownstone building of Walker, Evans and Cogswell's stationery store and come toward us. "Oh, there's your friend Dr. Chisholm," Aunt Ellen said to me. "Dr. Chisholm is an author," she explained to Helen.

Dr. Chisholm was the last person in the world that I wanted to see just then; I had told Helen about his book, and how he had omitted mention of the Major, and I was embarrassed at the prospect of their meeting. As the doctor came toward us I hoped that somehow he would fail to recognize us. But he looked in our direction and smiled, then came up to us.

"Well, well," said the doctor, "what beautiful flowers!"

"Aren't they just lovely?" Aunt Ellen agreed. "Doctor, this is Helen Gorman, from Philadelphia, and this is Billy Cartwright, whom she's visiting. They're both grandchildren of Major Frampton."

"Ah, yes," said Dr. Chisholm. It seemed to me at that moment that he smiled almost mechanically. "From Philadelphia, is it? Well, I hope you're enjoying your visit to our city, Miss Gorman."

If Helen remembered what I had told her about Dr. Chisholm and her grandfather the Major, she gave no sign of it. "Oh, yes," she said, "I'm having a grand time!"

"Fine, fine! That's as it should be." And Dr. Chisholm proceeded up the street, while the four of us stopped by the iron staircase that led up to Aunt Ellen's office, above a bank. "Dr. Chisholm," Aunt Ellen explained to Helen, "knows more about Charleston history than any other man alive. Did Omar show you his new book about the battle of Fort Sumter?"

"Yes, he did," Helen replied.

"And he's a great friend of Omar's, isn't he, Omar?"

"Yes'm," I said hastily. "What time does the Clyde liner leave? We'd better be going."

Bidding Aunt Ellen goodbye, we walked past the red stone façade of the Carolina Savings Bank and crossed East Bay Street, moving single file along the narrow slate sidewalk of Exchange Street, past the blue-lighted windows of the Charleston Engraving Company, through the narrow cobblestoned thoroughfare, until we reached the Port Utilities railroad switching track next to the marsh. Here the river was, with Castle Pinckney a mile offshore, directly opposite us, out beyond the ship channel. Immediately ahead of us lay the gutted wooden hulk of an abandoned launch, disintegrating in the black mud, the twin spars of its forward skeleton thrust upward like beseeching arms. Beyond was

Adger's Wharf. We walked along the crunchy black earth toward it.

The two docks of the wharf were the scene of widespread activity. Half a hundred small craft were moored alongside, with numerous men, mostly Negroes, working away at various tasks. There were shrimp trawlers with their festooned nets swung aloft on polished booms, broad-beamed launches of various sizes and descriptions, stub-nosed commercial craft with their hatches open and boxes of goods and produce piled on deck, ungainly barges lashed two-by-two to pilings. Beneath a tin shed on one dock a half-dozen Negro women were busily and loudly packing shrimp, while a man was scooping cracked ice into shrimp-filled lard tins.

Helen was enthralled. She stood for five minutes observing the women sorting shrimp. Then she walked out along the wharf and watched two Negroes mending nets aboard a trawler. Soon she had engaged them in conversation and was receiving a description of how the nets were used, what caused them to tear, what was involved in the business of trawling for shrimp. She listened attentively, and the Negro trawlermen responded to her interest by describing their occupation at great length.

We walked over to the wharf nearest the bay, and up to the edge of the concrete sea wall, where so often on Saturday mornings the Major and I had stood. Beyond us were the familiar sights—Fort Sumter in the center, Forts Moultrie and Johnson on either side of the harbor, the smudge of a ship against the horizon beyond Sumter. I tried to point out the landmarks to Helen, as the Major always did, but I felt very inadequate, standing here without him. I knew a sudden surge of affection for him, loyalty to him. If only he were here with us, to look out at the harbor, to curse Baitery's little ferryboat, to recite the Henry Timrod poem!

"Is that where the Celebration's going to take place?"

163

Helen asked, pointing across the harbor.

"Yes," I told her. "Right out there on the Fort. They'll get on the boats down at the Battery and go out there."

"Golly, I wish I could stay here for it! It'll be so exciting!" Helen exclaimed.

"Come on now," Billy Cartwright said. "We've been here long enough. Let's go see the Clyde liner."

We retraced our steps along the railroad tracks, walking back past the foot of Exchange Street to a point where we could see the steamship close by, barely two hundred yards distant across the tidal flat. The Clyde liner in port that day was the *S.S. Cherokee,* a bulky, single-stacked vessel with a black hull and rows of white-painted cabins. It was the smallest of the fleet of passenger ships which called at Charleston three times a week en route to and from New York and Jacksonville. Even so it was by far the largest ship I had ever seen close up, for the other Clyde liners were too large to berth there on the exposed side of the dock. They were always moored in the more commodious boat slips, where the buildings blocked the view and all that could be seen from the shore were the masts and funnels. The *Cherokee* was not my favorite Clyde liner; for no reason in particular I preferred the *S.S. Algonquin.* But I had never seen the *Algonquin* close up.

As for the *Cherokee,* it was small, but it was a genuine ocean liner, not simply a freighter that also carried passengers. True, it did not go far out into the ocean, running only along the coast, but in port its masts and rigging were bedecked with pennants and the superstructure was resplendent in white paint, polished mahogany railings, and clusters of circular white life preservers, each bearing in black letters the name, *S.S. Cherokee.* We could see the seamen working about the docks, and on the lofty bridge the officers were standing about, garbed glamorously in their white uniforms and gold-visored caps.

We stood for a while watching her, wishing that we could be passengers and could walk up the stairway to the long covered trestle that led from Vendue Range to the brown-painted docks, then across the fancy, railed gangplank, to be received by attentive stewards and ushered to our portholed staterooms. How splendid it would be to stand along the ship's railing and watch the waterfront pass by as the *Cherokee* moved out to sea, past Sumter and through the jetties, and onward to open water and the port of New York beyond!

"Let's go watch the banana boat unloading," Billy suggested.

"Sure. Let's go!" Helen agreed.

So we set off for the Southern Railway docks, stepping along the railroad tracks and past the old ferry wharf. "Here's where the Major's ferry used to dock," I told Helen. We peered within. It was empty; not a soul was nearby, even to wait for the little gasoline ferry of Baitery's. We walked along past the Custom House and the Bull Line docks, then cut across a field beyond the old Bennett rice mill to the Southern Railway Pier No. 2, the fruit company wharf. It was a low, black structure with large white lettering across its front, situated at the end of a row of warehouses and covered docks. The day was blazing hot now, and perspiration soaked through our garments as we hurried across the field to escape the intense humidity that rose from numerous pools of tidewater on either side of us.

At the fruit dock a smallish vessel, the *S.S. Miramar*, was tied up in the slip. She was painted white, with tan fittings. Many times I had seen the boats of the Great White Fleet (as the advertisements in the *National Geographic* described the fruit ships) pass by off the Battery; from that distance they had seemed pure white and gleaming. Close by, however, we could see that the paint was stained here and there and was more cream than white.

Great steel doors had been swung open in the white ship's sides, with tiers of rollered ladders slanting down from them to the wharf. We stood in the shade of the dock entrance and watched. Along the rollers stem after stem of green bananas was being steadily disgorged from the hold of the ship. Husky Negro stevedores, stripped to the waist, lifted the stems as they came sliding down off the rollers, hoisted them two at a time over their great shoulders, and trudged off to load the bananas aboard refrigerated railroad cars. As soon as one string of yellow cars was filled, a small, noisy Southern Railway switching locomotive would draw them away.

We stood with some others at the end of the boat slip, in the shade, watching the operation. Despite the shade it was hot; there was not a breath of air coming off the river. Below us, the dirty harbor water lapped against the dock pilings, its surface filmed with oil slick, sawdust, and stray green bananas floating about. Inside the covered dock the Negro stevedores worked steadily, chanting as they labored in a kind of sing-song made up of numbers sung in unison, interspersed with words:

Gib'um one, gib'um two, gib'um three, gib'um four,
Wanna one, wanna two, wanna three, wanna four, ho!

Then from the direction of the city came the shrill blast of a steam whistle. A bell rang on the dock. Foremen began blowing industriously on the whistles they carried on cords about their necks. The flow of green bananas from the ship's hold slowed, ceased. It was noontime, time for lunch.

In twos and threes the Negro stevedores dispersed along the dock and outside on the street, retrieving brown paper sacks and black tin boxes of lunch, then seeking out places of respite from the heat, which bore down everywhere.

166

"Say, isn't that your cook there?" Billy Cartwright asked, gesturing toward a group of Negroes clustered at the entranceway to the wharf. I looked. A woman was standing by the wall. Sure enough, it was Viola. The bandage on her arm made the identification certain.

Had she seen us? No, it was unlikely, or she would not be standing there so openly.

As we watched, a Negro laborer came shuffling along the dock and up to where she waited. It was Dominique, all right; there was no mistaking him.

"Quick!" I said. "Turn your backs!" We stood looking down at the water until Viola and Dominique had had ample time to walk past us. Cautiously I looked around and saw they had strolled on toward another pier just beyond the fruit dock. There they sat down in the shade of the building, under the narrow ledge of the roof.

"She's supposed to be home, sick," I said.

Billy snorted. "Doesn't look very sick to me."

Viola and Dominique were laughing and chattering away —with Viola, to be sure, doing most of the talking. She did indeed appear most hale and hearty—in the best of moods, apparently, her dourness and gloom of the previous weeks entirely gone.

Her high spirits angered me. What right had she to be so merry, so heedless of the sticky, stultifying heat which was blazing down upon us where we stood? Well, I would fix her, all right.

It was important that the three of us not be recognized. "Let's sneak through that crowd in front of the dock," I said, "and leave by the far side. I don't want Viola to see us."

So we slipped into the assemblage of people standing about the entrance to the fruit dock, and crossed over to the other side of a string of freight cars. Down the dirt road we walked, in sweltering sunlight, to Laurens Street, and then westward to East Bay, crossing the railroad tracks on the way. "We'll ride down to Broad Street and get the flowers," I said, "and then take the Rutledge Avenue car at the post office."

We waited for the streetcar for what seemed hours, standing against the front of a house to gain the feeble shade it afforded. The sun blazed down, baking the pavement, sidewalk, buildings. The stone house radiated heat—febrile, enervating. Light glinted on the flashing windshields of automobiles, glared from the unpainted corrugated roof of a warehouse. Across the fields we could still see the fruit dock; work had resumed there, and the switching locomotives moved back and forth, shifting the lemon-yellow refrigerator cars, sending clouds of coal smoke into the sky.

"God Almighty, streetcar, come *on!*" Billy Cartwright groaned. "I'm about to melt away."

Helen said nothing. We waited. The energy and enthusiasm of the earlier morning had all evaporated now; we were merely hot and uncomfortable.

Finally a streetcar hove into view, but from the south, moving uptown. If it were not for Helen's flowers, I thought gloomily as it rumbled along toward us, we could board it and get out of the sun.

The car was less than a block away when Billy Cartwright could stand it no longer. "Couldn't we leave the flowers?" he asked. "You could get some more another time."

Both of us looked at Helen.

"All right," she said.

We raced across the street to where the northbound trolley would stop. "Come on, come on!" Billy Cartwright begged, while the car bumbled along and the heat bore down.

For several blocks we rode without speaking. Then finally I said, "Maybe Billy's father can pick up the flowers and bring them when he comes home for dinner."

"It doesn't matter," Helen said. "They've probably wilted anyway, in this heat."

We got off the Belt Line car at Rutledge Avenue and waited under a store awning for the Rutledge trolley to come. It too was a long time in arriving. We were not so much oppressed by the heat now as simply tired. All our strength and energy had been sapped; we waited silently, dispiritedly, the happy banter of the morning vanished. I felt vaguely out of sorts, sullen.

Finally the streetcar came. It was crowded, mostly with Negro workmen. Helen and I sat down in one of the vacant seats at the very front, and Billy took a single seat farther back in the car. The seats for Negroes, in the rear, were not all filled, but even so other Negroes stood in the aisle of the car, talking cheerfully and gaily. Their merriment infuriated me. The air was oppressively sultry; I could smell the perspiration from their bodies. I thought again of Viola, the way she had been laughing and carrying on with Dominique down by the fruit dock. Too sick to come to work! Some sickness! As kind as my mother and father were to her, she too was like all the others, I thought, ungrateful, deceitful. Well, I had caught her at it, all right. Wait until I told my parents what I had seen.

She would come to work in the morning and tell my mother that she had been feeling sick and had stayed in bed all day with a fever. And I would say, slyly, "Are you sure that you didn't go down to the fruit dock for a while, Viola?" She would look at me then, and shake her head, and say, "No." But I would continue, "Are you quite certain that you didn't meet Dominique there at lunchtime and eat lunch with him?" She would still shake her head then, not in pretended indignation now so much as in dogged bewilderment, knowing that she had been trapped in her deceit.

God, but it was hot! The Negro workmen continued to laugh and joke among themselves as they stood in the aisle. Only Negroes, I thought, could laugh and be cheerful in weather like this.

Then, as if she had read my thoughts, Helen spoke up.

"How wonderful it is of them," she said, "to be cheerful even in the heat. I'm so tired that I've been sitting here feeling cross, when all I've done is to walk in the sun a little—and they've been working in it all day probably, and yet they're happy."

"They're like animals," I said.

"No, no," Helen said, her voice growing excited. "Not like animals. Like wise men who make the best of what they have, instead of being ugly about it. Think of those flower women—they didn't just want my dimes. They wanted *me* to buy *flowers*. They were selling beautiful things, and they loved it. Don't you see, Omar? Don't you?"

"But they're dirty, and they smell," I said.

"Suppose you'd been working out in the sun all morning, like them. Wouldn't you perspire too?"

"Maybe, but when I go home I'll take a bath and clean up. I'll bet they won't."

"How do you know? How do you know they've even got running water to take a bath in?" Helen asked. "My mother says that only a very few Negro families even have running water in their homes."

"You talk like a nigger lover," I said.

Helen's face turned white. "Don't you talk like that!" she said. "It's mean, and ugly. Just because you're all hot and uncomfortable, you take out your hatred on the colored people because they don't act mean and ugly too. You're unfair, and I hate unfair people!"

"And I hate smart-aleck Yankees who know it all," I shot back.

"Oh, shut up!"

I turned my face to the window. The sun glared on the gray sidewalks and porches of Rutledge Avenue.

Then as we rode on, and I continued to stare out the barred window, I wondered at what I had said and done. Why had I been so mean? Now I had talked ugly, and said cruel things, and had made Helen hate me. I had felt tired and hateful, and I had struck out, like a savage animal, at someone who was good and kind and who had refused to feel as hateful as I did.

And wasn't she right? I had hated the Negroes because they were enjoying themselves, laughing and joking; because the heat had not made them sour and angry as it had made me. Oh, God damn this heat! I thought. Now I had ruined everything, had made someone whom I admired and loved hate me. And in a very short time she would go away, back home to Philadelphia, and that would be the end, past recall, past change. In my anger, my hate, I had said what I did not even believe, in order to hurt, to spread my ugliness and hatred.

It was vicious, intolerable. I stared at the wicked iron bars of the trolley window, as if they were imprisoning me in my cursed weakness, holding me to my rage and filth. And at that moment I remembered Helen before St. Michael's with the flower women, running toward the flower women, laughing so delightedly among the purple and red nasturtiums and zinnias, so overwhelmed by their loveliness she could not choose from among the bouquets. That—*that* was what I was demeaning, scorning!

We were only three blocks from Versailles Street. Before we got off, I must do something to save the day, for otherwise we should have to walk home with Billy, silently, glumly,

171

and the breach would become irrevocable. What should I say?

Now we were only a block away.

"I'm sorry," I said.

Helen did not reply. I could see tears in her eyes.

"I don't hate colored people, and I don't hate you. I was feeling mean from the heat. I was wrong. I swear."

She reached out then and gave my hand a little squeeze. Her eyes were brimming with tears.

That evening at dinner my father said, "Well, where'd you go today with your true love?"

"Aunt Ellen said you stopped by there," my mother said. "She said Helen left some flowers and didn't come back for them."

"It was too hot to go back to get them," I explained.

"I told you it was going to be hot," my mother said. "Did you go down on the waterfront?"

"Yes."

"Where to? Adger's Wharf?"

"Uh huh."

"Anywhere else?" he asked.

"Yes, we went down to the fruit dock," I said.

"Did you see Dominique there?"

I looked right at him. "No, I didn't see anybody I knew. We didn't stay there for very long."

8.

8. The heat wave that had settled upon Charleston continued unabated; the mercury remained close to 100 degrees. We played indoors for the most part until evening, when it grew a trifle cooler. But even when the sun went down, the air remained hot; only the faintest of breezes came off the river, barely touching the leaves in the water oaks, brushing them ever so lightly in passing.

Billy Cartwright decided that the thing to do was to take advantage of the weather by setting up a drink stand down at the corner several blocks away, and marketing lemonade to the workmen at the several houses being constructed nearby. So we built a wooden stand and undertook to brew some lemonade. Unfortunately, the demand for ice-cold lemonade was somewhat under expectations, and by two p.m. we had sold only eleven glasses of lemonade, barely enough to cover our investment in lemons, sugar, and paper cups. Regretfully we closed out operations, drinking some of the watery lemonade ourselves and throwing away the rest, and retired to the shade of our basements.

On weekends and Wednesday afternoons there were the Municipal League games; baseball was endurable even despite the broiling heat. We went to all the games; Helen soon learned the names of the players and became as familiar with the teams as we were. She chose as her favorite team the Sokol Tigers, a club which was fighting a battle for first place with Billy's and my team, the Tru-Blu Brewers. Seated in the College Park grandstand, we watched all the games, listened to the shirt-sleeved crowds calling to the players, consumed soft drinks, and afterward walked home in the sullen late-afternoon heat.

It was the Major who suffered most of all from the weather. He lost all his energy, his vigor; he sat about the house a little, but mostly he stayed in his room, dozing now and then, while an electric fan whirred way in a feeble effort at stirring the hot air. On the morning after our visit to the waterfront and the fruit dock, I went by to see him. He seemed interested and nodded his head in agreement when I explained where we had been, saying, "Yes, yes," and "Good, good." But when I was through, he said something that puzzled me.

"Did you show her the *Sappho?*" he asked.

"No, sir," I replied. "We weren't over there. We were down by the waterfront."

"But you said you went past the Custom House," he insisted. "You must have passed right by the ferry dock."

"Ferry dock? You mean Baitery's dock?"

"Of course not," the Major said impatiently. "I mean the *ferry* dock. At the foot of Cumberland Street."

"But, sir, that's Baitery's dock now, isn't it?"

The Major frowned. His face had a look of puzzled concern. "Oh, yes. Of course. I'd forgotten for the moment. I was thinking of the old days."

The mistake perplexed me; many times on our walks we had passed by the dock where the old harbor ferries used to tie up, and the Major knew full well that it was used only by Baitery's little gasoline ferry now. It was as if, for the moment, he had been living in the past, before I knew him, when the bridge had not been built and the ferries connected Charleston and Mount Pleasant. He had spoken of the *Sappho* as if it were over on the Cooper River waterfront, as if it were in service, when of course, as he had told me many times, the *Sappho* had been decommissioned even before the World War. I had never once known the Major to make a mistake quite like that. It was the way he had said it that worried me.

When I left the Major's room I went out onto the Cartwrights' front porch, where Billy, Helen, and their mothers were seated. They invited me to drive over to Folly Beach with them. We drove out through the hot city, along the sweltering streets, and across the Ashley River Bridge. At Elliott's Cut we waited awhile for a launch to pass through the drawbridge. It was the sugar boat, and this time we saw it close at hand, with its galvanized tin roof that covered the rear deck, its green cabin, and the sign, DIXIE CRYSTALS, on the side. This was the same craft that we had seen that day when we had gone out on the *Sappho*, and which Helen had confused with the Major's old ferry run. I remembered the Major's slip of a few hours earlier, and I told them how the Major had for a moment forgotten that the *Sappho* was no longer in service. Mrs. Cartwright and Helen's mother looked at each other briefly.

"It's the heat," Mrs. Cartwright explained to me. "It's so hard on an old person, you know."

"I wish we could take him to the mountains until this hot spell is over," Helen's mother said.

"He wouldn't go," Billy's mother replied, shrugging her shoulders. "He doesn't want to set foot out of the city until after the Fort Sumter Celebration. He seems to think that unless he stays here, it won't come off."

When we arrived at the beach and changed into our bathing suits, we found that the fine dry sand was burning hot. We raced desperately for the water's edge and the strip of darker, moist beach where we could walk in comfort.

"Let's go up the beach a little," Helen suggested then. "It's nicer there."

We moved a hundred yards up the strand, away from the pavilion area, then headed for the water. The combers were crashing lazily in from the ocean, the surf was pleasantly warm, and the current swirled about our legs as we splashed about in the sea. Billy Cartwright and Helen dived through the breaking waves or crested them from behind as they came thundering in, riding them shoreward. I, who swam very poorly, lolled about in the water nearer shore, sitting on the cool bottom and submerging myself to my neck, then springing up in time to avoid being deluged by a wave.

I groped with my hands until I found a sand dollar on the bottom, and as Helen came wading in, I sent it skimming toward her. She dived into the water after it, and soon came up, dripping but triumphant, brandishing it in her hand. She was fascinated by the intricate design with the tiny pointed star at the center, and the five petals spread out like delicately etched leaves. "Is it alive?" she asked, noting the thick network of wriggling brush on the underside. I nodded. She held it up to the light for a moment, then placed it gently back in the surf.

Afterward we went back up onto the sand. Out of the water, we felt again the force of the baking sunlight upon our shoulders and arms. "We'd better put some more lotion on or we'll turn red as boiled lobsters," Helen said. First Billy and then I held still while she applied the oily lotion on our skins. Then she handed me the bottle and turned around, and I spread lotion over her slender shoulders and arms. As I touched her firm, clear skin, I hoped she did not feel my fingers tremble.

"Let's go beachcombing!" Helen said. We agreed willingly and set off up the beach.

"Do you suppose valuable objects float ashore sometime?" Billy Cartwright asked.

Helen told him that it was certainly possible. On some beaches, she said, there were people who made their living entirely from picking up things that the sea washed ashore. We walked far past the row of beach houses, up to where the dunes were barren save for clumps of sea oaks and twisted trunks of dead trees hollowed out by the sand. Then we turned and headed back, though Billy wished to go still farther along the beach to see if he could do some profitable beachcombing.

At length we neared the pavilion again, whereupon we stopped and stretched out for a while on the sand. Helen lay beside me, her bathing cap over her eyes to shield them from the sun. Seeing her small body there near me, I became aware, all at once, of her attractiveness. I was intensely conscious of her physical beauty; she was slim, well formed, desirable. For the first time in my life I felt a distinct physical yearning for a female body, and I felt my own body respond to such an extent that I had to roll over quickly onto my stomach in order to prevent my excitement from becoming embarrassingly obvious.

I knew about sex, of course, and like all my friends, was fascinated with talk of it. I knew that the automobile headlights I sometimes saw out in the Devereux woods at night, beyond the Cartwrights' house, were those of cars where grownups parked and, from certain unmistakable evidence sometimes found by us along the roadside, Did It. I had, secretly, done some experimentation of my own, and at times I imagined myself Doing It with girls. Never before, however, had I thought of this in relation to a particular girl, and while in the presence of that girl.

I lay on my stomach, my body pressed desperately against the sand, my chin resting on the back of my hands, and yawned in feigned ennui. Alas for my comfort, Helen likewise rolled over onto her stomach and lay there close by me, her freckled face cradled in her slim arm. She began talking about the plays she expected to see at Saturday matinees that fall in Philadelphia. The feeling of intimacy with her, there under the sun, with her tousled hair and clean, warm limbs stretched out, relaxed, so near me, was overpowering. I was physically uncomfortable, and my stomach seemed to be

177

twisted into a knot from the excitement.

In desperation, I said, "Shall we go back to the pavilion and try the rides?"

"Okay, let's," Helen agreed.

Whereupon I leaped to my feet, shouting as I did so that I would "race you to the pavilion!" and began sprinting down the beach. Halfway there I slowed to a walk, panting heavily for breath, and the two of them caught up with me; but the physical exertion and the fatigue had restored my composure, and I was safe again.

Mrs. Cartwright and Helen's mother were waiting for us before the pavilion, having brought sandwiches and a thermos jug of cold lemonade, and we set things up in the shade, spreading a blanket on the sand for the lunch. After we had eaten, Billy and Helen and I headed for the amusement park across the street. There was a Ferris wheel, a merry-go-round, an auto park in which little cars slid clumsily along a metal floor and bounced off each other's cushioned sides, a loop-the-loop that required two tickets per trip, and a caterpillar in which carriages were whirled around a circular track at great speed, and over which a canvas awning descended to blot out the daylight and add to the excitement.

The three of us rode the Ferris wheel together. As the great wheel bore us high over the beach, we could see the strip of island stretched out far below us, and the glistening ocean beyond, where the green waves flashed in the sun, while off in the distance several trawlers were moving back and forth. Then we all had a turn in the auto park, where we lost Billy to his principal joy.

"I don't want to ride on the cars again," Helen said, but Billy wanted to do nothing else.

Left alone, Helen and I walked somewhat self-consciously to the caterpillar, handed our tickets to the attendant, and climbed into a carriage together. There were no other riders. The caterpillar started off and soon picked up speed, and then the canvas roof arched in over us, leaving us in dim, shadowy light as we were whirled around.

I was acutely ill at ease; my insides shivered in nervous excitement. I knew that this was my opportunity to embrace Helen, and I was aware that Helen knew this too. But I was too timid to do so, and after several awkward minutes during which we sat in silence under the whirling canopy, the caterpillar slowed down, the canvas screen was withdrawn, and we were out in the bright afternoon again. Inwardly I cursed myself for my timidity. Blinking in the sunlight, we stood up to leave. Across the amusement park we could see Billy intently steering one of the cars in the auto rink.

"Let's go around again," I sugested nervously.

"Okay," Helen agreed. So we handed two more tickets to the attendant and resumed our places.

Again the caterpillar started off and gained momentum, and the protective canopy swung down over us. For some seconds we sat there uneasily. Then Helen spoke. "You can put your arm around me if you'd like," she said.

Timidly I reached my hand around her shoulder, and after a moment I drew Helen's firm, slight body close to me. She nestled down against my shoulder, warmly and deliciously, and as we rocketed around in the hot, velvet shadow, I gathered my courage and leaned over to kiss her. I had never kissed a girl before, however, and our noses bumped. Helen giggled. I shifted my face and pressed my lips close against hers for several seconds. My body tingled with a nervous exultance as we careened along, Helen close to me, her head on my shoulder and her cool forehead against my flushed cheek.

We felt the caterpillar begin slowing down then, and hastily we drew apart as the canvas canopy slid back and we were in daylight again.

"Golly but it's bright!" I said self-consciously, and Helen agreed that it was.

We saw Billy Cartwright walking toward the merry-go-round, searching for us there, and we got off. The ground felt dizzy beneath my feet as we stepped down from the wooden planking of the caterpillar platform and walked off together across the burning white sand to join him.

9. IT WAS NOT EASY FOR ME TO FALL ASLEEP THAT NIGHT. My mind was filled with fantasies. I imagined that I would go off to college after high school (during which time I would have been seeing Helen every summer and corresponding voluminously with her at other times), to the University of Pennsylvania or some other school near her home. After we had graduated together, we would be married, and live somewhere in the Northeast (where I had never been), and I would be a famous newspaperman, or a movie writer like my Uncle Ben. I kept seeing, too, the vision of that firm body in the yellow bathing suit near me on the sand. I thought of how it would be when she was a grown woman and I a grown man and we would experience the delights of complete bliss. It would be beautiful, noble, and also recklessly wanton and sensual. Afterward we would lie together, side by side, warm in each other's arms, contented in the sweet darkness. If only the years ahead could pass swiftly, and bring me to manhood, when I should be able to do all things, go to all places, see all sights. Eight years! Eight long years!

The next morning was hot, muggy; the sky was flecked with small clouds high up. The morning paper predicted hopefully that a cool front would arrive within twenty-four hours, and would lower the temperature to the 80s again, but the weather outside showed no sign of it.

Despite the heat, Viola was in unusually good spirits that morning, more so indeed than she had been in weeks. She sang at her work and laughed and joked a great deal while serving breakfast. I wondered what had happened to bring about this change in disposition. Was there some connection between this and the fact that the previous day, Dominique had been supposed to work in our yard but had not shown up? I did not know, of course; and besides, if connection there were, what could it be? There was no way of telling. Whatever the cause, however, it was good to have Viola acting like her old self again.

After breakfast I went over to the Cartwrights'. Neither Helen nor Billy was there. The Major was seated in the rocking chair in his room, the fan droning away by the window as usual. I thought he seemed even more tired and listless than on the previous day.

"It was a day like this when the earthquake struck," he said. "All during the day, people kept remarking how close and sultry it was."

"What time did it hit?" I asked.

"In the evening. At fifteen seconds after 9:51 P.M., to be exact. The clocks in the telegraph offices stopped when it struck. Yes, sir, it was the evening of Tuesday, August 31, 1886, and well do I remember it."

"Was there any warning?"

"Well, yes and no. That evening, of course, we didn't have any inkling. But several days before there were earth tremors up around Summerville. People said it was so violent that every dog in town started barking. We didn't dream it would happen to us, though."

"Where were you when it hit?" I asked. I had heard the story before, but it always interested me.

"Out on the *Sappho*, of course. We were right off Mount Pleasant, on the westbound run, when all of a sudden it happened. The water was perfectly smooth, without so much as a wave, when the *Sappho* pitched as if somebody had taken hold of it and was jerking it back and forth."

The Major reached over to his bed table and picked up a cigar. He removed the wrapper from it, placed it in his mouth, and fumbled in his pocket for a match. "You see," he continued, "the water was still, and it was the earth underneath that was moving. I remember old Captain Jervey—he was master of the schooner *Caroline*, and I knew him well —telling about how he was sitting out on the piazza of his home, when all of a sudden the northeast corner of the house rose up, and then the southeast corner, and after that it was like an old barge on a choppy sea, with the house rocking and pitching. Then they started coming from the other direction, and Jervey said he could see the way the shock waves were traveling, from the shadow the street lamp was throwing. And the noise! It was like all hell had busted loose. Jervey and I both agreed that the closest thing we'd ever heard to it was an artillery duel in the war. But the earthquake was worse."

While the Major was talking, Helen came in and sat for a while with us. After what had transpired the day before at the amusement park, I felt anxious in her presence. Would she be angry now? Was she ashamed, today, of what had taken place between us?

I questioned the Major some more. I was so glad to hear him acting like his old self, reminiscing away just as he had always done. I had not been able to put from my mind the incident of the previous morning, when he had seemed to forget for a moment that the ferryboats were not still operating. But now he seemed spry enough, alert enough.

Then just as I had become fully reassured that yesterday's slip was a momentary lapse, the Major did it again. Helen and I had got up to leave and were going out the door, when the Major said, "You wait till this heat wave ends, and I'll take you out on the *Sappho*. Nothing like a ride across the harbor to cool you off in this kind of weather."

I looked at Helen. This time I did not say anything to the

Major, did not remind him again that the *Sappho* had been out of commission for years and was rotting away in the mud flats off Gadsden Street. Instead I murmured goodbye and went outside, with Helen following.

"Omar," she whispered as soon as we were out of earshot, "don't say anything to Mother or Aunt Agnes about that."

"Why not?"

"Because it worries them to death. Grandfather's been forgetting things lately. He's all right when he's talking about the old days, but when he isn't, he forgets where he is sometimes. Mother says it's just a sign of old age, but I think it's more serious than that, from the way they worry about it."

I wanted to question her further, but just then her mother came into the room, holding a letter in her hand.

"It looks as if we'll be leaving for home next Monday instead of the week afterward, dear," she said. "Your father's landing in New York a week before he had planned, and we certainly want to be there when he arrives."

Helen thought a minute. "Why couldn't he come down here then?" she asked. "Then we could stay till it's time for school to start."

Her mother laughed. "Oh, child, you know that's out of the question. He'll have so much to do at the office that he won't be able to rest quietly until he cleans off his desk. After all, he's been away almost two months."

"I suppose so," Helen agreed.

The two of us went out onto the front porch. The news weighed heavily upon me; I had not allowed myself to dwell on the fact that Helen would soon be departing, and now that the day was suddenly close at hand, I was dismayed at the thought.

We sat for a while looking out at the Ashley River—the same river that in early June had gone sweeping by when Billy Cartwright and I had built the boat, and was still flowing on as always. The woods on the opposite shore

seemed as far away as before, the marsh as green, though a
yellower green now, faded by a summer of blazing sun. The
reed grass seemed as always to anchor the reflected sky, with
the fast little clouds floating across the surface, the sun
flashing in iridescent brightness upon the creeks, the marshland, the distant shore. All was just as it had always been.
What had happened to make the days go by so fast?

"Couldn't we go boating?" Helen asked.

"Okay," I said. "Let's go."

As we walked down toward the wharf I remembered that
when the Major had been telling me about the earthquake,
he had unwrapped a cigar. But he had never lit it.

There was a half-foot of water in the *Endymion of Charleston, S.C.* as it rocked in the creek, tied to the wharf behind
Mr. Simons' house. The two inflated inner tubes that Billy
and I had secured for life preservers floated atop each other
in the bottom of the boat. I found an extra bailing can and
Helen and I went to work together, scooping water out and
pouring it over the side, getting thoroughly wet in the process. After ten minutes of bailing we cast off. Paddling in
unison, we sent our blunt-nosed craft swinging along the
creek, bound for the edge of the river.

"It certainly handles nicely when it's not full of water,"
Helen said.

"Yes," I answered, "but it fills right up again, and we have
to keep bailing it all the time. It's much worse than it used to
be."

"I don't care," Helen said. "I think it's a wonderful little
old red boat, and I'll always remember it."

How nicely she said things!

We pushed along, following the winding creek bed, until
after a time we had come paddling up to the edge of the
river.

"Here we are," I announced, taking hold of some reed grass with one hand to keep us from drifting out into the current, while with my other hand I retrieved the bailing can and began scooping out some of the water that had leaked in through the seams on our journey to the river's edge.

Helen looked out at the river. "How far is it across?" she asked.

"Not too far," I said. "About as far as we've come from the shore, I guess." I looked back at the bank and Mr. Simons' house on the hill beyond the wharf.

"It's too bad," said Helen, "that we can't go over to the other shore. I'll bet it's lovely over there on those sandbanks."

"I'll bet it is too." Bright, white, clearly visible against the green forest beyond them, the sandbanks lay just beyond the water.

"Couldn't we go a little way out," Helen asked, "and see how it is? If it seems too rough, we can always turn around and come back."

I did not really want to do it. But I could not dare admit to Helen that I did not.

"Well, okay," I said. "Why not?" I released my grip on the reed grass, took up the paddle, and shoved the *Endymion's* bow directly into the current. Gripping our homemade paddles with tight fingers, we pointed for the far shore, and the *Endymion of Charleston, S.C.* moved into the river.

The current was strong, but the crests of the waves were broad and rolling, and the *Endymion* glided cleanly along, taking the swells evenly and smoothly. Neither Helen nor I spoke as we paddled away, intent on our work, watching the green water, many feet deep, slide steadily by us. The white line of the sandbanks across the river was still far away. Yet each stroke of our paddle blades was bringing us closer to them, nearer than I had ever been before. The nervous tension I felt was mixed with pride at what our little boat was doing. What would Billy Cartwright say when he came home from Orangeburg with his father that evening and heard that we had actually crossed the river in the *Endymion!*

On and on we went, saying nothing, still working away. Overhead the sky was filled with many small clouds moving eastward. There was a little breeze on the water, and it was not nearly so muggy any more. Occasionally I felt the tingle of spray on my cheeks. I looked back; the edge of the marsh from which we had come was far behind us now. We could not turn back. Ahead of us the white sandbanks were visible in detail; we could see the contours, the grass growing in clumps along the dunes. We were getting there, all right! With renewed effort we tugged at our paddles. River water, seeping in from the sprung seams, sloshed about in the boat, but we were too committed now to dare to pause for bailing, so that the water was up to our ankles by the time we neared the shore. Even then we did not stop to bail out the boat; right up to the sandbanks we paddled, until at last the *Endymion of Charleston, S.C.* grated against the sandy bottom and our boat shuddered to a stop. We got out, stepping onto the firm sandy bottom, and together we pulled the *Endymion* to the edge of the dry banks.

"We'd better bail it out, so we can get it all the way up on the shore," I said. We dipped pail after pail of water out, still working rapidly, as if even now there were some danger that we would not remain safely ashore if we slowed our pace. Only when the *Endymion* was once again fairly dry, and we had pulled it entirely out of the water, did we dare to breathe easy.

"Well," I said, "here we are."

We looked around us at the sandbanks.

"Here we are," Helen agreed.

Here were the banks of white sand that Billy Cartwright and I had so often regarded from the far shore, and which had seemed so remote, so inaccessible. Now we saw the sand was coarse and pebbly, with tiny fragments of shell and rock mixed in, gravelly to the touch. The banks had been formed several years before when the ship channel had been deepened by a large green-and-tan Army Engineer dredge, which had spent half a summer huffing and churning out in the river. They were quite dry, and grass grew here and there. Downstream and upstream they stretched out, in undulating contours, with little hills set back from the water's edge, sloping down toward the marshland behind and the woods beyond that. So far as we could tell, they seemed entirely isolated from the mainland.

We set out for a walk along the edge, and soon we came to several large brown mounds, which proved to be made up of thousands upon thousands of tiny stone sea shells, looking much like ordinary shells but hard and solid throughout.

"Why, they're fossils!" Helen exclaimed. She scooped up a handful. "They're many, many thousands of years old," she said. "They're formed by sand settling in real shells and gradually turning to stone. We studied about them in science class."

Poking among the mounds of shells, I came across a number of shark's teeth, long and pointed, sharp to the touch. "You ought to take some of these back and make a bracelet of them," I suggested. So we sat down on the shells and began combing through them. In a few minutes' time we had collected more than enough teeth for several necklaces and bracelets.

"Wouldn't Billy love to be here!" Helen said. "He'd probably want to bring back all the shark's teeth he could find and try to sell them."

We laughed. "Isn't he wonderful?" Helen declared. "When he gets an idea like that, there's no discouraging him."

"Soon as he sees these shark's teeth he'll want to be right over here on the next tide," I predicted.

I put the shark's teeth we had collected in my pocket, and

we continued our walk. For about a mile we strolled along, looking at the river, poking at objects half buried in the sand. Hermit crabs had set up operations along the water's edge, and we could see them staring suspiciously at us as we walked by, intruders that we were on what had until now been their solitary domain. In some places the sand was wet and springy, while in others it was quite dry and firm, almost like beach sand. Soon we had come halfway to the Seaboard trestle, over which the evening train that I so often listened to came rolling into the city each night.

"Do you think anybody could walk out here from the mainland?" Helen asked.

I looked around. A solid strip of marsh seemed to intervene between the sandbanks and the western shore. "I doubt it," I told her. "We can walk along the other side and see, though." We crossed over the banks, climbing the dunes, making our way along the inner shoreline, by the edge of the marsh. There seemed to be no place where it might be possible to get from the sandbanks to the shore on foot.

The isolation, and the knowledge that we had to cross the river again in our little boat in order to get home, made me somewhat uneasy. "Maybe we'd better be heading back," I suggested.

"Oh, not just yet," Helen said. "It's not even lunchtime yet. Let's sit down on the dunes and rest awhile."

We climbed up to the crest of the sandhills—they were not dunes, I decided, but simply places where the dredge had deposited the sand a little higher than at other points—and sat down.

"Isn't it lovely?" Helen said. So it was, for there before us lay the green river, but this time seen from the western shore, and beyond it the marshland in front of our houses, until today the farthest limit of our explorations in the boat. We could see Mr. Simons' house, with its grove of water oaks that surrounded it and partially obscured the old white structure

189

with its red roof and double dormer windows. My own house was almost entirely screened from view by the trees, but the Cartwrights' brick house was clearly visible, standing alone at the edge of the marsh, with no large trees to block the view. A little farther to the south the woods of Devereux were massive and green. Beyond all of this we could see the plumes of smoke from the factories on the Cooper River across the city, and past that the girdered peak of the Cooper River Bridge. The sunlight played over everything, broken sometimes by shadow as passing clouds obscured it.

"Do you suppose they know we're over here?" Helen asked.

"I don't imagine so," I answered. Unless someone had happened to see us crossing the river in the *Endymion*, it was unlikely. And besides, my parents were downtown that morning, and Mrs. Cartwright and Helen's mother had said they were going out again too. So only the Major was likely to be home, and he was keeping to his room these days.

"Do you think they could see us from over there if they were looking?" Helen asked.

"No, not unless they had a telescope or something."

We were quite alone, as isolated as if we were at the beach and had gone far beyond the last of the houses, out of sight of the area where people went bathing. Even more isolated, I thought, because to get to where we were now, it was necessary to come by boat across the water or through the marshland behind us. The thought of our isolation and our solitude made me think of that occasion when we had been in the caterpillar together, and I trembled nervously.

"Why does it worry your mother and Mrs. Cartwright," I asked Helen, "when the Major forgets that the *Sappho* isn't running any more?"

"Because when old people start doing that, it's a sign that they're losing their mind. Haven't you read about how old people sometimes go into second childhood, and live just like it was a long time ago?"

"I guess so." I had, to be sure, heard of that. It was not a pleasant thought. As long as I had known the Major, he had seemed so perfectly aware of everything, so completely alert and wise. I thought of that night in early June, at the Legion meeting, when he had stood up and said just the right thing to end the argument about postponing the Fort Sumter Celebration. To have him now confusing the past and the present, forgetting that things in the past were over, seemed a betrayal.

I had tried to overlook the business about the *Star of the West* and Dr. Chisholm's book. I *had* overlooked it. It had shaken me for a while, but I had managed it, had dismissed it on the grounds Helen had stated that other time in the boat: that he was an old man and sometimes got his stories mixed up a bit. *That* kind of forgetfulness was one thing, though; it was a foible, unimportant in the larger realization of what he was—a fine, clear-eyed, beautiful old man. This latest was another thing altogether. It meant that something was happening, something that could not be explained away or overlooked.

But was the Major breaking up? Perhaps it was only the hot weather, as Mrs. Cartwright had said when we were sitting in the automobile waiting for the Wappoo Cut drawbridge to close. He was old, and the brutal summer heat was momentarily dulling his senses. Once the weather cooled off, he would be his old self again, in plenty of time for the Fort Sumter Celebration, and for a long time after that.

"It's probably just the weather," I told Helen.

"I hope so," she said.

It had to be! The Major could not be declining, could not be —dying. I thought the ugly word, and shivered at the thought. Was the Major *dying*, now, this summer, this month? Was he going to die soon? He must not do that! He *had* to hold on to life, had to endure at least through the Celebration next month, for which he had waited so long, and which in my mind—and his too—would be *his* celebration, *his* great triumph. Whatever happened, he must not miss it!

And Helen . . . she must have been thinking what I was thinking, for just at that moment she said, "Wasn't it funny, that time by the *Sappho,* the way the skeleton frightened me so?"

We heard, far downstream, the horn of the railroad trestle, and looked up to see the long center span turning on its axis, its machinery clanking, as I had heard it do so many times at night for the launch. This time it was no launch that wished to pass through, however; beyond the bridge we could see the tall masts of a freighter moving toward the trestle.

"A ship!" Helen exclaimed. Its sharp bow loomed up in the gap between the bridge spans, and a large gray vessel moved through and glided upstream in our direction. We watched her as she came toward us; towering over the marsh, she moved in leisurely fashion, her bow smoothly parting the river water, her twin screws revolving at slow speed. We could make her name out plainly: *Cavalière.* She was French, and the tricolor floated out from her stern in the breeze. The hull was gray, the cabin and superstructure white. There was a single black stack, topped with a blue ring, from which a wisp of brownish smoke fanned out. We could even see members of the crew standing at the rail along the deck. Helen waved at them, and several of them returned her greeting.

The ship passed upstream; we read the lettering on the stern, the name again and the home port: *Cavalière—Bordeaux.* Her masts and cargo booms seemed like the framework of great inverted umbrellas, with the bare ribs craning upward at the sky. Now the swells of her wake came crashing one after another onto the shore of the sandbanks in churning staccato. They died down, and then all was silent.

Again I thought of our isolation there on the sandbanks,

and again I shivered. I wondered whether I dared put my arm around Helen. What was she thinking about?

I tried to get up enough nerve to do it, but I could not. Instead I sat there beside her, uncomfortable, acutely aware of her presence next to me. Was she waiting for me to do something? Or was she thinking about something else entirely? Whichever it was, she gave no indication, but sat quietly all the while.

"We'd better be going back," I said after a few minutes.

"All right."

After a moment I got up, and Helen followed my lead. We walked down to where the *Endymion* rested on the shore, its squat red bulk looking small and ungainly, while once again the river appeared exceedingly wide. Together we tugged away at our boat until it was afloat. Stepping over the sides and into our places, we picked up the paddles and set out for the far marshland.

The river was rougher now. From where we had sat on the sandbanks we had not noticed, but now the closeness of the day was gone, and there was a definite breeze. I remembered that when the freighter had passed, the flag at the stern had been flying straight out. There was some wind now, and the *Endymion* rocked and swayed in the current, so that it was considerably more difficult to keep our craft pointed straight across the river. The waves and the force of the current kept swinging her blunt prow downstream. Salt spray dashed against us as we rolled and dipped in the flowing channel. We made headway, but the going was hard.

"Keep paddling," I told Helen, and began scooping water out with the bailing can. The boat was pitching so that it was necessary for me to hold onto the side with one hand as I bailed, and when I bent over, there was the uncomfortable sensation of cool spray against my back.

193

After a minute I looked up to see that a shadow had fallen over the river, and I noted with alarm that a bank of gray clouds was arching over the sky from the west, with the sun already hidden behind one tier that preceded the rest.

Helen was straining away at the paddle. For a moment I looked back. We were already well out into the river, away from the sandbanks, but despite our efforts we were being forced farther downstream. We gave a concerted push with our paddles on the right-hand side of the boat. The *Endymion's* bow swung upstream again. We nosed over one oncoming swell, then slipped into the trough, and the next wave crashed against the boat, sending a heavy shower of water over the side and drenching us both from head to foot.

I was thoroughly frightened now. "We better move with the current and try to keep heading for the shore," I said. Helen nodded. We bent to the paddles. My mouth was dry with fear.

Several inches of water had again covered the bottom of the boat, but I was afraid to stop paddling. We kept at our task. The *Endymion* dipped and tossed, up one wave, down another, with spray crashing repeatedly over the side and drenching us. The edge of the marsh was still a long way off; we were moving downstream. I could see the woods of Devereux, remote and inaccessible now, far to our left.

Now the water was over our ankles. "You bail and I'll keep paddling!" I called to Helen. She put down her paddle and began dipping water out, while I continued to work away with my paddle. But without her help it was all I could do to keep the *Endymion's* bow from swinging directly downstream.

"We'd better put the inner tubes on!" I said. We stopped our paddling for an instant and draped the inflated inner tubes over us. They were large and clumsy, and we had to hold our arms well away from our bodies, and lean farther out, to work the paddles. This in turn made the seating more precarious, and each new lurch of the *Endymion* threatened to unseat us.

Finally we could see that the marsh was much closer now, less than a hundred yards distant. Never had the marshland looked so inviting; the thicket of reed grass would break the force of the current and enable us to make the land. With concerted effort we pulled hard, until at last the *Endymion* nosed into the grass. We moved well away from the river, until the waves no longer tugged at our boat, and then put down our paddles. We were safe again.

For some minutes we sat there, breathing heavily, our arms numb from weariness. I did not even bother to grasp the reeds; we let the *Endymion* drift up into the marsh while we rested.

"That was sure something, wasn't it?" I said at last.

"I was scared to death," Helen said. "I was certain that any minute we'd turn over."

"Me too."

After a while I stood up in the boat and looked around to see where we were. We had been forced a long way downstream, halfway to the railroad trestle at least. Devereux wood was far upstream. Across the marshland, below us, I could see the brick façade of the old peanut mill, many years abandoned, that stood near a creek that I had crossed on numerous occasions when bicycling over to The Citadel.

"Maybe if we could work along the edge of the marsh to the creek that flows past that mill, we could get in to shore," I said. There was no thought of trying to make our way upstream to the place where we had entered the river. Even if we could keep to the marsh's edge and away from the heavy river swells, it would be an arduous push of almost a mile against the current.

So we eased the *Endymion* hesitantly back toward the river, clinging to the fringe of marsh, and crept downstream, taking care not to swing away from the reeds and out into the stream again. We were a long time finding the mill creek, but at last we reached it. It was wide, much wider than the creek in front of my house. We poled along, following the turns and bends, until finally we drew up onto a point of land just beyond the old mill. We hauled the *Endymion* as far onto the grassy bank as we could get it without bailing, and I tied it to a tree.

"I hope nobody takes it," Helen said.

"Small loss if they do," I declared. I had had enough of the *Endymion of Charleston, S.C.* for quite a while, I thought. I looked at her there, lying empty and clumsy upon the bank, the grass about her sides wet from the water that was draining from her leaking carcass, her crude red planks slick and glistening from the river water. A mere wooden box she was: some planks and nails, a coat of red lead to hide the raw lumber. In that flimsy, coffinlike contraption we had risked our lives crossing the Ashley River!

We walked back along the rutted dirt road that led through the fields and toward Devereux wood, saying little. "I wonder what time it is?" Helen asked.

I could make out where the sun was positioned behind the clouds that now covered the sky. "About two, I'd say," I told her.

"What shall we tell them?" Helen asked.

I considered. "We'll just say that the boat got stuck in the marsh and we had to pole downstream in order to get to shore."

"All right."

Now we were walking through Devereux wood, along a line of oak trees and past some abandoned stone columns. It was just off to the left here, on the hill, that the Major and Billy Cartwright had been standing that day when Billy had thrown the stones at us in the boat and had flushed the man and woman out of the bushes along the marsh's edge.

I glanced at Helen; she was plodding along, face turned

toward the ground. We passed through the woods and the clearing and continued along the path, the thickets stretching high up on either side of us. Just ahead was the bend in the trail that would bring us out near the Cartwrights' house.

Helen stopped then, and turned toward me.

"Omar?"

"What?"

"Omar, would you kiss me again?"

I put my arms around her and drew her awkwardly to me. For some seconds we stood there in the center of the path. I could feel her small, moist lips against my own, and I felt my body tense as her own body pressed against me. When we drew apart, I felt weak.

We walked on down the path, around the bend, and toward the houses.

10.

IT WAS LONG PAST MEALTIME WHEN I ARRIVED home, and my parents scolded me for my tardiness. Afterward I went up to my room and I lay down for a minute, for I was quite tired from the strenuous exertion of the morning. In no time, it seemed, I felt my mother tugging at my shoulder and calling, "Wake up, wake up!" I shook my head to dispel the blur. "Wake up, Omar!" my mother said again. "This is the evening you're to go down to Dr. Chisholm's. Wake up! It's almost time to go!"

With all the excitement of the morning I had forgotten about it. Outside it was dusk; I realized that I must have slept all afternoon.

"Go take a shower and dress," my mother told me. "Hurry up now, or you'll be late. It's after five o'clock."

I stood under the warm shower, letting the water pour down on me, feeling the sharp streams drumming on my head and shoulders, slowly restoring me to wakefulness. I could not remember when I had ever been so deeply asleep. There was no memory of dreams, no sense of time having elapsed; there was simply a blank in my experience. Minutes passed by, and at last I was able to turn off the shower, step out, dry myself and dress for dinner.

I rode downtown on the Marvelous Ringgold's trolley. Under my arm I carried an envelope containing poems and verses that I had scraped together the previous evening for the occasion, adding verses and lines hurriedly to make them appear to be what they certainly were not—any kind of serious, sustained attempt to write poems, to be a poet.

How my resolve had slackened since that evening long ago
—in June it was—when, inspired by my first encounter with
Dr. Chisholm, I had vowed to carry a notebook about with
me to capture the golden insights, and then to turn them
into poems. A few stanzas, some halfhearted lines scribbled
on loose-leaf paper: such was what my literary resolve had
come to.

Aunt Ellen was already home when I arrived. "I thought
you must be sick, when I came home and didn't find you
here," she said. "I was about to go downstairs and telephone
your mother to see whether anything was wrong."

It was already time for us to go down to Dr. Chisholm's, so
we set off immediately along the corridor and down the circular stairway at the other end of the building, to the sec-
ond-floor corner apartment occupied by the doctor.

He greeted us at the door. "Well, well, come in!" He
beamed. "Young man, I'm delighted to see you. Miss Ellen,
how are you?" He ushered us into his parlor, a large room
that opened onto a balcony and was decorated with black-
and-white etchings of Charleston scenes.

"Will you have a martini, Miss Ellen? Or will it be some
sherry? I have an excellent dry sack."

"Some sherry would be very nice," Aunt Ellen said.

"Fine. I believe I'll just have a martini. Young man, what
will you drink? How about a Coca-cola?"

"Fine, sir," I said.

The Doctor disappeared into another room, and my aunt
and I could hear the sound of glasses and bottles clinking, as
well as of someone else moving about the kitchen, and Dr.
Chisholm's voice conversing in low tones.

"Aren't these lovely drawings?" Aunt Ellen said.

"Yes, ma'am." I tried to appear at ease, but I was quite
uncomfortable, seated upright in the high-backed chair.

"I have always felt," said the Doctor, emerging from the
kitchen with a tray on which there were various glasses and

bottles, "that it is not what an artist actually paints or draws, so much as in the overtones surrounding those objects, that the true meaning of his work resides." He set the tray down on a small mahogany table, and poured Coca-cola into an ice-filled glass, twisting the bottle deftly to catch the last residue of liquid, then handing the glass to me on a small, cherry-colored doily. Next he drew out the cork from a green wine bottle and carefully measured out a glass of amber wine. He presented it to Aunt Ellen, together with another cherry-colored doily. After that he poured a clear liquid from a little cracked-glass pitcher into another and different-shaped glass, holding a spoon over the lip of the pitcher to keep the ice from slipping into the glass. He held the glass to the light, tasted the clear beverage, and sat down opposite us in a large, barrel-like chair. He tasted the drink lightly with his tongue.

"Yes, indeed," he said. "Just as in this martini—not the actual taste of the gin, but the something else, the breeding of the vermouth—fine wines have it, just as great paintings do, and the great poems. We poets, young man," Dr. Chisholm went on, addressing himself to me, "are artists with words. The word—that's our pigment, our oils. We must choose our words so as to give to the picture we paint not simply lines and colors, but the elusive quality that lies behind the artist's draftsmanship. To communicate that luminous softness that's more than mere accuracy of detail, to give tone to our words—that's what you and I must strive for, young man. More sherry, Miss Ellen?"

"No, thank you," my aunt replied.

The doctor took up the pitcher and refilled his own glass. "You don't mind, do you, Miss Ellen, if we poets talk shop like this? Let two poets get together, you know, and they say that the world can collapse around them and they'd never know it."

"Oh, do go right ahead," Aunt Ellen assured him. "I'm just fascinated."

"I'll never forget the time," Dr. Chisholm declared, "when the poet Seamus O'Doyle came to Charleston to address the Poetry Society. He spoke on Hawaiian folk songs, and afterward we had a little gathering at John Bennett's. And what a session that was! We settled all the problems of the literary world, I can assure you. The stories Seamus O'Doyle told us—of Yeats, Gogarty, Synge, Russell, Joyce—though I must say I don't share his high estimate of the last named, and I told him as much. The others, though—pure lyricists, every one, so steeped in the Celtic magic of that enchanted green isle."

"You spoke of your next book of poems, Doctor," Aunt Ellen said. "Will it be published soon?"

Dr. Chisholm smiled and poured himself another glass from the little pitcher. "No, Miss Ellen, I fear not. I haven't quite enough for another book yet, but I'm working. You see, I've embarked on a rather ambitious plan, and it isn't the sort of thing that one can do overnight. In fact, I've been at it for several years already."

"Can you tell us about it?" my aunt asked.

"I want," said the doctor, "to describe a summer in the life of a Charleston boy, in a series of lyrics, one for each day of the months of June, July, and August. Not what the boy says, of course, but what he *feels*, and would say if he had the words to express it. That's ninety-odd poems in all, you know, and I haven't done nearly that many yet. In fact, chronologically speaking, I'm still in late July! I keep working away, though. I just completed a little verse the other evening, as a matter of fact. It describes the day before a hurricane."

"Won't you read it to us?" asked my aunt.

"Aha!" the doctor laughed. "It so happens that I have the

201

draft in that cabinet there." Dr. Chisholm reached into the small mahogany cabinet and drew out a piece of paper folded over several times. With great deliberation he unfolded it. "Yes, here it is," he said.

The doctor cleared his throat. "It is called 'Before the Hurricane.'

> *"Let the gray clouds gather*
> *The south sky over;*
> *Let the sea bird issue*
> *His high-pitched warning.*
>
> *Let the fierce wind shatter*
> *The crests of the billows;*
> *Let the furious rain*
> *Send the white water leaping;*
>
> *Let two square flags,*
> *Red with black centers,*
> *Call the poor fisherfolk*
> *Back from their seining.*
>
> *I shall laugh with the wind,*
> *Exult in the salt spray,*
> *Shall bare to the storm*
> *My own heart's wild yearning."*

"How beautiful!" my aunt said when he had done.

"Thank you," replied the Doctor. "The idea for that poem came to me one day as I stood upon the ramparts of Fort Sumter, while working on my last book, and looked out at the ocean. When I viewed the sea, the wild Atlantic stretching from the shores of one continent to the other, I thought to myself, How to give tongue to that immensity, how to capture in words the heroic ebb and flow of the tide? Then I remembered, as a lad of eight years, standing upon the Battery with my father the day before the hurricane of 1898, and watching the growing anger of the waves as they dashed against the sea wall, sending towers of spray over the railing and onto the street. To a child, heedless of the danger of the hurricane, it was only exciting, pleasurable. And even to the adult, who knows the great damage that a hurricane can do, there is still something exultant and mad in the wind, the spray, the driving clouds. So I sought the words to express that, and it seemed to me that the most important thing was the rhythm, because after all, the hurricane weather was a matter of mood—surging water, crashing waves, moaning wind. And *that* is how the poem came to me."

There was a moment of silence, and Dr. Chisholm seemed almost to bow, as if concluding a speech. He examined the little pitcher, but it was empty of martini. "Well, it's almost dinnertime, I believe," he said, glancing at his watch. "I'm sure that Evalina is ready for us. Aren't you, Evalina?" he called.

"Yas, sir," came a Negro voice from the kitchen.

"Fine," said the doctor, rising to his feet. "Won't you come with me?"

We walked into a small dining room, with an ornate mahogany sideboard, a large gold-framed mirror on the wall behind it, and several portraits of distinguished-looking people in gilded frames. In the center of the room a table, with places set for three, was covered with a brown lace tablecloth and numerous silver dishes and bowls. Overhead there was a small but glittering crystal chandelier.

"Please sit down, won't you?" Dr. Chisholm invited, gesturing toward the table.

A Negro woman, immaculately garbed in gray and white, came in from the kitchen bearing a tray on which were three small glasses of fruit juice. "Thank you, Evalina," said Dr. Chisholm.

Evalina left the room. "A fine servant and friend, Evalina," he said to us. "She has been in my family for many years. The old-time type, you know." The doctor downed his fruit juice.

203

"Well, young man," he declared, turning to me, "I trust you have had a profitable and enjoyable vacation time?"

"Yes, sir."

"For myself," said the doctor, "it has been a summer of activity. There has been so much to do in connection with the Fort Sumter Celebration, and so many odds and ends to tidy up, things I had let slide during the final preparation of my little book of history. And it has also been a summer of meditation; a stock-taking, as it were. I had so drawn upon my reserves of emotion and imagination during the past year that it has been necessary for me to replenish them. And the way to do that, for myself at any rate, is to walk about the streets of our city and force my tired eyes and heart open to its loveliness, to teach myself to experience things again. I walk down Stolls Alley and down Church and Longitude Lane, and the old buildings, the lovely gardens and passageways, unfold in their magic color for me, and then, one day— a poem!"

The doctor had neglected his salad. Now he proceeded to attack it. Deftly he sectioned the sprouts of cold asparagus and popped them into his mouth one after another. Then, seeing that Aunt Ellen and I had already finished ours, he rang the little silver bell at his plate, and the Negro maid appeared to remove the salad plates and bring in a salver of lamb chops garnished with mint sprigs.

"Isn't it wonderful," said Aunt Ellen, "about Mr. Heyward's opera? I understand that it's a tremendous success on the road."

"Yes, I'm told it is," Dr. Chisholm replied. "Certainly I am overjoyed at DuBose's good fortune. Still, I confess to being somewhat irked when tourists approach me on the street and ask me to direct them to Catfish Row!"

"They say the music is very fine," Aunt Ellen said. "I heard it on the radio, and it seemed quite nice."

"Oh, it's all *right*, I suppose. But essentially what does it have to do with Charleston? After all, what does someone like Gershwin really know about Charleston and the South?"

Dr. Chisholm reached over and withdrew a bottle of red table wine from a frosted silver bucket. "I'm dreadfully sorry, but I completely forgot the wine. Here, young man," he said to me, pouring some into the glass by my plate, "you try a little of this, too. It won't hurt you, not just a glass. Miss Ellen, may I?" he asked, pouring wine into her glass as well.

I raised the wine glass to my lips and sipped a little wine. It tasted bitter.

"Now you tell me, Miss Ellen," Dr. Chisholm continued, "why, with all the beautiful Negro songs that exist, was it necessary for them to introduce all those fake blackface numbers? Alas, the answer is only too plain: money. Why, do you know that before agreeing to collaborate with Gershwin —as if that weren't bad enough—DuBose actually held up signing the contract for some months because *Al Jolson* was interested in doing the show?" He sipped some wine. "A vaudeville comedian like Jolson as a Charleston Negro!"

We were finished with the main course now, and Dr. Chisholm's maid was clearing off the dishes from the table. "You understand, of course," the doctor added, "that I love DuBose very much, and I'm delighted at his success. And I suppose I'm old-fashioned and foolish to think this way, nowadays when money is everything and it isn't who you are that matters, but how much you've got. But I cling to my outmoded values, and care not what the world thinks."

Dr. Chisholm's maid brought in plates of pineapple sherbet and small demitasse cups, which she filled with black coffee from a small bronze pot. The coffee was quite bitter. Dr. Chisholm lifted a tiny spoon of sherbet to his lips and tasted it thoughtfully. "No," he said after a moment, "I don't envy him. For me, art is art, and money is money, and never the twain shall meet." And he threw his arm out, palm downward, in a sweeping gesture of abnegation.

Unfortunately, the sweep of his arm was too low, and the tips of his fingers caught the small handle of the bronze coffeepot, overturning it on the table. The dark liquid ran out onto the tablecloth.

"Damn!" Dr. Chisholm swore, leaping to his feet. "Evalina! See what you've done? I've told you to be careful where you set the coffeepot!" He grabbed up a damask napkin and began sponging up the coffee, which slowly spread along the table. The Negro maid came hurrying into the dining room with a towel and washcloth. "Get this out at once," Dr. Chisholm ordered, "before it stains the cloth. Miss Ellen, I'm sorry," he said, turning to us, "but this tablecloth belonged to my great-great-grandmother, and I can't bear the idea of its being ruined."

"Oh, it'll be all right, Doctor," my aunt assured him. "Just pour some boiling water over it," she told the maid. "Hold the pot about two feet away and let the water pour onto it. It will come right out."

"Yas'm, I'm gonna do that right away," the maid assured her.

"Sorry I grew excited for a moment," Dr. Chisholm told us. "Let's go into my study, shall we? These servants are so trifling nowadays. If I've told her once, I've told her fifty times not to place the hot coffeepot too near the edge of the table. But it does no good. I might as well be talking to a stone wall."

We rose from the table and followed Dr. Chisholm out of the room and into another, this one lined with bookcases, and with several framed maps and historical prints on the walls.

"Will you have an after-dinner liqueur, Miss Ellen?" Dr. Chisholm asked my aunt.

"No, thank you," Aunt Ellen said.

"I believe I shall, if you don't mind," the Doctor said. He opened a door in the desk, removed a bottle and a brandy glass, and poured himself a drink. "A Coca-cola, young man?" he asked me.

"No, thank you, sir."

Then the Doctor went up to one of the maps on the wall. "This may interest you," he said. "It's a map of the harbor defenses. There is Moultrie, and there's the battery on Cummings Point, and there's the old ship channel, and that point there is where Battery Wagner was located." He indicated a place on the map.

Aunt Ellen and I stood with him in front of the map. "Isn't that the map that was on the inside cover of your book?" I asked.

"Yes, indeed," Dr. Chisholm said. "Delighted that you recognized it."

Dr. Chisholm went back to the desk, picked up the brandy bottle again, and refilled his glass.

It was then that I said a daring thing, so incredible that even as I was speaking the words, I was astounded at my brashness in saying them.

"Dr. Chisholm, why isn't Major Frampton in your book?"

He looked at me for a moment, startled. "Major Frampton? What do you mean, why isn't he?"

"I mean, all the stories he tells about Fort Sumter and the *Star of the West*—didn't they happen to him?"

Dr. Chisholm seemed puzzled. "You mean, you believe those stories? You've heard them?"

Aunt Ellen broke into the conversation. "The Major and Omar are great friends, Doctor; they go for walks down to the waterfront together." Aunt Ellen spoke queerly, as if she were embarrassed.

"Oh, yes, yes," Dr. Chisholm replied. He too seemed embarrassed now. He looked at me, then at Aunt Ellen, then back at me again. His face was red.

I understood then.

They all knew it.

Everybody in town knew it.

Everyone except me.

"Was he," I asked, in desperation, "the captain of the *Sappho?*"

"Oh, yes indeed," my aunt said hastily. "He most certainly was. I remember him looking so handsome in his uniform. Don't you, Doctor?"

"Why, I believe I do," Dr. Chisholm agreed.

"Oh, there's no doubt of that," my aunt repeated. "I remember him very clearly. And he was a city councilman, too, and everyone thought very highly of him!"

So there was that much, anyway. But now I knew at last what, I now realized, I had felt in my heart ever since I had first read Dr. Chisholm's book, back in June.

I heard Dr. Chisholm talking on as he poured himself another drink of brandy. He was telling about his ancestor who had rowed General Beauregard about the harbor. While he spoke, Aunt Ellen was looking at me. She thinks I'm disappointed, I thought; she doesn't realize that I came here to hear Dr. Chisholm say that.

"Tell me, Doctor," Aunt Ellen said, seeking to change the subject, "what is your next book going to be about?"

"Well, there is the sequence of poems, of course," Dr. Chisholm began.

"Oh, that's right, I forgot," my aunt said.

"But then, poetry is not something that one can write at will," the Doctor continued. "I should not be surprised if several years go by at the very least before the book of poems is ready. In any event, I have another idea that I'm toying with."

"What is that?" Aunt Ellen asked. "Or do you mind telling?"

"Not at all," declared the Doctor, pouring himself still another drink from the brandy bottle. "I am thinking of writing a little book about the South. Not a work of history, though of course it's impossible to write about Charleston and the South without bringing history in. But my main intention will be to portray our way of life. I want to try to tell outsiders—and ourselves as well, for sometimes we need to be reminded—what the South *really* is."

"How interesting," my aunt said, as she had so often said that evening.

Dr. Chisholm picked up the brandy bottle once again and poured some into his glass. The bottle, which after dinner had been almost full, was now more than half empty.

"And do you know, Miss Ellen, I've got a hunch that a book like that might really do well. Just for once, you know, I'd like to make a great deal of *money* out of a book! Call it commercialism if you will, but I've been noncommercial long enough. I just may haul off and do something that will *sell*. Yes, ma'am. Something that a great many people will read." Dr. Chisholm laughed. "Do you think I'm awful for feeling that way?"

"Not at all," Aunt Ellen replied.

"Of course, I don't mean to say that I would write anything that I would be ashamed of. Not at all. I'm simply going to show those boys what happens when a real writer decides to get in on the gravy train. Ha ha ha! We'll just see what happens then. Ha ha ha!"

My aunt joined in with Dr. Chisholm's laughter. Afterward she got up. "Well, Doctor, it's been simply delightful, but Omar must be getting home, and it's quite late. I just know that Omar has had a wonderful time, haven't you?"

"Yes, sir," I said.

"Delighted that you could come," Dr. Chisholm said, setting his empty brandy glass on the corner of the desk. "I only hope that I haven't bored you with all this talk about books and the like. I'm afraid we writers think that our little schemes are the most important things in the world. Well, it's been a pleasure to have you, and we must do this again soon."

Dr. Chisholm followed us to the door. He was walking rather unsteadily, and he leaned on the door frame as we exchanged farewells. "Bye-bye!" he called. "Remember, young man, keep on with the writing! Perseverance is what counts! Bye-bye!"

The door closed behind us as we walked up the hall.

"I'd better be getting on home," I said when we reached the staircase. "It's getting late."

"All right," Aunt Ellen said. She leaned over. "And, Omar, I wouldn't worry just because every one of Major Frampton's stories may not be true. He's an old man, you know."

"Oh, I won't," I assured her. "It doesn't matter."

"He's a mighty fine old gentleman," my aunt told me.

"Yes, ma'am. Nighty-night."

My aunt bent closer and kissed my cheek. "Nighty-night. And watch out for the steamboats!"

We both laughed. I walked down the steps two at a time, skipped along the hall and out into the courtyard. In my hand I clutched the manila envelope with my poems. He had not even asked to look at them! Thank God for that, anyway, I thought.

11. AT ONCE I WAS AWARE HOW MUCH COOLER IT HAD become. Not that it was cold, but simply that the heavy, sultry heat of the previous evenings had vanished. It was a clear night; the clouds that had spread over the sky in the morning were gone, and the stars were all out.

The physical impact of the night was what I knew; all that had taken place during the hours just past was so crowded and confused in my mind that I could not even separate it into understandable thoughts. I saw the houses, the street lamps, the palm trees, the iron railings of the fences with the oleander bushes beyond, the A&P store on the corner. I smelled the air. It was the air, I realized at once, of the north, the autumn, even though this was an early August night. Though it was not at all cold, there was a faint sharpness to it, a remote kind of keenness that came from faraway cold places, from Canada, the winter. Though more than a month of summertime was still to come, it meant that, inexorably now, fall was on its way.

I would not have to wait for the streetcar tonight; there was one coming down Wentworth Street. I wished to get inside, to sit down, to be quiet. If it were the Marvelous Ringgold at the controls, I thought, I did not know what I would do. I simply did not want to hear him talk, did not want to listen to him as he chattered away. How strange, I thought, for me to be *hoping* that Mr. Zinzer was the motorman!

Mr. Zinzer it was, fortunately. I handed him my fare, selected a seat halfway back, and sat down. I still could not think. I was trying to focus my mind, but it was as if I were peering through some binoculars and could see only a blur, and was attempting to work the lenses so as to sharpen the objects into their proper form. This is a streetcar. Those are tan wicker seats with brown casings of mahogany around them. There is a passenger in a blue work-jacket. There is another passenger in a blue serge suit, the collar of which is stained dark. That is a fare register, indicating that eight fares have been collected on this trip so far. Above it is a number in gold paint on brown woodwork, indicating that this is car No. 403. There is the motorman, Mr. Zinzer, whose complexion is pimply white, and who is seated on a green cushion in order to see over the ledge of the front window. Outside there are automobile headlights, lights of houses, street lights. We are riding up Rutledge Avenue, in an iron drone along steel tracks, and the trolley is rasping overhead.

When I saw the Major asleep on the Sappho, that day, I knew he was going to die. He is not dead yet but he will die. He is an old man with a fading memory, and he is going to die some day soon. Some day soon. He was leaning back on the post, his cigar placed on the edge of the wooden box next to him, his head low on his chest.

Dr. Chisholm does not like Mr. DuBose Heyward because he says he is commercial and makes money. Dr. Chisholm says he is going to write a book that will make money. The Major is going to die. He is old. Some day soon. He most certainly was the captain of the Sappho. But he was not at Fort Sumter. They all knew that, all but me.

And what of Dr. Chisholm? He is round-faced, and wears pince-nez, and when he knocked over the pot of coffee he blamed the maid. That was because he was already tipsy, even then.

That time when the Major stood on the bank in Devereux with Billy, he said, "Turn back or we'll open fire on you!" and he held up his walking stick like a rifle. And I thought, He is playing a game. But we always were, weren't we, from the start?

Billy Cartwright threw the second stone. The man came out of the bushes. He said, "What the hell's going on here?" He was buttoning up his pants. He and the woman had been Doing It.

Helen said, "Omar, would you kiss me again?" When I did I could feel Helen's bosom against my shirt. And if I could, then Helen could feel my body too.

When Dr. Chisholm poured the wine into the slender glass, he placed it on a cherry-colored napkin and with his elegant fingers he handed the glass to Aunt Ellen. Poets are artists with words, he said. He said, "What does Gershwin know about Charleston?"

Gershwin is a Jew. I am from a Fine Old Jewish Family of Charleston. When is a Jew not a Jew? When he is from a Fine Old Jewish Family.

But the Sabbath School hymn does not say that. It says,

> There is a mystic tie that joins
> The children of the martyred race
> In bonds of sympathy and love
> That time and change cannot efface.

That is what it says, and that is what is true.

The streetcar lurched onto a stretch of double track. I looked out the window; we were already at Poplar Street, and up ahead I could see the single headlight of the southbound car moving along the track toward us. Silent and untroubled, Mr. Zinzer waited. The approaching headlight bent to the left as the southbound trolley entered on the double track. Mr. Zinzer started up our car, then waited as the other drew alongside. I could see the Marvelous Ringgold there, leaning out of the cab window. "Everything all right?" he asked. Mr. Zinzer nodded.

The Marvelous Ringgold's car swung by us, headed downtown; we heaved into motion, forward, along the siding, back onto the single-track line.

Why did the Marvelous Ringgold insist on asking Mr. Zinzer if all was well? I wondered. As if anything could go wrong on the Rutledge Avenue Line. Because he too was playing a game. A game in which he pretended that what he was doing was exciting, that something different, adventurous, could happen to a streetcar conductor who made fifteen trips each day along the same five miles of track, month after month, year after year. That was his game, just as the Major's was that he was a hero of the battle of Fort Sumter, and Dr. Chisholm's that he was a Distinguished Poet and Historian, and my father's that he was a renowned grower of roses.

And Mr. Zinzer, what was his game? I wondered as I watched him sitting there, his stolid face registering no emotion, no awareness. It was as if *he*, at any rate, knew that it was only games that people played, and could not deceive himself into playing. But I could not imagine Mr. Zinzer thinking such thoughts, could not imagine him thinking at all.

Now we were almost at Versailles Street. I reached up and pressed the buzzer; the sound was flat in the rocking cab. I got up to leave, walked toward Mr. Zinzer at the front of the trolley car. He slowed the car to a halt; the iron roar of the wheels ceased.

Mr. Zinzer turned around then, and he looked at me with his little red-rimmed eyes.

"Come on," he said, "ride up to the end of the line and back."

I sat down in the seat across the aisle from him. The streetcar resumed its forward motion.

In an amazing evening, was this not the most amazing occurrence of all? For he had never said anything, to me, to anyone, so far as I knew. Now he had spoken to me, had asked me to ride with him to the end of the line and back. To have him, of all people, say something friendly, act as other human beings acted, was incredible. He *was* a human being, after all. What was he like? What was he thinking? He sat there in his dingy black conductor's uniform, his pale, chubby hand on the controls, the peaked motorman's cap set low on his head, himself small, plump, unprepossessing. On the floor by his side sat a black-enameled lunch box, bulged at the top to house the thermos jug within. He perched on the swiveled motorman's seat with its circular, cast-iron base, its black seat cushion topped by the green cloth cushion diligently steering: so much I could see as I looked. And who was Mr. Zinzer?

The trolley car rounded the corner at Herriott Street and moved slowly up to the end of the tracks. It was night, and all the buildings and stalls along Magnolia Crossing were closed, except for one filling station on the corner, forlorn and still. The railroad tracks across the highway were unused, empty. We drew to a stop beneath the single street lamp.

Mr. Zinzer stood up, gathered his seat cushion and lunch box, removed the throttle and brake lever from the transformer, and took them to the other end of the car. He came back along the aisle, reversing the seats. I helped him with the last two, then followed him to the other end of the car. Mr. Zinzer attached the controls to the transformer box

215

there and turned the throttle handle. The cab doors opened. He walked over to them; for a moment he looked around at the night as if he were teetering at its edge, then he stepped down onto the ground.

He went around to the front of the cab, lowered the trolley from the wire, fastened the loose rope to the cab. The motor ceased throbbing and the cab lights went out.

I watched him proceed to the rear of the car, heard him undo the fastened trolley there, raise it, felt it thump several times against the overhead catenary, slip into place. The motor commenced to throb again and the cab lights came back on.

Mr. Zinzer came back around to the front of the car, climbed aboard again, closed the doors. He reached up to the fare box and twirled the lever. The three white numbers spun until all displayed the same number,

1 1 1

and then in swift unison up the table to

9 9 9

and then to three zeros.

Mr. Zinzer resumed his seat. He adjusted the cushion and grasped the brake handle. With a hiss of escaping air the brakes disengaged.

He nudged the throttle forward and opened it a little. The trolley car lurched into motion.

Down the tracks into the darkness of Herriott Street. Onto Rutledge Avenue.

And all the while I kept waiting for Mr. Zinzer to say something, to follow up his act of inviting me to ride with him by speaking a few inconsequential words about the weather, the night, or some such talk. But he said not a word.

He guided the trolley car slowly down Rutledge Avenue, and at Versailles eased it to a stop. He opened the doors and I stepped out. "Good night," I said.

He did not say a word.

The doors closed behind me, and trolley car No. 403 continued on its way.

Sooooooo—it was rutty old Versailles Street that I walked along now, toward the river, as I so often had, stepping along the paved sidewalks, my shoes tap-tapping solemnly, my body slanted under the street lamps to crazy shadows that came and went, frontways, sideways, one shadow meeting the other, sliding from under it, past houses with lighted windows, houses with windows dark, shades drawn, the streetcar humming in the distance, an auto horn sounding down Darlington Street somewhere, my steps hushed and crunching as I crossed the dirt side streets, up onto the sidewalk again, shuffling, scraping the pockmarked cement squares, along open fields adjacent to the sidewalk, rank with high weeds, fennel, chicory, dew. Crickets of August blared heartlessly in the dark, their pulsating whir rising, falling, weaving in and out. This is fresh cool air, come from Canada, clear as the sharp stars in the remote, receding sky, and all the crickets sighing *end of season, end of season.*

But that is still a long time off, I thought. Now along Versailles Street past where the sidewalk ends and the weeds hide the unset slabs of granite coping, the thick foliage crowds in on the dirt road, and the white moths of summer spin about the arc lamps, while pale toads vault across the street.

I turned into our driveway, walked along the grass horseshoe drive, past the cinderblocks, past the rose arbors and hydrangeas, past the crocuses along the slate-slabbed walk, and up the brick steps to the porch, where through the window screens I saw my parents reading in the living room. I opened the front door and went inside.

"Where in the world have you been?" asked my mother.

"We stayed late."

"It's after eleven o'clock. You'd better go right to bed."
I sat down in the wicker rocking chair and picked up the sports page.

"Did you have a good time?"

"Yes, ma'am."

"Guess what?" my father said. "We got a letter from Uncle Ben today."

"Is he coming?" I asked.

"Yes. For the Fort Sumter Celebration next month. Now you stop reading and go on upstairs."

"All right." I got up to go.

"Maybe you'd better take a light blanket," my mother said. "It's turned cool."

"It's not that cool," my father said.

"No, ma'am," I agreed. "It's not that cool."

Upstairs I closed the door to my room and turned on the radio. I lay across the bed watching the yellow glow of the pilot light spread over the dial. I reached out and turned the pointer all the way to the right-hand side of the dial, where there was a station in Cincinnati that played hillbilly music all night long. A man with a high nasal voice was singing the "Wabash Cannonball," with an electric guitar imitating a train whistle behind him. I listened to the stanza about "Here's to Daddy Claxton" and tried to make out whether the words were "the courts of Alabam'" or "the courts throughout the land." I could not tell this time, either. As often as I had heard that song, I could never make out which it was. I wondered whether I would ever find out.

Jee-zus, what a day! The river, Helen, the *Endymion*, Dr. Chisholm, the Major, Mr. Zinzer . . . ! I undressed, got my pajamas from the closet, stepped into them, turned off the overhead light, climbed into bed. The radio was still playing, its warm yellowness faintly lighting the room. I reached over, shut it off, watched as the pilot light faded to dark.

I wondered whether Helen was still awake. Again I remembered the morning, the walk along the banks—the shark's teeth were still in my pants pockets, probably—the great ship passing along the river, the dry bitterness in my mouth when we were fighting for safety from the waves. Tomorrow or the next day I would have to go with Billy Cartwright and fetch the *Endymion* from the spot where Helen and I had left it. Or was it even worth reclaiming?

She had kissed me as we stopped on the path in Devereux, just before the bend in the trail by the Cartwrights' house. Before she left for home on Monday I would try to kiss her again. When she went back to Philadelphia we would exchange letters, keep in touch always, until years from now when . . .

But now, as I entered sleep, I could hear, faintly, the whistle of the night train wailing over on the island far away.

12.

"Going to lose your girl friend on Monday, eh?" my father remarked at breakfast the next morning. I concentrated on my fried eggs.

"Well," he said, "don't worry. A few years more, and they'll be coming along regularly, just like streetcars."

I thought momentarily of Mr. Zinzer's strange conduct of the previous night. I wondered whether it had really happened, whether he had in truth spoken to me, invited me to ride with him—so incredible did the whole idea seem now.

"Of course," my father continued, "you won't find many girls who can write love poems to you, like this one."

"Stop teasing him," my mother said. "You wouldn't think it was so funny if *your* girl friend was going away."

My father laughed and patted my mother on her head. "But my girl friend wouldn't dare leave me, would she?" he said. "Who else would pay her department store bills for her?"

"Oh, you never can tell," my mother responded. "I just might elope with a millionaire one of these days."

"I'll bet he couldn't grow roses like mine," my father said. "Anybody can earn a million dollars, but not many people could grow the rose crop I'm going to have this fall. A rose is a rose is a rose, eh, Omar?"

"If you're finished with the sports page," I said, "could I have it?"

My father handed me the newspaper. "Roses are red," he recited, "violets are blue. Where you see three balls, you'll find a Jew."

"Hush," said my mother, giggling, "that's not nice to say."

220

"How about that, Omar?" my father insisted happily. "Is
that real poetry?"

"It's rotten," I said, trying not to laugh.

"Oh, yeah? Well, let me hear you do better, then."

I said nothing, and continued to read the ball scores.

There was a letter in the morning mail for me from my
Uncle Ben. I had written him earlier in the summer about
Major Frampton and my talks with him.

"What you say about your friend and his stories," he wrote,
"reminds me of a book that you may read and enjoy some
day when you are older. It's called *Tristram Shandy*, and one
of the characters is a retired army officer who spends most of
his time talking and thinking about the battles he once
fought in Flanders. The old soldier's brother thinks him silly
for carrying on about such things, but the brother does
exactly the same thing about other things. The point is that
sometimes it's very hard to know who's being silly and who
isn't."

Uncle Ben also repeated what he had told my parents in
his letter to them the previous day, that he would be paying
us a visit next month, because his studio wanted him to write
a movie script about the Civil War. It was too bad, I thought,
that Helen would be gone then; I would have liked her to
meet him.

Afterward I went over to the Cartwrights'. Helen and
Billy were in the living room, reading the paper. I felt a sudden pang of resentment at Billy's presence. If only he could
go away for the two days that Helen would still be here.

I handed Helen the shark's teeth we had found on the
sandbanks the previous morning.

"What are those?" Billy asked.

Helen showed him.

"What are you going to do with them?"

"Make them into a bracelet, I suppose," Helen said.

As I had anticipated, Billy was immediately eager to go back across the river and get some for himself. Helen had already told him about the *Endymion*, and Billy was all for going over to the peanut mill that minute and retrieving our boat, so as to return to the sandbanks when we got back from the beach.

"Nothing doing," I told him. "That boat's too small for that river. Besides, it's choppy out there today."

Billy went over and looked out the window at the river. "Okay," he said, "but the first calm day, let's go."

"You'd better not go over in your boat," Helen declared. "Wait till you get a bigger one."

"If we could sell the shark's teeth to a jewelry manufacturer, we could buy a big boat," Billy suggested.

"How do you know they're worth anything?" Helen asked him.

"They must be," Billy said.

He looked out the window at the sandbanks across the river. "Thousands of dollars' worth of rare jewelry over there," he said, "and we can't get to it."

"That's life," Helen declared.

"Well, don't tell where you got them," Billy told her. "We don't want to tip them off."

"Tip *who* off?" Helen asked.

"Other shark's teeth collectors. They'd be down here in no time."

"All right."

"How much," Billy asked after a moment, "do you think shark's teeth are worth on the open market?"

I looked through the open door into the Major's room. He was seated in the armchair by the window, half asleep.

Should I go in to see him? Now that I knew? Yes, I would, of course; I walked over to the door and entered the room. He saw me, blinked, and smiled. "Well, boy, how's it going?"

"All right, sir."

"A beautiful day for sailing, isn't it?"

"Yes, sir."

"You don't see many sailing ships any more," the Major declared. "When I was a boy, the waterfront was crowded with them. Nowadays, though, if I see two of them on an entire day's run across the harbor, I'd be quite surprised."

There it was again. He was speaking as if he were still the captain of the *Sappho*. The cooler weather seemed not to have helped at all, as Helen's mother and Mrs. Cartwright had hoped it would. He talked on, sometimes about the *Sappho*, sometimes about other matters. At times, as when he got on the subject of the Fort Sumter Celebration next month, he seemed perfectly sensible, quite aware of things. He talked eagerly then, anxiously, holding onto the subject tightly, fighting to keep his mind focused on it, as if it were a difficult and important thing to do. He would frown and fall silent a moment to collect his thoughts. Then the frown would disappear and his face would assume a tired and faraway look, and he would lapse back into talk of the *Sappho*, or the earthquake, or something else in the long-ago past, as if his effort had failed and he had given up trying to hold on. It was very strange; the Major seemed to be traveling back and forth between one time and another, and I could never tell exactly what time he thought he was living in when he was speaking.

He seemed changed physically, too; his eyes, though still a bright blue, were somewhat watery and filmed, and his chin seemed to have sagged a little. I noted, too, that he was in great need of a shave. I could hardly recall his being so unshaven before; he had always been so immaculate and neatly groomed.

Mrs. Cartwright came into the room. "Father, you'd better stop talking with Omar so much now and take your nap,"
she told the Major. "You don't want to get overtired, you
know."

"All right," said the Major, "all right." He got slowly to
his feet and began removing his bathrobe. He was wearing
long white pajamas with a thin pink stripe. I had never
seen him quite so shaky. After I said goodbye and left the
room, I heard the Major easing into his bed, and Mrs.
Cartwright asking him how he felt, and the Major mumbling
something about being a little tired but he would be all right
in a day or two.

We played around the house that morning. After lunch
Mrs. Cartwright took us downtown to the movies while she
went to her bridge club. I kept remembering that Helen
would be leaving in two more days, and I wished that Billy
Cartwright would leave us alone together for a while at least.
We sat through the movie in silence. I thought of trying to
put my arm around Helen, or to hold her hand, the way I
had seen older couples do in the movies, but with Billy there
I couldn't, even if I had been able to gather the nerve to do
so. When the movie was over we went to Cheeseman's
Double Dip on Wentworth Street and had some ice cream,
then walked to Billy's aunt's house over on Smith Street,
where Mrs. Cartwright was playing cards, and waited for her
to take us home.

As we drove back uptown I felt gloomy. Helen was going
home the day after tomorrow. I would probably not have a
single opportunity to be alone with her again. If only Billy
were going away tomorrow on another business trip with his
father to Orangeburg. But he was not. The less than two
days remaining of Helen's visit would pass and then we
would say goodbye, and that would be all.

Billy talked away about the movie, relating the plot in great detail to his mother. Helen said little; neither did I. It was as if there were a wall between us, and both of us knew there was no use trying to scale it. So we rode along without speaking, listening to Billy rattle on.

At Martschink's Cash-and-Carry Mrs. Cartwright pulled the car over to the curb and she and Billy went into the store.

"I wish we could go for a walk tonight," I said to Helen after a minute.

"Mother and I have to go down to Aunt Phyllis's," Helen said. "I wish we could, too."

That was out. So there was only tomorrow, and then the next day Helen and her mother would leave for Philadelphia, and it would be over like this, inconclusive, unsatisfactory.

"Tomorrow night," Helen said, "we'll probably have to stay in with Grandfather. Mother's so worried about him."

"Uh huh."

"Maybe," Helen said, "I'll go outside tomorrow night and take a walk."

"Maybe we could go for a walk together," I suggested. "I'd like to take a walk about then, too. I often go out walking in the evening."

"All right," Helen said. "I expect I'll feel like going for a walk about eight o'clock. I'll come walking by your yard and see whether you're leaving for your walk about then. Okay?" She spoke rapidly, for Mrs. Cartwright and Billy were coming toward the car.

"Yes," I agreed. "Fine."

Once more I was in high spirits. We continued on home, along Peachtree Street, and Helen and I chattered volubly about various things. Our sudden garrulousness puzzled Billy Cartwright. "Are you all going crazy?" he asked. "You must have been scratched with a phonograph needle." Helen giggled merrily, and I laughed too. "You must be losing your grip," Billy observed. We laughed some more.

"Couldn't we go for a picnic tomorrow?" Helen asked, after we had arrived at the Cartwrights' and Billy's mother had gone inside with her groceries.

"Where?" Billy asked.

"Oh, just out in the woods," Helen said. "How about that tree house of yours that you told me about?"

"A picnic out in Devereux?" Billy demanded. "What for?"

"Just for fun," Helen said. "We could pack lunch and go out in the tree house and eat it."

Billy shrugged his shoulders. "All right. I don't mind, if that's what you want."

So it was agreed. I was to provide the lemonade, and Helen and Billy would bring the sandwiches. We would take our lunch out to the tree house in the long tree that hung over the marsh, and picnic there in Devereux.

Why was the very word so exciting, I wondered—so mysterious, so alluring? *Devereux.*

13. THIS IS HELEN'S LAST DAY, I REALIZED WHEN I WOKE up the next morning. I shivered momentarily in excitement. There would be the picnic; my mother had readily agreed to supply the lemonade and had insisted upon providing a chocolate cake as well. Then, in the evening, there was the walk we would take, the final walk, down by the marsh along the river bank perhaps, in the darkness. And it was *she* who had suggested both, I thought exultantly. *She* had suggested them, because she wanted to be with me!

My father had the expected remarks to make at breakfast. Was I aware of the ways of red ants? Was I going to bring along Dr. Chisholm's book of poems to read to Helen? Had I ever heard the poem that went

> *A book of verses underneath the bough,*
> *A jug of wine, a loaf of bread, and thou*
> *Beside me singing in the wilderness;*
> *Ah wilderness were paradise enow!*

My mother told my father to stop teasing me. My father said that he wasn't teasing me, he was just trying to be helpful. "Well, don't be so helpful," my mother told him.

"Very well, son," my father said, "but I warn you: Many a woman with stars in her eyes has matrimony on her mind."

"Where are you going on your picnic?" my mother asked.

"Oh, just out in the woods somewhere."

"Where in the woods?"

"Out in Devereux." I tried to look casual.

"You'd better be careful out there," my mother said. "There are all sorts of strangers in those woods. Why don't you go down by the marsh instead?"

"We go out there all the time," I said. "What's wrong with it?"

"Well, I don't know," my mother said, "But I just don't like it. Does Helen's mother know that's where you're going on your picnic?"

"Sure," I told her. "Sure she does."

"Well, I wish you'd go down by the wharf."

"It's too hot down there," I said. "Don't worry; we go out to Devereux all the time. We'll be all right."

When I left for the Cartwrights' my father was working in the side yard, pruning his North China elm. Dominique had not come to work that morning either; it was the third time in succession he had failed to show up. "I'll have to go down to the fruit dock and see what's the matter," my father had told my mother. I had the feeling, however, that both of them were relieved that things had worked out this way. As for Viola, she had professed to know nothing about it, declaring that she had not seen Dominique for more than a week. But she sang at her work and was in high spirits.

"Be careful," my father told me as I walked past him toward the gate.

I strolled across the open lot that separated our house from the Cartwright place, carrying a basket with a thermos of lemonade and three big slices of chocolate cake wrapped in waxed paper. It was a bright, radiant morning, like the previous day, but much hotter. Summer was back again in full force.

I did not go in to see the Major when I arrived at the Cartwrights'; he was taking a nap, I was told. Helen and Billy were out on the porch reading the paper. I joined them, and we sat around for a while. Helen had acted almost studiously casual when I had come in, I noticed—as if she wanted to hide any obvious interest in my arrival.

We finally set off together down the path and into the woods. The heat was intense now, but we were in high spirits. Billy began whistling "The caissons go rolling along," and we sang together. Helen knew the names of all the trees and flowers and pointed them out as we strolled along, stooping over into a clump of weeds to pick out the blossom of a trailing Meadow Beauty, spying its elusive blue flower where I had noticed nothing but leaves and brush. Into the grove along the bank of the marsh we walked, leaving the road, treading single-file along the narrow pathway lined with vines and thornbushes. We went up the hill where the Major and Billy Cartwright had stood that day when we were in the boat, then down the opposite side to the green grass along the water's edge. No one was there, I noted with relief. We climbed up into the branches of a huge, spreading live oak, making our way to the tree house—not really a house, but a wooden platform with low walls, all but hidden from view by the foliage. Billy and I had built it the year before, having stolen some boards from a house under construction.

Billy scrambled up first, and I handed the lunch baskets to him. Then we both helped Helen up, and I followed. We sat down on the cool planking and spread our baskets of lunch on the floor. The thick foliage of the oak tree partially obscured our view of the river to the front as well as of the grass bank below, and the sunlight was filtered through a heavy mass of green leaves.

"Isn't this enchanting!" Helen declared. The morning was still, and the trees and foliage screened out the noise of the city across the fields. We could hear only, far off, the thumping of hammers from the houses being built on Peachtree Street, and the faint iron hum of a streetcar moving up Rutledge Avenue, a long way distant across the fields. Somewhere in a nearby glade catbirds were jangling their harsh cries, and off in the reed grass a marsh bird called brazenly.

Billy and I talked about building another and larger boat.

This time we would not hurry the job. We would make our plans carefully, measure everything, and follow the specifications exactly. We would not commit the error with the tar paper this time; we would get some calking cement and pack the seams thoroughly. It would be a much more presentable and seaworthy craft, we agreed. We wanted something that could cross and recross the river without difficulty in any but the roughest weather. We would have real oars with oarlocks, not homemade paddles.

"Let's eat!" Billy said after a few minutes. We began unwrapping the lunch. Helen poured the cold lemonade into paper cups and passed them around and we began eating the sandwiches. There was a double supply of cake, because Mrs. Cartwright as well as my mother had provided slices for each of us, and there were also some hard-boiled eggs that my mother had included.

We were halfway through lunch, chattering happily as we ate, when Billy suddenly said, "Shh! Listen!"

I heard the sound of a small animal moving about in a thicket nearby. "It's just a rat or a squirrel," I said.

"No, not that," Billy whispered. "Listen. There's a car coming along the road."

Sure enough, we could hear the sound of an automobile, off toward the south. Soon it hove into view, an old Ford sedan with red-spoked wheels, making its way along the rutted road from beyond the old peanut mill and into the grove. It pulled up to a clearing several hundred feet away, and we watched a man and a woman get out, the man clutching a rumpled paper sack. They began walking in our direction, along the path that led to the grassy bank below us by the water's edge.

Hidden by the foliage of the tree, through which we could

see but not be seen—unless someone knew we were there and was especially looking for us—we watched as the man and woman proceeded through the thicket. At one point the woman snagged her skirt, a dark-blue affair, on a thornbush, and the man helped her free it. They came on down the path until they were only a short distance from our tree.

"How's this?" the man asked. He was short, with a dark face and an unkempt shock of black hair that came down in sideburns.

"Why, I think it's real nice," the woman answered. They sat down on the thick, closely woven grass carpet in the sunlight.

The man leaned back and stretched, while the woman lay full length on the grass, placing her arm across her eyes. She was sallow complexioned, with straw-blond hair. They were talking about an office where they both evidently worked. We could hear some of what they said.

After a time the man reached over and took up the paper sack. He rolled back the top of it, displaying the neck of a bottle. Without removing the bottle from the sack, he unscrewed the cap and took a swallow. Then he too lay back until his head rested on the grass.

We ought to make a noise, I thought to myself. *Now, before anything happens.* But I was afraid to. We watched in silence.

For a while they both lay there immobile. Then presently the man reached out his hand, vaguely, seemingly without looking, and let it come down on the woman's blouse. For a moment he kept it there, and then he slipped it inside the blouse. The woman lay with her arm still over her face, seeming not even to notice what the man was doing. The man kept groping around with his hand. The woman stirred, moving her legs slightly.

Suddenly the man turned over on his side, placed his other

231

arm around the woman, and drew her to him. They rolled over together on the grass, writhing in a deep embrace, as we watched unseen above them.

My insides were constricted with excitement. I looked at Billy Cartwright; he was watching, wide-eyed. From the corner of my eye I glanced at Helen. She too was staring, her eyes fixed, her mouth half open, her face white.

The man and woman rolled over together, partly out of sight behind a thick branch that blocked our view. We could see their bodies moving, hear them breathing heavily, as if in great exertion.

After a little while the man sat up, crawled several feet away to where the bottle in the paper sack lay, and took another drink. He offered the bottle to the woman, who accepted it and held it up to her lips for several moments. They remained there for some minutes, the man sitting watching the marsh, the woman still lying on her back, her skirt high on her tan-white legs.

Finally both of them got to their feet and dusted off their garments. After the man had replaced the cap on the whisky bottle in the sack, they walked off together toward the automobile, arm in arm, oblivious to the vines and thorns along the path. I watched them go up to the automobile and get in. I heard the motor cough, start, then the automobile backed up, turned around in the clearing and drove off, trailing a thin dust cloud after it.

Billy Cartwright was grinning. "Boy, if they'd known we were up here!" he said.

I looked at Helen then. She was staring out at the clearing where the man and woman had been as if in a trance.

Then slowly she rose to her feet. She stepped out of the tree house onto the limb and made her way down stiffly, mechanically. When she reached the ground she looked once at the place where the man and woman had lain, then began walking off along the path through the woods, toward home.

"Hey, where are you going?" Billy called.

She did not reply. She continued walking, not looking to right or left. When she reached the clearing she stopped for a moment, and looked around again. For a moment she threw up her hands, as if to ward off a blow, and then began running toward home, down the path, until she disappeared from sight.

I wanted to go after her, to tell her it was a mistake, that what we had seen did not matter. But I knew that if I did, she would not listen; that I could do or say nothing now.

"I hope she won't tell what we saw," Billy said after a time. He reached down for the thermos jug. "Well, let's have some more lemonade," he said.

I shook my head. I was not at all hungry. My heart was pounding violently, sickeningly, inside my chest, and my stomach was heavy and solid.

"Let's go on back," I said.

"Why? We've still got all this cake to eat."

"I don't care," I told him. "I'm going."

"Oh, all right," Billy agreed.

Bearing the remains of the picnic, we clambered down from the tree and started back along the path, slowly, in single file.

It had been my fault, it seemed to me. In some way what had happened had been allowed by me to happen, had been willed by me. It was not simply that I might have cried out, made some noise, contrived in some way to alarm the man and woman, so that they would have known we were there and gone away. It was also that I had gone out to Devereux, had taken Helen there, for that purpose; had known that something would happen in Devereux that was wrong for us to see and know.

It was as if I had planned it, caused it.

I left Billy at his house and walked home quickly. Fortunately my parents were not around when I returned, and I went straight to my room.

I stayed there all afternoon, reading and listening to the radio, and sometimes I thought of what we had seen, and then of the look on Helen's face.

At dinnertime I was not hungry. To my parents' questions about whether we had enjoyed our picnic in Devereux I replied briefly and evasively.

As soon as it was dark, I went out of the house into the yard. Eight o'clock came and went and Helen did not appear. Until long after the appointed time I waited, hoping against hope, sitting by myself in the dark on the bench by the rose arbor.

14. THEY WERE GONE. I THOUGHT OF THAT AT ONCE THE
next morning. Helen and her mother had departed
for Philadelphia by now. It was all over. The two months
which had meant so much, promised so much, had ended.

That afternoon Billy Cartwright and I went off together
to retrieve the *Endymion* from where Helen and I had left
it by the old peanut mill. On the way, we passed once again
through Devereux, along the same path down which Helen
had retreated the day before.

"Wonder whether anybody's out there now cutting it?"
Billy mused as we walked by the clearing.

"I don't know," I said.

"They say that by the time you're twelve or thirteen, you
can do it."

"I know."

We walked along silently for a bit. "Did Helen and her
mother get off this morning?" I inquired, asking what I had
been wanting to ask from the outset.

"Uh huh."

Billy volunteered no more information. After a minute I
asked whether Helen had said anything about yesterday.

"No, she didn't say a thing. She stayed in her room. She
didn't even eat any dinner; told her mother she had a head-
ache."

I thought again of her white face, the way she had looked.

"We shouldn't have gone out there in Devereux for the
picnic," Billy said. "But she's the one who wanted to."

"She probably didn't know about it," I suggested.

"Sure she knew," Billy said. "She was there that day in the
boat, wasn't she?"

235

"Maybe she didn't know what they were doing."

"Aw, everybody knows about that. I bet she knows just as much as us."

We turned off the road onto the old railroad spur that led to the peanut mill. When we reached the bank where Helen and I had tied the *Endymion* to the tree, the boat was not to be found.

"Somebody must have stolen it," Billy said.

I looked all around but could find no trace. At length I climbed up into a low tree and scanned the nearby marsh. Some yards distant I saw something painted red, almost hidden in a high clump of reeds.

"It's out there," I said. "It must have floated away."

"Aw, let's just leave it," Billy said. "It's not worth the time and trouble it'd take to get to it. It leaks like a sieve anyway, and we can build a better one."

"All right." I had been waiting for him to say that.

"Come on," Billy said, "let's go over to the ball game." He started away.

Before I followed, I took one last look at the *Endymion*, its flat red paint, its squat, clumsy bulk. Billy was right; it was in no way worth bothering with. We would build another boat next spring that did not leak so, that was sharp-prowed and seaworthy and did not rock precariously with each swell of the river current; a boat that would navigate the river as well as the marsh creeks. Last spring, when we had built the *Endymion*, it had seemed like quite a boat. Then, all we had wanted to do was to paddle about a little in the marsh. Now we wanted a craft that would take us on deep water, in strong currents, like any other boat. The *Endymion* had served its purpose, I thought, but its usefulness was done.

On the way back from the ball game, I told Billy Cartwright about my strange experience of several nights ago with

Mr. Zinzer, which in the excitement of the past two days I had almost forgotten. To my surprise, Billy said that exactly the same thing had happened to him, not once but twice in recent weeks. Each time he had accepted Mr. Zinzer's invitation to ride up to the end of the line and back, and each time Mr. Zinzer had not spoken a word to him during the entire time.

Neither of us could make any sense of the whole thing, and we decided that Mr. Zinzer was simply losing his mind.

At supper that evening, my father began telling about his discovery that not only had Dominique been absent from his job at our house, but that he had not worked at the fruit dock all that week. My father had talked to the superintendent of the pier, who was a friend of his, but had found out no more than that Dominique had not reported for work. Whether he was sick, or had left town, nobody knew.

While my father was talking about this, the telephone rang, and I got up to answer it. It was Billy Cartwright's father, who wanted to speak with my father. They conversed for several minutes, with my father talking in a low voice as if he did not wish my mother and me to overhear him. Several times, however, I heard the words "Billy" and "Omar," and once I thought I heard him say, "Do you think I ought to call Pete Connolly at the power company and tell him?" and then, "Why don't you come on over after dinner and bring him, and we'll find out?" When my father returned to the table he gave no indication of what the conversation had been about. I was afraid that perhaps Mr. Cartwright had found out what had happened on the picnic in Devereux, and that the reference to the power company meant that Mr. Cartwright had somehow learned that the man and woman we had seen worked there. But if this was what Mr. Cartwright had called about, my father gave no sign of it, though he seemed preoccupied, and for the rest of the meal had little to say.

After dinner I went up to my room and began trying to decide what I was going to say to explain away the incident in Devereux. The only feasible course seemed to be to pretend innocence and ignorance of what had gone on there previously, and to take the line that we had never dreamed that anything like that could happen. This would probably not be thoroughly convincing, but our parents would have to pretend to believe that we did not know, for the sake of form. If I insisted, then, that I knew nothing about what went on in Devereux, my parents would have no recourse but to seem to believe me, though all of us would know better.

There was the sound of voices on the front porch, and my father came up the stairs, followed by Mr. Cartwright and Billy. I glanced at Billy; he seemed to be somewhat puzzled but not perturbed. Perhaps they had not found out, after all.

"Omar," my father began, "what's this about a streetcar conductor asking you to ride up to Magnolia Crossing with him the other night?"

I told him what had happened.

Mr. Cartwright turned to Billy. "Is that what happened to you too?"

"Yes, sir."

There was silence for a moment. Both my father and Mr. Cartwright seemed to be ill at ease, as if they were embarrassed about something.

"Are you quite certain," my father said to me, "that that's *all* that happened?"

"Yes, sir."

"You're sure the motorman didn't try to, uh, touch you, or come close to you, or anything like that?"

"No, sir." I was at a loss to understand what he had in mind.

"How about you, Billy?" my father asked. "Are you sure he didn't do or say anything, except drive the trolley?"

"No, sir." Billy shook his head. "He acted just like I wasn't even there, like he always does. I couldn't figure why he even wanted me to ride with him."

Mr. Cartwright spoke up. "Well, uh," he began, his face red, "uh, you see, uh, sometimes—I'm not saying in *this* case, of course—but sometimes older men are attracted to little boys."

I was quite perplexed at what he meant, and I could see that Billy was, too.

"But Mr. Zinzer didn't even speak a word the whole time," I said. "All he did was run the trolley, just as usual."

"Of course," said my father at once. "He probably just thought you'd like the ride. We're not saying that Mr. Zinzer's like that. But you see, some men are, as you'll find out some day, and you have to know about these things, and watch out for them."

"You mean Mr. Zinzer might want to do something bad to us?" Billy asked.

"Not at all," Mr. Cartwright replied hastily, "not at all. That isn't what we mean. It's just that, well, even though Mr. Zinzer very likely meant no harm at all, nevertheless you have to be careful, and not let yourself get in a situation where something might go wrong. Do you see what I mean?"

Billy frowned, looking just as puzzled as I was. "I think so . . ."

"At any rate," my father said, "I want you to promise me, Omar, that from now on you'll get off the trolley car at Versailles Street and come straight home at night, and not ride up to the end of the line with the motorman, no matter what the circumstances are. Okay?"

"Yes, sir."

"That's right," Mr. Cartwright added, "That goes for you too, Billy. You are not under any circumstances to ride up to Magnolia Crossing at night with the motorman. Do you understand?"

"Yes, sir."

Mr. Cartwright and my father got up. They were still rather flushed, as if they were embarrassed by the conversation and were relieved that it was over. "Well, that's all," Mr. Cartwright declared. "You coming home, Billy, or are you going to stay over here with Omar for a while?"

"I'll stay for a little while," Billy said.

As my father and Mr. Cartwright started out the door, Mr. Cartwright turned. "Oh, one more thing," he said. "If this motorman Mr. Zinzer asks either of you to ride up there with him at night again, will you promise to tell us right away?"

"Yes, sir," we agreed.

"What do you figure they're worried about?" Billy Cartwright asked, after his father and mine had gone back downstairs.

"I don't know," I said.

Billy thought a moment. Then he looked up. "I bet I know!" he said.

"What?"

"I bet they think Mr. Zinzer's a fairy!"

That was it! "I'll bet you're right," I said.

"That's what they meant about being attracted to little boys, and all," Billy declared.

"Yeah, that must be it!"

"Do you think Zinzer's really a fairy?" Billy asked after a moment.

"I don't know." I had never thought about it. "I don't think he's much of anything."

"If he's a fairy, you'd think he would have said something, or at least noticed us."

"Uh huh."

"Well, anyway, it's none of our business," Billy said. "I wouldn't ride up there with him again anyway."

"Boy, I was really worried when I heard my father talking to yours on the phone," I said. "I thought they'd found out about the man and woman in Devereux."

"No," Billy assured me, "there's no possible way they could ever find out, unless Helen tells her mother, and I don't reckon she will."

We thought about it for a moment. "Well, let's go catch baseball under the street lamp," Billy suggested.

"Okay," I said, and we went on outside.

What would happen next? What was there left to happen? I thought to myself. Devereux. Dr. Chisholm. The Major. The boat trip. Now Mr. Zinzer. What in the world could take place that had not already taken place?

The next morning the newspaper headlines shouted their answer.

TROLLEY MOTORMAN
SHOT TO DEATH

ESTRANGED WIFE

HELD IN MAGNOLIA

CROSSING SLAYING

Mr. Zinzer!
Dead!

And that woman I had seen on his trolley once, the red-faced one who had yelled at him—his wife! For the newspaper story told how for months he had feared for his life because of his estranged wife's threats. Twice before she had been committed to mental asylums, the story said.

And when the Marvelous Ringgold had stopped his cab to ask, "Is everything all right?" *that* was what he had meant! And I had thought he was playing a game.

241

And when I had watched Mr. Zinzer step to the door of his cab that evening at the end of the line, and he had seemed to teeter on the edge of the night before stepping down to the ground, he had been looking for her! He had been looking to see whether, out there in the darkness, she was waiting for him with a gun.

Over and over again I read the story.

He stopped at the end of the line, and his wife stole aboard the cab while he was reversing the trolley outside. When he climbed back inside, she pulled a revolver from her purse and began shooting at him.

He tried to flee, but two bullets struck him, one in the shoulder, the other in the stomach. He staggered to the open door, fell out onto the ground.

His wife stepped over him and tried to escape across the highway and the railroad tracks, but two attendants at a service station overtook her and held her for the police. A .38 revolver, with one bullet remaining in its chambers, was found in her purse.

Mr. Zinzer was rushed to the hospital in an ambulance, but died en route.

His name was Henry M. Zinzer. He was fifty-three years old. He had been employed as a streetcar motorman for twenty-eight years, the last thirteen of them on the Rutledge Avenue line.

Police found three bullets imbedded in the woodwork inside the cab.

The trolley car was Number 403.

On the Rutledge Avenue line.

While I was reading the paper, my father came into the living room.

"Did you see?"

"Yes," my father said.

I looked at him. "That was why he wanted Billy and me to ride to the end of the line with him."

"Yes."

"It was Number 403."

"Yes."

Yes, yes, yes, yes, yes.

My father said, "Look, you see he had no right, he had absolutely no right to ask you to do that. He was risking your life, and Billy's. She was insane, she would not have cared, you might have been killed."

"Yes," I said.

I saw him, standing at the door of the cab, looking into the dark. For a moment I saw his cheese-white face, his slumped shoulders, his worn black uniform with the brass buttons, his dully glossed shoes.

He is dead now, I thought. *He is the first person I have ever known who died. Except Mr. Weinberg across the street, when we lived on the Terrace and I was six or seven, and he was old and blind. Mr. Weinberg did not know me. Mr. Zinzer did, though he never said anything. Now he is dead.*

His wife had threatened his life before, the newspaper said, and he had asked for permission to refuse to transport her on his car, and had received it.

So she had waited around in the shadows at the end of the line, and while he was outside lowering the trolley for the downtown run, she had crept around the front of the cab and inside.

When he stepped back aboard, he saw her, pointing a pistol at him.

I wondered whether, when he saw she was there, his little round pig eyes blinked their granulated lids, expressing surprise at last.

"That business," my father said, "the other night, that we spoke to you about—that was mistaken. But it's worse,

243

really, because he had no right to expose children to danger like that."

"Why didn't he get the police to lock her up?"

"I don't know. Maybe there was no way he could prove that she threatened him. You can't just have people locked up without a good reason, you know."

All that time, when he was driving along, saying nothing, looking straight ahead, keeping the trolley car moving forward down the track, this had been what Mr. Zinzer was thinking about.

Thinking, every time he stepped out of the cab to change the trolley at night at the end of the line, that this time she would be there.

Number 403 was the car.

On the Rutledge Avenue line.

At midnight, at Magnolia Crossing, the end of the line.

I wanted to go and talk to the Major about it, to tell him about it all. But the Major was sick now, living in the past, and Helen was gone, while outside it was still summer, with everything so full and heavy and the weeds grown thick-green and rank, and there was no one I could tell.

PART THREE

The End of the Golden Weather

1. For several September days the sky had been high and blue, with feathery little white clouds scattered across it at a great height. Mares' tails, my father called them, and said they were made up of millions of tiny particles of ice. Now the white clouds had filled out until they covered the sky, and the sun shone through them with a halo-like ring. They had become darker, too, and heavier. The weather was warm and humid, hurricane weather, my father said. He followed the radio reports intently, for a tropical storm had been reported off the coast and was moving in our direction.

My father's emotions were mixed. He had followed the changing cloud patterns, noted the steady fall of the barometer, enjoyed the opportunity to try out his meteorological lore, to watch the weather happening around him. On the other hand, there were his roses. All summer long he had tended his precious garden, replacing the soil with black loam, watering it during the days of drought, feeding nourishment to it against the fierce midsummer heat, until now the fall season was coming closer and the buds were already forming for what would soon be his triumph. If a hurricane struck, what might it not do to his rose garden? So he had looked apprehensively at the procession of clouds that signified the increasing likelihood of a blow, until now the portents were ominous and imminent.

"If it comes," he said, "it'll hit tomorrow morning." He drove stakes into the ground by the rose bushes, tore up white cloth into strips, and fastened the stalks to the stakes for support against the wind. He shook his head. "The buds are

247

exposed," he told my mother. "They're just far enough along to catch it, if the hurricane hits." And barring an unforeseen turn in the direction of the hurricane, that was what it was going to do.

I was going downtown that morning, to get a long-postponed haircut and deliver a package to Aunt Ellen's apartment. Before I left, however, the telephone rang and Mrs. Cartwright asked me whether I could come over for a little while. Some men were coming to interview the Major about a radio play they were writing about the Charleston earthquake, and she thought that I might be able to help the Major refresh his memory. The way the Major had been acting in recent weeks, there was no knowing whether he might be able to concentrate on the subject. So I took the package for Aunt Ellen and went on over to the Cartwrights'.

I got there just as the automobile with the letters wcsc— RADIO CHARLESTON painted in gold on the side drove up to the house. Billy Cartwright was already in the Major's room. The two radio men, whose names were Mr. Bunker and Mr. Koger, told the Major what they wanted.

At first the Major did not quite understand. "Earthquake?" he said. "There's not going to be an earthquake. Hurricane, maybe. Reminds me of the one in '93, when—"

Mrs. Cartwright interrupted. "No, Father, they know about the hurricane. They're going to do a radio broadcast on the Charleston earthquake, and they want to ask you about it."

"Oh," said the Major. "Want to know about the earthquake, huh? It was bad, plenty bad. Frightening thing."

"Were you in it, sir?" one of the men asked.

"Of course I was in it. The whole thing."

There was a pause, while the Major sat there in his rocking chair and frowned.

"Tell them," I said after a minute, "about Captain Jervey and the earth waves."

248

The Major smiled, and his eyes seemed to grow brighter. "Oh, *that*. Yes, sir, old Captain Jervey, master of the schooner *Caroline*. A good friend of mine, too. Well, he was sitting out on his piazza when it happened—fifteen seconds after 9:51 P.M., to be exact. You see, there was a clock in the telegraph office, and when the earth tremors hit it stopped at exactly . . ." And the Major was off, in his old form, the way he used to talk, while the two radio men were busily scribbling notes. Occasionally he would falter, but Billy and I knew the whole story by heart, so we would remind him about this or that episode he had not yet mentioned, and he would resume his narrative at once.

After the Major had talked for almost an hour, Mrs. Cartwright came back into the room and suggested that he was getting tired. The radio men thanked him and prepared to leave. They offered me a ride downtown as far as Calhoun Street, and I got into their car and rode off with them.

One of the men had talked with the Major back in the spring. "He's certainly slipping back," he remarked. "Last April he was just as alert and vigorous as could be. It's too bad."

"I wonder whether he'll still be able to take part in the Fort Sumter Celebration," the other man asked.

"Oh, yes, sir," I answered at once. "He wouldn't dare miss that. He's been waiting for it all year."

"Hope this hurricane doesn't blow Fort Sumter away," one of them remarked.

"Oh, well, even if it does hit us, there'll be a week to tidy it up and make repairs before the big day," the other said.

The idea—it had not previously occurred to me—that the hurricane might have any effect on the Fort Sumter Celebration was disturbing. The Major had been waiting so long for it. If it were once again postponed, might he not have drifted so far away by the time it was held that he would not even know what was happening?

249

I thought about this as I got out of the automobile and walked toward Aunt Ellen's apartment. The Fort Sumter Celebration *must* come now, while he could still be part of it. To wait so long, only to lose—that must not be. Whether or not he was actually at Fort Sumter during the war was unimportant now; he must not miss it!

At the Warwick Apartments I found Mrs. Bready and left the package for Aunt Ellen with her. We talked for a little while and then I said goodbye and walked out the front entrance into the courtyard. *Zoom!* the wind hit me. A crazy, tilting wind, mad, careening, blowing salt air every which way. Not savagely, not even too strongly, but wildly, excitingly.

On the sidewalk by the Warwick Court Pharmacy a Negro delivery boy was leaning from a bicycle whose seat was elevated as high above the frame as it would go. His long legs were touching the coping, his trousers flapped in the breeze, and his scuffed shoes tapped a syncopated rhythm as he whistled into the wind: "Who dat climbin' on de wall? Look lak phenobarbital." Overhead the palmetto fronds swayed back and forth. Green and tan awnings slapped sharply above the iron-railed apartment balconies above my head. The wind cut along the hedges, swirled in the courtyard, moaned wickedly under the overhanging marquee of the drugstore. A sheet of newspaper, sucked up by the wind, was sent dashing and sliding along the gutter. Over Colonial Lake a sea bird dipped low. Riding the currents of air, it was borne aloft and away.

Off the coast the hurricane was brewing; tomorrow it might come blasting ashore. Meanwhile the salt spray, flying leaves, tingling air. And the delivery boy, lolling on his bicycle at the curb by the drugstore, whistled his song: "Since my gal and me ain't together, It's all I can do to keep warm."

I walked along Wentworth Street. Automobiles came and

went, a streetcar rumbled by (the motorman someone new, not Mr. Zinzer—never again Mr. Zinzer. There was a new man on the night shift with the Marvelous Ringgold). At Coming Street I sniffed the rotten produce from the open stalls of the grocery store at the corner—stale cabbages, wilted lettuce, banana stalks with fruit ripe and blackening. (Had Dominique carried them ashore from the fruit boat? No, for Dominique had not worked there for over a month now. He had gone away; no one knew where.)

At St. Philip Street I passed the open waiting room of Dr. Jenkins' optometry offices, and peered within, observing the waiting patients grouped about the room in the dim light. In the recesses at the rear a door opened, and through it I could see the lighted chart with its black block letters:

E

N Z

Y L V

U F V P

N R T S F

O C U G T R

I passed Cheeseman's Double Dip, with pale-pink and green froth and little tin spoons, bleach-blonde waitresses in stained pastel uniforms, a radio pulsating cheap sounds. Past the imitation marble façade and into the L-shaped confusion of the S. H. Kress & Company five-and-dime.

Now out into the fresh, sharp air of King Street, along its narrow, busy way, past a millinery store (*Charleston's Exclu-*

sive Style Center), bookshop (*Legerton's*—sign showing ledger and ton, equally balanced on scale), bakery (*the freshest cakes in town*), music store (*the South's oldest music store*). In the windows of the W. T. Grant Company—10¢– 25¢–$1.00—I saw book bags, pencil boxes, tablets, rulers, lunch boxes, fountain pens, bottles of ink, pencil sharpeners, scissors, paste, and a lettered sign depicting a fatuous, rosy-cheeked schoolboy, reading SCHOOL DAYS AHEAD! But not for two weeks yet, at least. Perhaps the storm. . . . Sufficient unto the day the evil thereof, I thought, with a quick glance up Hasell Street to where the temple, still closed for the summer, stood behind its iron railing.

Before Felder's Palace Barber Shop the spiral pole twisted in endless revolutions, the red and white stripes rising bloodlessly from the base, curving upward one after another until they vanished abstractly into the air. I opened the glass doors, stepped down onto the black-and-white tiled floor.

"There you are!" said Oliver, thin and tan-skinned, with long hair that spread out from his temples in two gray tiers. He removed the striped sheet from the black leather arm of the barber chair, grasped the crank underneath, and lowered the seat several notches. "Trying to make the barbers all starve?" he asked as I stepped onto the chrome footrest and vaulted into the cushioned seat.

"How's the Major these days?" the barber at the next chair asked. It was Dash, the only man to whose hands the Major ever used to entrust his shave.

"He's all right," I said.

"He hasn't been in for quite a while," Dash said. "I heard he was sick."

"He hasn't been feeling too good in this hot weather," I explained.

"I'll bet he perks up next week for the Celebration," someone said, and chuckled.

"He's told me many a time that he wasn't going to let anything happen to him until after the Fort Sumter Celebration," Dash declared. "He said he's been looking forward to it for too long."

The hurricane news came over the radio. The storm was approximately 100 miles off the coast, the announcer said. If its present direction and rate of speed were maintained, it would come ashore about 11 A.M. tomorrow. Small craft were urged to keep to their bases, and all precautions should be taken. People in low-lying areas were advised to prepare to evacuate them by 6:00 P.M. unless the storm changed course. High tide tomorrow would be at 2:03 A.M., and low tide at 8:16 A.M. For further details keep tuned to this station.

"Man, if that thing smacks in here on high tide, we're going to have a rough time," someone remarked.

"According to what the report said, it's going to be closer to low tide," said another.

"I hope so, but you never can tell."

"I just hope it doesn't tear things up like in 1911. You remember that?"

"I'll tell the good Lord I do. I was living down on Magazine Street then, and the water rose up two feet in our bedroom."

"Man, I was worse off than that. I was over on Sullivan's Island, Station 9. My father was in the Army over there, you know. Before that wind stopped blowing, our house shifted a foot and a half off the pilings."

"How high did the tide get that time?"

"Over thirteen feet, I believe. I remember it washed that lumber schooner right up onto East Bay Street."

"Yeah, man, I remember that."

"Yes, sir, that was some blow."

"It sure was."

Afterward I walked along Market Street, through the almost deserted stalls of the city market, crowded ordinarily with Negroes come in from the sea islands with produce, but empty of life today save for one old woman with a few ears of late-season corn for sale. "Corn, suh?" she asked, though she knew I would not want any, and spoke to me more in greeting than in question. "No thank you," I replied.

" 'e sure blowing up," she said.

"It sure is."

I came out opposite the Custom House. Atop that stone structure with its wide tiers of steps and tall, thin marble columns, a wind gauge spun vigorously in the air, while above that, on a swaying flagpole, the signal of peril swung briskly out in the wind: two red warning pennants, each with a black square in its center. I remembered Dr. Chisholm's poem about the hurricane flags calling the fisherfolk back from their seining. Were the trawlers out at sea in this? I would walk down to Adger's Wharf, I decided, and see for myself.

Along East Bay Street, scraps of paper blew in all directions. Awnings were lashed up tightly against sides of buildings. A red wagon wheel, suspended by chains, swayed back and forth over the doorway of the I. M. Pearlstine Hardware Company. In front of the William Bird Paint Company a Negro man perched halfway up a stepladder, removing a golden whale from its moorings. Automobiles hurried by, their tires swishing along the damp pavement.

Before the restaurant of Pete Demos, at the corner of Broad and East Bay, two men stood talking. One was our neighbor, Mr. Simons, the other a friend of my father's whom everybody called Strong Cigar, and who wrote a column for the evening paper under that pen name.

"Boy, don't you think you'd better go home before you get blown out into the harbor?" the man named Strong Cigar asked.

"I just saw your father," Mr. Simons said, his eyes twinkling. I knew there was a joke coming, for of course my father was at home. "He said he was going out to sea with the Coast Guard to get some first-hand information on *this!*" Mr.

Simons chuckled happily at his own fancy, and the man named Strong Cigar grinned, for my father's passion for the weather was notorious.

"Yes, sir," Mr. Simons continued. "He said he wasn't going to settle for any of this radio baloney. He said he was going out to get the *facts!*" They laughed again, and I joined them.

The man called Strong Cigar turned to leave. "Now, Herbert," he said, "you stay right here and make sure that this corner doesn't blow away."

"You can just bet your sweet life I will," Mr. Simons told him. "Pete Demos and I are going to ride it out together!" And they laughed at the thought.

Mr. Simons told me that he would be driving home in an hour if I wanted a ride, and I arranged to come by his office. He walked away, up Broad Street, and I crossed over to Exchange Street, walking past the blue-flared windows of the Engraving Company and out toward Adger's Wharf.

There was no Clyde liner in port today. From the open water beyond the harbor, the wind streamed briskly. The trawler fleet, moored to the docks for safety, rose and dropped with the tide. They had not needed Dr. Chisholm's warning after all. Over the low concrete seawall the spray came crashing, forming pools of water on the shell soil beyond. In unison the tugboats of the White Stack Towboat Company rocked away as the harbor swells tugged at their hawsered hulls. From the high white stack of the *Cecilia*, largest of the three, a trace of smoke planed out. A helmeted man carefully picked his way along a narrow gangplank leading from the wharf toward a gray launch.

I went up close to the seawall, until the salt spray pricked my cheeks. The surface of the water was split into a million planes and hollows, and as the waves came thudding into the wall they slipped and slid into each other, forming wild patterns of froth.

I missed the Major then. I missed his set speech, his recitation—"But still, along yon dim Atlantic line, The only hostile smoke Creeps like a harmless mist above the brine . . ." Now I was alone, and the green combers were crashing in from the Atlantic, the wind was whistling ominously, and the spray was cold and drenching.

To the southeast I saw the low bulk of Fort Sumter pressed close to the horizon, as if braced for the hurricane. A lone green launch cut choppily through the waves on its way around the point of the harbor. Far beyond Sumter, scarcely visible at all on the expanse of heaving water, a ship beat out to sea, perhaps to ride out the blow, its smoke a black smudge on the lowering face of the deep. Behind, a bank of gray-black clouds leaned terribly toward me where I stood.

2. By late afternoon the wind was blowing steadily, and the rain had begun to fall, slashing downward in sheets, rattling against the windows of our house. Soon it was quite dark, and we could see nothing but a shimmering wall of rain outside. On my father's cyclo-stormograph barometer a receding line dipped lower and lower, and my father was certain that the full force of the hurricane would be upon us by the coming morning.

He had spent the day while I was downtown making all the preparations he could against the hurricane's advent. Not only had he fastened the rose bushes to sticks to protect them, but he had procured a quantity of waxed-paper sandwich bags and a box of rubber bands. These he had fastened around many of the rosebuds for protection, until the garden, when I saw it upon my return home with Mr. Simons, looked like a bizarre kind of Christmas tree with bulbous white ornaments.

Mr. Simons saw it too, and he chuckled merrily. "What's that you've got there?" he shouted out to my father from his car. "A toadstool bush?"

"You go to hell!" my father had yelled back.

"Why don't you make them waterproof?" Mr. Simons called to him. "It might cost a little more, but you could use them again later!" For some reason, both he and my father laughed uproariously at this.

Until the rain became so heavy and the darkness so complete that it was no longer possible to see anything from the windows, my father kept pacing nervously about the house, glancing again and again at the rose garden and then at the cyclo-stormograph. Meanwhile my mother placed candles about the house, filled all available pots and jugs with drinking water, and saw to it that the flashlights were working properly.

We sat down to dinner with the wind moaning and howling outside, setting up a continuous roar in the oak trees across the lawn, while the water sang through the open gutter pipes along the roof. My mother served the meal, for she had sent Viola home early in a taxicab before the rain became too heavy.

"I hope Viola's house has a good roof on it," my mother said.

"Those old houses over on Meeting Street have weathered more than one hurricane," my father assured her. "I expect they'll weather this one."

"Where do you suppose Dominque is these days?" my mother asked.

"No telling," my father said. "But I don't think Viola cares any more, at any rate."

"Well, I certainly am glad for that," my mother declared. "She was in a foul mood for a while, whatever the cause."

"Did the cut on her arm ever heal up?" I asked.

"Yes, indeed," my mother told me. "She hasn't had any more trouble with it whatever."

I plied my father for descriptions of previous hurricanes. How strongly did the wind blow? How long did they last? Would it get worse as the center of the hurricane approached? I remembered the Major's tales of the ravages that previous hurricanes had worked, of large ships being blown up onto the shore, roofs ripped off buildings, church steeples blown down. My father assured me that in our house, new and sturdily built as it was, there was nothing to worry about. The roof would be certain to withstand whatever winds the hurricane might develop. "Might blow a few shingles off, that's all," he said. The damage a hurricane did, he told me, was usually confined to uprooted trees and blown-down wires, except in sections of town where houses were in poor repair.

But the wind blew ever more strongly and steadily and the rain cascaded down, and I was apprehensive. My uneasiness was not helped by my father's going to the window every few minutes and glancing out toward the rose garden, even though he could see nothing at all. My mother would tell him to sit down, because he was making everyone nervous, and my father would agree, but minutes later he would be back on his feet again and mopping with his handkerchief at the condensation on the windowpanes in a vain attempt to see how his rose bushes were doing.

To divert our minds, my mother began speculating on when Uncle Ben would arrive. He was driving across the continent in his automobile, with stops in Houston, New Orleans, and Birmingham. Though I had not seen him in more than two years, I remembered his last visit vividly, for he had arrived with a new bicycle for me, the first I had ever owned. I asked whether the hurricane might delay Uncle Ben's arrival, and was assured that it would not. Would the hurricane be likely to cause any hitch in the plans for the Fort Sumter Celebration? Of course not, my mother said. But my father declared that it might, if too much damage was done. "It probably wouldn't hurt the Fort, though it might cause some damage to the dock," he said, "but if it tears up the downtown area too much, they might have to postpone it a few weeks."

"That's not fair," I said. "It's been postponed twice already, and the Major's waited too long as it is."

My father laughed. "Whether it's fair or not doesn't make the slightest difference, buddy. Hurricanes aren't ever very fair."

"But if God makes hurricanes, why would He do it?"

My father shrugged. "You'll have to ask God about that."

After dinner we sat around in the living room, listening to

the radio, with the wind and the rain battering away outside. The static was so bad, however, that after a little while my father turned the set off. "Must be blowing fifty miles an hour out there already," he said. He got up and went over to the window for the hundredth time, swabbing at the fogged panes with his handkerchief, peering out in vain and shaking his head.

I decided to telephone Billy Cartwright and exchange views of the hurricane. When I picked up the receiver, however, there was no sound. The line was dead. I flicked the bar several times to no avail.

"The phone's off," I told my father.

"The wind must have blown some wires down," my father said. "Service probably won't be restored now until after the hurricane passes."

I remained in the living room with my parents for a long while, for I was nervous about going upstairs to my room by myself, though I did not want to admit it. But at last I yawned once too often and my mother insisted that I go up to bed. She handed me a flashlight. "Here, take this," she told me, "but don't use it unless you have to. You might need it later if the power goes off."

I trudged on upstairs, stopping by the phone to see whether by any chance it was back in operation. It wasn't. Once upstairs I walked down the hall toward my room, the rain drumming on the roof over my head as I went. I had the odd feeling of expecting to find something wrong in my room, something connected with the storm. Exactly what I expected I was not sure, but the fact that here upstairs I was nearer to the storm made me so apprehensive that it was only with an effort that I could force myself to turn on the light in my room, as if some unknown peril awaited me there. I gritted my teeth, reached inside the open door, and flicked on the light switch.

All was as it should be, however: the single bed, the bureau with the framed photograph of Carl Hubbell on it, my desk and typewriter, the sofa along the side wall, the low fiberboard walls that slanted inward and upward to conform to the shape of the roof overhead. What was different was the sound of the storm—much closer and more relentless than it had seemed downstairs.

Beyond the two curtained windows near my bed, the blackness of the night and the driving rain obscured all vision, and I could hear the boughs of the great oak trees outside as they strained and creaked under the impact of the hurricane, while the furious rush of the rain in the gutters produced a metallic singsong, high pitched and frenzied. The rain thudded against the roof, rattled and beat at the dormer windows across the room that faced to the south.

I undressed for bed, placed the flashlight on the bed table, climbed into bed and turned on the radio, to see whether I could hear any further news about the hurricane. The static was so bad that after barely managing to hear the local station announce that the blow was due to strike the coast about 6:00 A.M., I had to turn it off.

I lay there listening to the storm. There were lightning flashes now, and the momentary flares of light made it possible for me to see the dim outlines of the oak boughs pitching and tossing as they bent away from the wind and rain. The crash of the thunder was muffled by the general din of the hurricane.

So this was a hurricane! I had imagined something dramatic, exciting, something in which I would be actively, even perilously involved. Instead, here I was in my room as usual, lying in my bed, with the elements raging outside, but with nothing to do myself but listen to the storm and think about it.

The wind roared on, the rain continued to drive against the windowpanes and the clapboard sides of the house, coming in bursts, drumming on the roof, rattling on the dormers,

261

flailing against the outer walls. With rumbles of thunder and quick flashes of lightning it bore down upon the house, the trees, the garden, the city. Nothing mattered but the storm. There would be no launch making its way down the Ashley River tonight, no late train rumbling across the railroad bridge. The streetcars had probably ceased to run; even if they had not, I would not be able to tell, for they would not be audible half a block away, so frenzied was the onslaught of the storm. There was nothing I could hear or see, nothing but the furious hurricane.

The overhead light in my room was still on; I got out of bed and turned it off. Then on an impulse I reached out and drew the door to my room shut as well, closing my room off from the rest of the house. I was too tired to read, so I turned off the bed lamp. Before I closed my eyes for sleep, however, I picked up the flashlight my mother had given me and flicked on the switch. I trained the beam upon the window near my bed. The light pearled against the rain-fogged windowpane, making a glistening circle of bright droplets that streaked and ran down the glass, reflecting the light in ripples and beads, letting in the black night not at all.

Insulated against the hurricane's force, I felt cut off and insulated from the world. The knowledge that the telephone was out of commission only increased this feeling. It was as if I were in a ship, alone on a savage and inhuman ocean, while outside, elsewhere on that ocean, there were other such ships, each one alone, solitary—and for each one of them it was as if the others did not even exist. There was a kind of finality to it, a sense of entire separation. I felt almost as if all the calm, sunny days, the months when people went about their business, were only temporary interludes, impermanent, while this was the true weather.

For some reason, then, I remembered that evening last spring when I had sat in the temple while Dr. Raskin was delivering his sermon. I remembered the vision I had had of myself as honored and selected, certain that all would be untroubled and serene. How innocent and naïve I had been then, how arrogant and smug in my self-esteem! For so much had happened since then. Here I was now, with the hurricane howling, warm and dry for the moment to be sure, but alone and at the mercy of great forces. For if the wind rose and rose in its intensity, became powerful enough, could it not rip off this roof, demolish this house, all houses, the entire world? My father's words at supper returned to me. "You'll have to ask God about that." Less than a week ago it had been warm, sunny; now the hurricane ripped savagely at the city, tremendous, inhuman.

If I were a German instead of an American, and lived in Germany, I thought, where would I be tonight? In a concentration camp? Or forced to go about with a yellow six-pointed star on my arm, exposed to the jeers and blows of all the toughs? Would my father come home one day, his face bruised and cut and blood trickling from his mouth? Every day the newspapers were full of such doings. But I was not a German; I was an American, and that was far away, across the ocean. It could never happen to me. Here I was no mere Jew, no kike with thick lips and a hook nose; I was a member of one of the Fine Old Jewish Families. Everyone knew that. But the hurricane wind tore at the windows, the rain pelted the roof, growing ever more violent, pounding, slashing. If that roof were removed, if that thin layer of boards, tar, asphalt tiles were suddenly whipped away . . .

I remembered the hymn again:

> *There is a mystic tie that joins*
> *The children of the martyred race,*
> *In bonds of sympathy and love*
> *That time and change cannot efface.*

And the hurricane roared on.

*   *   *

Much later, in pitch blackness, I was awakened suddenly by footsteps in the hall outside my bedroom. I reached over in haste to turn on the bed lamp. It did not go on. Thoroughly frightened, I grabbed for the flashlight as the door to the bedroom opened, and I recognized my father with a lantern in one hand and towels in the other. "The light's out," I said, shivering.

"I know. The wires must be down somewhere," he replied. "The rain's coming in around the windows, and it's leaking through to the ceiling downstairs. The floor over here is sopping wet."

Outside, the storm thundered. Uneasily, I got out of bed and helped my father as he mopped up the floor and wedged towels along the window ledges, and then I followed him downstairs, for I did not want to be alone.

My mother was in the kitchen, brewing coffee on the gas range by kerosene lamplight. "It's only four o'clock," she said. "Why don't you go back to sleep?"

"I'm awake," I said. "I don't want to."

She looked at me a moment. "All right, then, but go back upstairs and get into your clothes."

"I'm all right," I insisted. "I'm not cold."

"Yes, you are. It's chilly. Now go on upstairs and dress. There's nothing to be afraid of."

I stood there a few seconds, then went off to do as she told me. "Try not to step in the water by the windows," she called after me, "or you'll track up the house."

Afterward we sat in the kitchen around the table, my mother in her long, flowing dressing gown, my father and I dressed.

"Is this the worst part?" I asked.

My father nodded. "That wind's probably blowing close to a hundred miles an hour in gusts."

My mother placed two coffee cups on the table and poured

hot, black coffee into them. She looked at me. "Would you like some?" she asked.

"Yes." I had never been allowed to drink coffee at home.

"All right," she said, and poured a cup for me as well. I stirred some sugar and cream into the smoking liquid and sipped it. It was strong and very hot, and as I drank it the warmth spread along my throat and chest.

All at once there was a loud thumping out on the porch. I jumped in fright.

"The porch chairs!" My father sprang to his feet. "They've come loose from where I had them wedged. That wind must be terrific."

I started after him. "Omar, you stay in here!" my mother called, but I paid no attention.

My father removed a raincoat from the stairway railing and put it on. I opened the hall closet, took out my own raincoat, and slipped into it. As I did, my father glanced at me but said nothing. He unbolted the front door, forced it open against the wind, and went outside. I followed him out, onto the rainswept porch. The water was cascading upon us in great sheets, and the wind blew so fiercely that it was necessary to hold onto the side of the house to keep our footing. The three oaken porch chairs were lying on their sides on the slippery porch floor.

"Push them against the railing and leave them!" my father called. We caught hold of the chairs and slid them over to the railing, where my father shoved the backs under the bottom rail to anchor them. Then we crept back along the wall to the door, tugged it open, and slipped inside. Despite our raincoats, we were drenched from head to foot.

"Take off those clothes right away!" my mother told me. I trudged upstairs to do her bidding, leaving a stream of water behind me as I went.

Upstairs, I pulled off the wet clothing, dried myself off with a bath towel, and climbed into fresh clothes. I heard the wind blowing ever more violently, the rain crashing against the house, and I felt that surely the hurricane's entire force was at that moment being turned upon us. Yet, though windows leaked and water dripped from a wet spot on the ceiling, our home was proof against it.

I felt a thrill of exhilaration.

Let the storm blow! I said under my breath. Goddammit, let it blow!

So the hurricane droned on. Periodically we made trips to the windows to replace drenched towels. Gradually the blackness outside grew somewhat lighter, and we knew by the clock that it was morning, but the force of the hurricane did not seem to abate. Then, at length, as we sat listening, the wind gradually died down to a low moan, and the rain slackened in its force. I went over to look out the window. The yard was a solid sheet of water, and the bushes and shrubs were leaning away from the gale. Across the way in the Simons' yard great limbs of trees lay on the ground, and branches were scattered everywhere. Over everything there played an eerie green-white light.

"Is it finished?" I asked my father.

He shook his head. "I don't think so. We're probably right in the eye of the hurricane."

He was staring at his rose garden. The plants were twisted and bent, and the paper bags he had placed over the buds were all gone.

Minutes later, as I watched and listened, the rain began again, the wind resumed as before, and the hurricane was back in full force.

For an hour or more the storm raged, the rain falling in sheets, the wind howling, but from a different direction now, coming from the west and north instead of the south and east. At last, gradually, the force subsided, the sky grew visibly lighter, and it became possible to see out of the windows for some distance.

Eventually the rain was no heavier than in an average shower, and the wind blew only in occasional gusts.

Later I put on my raincoat and helmet again and went outside with my father to examine the damage. In the front yard, there were a few shrubs uprooted, and the impact of the storm had knocked over and shattered a concrete birdbath, but save for the pools of rain water spread over the lawn, and stray branches and leaves scattered about, no other damage was visible. The North China elm tree in the side yard was intact and unharmed.

Beyond the fence, though, the great water oaks were torn and gashed, with large limbs ripped off and dangling helplessly, while still others, split completely from their sockets, lay flat on the ground.

As for the rose garden, it was devastated. It lay three inches deep in water, and the bushes were bent and split, with leaves and twigs strewn everywhere. The trailing vines were hanging off the arbors, and the plants were bare and denuded.

All my father's work, all the months of pruning and planting, seemed wasted. It would be a year at least before his rose garden could reach full bloom now.

My father looked at the havoc. "Lord Almighty," he said.

Overhead the sky was clearing now, with tiny white clouds up in the remote blue. The rain had all but ended, and the air, though scented heavily with the odor of brine, was fresh and bracing. In the fields toward Rutledge Avenue, frogs by the thousands were singing happily.

"Well, the North China elm wasn't hurt, anyway," I remarked, trying to say something cheerful.

My father shook his head.

3. Later that afternoon my father drove downtown, taking Billy Cartwright and me with him, to see what the storm had done. Roofs of houses were torn off and crumpled in heaps of rusty red tin. Store windows were smashed, with scattered glass spread over the street, and some streets were blocked by trees, with severed branches lying in every direction. Wires were looped in crazy patterns over bent power poles. In some of the low-lying districts the water still stood two feet deep along the streets. The spire on the Lutheran church in Citadel Square was twisted into a bent, oddly cocked design, like the peaked tassel on a circus clown's cap. At Washington Park, by the courthouse, the shade trees were down in all directions; less than half were left standing. Mailboxes were toppled everywhere, and store signs set awry. Down along the waterfront small craft, up-ended, were strewn about, with one sizable launch lying squarely across the railroad tracks by the Custom House.

I kept wondering how Viola had fared during the hurricane. Some of the most severe damage we saw had taken place in the neighborhoods occupied by Negroes. We saw homes with roofs ripped away and the interiors exposed and open to the elements, and the Negro occupants, now that the rain had ceased, working away at salvaging some of their possessions.

"Let's go and see how Viola made out," I suggested to my father.

"Oh, she's all right. It's high ground up there where she lives," he told me. But he turned the car up Meeting Street and toward her house.

268

A few sheds and garages were down in her neighborhood, and several houses had layers of clapboard ripped away from their sides. Viola's house, however, appeared, when we drove up to it, to have come through unscathed.

"Well," said my father, "as long as we're here, we might as well go and ask." He parked the car and the three of us went up to the front door of Viola's house, a two-story, unpainted building with a side porch.

Viola came to the door herself in response to our knock; it seemed odd to see her there, so accustomed was I to seeing her only at our house. She was dressed in a white blouse and green skirt, quite different from the gray or black dresses she customarily wore to work. If she was surprised to see us there, she gave no sign of it.

"How did you make out in the hurricane?" my father asked.

"We did all right, sir."

"Any damage?"

"No, sir; a couple of bricks come off the chimney, that's all."

"Where do you mean, on the roof?"

"No, sir, in the house."

"*In the house?* You mean the chimney cracked on the inside?"

"I don't know, sir. They fell in the fireplace."

"You'd better let me take a look at it," my father said. "It might be dangerous."

Viola led us along the porch and inside the house. Several small colored children looked curiously at us from across the hall. The room was small and dark, with some old furniture placed about it, and several kerosene lamps glowing. There were some printed curtains at the windows, and on the wall there was a colored picture of Jesus, evidently taken from a magazine, with a round halo above his head and a brown beard. By the door, on a green table with a scarred porcelain

269

top, was a bowl with several large hydrangea blossoms.

It struck me that I had never before in my life been inside a Negro home. There was a sparseness to the room, with its rickety furniture and the single faded cloth rug on the unwaxed floor, and yet there was a kind of warmth to it. I thought, *This is Viola's home.* It had never really occurred to me to think of her as having a home of her own; I had always thought of her as existing only in our house, for us, as if that was all she was meant to be. I had vaguely resented the business with Dominique, I realized then, because it was something independent and private, apart from her role in our life. But she is not only our cook, I told myself. To her this house is just as important as our house is to us.

My father was inspecting the fireplace. I could see several loose bricks lying at its base.

"I don't see any cracks in the face," he told Viola after a minute, "but something must have jarred those bricks loose. You better see that this gets fixed before you start using the fireplace again."

"Yes, sir."

"Who's your landlord?"

"Mr. Muhlendorff."

"Well, you tell him you want this fireplace repaired, you understand? Tell him you want it done right away, before cold weather comes."

"Yes, sir."

"And if he doesn't take care of it, you let me know and I'll call the building inspector and he'll make him do it," my father told Viola. "You understand?"

"Yes, sir, I will."

"All right, then," my father said, turning to leave. "We'll see you tomorrow morning."

"Yes, sir," Viola said. "Thank you for coming by."

For some reason, what was happening had made me feel somewhat strange, even uncomfortable. There was a sense of having intruded. Perhaps it was the presence of the two little children standing across the room, watching silently, saying nothing. There was also a feeling that something was missing, as if I expected to find something that was not there. Whatever it was, I felt ill at ease and anxious to leave.

As my father was going out of the room, he noticed the two little Negro boys still standing there, watching him intently. "Are those your boys, Viola?" he asked.

"No, sir, they my sister's children."

My father walked over to them. "You boys like ice cream?" he asked.

They were silent for a moment. Then one of them murmured, "Yassuh."

My father reached into his pocket and extracted a twenty-five-cent piece. He handed the coin to one of the boys. "There you are," he said. "Have some ice cream on me."

"Tell Mr. Kohn thank you, Calvin," Viola prompted.

"Thank you, suh," the boy whispered.

My father walked on out the door, with Billy and me following. "Well, so long, Viola," he said. "You see that that chimney gets fixed, now."

"Yes, sir, I will," Viola assured him.

As we went out the door, I happened to look up.

There, under the doorsill, painted crudely but distinctly, I spied a small blue cross.

"How did the Major take the hurricane?" I asked Billy Cartwright a few minutes later, as we were riding back home.

"Slept right through most of it," Billy said. "He didn't even seem to notice it. When he woke up this morning he asked whether it had rained all night."

"Did you tell him it was a hurricane?"

"Yes, but half the time he thought we were talking about that one in 1893."

271

My father drove us by the baseball field at College Park to see whether the diamond looked too damaged for the Municipal League play-off game to be held Saturday. There was some water standing on the infield, but otherwise the field seemed playable. Across the way in adjacent Hampton Park, however, numerous trees were split and uprooted. "Washington Park's the one that's really going to look funny," my father said. "It's hard to imagine it without shade trees."

We drove up Versailles Street. When my father saw his rose garden again, he became glum once more. A little of the water had drained away, but the damage to the rose bushes seemed catastrophic. Many were bent low to the ground and almost denuded of leaves.

We went on into the house.

"How was it downtown?" my mother asked.

"Pretty rough in some places," my father said. "Ripped up the waterfront, and some of the Negro houses over by Fiddler's Green had their roofs blown off."

"We went by Viola's," I said.

"How was she?" my mother asked.

"All right," my father told her. "Might have had her chimney cracked, though. I told her to be sure that her landlord has it fixed before winter."

"Dominique wasn't there," I said.

My mother looked at me. "Of course he wasn't," she said. "He isn't Viola's husband. Besides, he's probably gone away for good, anyway."

"Do you think Viola was in love with Dominique?" I asked.

My mother shrugged her shoulders. "Heavens, child, I don't know."

"Why do you think he left?"

"I'm sure I don't know," my mother told me.

*   *   *

My father sat around, listening to the radio reports of the storm damage, saying little. "Aren't you going to try to tidy up the garden?" my mother asked him after a while.

"What's the use?" my father said, shaking his head. "I've got all fall to do it now. There won't be a dozen blooms this year."

"Oh, I wouldn't be so sure," my mother told him. "It probably isn't nearly as bad as it looks."

"It's just about ninety per cent ruined. That's how bad it is."

Late in the afternoon, the telephone rang, and my mother answered it. "It's for you," she called to my father.

He got up and went to the phone. "Yes," he said, wearily.

But soon his tone of voice changed, and he was talking eagerly about something having to do with the garden. "You come on up tomorrow morning," he repeated several times. "I'll be glad to show it to you."

When he put down the phone, he came hurrying back to my mother. "That was Sam Russell, down at the Bureau of Parks and Playgrounds. He was looking at the damage in Washington Park, and somebody told him about my North China elm tree, and how fast they grow. He thinks maybe they could plant some in the park and have shade trees back in a few years. They're coming up tomorrow to see it!"

"Oh?"

"I knew there'd come a time when that tree would serve a good purpose," my father said. "People thought I was crazy to order it. Said it would never grow around here. Now it's going to save Washington Park."

"Isn't that nice?" my mother agreed. "And just to think, you grew it yourself!"

My father hurried down the basement stairs to get the pruning shears, and then headed for the side yard. When I went out onto the porch a few minutes later, he was working away at the North China elm and humming as he worked.

273

*   *   *

Within two days after the hurricane had struck and passed, our yard had been cleared of debris and everything was in order. The rose garden had been repaired as well as possible, with the trailing vines put back on the arbors and trellises, the bent bushes staked to an upright position, and ditches cut to drain away the standing water. A cloudless sky and bright sunlight had aided in the work. The authorities had come up to inspect my father's North China elm, and the evening paper published a photograph of my father trimming its branches, together with the information that the Bureau of Parks and Playgrounds was strongly considering planting North China elms in Washington Park and other areas where hurricane damage to trees had been heavy.

Elsewhere in the city the work of restoration was under way. The Fort Sumter Celebration, it was announced, would take place next week as planned; the damage out at the Fort had been inconsequential, and the landing dock was in satisfactory condition to handle visitors. The President would arrive on Tuesday as scheduled, but he would not leave for a Caribbean vacation as previously planned. Instead he would make a speaking tour in the Midwest, for the presidential election was only two months off and the campaign was at its height. The morning newspaper was thundering editorially against the President, and the evening paper muttering about him, but my father said he was sure to be re-elected.

As for the Major, he was ready for the big day. He did not talk very much, but he was determined to be there. He seemed clearer, firmer. He squared his jaw, refused to allow his thoughts to wander. "It's going to be a great day," he kept repeating. "It'll be like nothing that ever was before."

4. WHERE WE SAT WAS AT THE VERY TOP OF THE GRAND-
stand, high above the playing field, almost on a level
with the tops of the trees across the way in Hampton Park.
On the turf beyond us the Tru-Blu Brewers, in blue-striped
white flannel uniforms, were meeting the Sokol Tigers, in
solid gray with orange and black lettering, for the Municipal
League championship. It was September 5, end of the baseball season: this was the last game. In the seats below us
several thousand spectators were hunched, calling, shouting,
arguing. It was a bright, hot day; the crowd was shirt-sleeved
and perspiring, and dark circles of sweat spread under the
arms of the ballplayers, soaking through their flannel uniforms.

All season long these two clubs had battled. Tru-Blu had
been the favorite all the way; nobody had thought that the
Sokol team would ever come up to the end of the season tied
for first place, and forcing the championship into a play-off.
Yet here they were, chiefly on the ability of their little pitcher,
Turkey McNeil, to beat Tru-Blu. The two clubs had tied for
the championship; today's game would determine the
winner. And the question was whether Turkey McNeil could
do it once again.

The game started out as a pitchers' battle. McNeil, a small,
active pitcher, the one Helen had so admired, was in fine
form. Time after time he went through the contortions of his
peculiar delivery, working the ball over, under, pumping his
leg, then serving up tight curves and tricky change-ups that
had the Tru-Blu batters lunging vainly at the air, or tapping
weak rollers to the infield. Equally effective, Gabbo Jones, the

275

Tru-Blu pitcher, was rearing back and blazing his fast ball past the Sokol batters, rocketing it into little Joe Watson's black catcher's mitt for repeated strike-outs. The infielders called encouragement, the outfielders lolled about far out on the green turf, with little to do except watch and wait.

As batter after batter went down, and the twin rows of zeroes on the scoreboard in right center began to extend out across the board, a deep quiet settled over the crowd. Applause was less wild, less exuberant; notice was taken of the fine points, the individual excellences of the players; attention centered on the two pitchers, on the authority with which they toed the rubber slab, worked on each batter, kept the ball low and just inside the strike zone. "This could go on all afternoon," Billy Cartwright said. "At this rate we might be here till dark."

Then in the fourth inning, the Sokol Tigers struck. Frenchy Marivaux, the square-jawed, swarthy center fielder whom many people considered the best ballplayer in the league, swung on a Gabbo Jones fast ball, met it solidly with his bat, sent the white ball plummeting out between the left fielder and center fielder and rolling toward the fence. He streaked around second base and went sliding into third with a ringing triple, as Shouting Sam Cannon stabbed at him in vain with the relayed ball. He got up, dusted off his trousers, and took a long lead off the base. When the next batter lofted a fly ball into short center, he came storming in ahead of the throw to score the first run, and it was Sokol 1, Tru-Blu 0.

The Tru-Blu Brewers fought back. Redbird Heintzelman worked Turkey McNeil for a 3–2 count, then ducked under a change-up, inside and high, to take his base on balls. Pelzer Hughes advanced him to second with a neat sacrifice bunt. Jim Coberly drove a fly ball to right field and Redbird went to third. But then Turkey McNeil called on all his craft and forced young Billy Sykes to swing furiously at a third strike, and the threat was over. The little Sokol pitcher nodded his satisfaction, placed his glove under his arm, and strode briskly in to the bench.

"Day in, day out," somebody remarked, "he's the most consistent pitcher in the league."

"He's got a long way to go yet today, though," another declared.

And the game settled down again. The goose-eggs spread farther across the scoreboard, until there were seven of them for the Tru-Blu Brewers, and six more, with that lone number 1 in the center, for their opponents. The crowd was excited, tense, waiting and watching with a suppressed nervousness, knowing that the grim contest going on in front of them might at any moment break wide open into a savage explosion, that one pitch thrown to the wrong spot at the wrong instant could unloose the pent-up violence, that on every dip and weave and arching blur of the pitcher's windup and delivery, a city championship rode.

And most of all the ballplayers knew this, and they crouched at their positions, pounding their sweaty fists into their gloves, flicking their spikes at the infield dust, pacing the lines, and whistling, chattering, calling.

Now the sun was slipping down into the tops of the trees in the park, and there were long shadows on the grass where the outfielders paced, and a lemon brightness over everything, the golden crispness of late summer color, with every object sharp and distinct, palpable, real.

I thought suddenly of Helen then. Was she at this very moment watching the Phillies play up in Philadelphia? She might well be. And if so, was it like this there too?

I had not thought of her very much these past several weeks, not very much at all. By leaving when she did, it was as if she had simply vanished, and a segment of my life had closed and been put away. I had imagined, back before that last cataclysmic day out in Devereux when all had changed, that I would miss her intensely, think of her all the time, yearn for her. But I had not. There had not even been time.

There had been Mr. Zinzer's death, and then the hurricane and its aftermath, and now the city championship, and my Uncle Ben's arrival only two days away, and the Fort Sumter Celebration about to take place—and she had been out of my mind, a fleeting image now and then, a moment's pang, but never for long. It was strange—and yet I was grateful for it; for otherwise, I thought, it might have been unbearable.

As if it were so large that I could not bear to think of it at all, was not ready to think of it; so I had simply put it away!

I was brought to my senses by a terrific roar; everyone around me was suddenly shouting and yelling, and I looked up to see a Tru-Blu player rounding second and streaking for third, while another tore past first base, and in deep left-center field, Frenchy Marivaux was in the act of picking up a line drive that had carried almost to the fence.

When the din had subsided somewhat and the next batter came walking up to the plate, Redbird Heintzelman was taking a long lead off third base, his arms outstretched, his barrel chest and tapering torso swaying, taunting the pitcher, while at second base Pelzer Hughes moved off the bag, alert, menacing. I looked at the scoreboard: top of the ninth, two out, tying run on second, Jim Coberly at bat.

Will they give Jim Coberly an intentional base on balls, to get a play at every base? Yes, they will. Turkey McNeil loops four wide pitches in to his catcher.

Now the bases are loaded, and the excitement of the crowd is at a peak. There is a high-pitched roar and then, silence, stillness, and Turkey McNeil and Billy Sykes stare at each other. The batter stands at the plate, slim, agile, waving his bat back and forth in a short arc, ready. His face is thin and brown, his eyes are intent upon his opponent. Turkey McNeil pauses. He looks momentarily at the base runner on third, who flicks his hands at him in challenge. Turkey looks back. *Steal home,* he dares him, *come on, try it. I dare you to try it.*

Turkey wheels, throws to the plate.

And there is a sharp crack, and Billy Sykes lines the ball over the second baseman's head and into deep left field.

The rest happens swiftly. The next Tru-Blu batter grounds out, and the Sokol Tigers, their backs to the wall, come in to bat for a desperate try at retrieving the game, trailing 2–1 in the bottom of the ninth. But Gabbo Jones is invincible now. Disdaining the use of curve balls, he blazes his fast ball in, relentless, unbeatable, throwing strike after strike, until there are two outs and only Frenchy Marivaux, the best of them all, stands between Tru-Blu and the championship of the city. Twice Gabbo Jones rears back and throws, and twice Frenchy Marivaux swings and misses. The third time he sends a fly ball deep into center field. Up into the sky it arches, high up, and now Jim Coberly waits for it, places himself under it, watches it settle down, down . . . takes it for the final out.

Billy Cartwright and I rode the streetcar home that day, traveling up Rutledge Avenue with the Marvelous Ringgold, listening to some of the other riders discussing the game.

"Let's go up to the end of the line," Billy said suddenly as we neared our corner. I nodded, and we kept our seats while the trolley car passed Versailles Street and headed toward Herriott, rounding the corner there and moving up to Magnolia Crossing.

This was where it had happened. I had not been up here since. I glanced up at the number of the trolley car. Sure enough, it was Number 403.

Out of this car, in this very spot, Mr. Zinzer had stepped,

just as the Marvelous Ringgold was now stepping outside, to reverse the trolley arms; and through those very doors Mr. Zinzer's crazed wife had crept, had leveled the revolver at him when he came back inside, and fired two bullets into his body.

Billy Cartwright walked up to the front of the cab. "Look," he said, and pointed to a place on the dark woodwork where a little round hole had been plugged with plastic wood.

"Do you suppose it's a bullet hole?" I asked.

"I bet it is," he said.

The Marvelous Ringgold stepped back into the cab and saw what we were looking at.

"That's one of them," he said. "They found three bullet holes in the woodwork. See over here? She fired five shots and hit him twice, once in the shoulder, once in the stomach." He shook his head. "Poor little guy."

We stood there silently, looking at the bullet holes.

"Well, let's go," the Marvelous Ringgold said after a moment. "Come on, help me reverse these seats." We went down the aisle together, grasping the brass handles of the wicker seat backs, pulling them toward us, until we reached the other end of the car and the Marvelous Ringgold began placing his equipment on the transformer box for the downtown run.

The Marvelous Ringgold glanced at his watch. He looked back questioningly toward the railroad tracks across the highway. At that instant, as if on signal, a bell began clanging. The striped guard rails at the crossing began lowering. For a second they hung there, bell tolling, and then we heard the gathering roar of an approaching train.

Seconds later a green-and-white passenger engine streaked through the crossing, whistle shrieking wildly, drive wheels flashing, black smoke fanning from its stack, noise reverberating everywhere, six coaches in tow, the flanged wheels clattering over the switches, in a whirl of dust and sound, barreling northward up the line.

Flinging the throttle forward, the Marvelous Ringgold slammed shut the doors of the trolley car, sent it lurching into motion, and headed back toward the city.

5. THERE WAS A TREMENDOUS MASS OF PEOPLE MILLING around down on the Battery. Along every street, cars were parked for blocks away, and traffic cops busily routed additional automobiles away from the scene. We left our car on Tradd Street and walked along King toward the harbor tour pier, from which the boats would depart for the Fort.

It was early afternoon. In the morning there had been the parade, a miles-long procession of bands, troops, open-top automobiles and floats. It had made its way down King Street, then onto Broad to East Bay, while thousands of spectators had crowded along the sidewalks to watch. As for us, we had enjoyed a privileged view, watching from the second-story windows at Aunt Ellen's office. Billy Cartwright and I had gone there with Uncle Ben. My father, as adjutant of the Legion Post, had ridden in one of the many official cars, and of course the Major had occupied a place of honor at the reviewing stand on the steps of City Hall. It had been a magnificent parade—especially the bands: the United States Marine Band itself, Navy bands from the fleet, the Citadel Drum and Bugle Corps, several Legion bands from upstate, the Eighth Infantry Band from Fort Moultrie, the Parris Island Marine Band, the Infantry School Band from Fort Benning, and, last in line but a center of attention, the Jenkins Orphanage Band, clad in the spangled gray Charleston Light Dragoons uniforms my father had given them, and playing away with matchless fervor. I had never seen so many military bands in my life, or so many marching men. The newspaper accounts had said that more than ten thousand troops were participating, including the Summerall Guards of the Citadel cadets, who performed intricate rifle drills as they stepped along.

Now, in the afternoon, we were going out to the Fort to observe the commemoration ceremonies. My father had procured passes for us on the official boat which carried the Major, along with five other Confederate veterans who had come to the ceremonies from upstate. *Of course* he belonged there, I thought; in my eyes, in everyone's eyes, he was a Confederate veteran. It was *his* day!

Uncle Ben had arrived in the city the evening before, from California, driving a big gray automobile. I was surprised to find that I was almost as tall now as he was. He was staying down at Aunt Ellen's and planned to spend a week with us. He wore smoked glasses and smoked one cigar after another.

The four of us showed our tickets to the policeman at the dock entrance and went out onto the boat. It was already crowded, and among others I recognized Dr. Chisholm standing on the upper deck talking away. It was a warm, calm day, with a very light breeze and almost no choppiness to the harbor water. We stepped down the gangplank and found some seats over against the rail, by the stern.

Billy Cartwright and I set off at once to explore the boat, slipping through groups of people clustered here and there, down a stairway to a glassed-in deck where there was a soft-drink counter doing a brisk business, then up again and onto the forward deck, where we saw the Major seated in the center of the group of the other old veterans, talking and smiling to everyone. If the Major was tired, he did not look it; the haziness of recent weeks seemed vanished. He was enjoying himself, taking in everything, and seemingly his old self again. I was immensely happy; the day for which he had waited so long had come, and the Major was ready for it after all. Soon the boat cast off and swung out into the channel, making a wide curve as it headed for the Fort far out in the harbor. We stood at the rail and watched the crowds of people along the Battery. The harbor was dotted with boats large and small, including a dozen or more naval ships decked out with rows of colorful pennants, with the crews dressed in white and lined up along the decks. "They're waiting for the President," Billy said. "He's their commander-in-chief, you know."

I went back to look for my father and Uncle Ben. My father had gone off somewhere, but Uncle Ben stood near the stern, conversing with a tall, gray-haired man.

Presently Dr. Chisholm came hurrying up, hand out-stretched in greeting. "Why, DuBose," he said, "I had no idea you were coming down from the mountains for this. How *are* you?"

Dr. Chisholm looked at my uncle. "Why, *Ben!*" he declared. "How are you, fellow? Why, I haven't seen you in ten years. You're in Hollywood now, aren't you?" My uncle nodded. "We're certainly proud of you," Dr. Chisholm told him.

Next he looked down at me. "Well, well, young man," he said, "how are you? How's the poetry coming?" I blushed and murmured something. "Keep it up!" the Doctor told me. "That's the way!"

He turned to Mr. Heyward again. "DuBose, I'm just delighted with *Porgy*. It's a wonderful thing. I couldn't be more pleased if I'd written it myself. A real work of art. Don't you think so, Ben?"

My uncle agreed, and Dr. Chisholm continued. He spoke of various writers, with my uncle and Mr. Heyward joining in occasionally. I had not realized how many famous writers Dr. Chisholm actually knew, but he rattled off the names of one after another. When Mr. Heyward asked him about his own work, he blushed and said that it was "nothing, nothing, just a little local color." After a while he excused himself, declaring that he had to check on some arrangements, and headed off toward the front of the boat.

When Mr. Heyward had left, my uncle and I sat at the rail, watching the green shore line along James Island and the buildings at the Quarantine Station at Fort Johnson.

On my way to find Billy I passed Dr. Chisholm again. He was talking earnestly to a man who was making notes in a little book, gesturing toward various areas in the harbor as he spoke. The man was thin and dark-complexioned, and very Jewish looking. "We have grown up with history," Dr. Chisholm was telling him. "From earliest childhood it has been part of our life. For every Southerner, there is the memory of defeat, and the birthright of a Lost Cause. Whatever we may lack in worldly goods, we have a pervading historical view of life. I shall never forget, myself . . ."

I went up the stairway to the front deck. The Major was there, seated in a deck chair, surrounded by well-wishers, and smiling away. Billy stood nearby. "Here's the other member of my color guard!" the Major declared as he caught sight of me. "Come over here and tell me what you think of all this!" I went up to him and he placed his arms around Billy and me. "Did I ever tell you boys," he said, "about the time when . . ."

At that moment the whistle on the boat cut loose with a short blast, and a bell rang. "We're coming alongside the pier!" someone said. Sure enough, Fort Sumter was just off the bow of the boat, its red bricks glistening in the sun. Atop the ramparts near the dock the United States Marine Band was playing.

The ceremonies would not begin until the President of the United States had arrived, together with the governor and the mayor and Senator Jimmy Byrnes and others, so there was a half-hour's wait. We walked about the Fort, observing monuments, esplanades, casemates, and memorial plaques of various kinds, and listening to the band as it serenaded the

285

visitors. Soldiers stood alongside the two immense disappearing rifles of Battery Huger, and we noticed ammunition placed nearby. After a while a whistle blew, and the gun crews went into action, loading the cannon.

"We'd better step farther away," my father said. "They're getting ready to fire the salute."

Seconds later there was a thunderous roar, and the ground vibrated beneath us as the two cannon began a 21-gun salute, firing in sequence at exactly 10-second intervals. There was white powder smoke everywhere, with a strong, acrid odor. The soldiers worked swiftly and methodically to the terse commands of the officers, swinging open the breach, inserting the brass-cased rounds, slamming the breach block home, stepping away, working the lanyard controls; and the immense guns recoiled with a blasting discharge. Afterward my ears rang, and the sound of voices seemed far away.

"Here he comes!" people began yelling shortly after the salute was over, and Billy Cartwright and I ran over to the edge of the parapet to see. A large gray naval launch with a starry blue flag flying at the bow was cutting through the harbor waters toward the fort. We could see a good many people under the canopy, some in civilian clothes, others in white or khaki uniforms with gold epaulets and brass. The launch drew up to the pier and was made fast. The files of soldiers along the wharf snapped to attention and the Marine Band struck up "Hail to the Chief" as the Presidential party made its way into the Fort.

There he was, finally—moving with a limp, leaning on a naval aide's arm, Secret Service men alongside him, waving, wearing an old gray hat, his grin evident even from where I stood. That was the President!

At length the President took his seat on the rostrum and the ceremonies began. Mayor Maybank, a tall, good-looking man with a chin almost as square as the President's, officiated. The Reverend William Way, D.D., offered a prayer. Mayor

Maybank introduced Senator Jimmy Byrnes, Governor Olin D. Johnston and others.

"We have many other distinguished guests," he continued, "but before we introduce our great Chief Executive, I want to present a group of men in whose honor we are convened today, the last survivors of all the brave soldiers who defended their homeland three quarters of a century ago. For us they will always be the bravest of the brave, the heroes of a Cause which may have known military defeat but whose spirit was never vanquished. We are honored and proud to have them with us today!" He gestured with his hand toward the gray-headed old men on the rostrum, who rose hesitantly to their feet while the crowd yelled madly and the Marine Band swung into the strains of "Dixie."

I felt the hair rise on the back of my neck, and my heart was filled with emotion, for Major Frampton was there among them, standing frail but tall, waving his hand lightly, taking in the tumult and the acclaim. The tears blurred my eyes as I watched him. All the spectators were yelling fiercely, not simply cheering but raising their voices in a wild, exuberant shout that I knew instantly could be only one thing— the rebel yell! And the old-timers on the platform were waving back, smiling, enjoying it all, with the band crashing out "Dixie" all the while.

It was as if all there—young and old, the six old men standing so frail on the platform in the September sun of Charleston Harbor, the governors, mayors, senators and dignitaries on the platform around them, the hundreds of men, women and children in the audience below—were caught up as one in a sudden outburst of affection and pride; as if in our cheering we were saying that we were all together; and a great joy ran through me that this moment existed, while the music and the shouting reverberated through the salty harbor air. Often since then I have thought about that moment, and even today I feel the same tightness in my throat each time I hear that song played, and I think of those old men.

Afterward the President spoke, and we all cheered for him, too, the old men on the platform leaning forward in their chairs and applauding most vigorously of all. I watched the Major, for I knew how he loved the President, and I could see the excitement and pride in his face as he clapped his hands together steadily while the President waved cheerily at the crowd. Then there was quiet, and he began to speak. Everybody laughed at first when he said that as a Democratic President he for one was grateful every election year that the Southern states were still in the Union. He talked about the bravery of the soldiers during the Civil War, and he went on to speak of the need for making the South economically strong and prosperous, and how under the Democratic Administration the South was at last exercising its rightful voice and leadership in national affairs. He spoke of the great human heritage of Forts Sumter and Shiloh, of how both the natural resources and the human resources of the Southern states had been abused and squandered for so long, and of how a healthy and thriving South was essential to the well-being of the American nation. He said that now, seventy-five years after the firing upon Fort Sumter, it was time for a new dedication of hearts and minds to the never-ending fight against poverty, intolerance, greed and ignorance. He declared that he was confident that the South's long heritage of bravery and leadership would place it in the vanguard of the battle for human freedom and dignity.

When he had finished everyone cheered some more, and the President shook hands with the Mayor and the Governor, and then he hobbled over and shook hands with the Major and the other Confederate veterans. A color guard of Citadel cadets fired three volleys in honor of the dead of the Civil War and the Marine Band played the "Star Spangled Banner." Then the President and his party departed, back down the platform steps and across the parade ground to the pier, along the ranks of soldiers drawn up at attention, onto the launch again. Soon the gray launch was cutting through the green harbor water toward the city, with the escort vessels fore and aft, and the Celebration, the Fort Sumter Celebration, was over.

It was over, and the crowd trailed back to the pier for the return trip. Our launch, which had stood offshore while the President's craft was docked at the Fort, maneuvered back into position. Everyone was quiet now for the most part, as if all the passion of the crowd had been expended in the applause and cheering, and now everyone wanted to think about what had taken place.

How strange, I thought as I took my place on the boat along with my father, Uncle Ben and Billy Cartwright, that this event should be all over now. The planning, the talking, the anticipation—all had culminated in a single day's doings; months of argument and discussion, making of plans, issuing of invitations, dozens of meetings, thousands of hours—all for this, so soon ended. Good as the President's talk had been, thrilling as it had been to hear the bands playing and see the troops marching, it hardly seemed enough. It was odd. I had noticed before how something could be looked forward to, thought about, experienced a hundred times in anticipation, and then take place so quickly that, when it was over, one had to remind oneself that it had really occurred, try to remember exactly what *had* happened, since while it was taking place there had not even been time enough to absorb it.

And the Major, I wondered—was *he* disappointed? I saw him seated there on the front deck, the sunlight bright on his white hair and gaunt, sharp face, with the other old gentlemen around him. Having waited so long for this day, looked forward to it in such anticipation, thought of little else but this day, lived for it—did he too wonder now what it had all been for?

No. For he was smiling, not broadly, but lightly and gently, as if entirely contented and happy, as if it had been quite enough. It had been his day, and he was satisfied with it. All his long life had been summed up and amply justified, I thought, in those few moments when he and his comrades had stood there straight and proud, while the frenzied cheers filled the air and the band played. He had lasted until it took place: that moment. He had fought back age and the sapping heat of summertime, shaken off the gathering haze, stood clear-eyed and ready for the climactic occasion.

6. THE DAY BEFORE MY UNCLE LEFT HE CALLED FOR ME in his automobile, a gray Cadillac, the largest and most sumptuous car I had ever ridden in. So much had been going on that there had been no opportunity to have the conversations with him that I had so looked forward to having, ever since I had learned that he was coming. I had not seen him in two years, and it was during that time that I had written the little poems that made the family all declare that I "took after Ben." I had dutifully sent them to him, and he had written to me as if he were really interested in them. The letters I wrote to him, and received from him, had been quite different from those I occasionally exchanged with other relatives who lived out of the city. I had written to him, and been answered, not so much as if he were an uncle but a friend—a wiser, more knowledgeable friend to be sure than Billy Cartwright or my other companions in school, but one with whom I did not have to make the expected adjustments for grown-up manners and interests. There was the Major, to be sure; but with him it had been *his* memories, *his* concerns that mattered. He had been sympathetic about the troubles Billy Cartwright and I had had with Miss Mason and others, of course, but from a distance. With Uncle Ben it seemed different; I felt he was interested in things in the same way I was, and I wanted very much to talk with him about various matters.

He telephoned the Saturday after the Fort Sumter Celebration and invited me to have dinner with him the next day. Shortly before one on Sunday he drove up to our house and we went to a restaurant called Henry's, where we sat down at a table and—a rare experience for me—ordered our dinner from a menu. My uncle had a Manhattan before the meal; I had never before been in a restaurant which served drinks. While we ate, he asked me about my school work and my writing and how I had spent the summer. I told him about the Major, and the *Endymion of Charleston, S.C.* So understanding did he seem that I told him about Helen as well, and I even hinted at what had taken place out in Devereux that final, horrible day. My uncle only grinned and assured me that the older I grew, the more peculiar I would find the ways of women. He also said something similar to what Billy Cartwright had said: "Of course she knew what went on out there. Women are always aware of that sort of thing; don't you ever fool yourself that they aren't." Afterward he told me about his own house on the Pacific Ocean, and of his work at the RKO studios with actors and producers. He knew some of the movie stars quite well, and told me about them.

When dinner was over we went driving out toward Fort Johnson, and as we moved across the Ashley River Bridge and out the Folly Road in the Sunday traffic, he talked a little about DuBose Heyward and other writers, and what he called "the Southern self-consciousness." "You live in a city," he said, "where everyone is not only highly conscious of living in that particular place, but is always trying to measure himself as a man by it. There's not a single one of them who doesn't constantly think of himself as a Charlestonian, as if it were a role in a play. They don't just live; they act a part, and they're always thinking about how to play it best."

We parked the car at Fort Johnson and walked out onto a wooden pier that led out over the water, high above the swirling harbor current. Across the harbor was the city, several miles away, presenting much the same view as we had seen from the launch that had borne us to Fort Sumter several days before. We could see the Battery and, beyond that, the cream-colored block of Fort Sumter Hotel and the tall homes along the waterfront. There were the docks, the roof-tops of the city, and the church steeples jutting up at intervals. Nearer and to the right of the Battery was the brick bulk of Castle Pinckney on its harbor island, and past that the long, looping, twin-cantilevered arches of the Cooper River Bridge, stretched across the harborscape like an immense swinging gate, hinged on the right to the low shoreline of Mount Pleasant.

It was an unaccustomed view of the harbor for me. I had stood many times at Adger's Wharf and gazed seaward over the bay, but I had always been looking *from* the city and *toward* the point where I now stood. Though it was no more than a few miles from the city across the water, by land it was a great deal farther, since to get there one had to cross the river upstream and come down along the James Island shore, at no time more than several miles away from the city, but increasingly removed from it the longer one traveled. Now, as my uncle and I stood there, the city was directly in front of us, just over the water, yet quite inaccessible from where we watched.

"Yes, it's quite a city," my uncle said. "Nobody ever leaves it, really. They carry it right along with them, except that what they carry is what it used to be, never what it still is."

"Have you ever written about Charleston?" I asked.

My uncle laughed. "Me? No, I'm not a novelist, I'm a writer of dialogue. I'm not the kind of writer who writes about places."

"What kind of a writer do you have to be to do that?"

"Oh, I don't know. You'd have to have a strong feeling for a time past, in the first place. I mean, you'd have to be the sort of person who's preoccupied with what *used to be*. Actually there haven't been any really big Charleston writers. That is, some of them, like Heyward, have done some very good work, but we haven't produced any of the important ones. Ours have been mostly for the tourist trade."

"How about Dr. Chisholm?"

"Who, *him?*" My uncle laughed. "Oh, Horatio Chisholm's no writer. He just dabbles at it. There are places within his mind where he has never looked, and he won't look, but where, if he wanted to be an important writer, he'd have to look. And we've never had anyone in Charleston who has looked—not even Heyward, good as he is. Probably nobody ever will. I sometimes think that Charleston exists so that people won't have to. It's hell on the writers, but it's great for living."

"Dr. Chisholm says that Mr. Heyward writes for money."

My uncle laughed. "So what? He's still a fine writer. Chisholm's just jealous of Heyward's success, that's all."

"How do you know if you're going to be a writer?" I asked.

Uncle Ben smiled. "You don't, I guess. It's like the priesthood; though many are called, few are chosen. But I suppose the most important thing is to have something to write *about.*"

"What sort of thing?"

"It doesn't matter. You can write about anything, the slightest, most trivial thing, but you have to know what you *really* think about it. And that means you have to find the words, because you don't actually ever know anything until you have the words for it. You take right now. When we look out there across the harbor at the city, you probably see more things than I do. I mean, little details and the like. Children always do, though they gradually lose the knack. But even though you see it, you don't *know* it, because you don't have the words for it. But when you get older, if you're lucky, you may discover the words for what you already see right now, and then for the first time you'll really *know* it. You've got everything now except the words, but the words *are* everything. You don't even *know* what you know, even though you see more than I do."

294

"I don't understand."

My uncle laughed. "It does sound silly, doesn't it? Well, don't worry about it. I don't even know quite what I mean, myself."

We watched the harbor current for a while. It was at the full turn of the tide. Along the edge of the channel there was a visible line of foam marking the flowing water off from the tidal recesses along the shoreline. Here and there were little whirlpools and cross currents, tucks in the flat sheen of the water's surface. Pieces of debris, caught in the whirlpools, would spin round and round, their pace accelerating as they moved toward the center. Then they would be caught and pulled under the surface, to reappear beyond the circumference of the whirlpools and float tranquilly in the calm backwater.

"Soon it should be the right time for flounder fishing," my uncle said. "Your father and I used to come out here on hikes and fish off that point right over there. The flounder converge on that spot and lie on the bottom as the tide comes in, waiting for little fish. If you could see beneath the surface of the water, you'd soon see dozens and dozens of eyes staring back at you from the bottom. They have both their eyes on the same side, you know. They hug the bottom, so that you can hardly tell them from the mud."

My uncle looked over at the city again, across the bay. "Some city," he said.

On the way home I told Uncle Ben about my school, and he told me about a movie he had just written and how movies were made. When we drove up to my house and into the driveway, my uncle opened the car door for me. "I can't come in," he explained. "Have a supper engagement downtown. Tell your folks I'll see them before I leave."

I tried to thank him for taking me to lunch and for the

295

afternoon. "Think nothing of it," he told me. "We Wandering Jews have to stick together, you know!"

I closed the car door and waved goodbye to my uncle as he drove away. The gray Cadillac disappeared up Versailles Street, and I went on up to the porch, where my parents were sitting.

"Did you have a good time?" my father asked.

"Yes, sir."

"What did you do?"

"We went to Henry's for lunch, and then we drove out to Fort Johnson," I said.

"Your Uncle Ben and I used to hike out there and go fishing when we were kids," my father said.

"That's what he said."

"By the way, I found out something that might interest you," my father told me.

"What?"

"Dominique has gone to Jacksonville to live."

"How do you know?"

"Frank Bishop told me." Frank Bishop was the superintendent at the fruit dock.

"Do you suppose Viola is sorry he's gone?" I asked.

"I haven't any idea," my mother said.

My father laughed. "Just between you and me, buddy, I don't think she is," he told me. "I think it was the old cat-and-mouse game."

"What do you mean?" I asked.

"Well," my father said, grinning, "it's like this. As long as Viola was losing, she wanted him. But some way or other, she got the upper hand, and when that happened, it became a different matter altogether."

"I don't understand," I said.

My father laughed again. "You will when you get older. I wouldn't worry about it."

296

"But why would she want him at first, and then not want him later on?"

"The answer to that," my father declared, "is that Viola is a woman."

"Oh, go on, Quin," my mother said to him. "Stop talking like that. You'll just confuse the boy."

"Okay," my father said, "okay. Let him find out for himself." And he chuckled.

Later, when I went into the kitchen, I found Viola at the sink washing dishes. "Viola, has Dominique gone to live in Jacksonville for good?" I asked.

She turned around and looked at me. "Uh huh. Far as I know."

"What's he going to do there?"

"I guess he's going to work on the fruit dock."

"Viola," I asked, "was Dominique your sweetheart?" I looked at her closely to see her reaction.

She grinned. "Well, if he was, he ain't any more," she told me. "Now you get out of the kitchen with your questions. It's late already, and I got too much work to do to listen to you!"

I went on upstairs then. All at once I felt quite tired from my afternoon out in the open air on the pier, and I stretched out on my bed.

I lay there for a long time, with my eyes half closed. After a while it began to seem to me that we were still looking out across the water at the city, and that my uncle was talking, talking, and the words and thoughts flowed into each other like the current in the harbor, while the lights and shadows came and went in little patterns over the face of the city, changing its contours each time my uncle said something, so that although the shapes of the buildings and wharves and steeples were fixed, the city itself never seemed twice the same.

EPILOGUE

❝ AND THAT IS ALL THERE IS TO IT. THE SUMMER WAS OVER. It was really over the day the Fort Sumter Celebration was held, though there was still another week before school opened. Since then I've thought about that summer a great deal, and even though it happened only a short time ago, it seems so far in the past that I sometimes find myself wondering whether it was in a different century or something.

Once high school began the days went by so rapidly that there wasn't much time to puzzle over things. High school was strange at first, but after I got accustomed to it, it wasn't too bad. The hardest part has been Latin class; we have a new vocabulary to memorize every day, and another page to translate, and each chapter in the book is worse than the one before. The teacher is quite good, however.

My chief interest has been the school newspaper. Last fall before school opened I promised myself that this year I was going to study hard and not do anything else, but when the announcement came around about the newspaper staff meeting, I couldn't resist. It's kept me very busy, but I wouldn't give it up for anything.

One thing that's different about high school is that there are no girls in the classes. I can't say that I miss them too much, though; I'm too busy. But speaking of girls, a surprising thing happened in December—I got a letter from Helen.

298

I was sure that I'd never hear from her again, and had even stopped thinking about her very much, when one day there was a letter from her. She didn't make any reference to that last day out in Devereux, naturally, but she did say how much she had enjoyed *every minute* of her visit to Charleston. Mostly she wrote about her school work, and the plays she had been to see at Saturday matinees in Philadelphia during the fall and winter. She said she had seen *You Can't Take It with You,* and Eva Le Gallienne in *Prelude to Exile,* and Sigmund Romberg's *Blossom Time,* and Margaret Sullavan in *Stage Door,* and the Ballet Russe de Monte Carlo. She also said she had written some poems, including one about Folly Beach, which she said would be published in the spring issue of her school magazine. I wrote her back, of course, and we've exchanged several letters since then. Yet it's strange, but though I was glad to hear from her and all that, I haven't been lying awake at night thinking about her, the way I did in July and August. I haven't cared that much. It's odd but it's true.

When I told Billy Cartwright that I had heard from Helen, the first thing he asked was whether she had received any offers for the shark's teeth. If she had, she hadn't said anything about it in her letter.

Billy has had several projects on his mind to take the place of that one, however. One day he decided that he and I ought to go into the stamp business. His idea was that we would answer some of the advertisements in the *American Boy* and the *Open Road for Boys,* which offered free stamps if you let them send approval books. Billy figured we could simply return the stamps that were sent on approval and sell the free ones. We tried it, but unfortunately the few stamps we sold did not pay for the postage needed to write for the stamps and then send back the approval books. After a couple of weeks we were out something like fifty cents, so we retired from the stamp business.

His next idea was to sell tadpoles for scientific research. Every time there are heavy rains, the ditches along the roads near our house fill up with standing water, and soon the ditches are filled with swarms of tadpoles. Once, after a week of rain had left the ditches packed with them, Billy got the idea that tadpoles were probably very valuable for medical research; so we got some washtubs and collected thousands of them. At ten cents a dozen, Billy estimated, every time it rained hard we could make a tidy sum. After we had filled the washtubs with tadpoles, he called the Medical Hospital on the telephone to offer the tadpoles for sale. They didn't want them, however, so we had to take all the tadpoles back to the ditch and dump them again. Before we did, Billy proposed that we keep them and raise them to be frogs, and then sell them for frogs' legs. However, my father said that under no circumstances could we keep the tadpoles in the basement, and that besides, this kind of tadpole wasn't the kind used by restaurants for frogs' legs. So back to the ditch the tadpoles went. My father says that when Billy grows up he is going to be either a used-car magnate or a literary agent.

And, speaking of my father, he had a very successful fall gardening season after all. He got a lot of publicity when the city planted North China elms to replace the trees damaged by the hurricane. It also turned out that his rose bushes were not nearly so badly damaged as he thought they were. Most of them produced blooms, after all, so that in the month of October the automobiles were lined up on Sunday afternoons all the way to the corner, with people coming to see the roses in bloom. Now that winter has come, he has been making plans for the spring season, which he is sure will be his best so far. My mother is still tending her part of the garden, of course. She never did move those crocus bulbs away from the walk.

* * *

In November there was a sad event. The Major died, just before Thanksgiving. He had been sick for several weeks before. In fact, he had come down with a bad cold immediately after Fort Sumter, and although he recovered a little for a while, he was never the same. There was a steady decline from then on, until after a while he couldn't remember anyone, not even Mrs. Cartwright. The last month of his life I wasn't even allowed to see him. Everyone said it was a blessed relief for him to die when he did. After all, he *was* ninety years old —his ninetieth birthday was in October, though he scarcely knew it.

My parents took me to the funeral. It was held in Magnolia Cemetery, and the Major would have liked it, because he was buried with a Confederate flag draped over his coffin. There was a color guard there from the Legion Post and a bugler from Fort Moultrie to blow taps over his grave. When he died the evening paper had a long story about it. I found out that he was born in Georgetown, not Charleston, and that in 1864, when he was seventeen, he enlisted in the Confederate Army and was with the 19th South Carolina Infantry all through the campaigns in Tennessee and the Carolinas. So he *was* a Confederate veteran after all. He had evidently not been at Fort Sumter, though; to that extent Dr. Chisholm was right.

A few days after the funeral Mrs. Cartwright asked me to come over to their house, and she gave me the Major's photograph of the *Sappho*, the one taken while it was still in service, showing the tall smokestacks, the wheelhouses at either end, the walking beam and the paddle wheels. She said the Major would have liked me to have it. It was very nice of her, and I keep it framed on my bureau.

I haven't spoken with Dr. Chisholm since the summer, except once in a while to say hello when I see him on my way to Aunt Ellen's. He always asks about my poetry and says he wants to see it sometime. The fact is, though, that I haven't written any poetry for a good while; my work in high school has kept me too busy.

I asked my father once what *he* thought of Dr. Chisholm, and he said that as far as he was concerned, the Doctor reminded him of the cotton candy on sale at the circus each fall. It was pretty imposing at a distance, he said, but there was actually very little to it except air and a little sugar. I ought not to say that, though; after all, he *was* nice to me. And besides, I feel kind of sorry for him; I keep thinking about what Uncle Ben said.

Another sad event is due to happen soon. The trolley cars are being taken off, and replaced with buses. The motormen are all being trained to drive them, and soon there won't be streetcars on the Rutledge Avenue Line, or anywhere else in the city for that matter. I can understand why; the trolley cars are very noisy if you live next to them. When one goes by the high school, for example, the teachers in the classrooms facing the street have to stop talking until it passes. Furthermore, the streetcars do tie up traffic on King Street for blocks sometimes. However, I'm a little frightened at what the Marvelous Ringgold is going to be like with a bus. At least the trolleys run on tracks, but there is nothing to hold a bus down.

For my birthday in November Uncle Ben sent me a check for twenty-five dollars, with a note saying that I might want to use it to replace the *Endymion of Charleston, S.C.* 'For a firmer guide to the near meadows,' he wrote in his letter. He also suggested that if I wanted to be a writer, I ought to sit down sometime soon and write out, as well as I could remember, everything that had happened to me last summer. I tried it, but I gave up very soon; it seemed awfully thin, even to me. Thinking about it is one thing, but writing it is another.

Last Saturday I was downtown at the barber shop after

temple, getting a haircut, and when I was done, I walked down to the waterfront. It was the first time I'd done that since the Major died. It was a warm day, especially for February, and I stood out there on Adger's Wharf for a long time. But without the Major it was different. I miss those Saturday morning walks and the stories, even if they weren't all true. Incidentally, Billy and I have decided that next spring, when we build or buy a new boat, we are going to name it the *Major William I. Frampton.*

One day soon Billy Cartwright and I intend to walk over by the old peanut mill and just for curiosity climb a tree and see whether the *Endymion* is still out there in the marsh where we last saw it, or whether it's floated away, perhaps in the high tide during the hurricane. This fall and winter, however, I simply haven't had the time to do it. But some day soon I shall. I think I'll wait until spring, when the marsh begins turning green again and the tide covers the tips of the reed grass, so that the clouds are reflected in the water and it looks as if the sky was pinned there, while the sunlight flashes on the current—the way it always was, and I suppose it always will be.

$\mathcal{V}$OICES OF THE $\mathcal{S}$OUTH